WARRIOR PRINCESS, ERRANT PAGE

NIGEL OAKLEY

Paperback ISBN: 978-1-915981-70-7
Ebook ISBN: 978-1-915981-71-4

Published by Resolute Books
www.resolutebooks.co.uk

Cover design by Liz Carter at Capstone Publishing Services
Interior design by Amie McCracken

For Alastair and Jonny, the best sons a Dad could wish for.

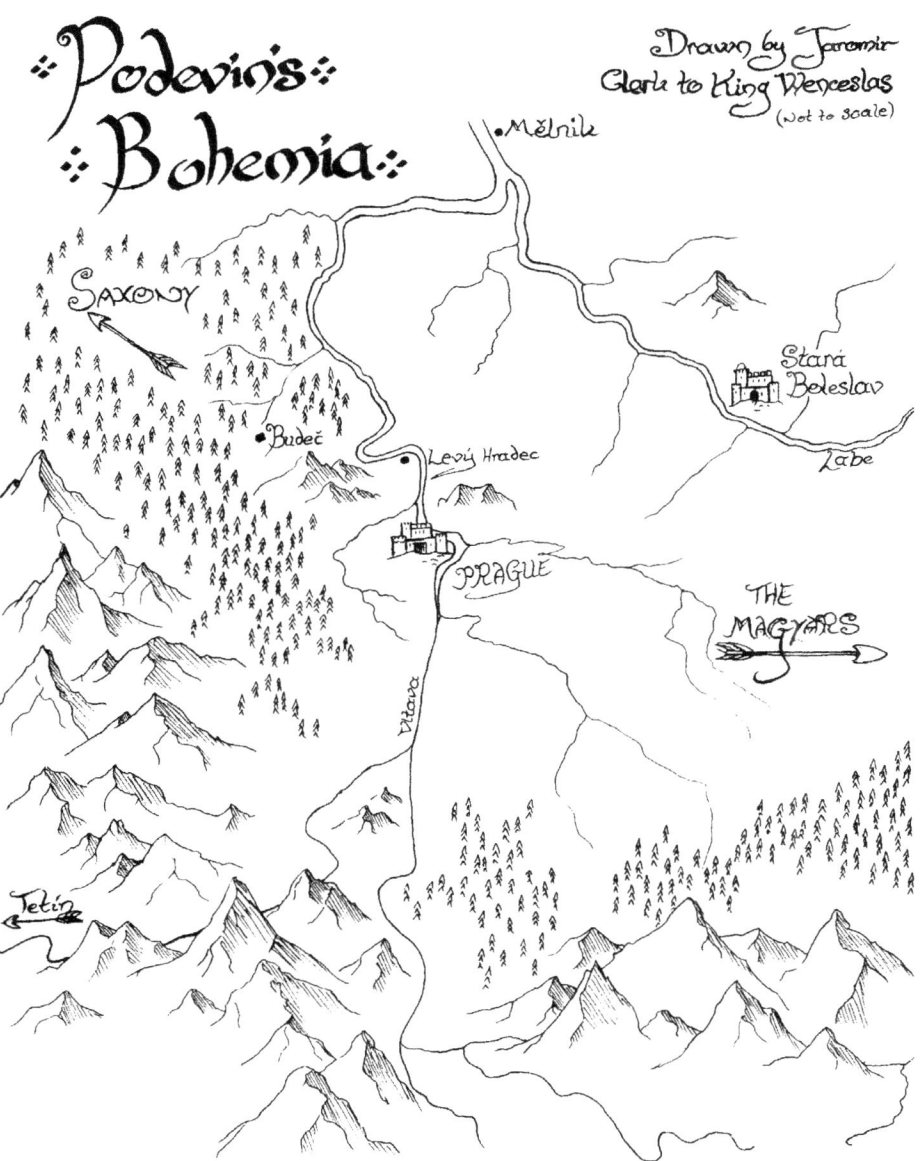

☙ Podevin's ☙ ☙ Bohemia ☙

Drawn by Jaromir
Clerk to King Wenceslas
(Not to scale)

• Mělník

SAXONY

• Budeč

Stará
Beleslav

Labe

• Levý Hradec

PRAGUE

THE
MAGYARS

Vltava

Tetín

Characters

Anglo-Saxon

Æthelflæd – deceased, former ruler of Mercia, Emma's aunt (and Alfred the Great's daughter)

Athelstan – King of the English

Beatrice, Hilde, Mabel, Ursula – ladies-in-waiting to Emma

Emma – Princess of the ruling house, Athelstan's half-sister

Edfleda, Elfleda, Ethelfleda – half-sisters to Athelstan, all nuns

Matilda – Princess of the ruling house, Emma's older sister, also half-sister to Athelstan

Geraint – captain of the Royal Bodyguard

Brother Mark – former warrior, now a Benedictine Monk; appointed as Emma's Chaplain

Bohemian

Duke Boleslav – Wenceslas's younger brother, father to

Young Boleslav (also known as Mladenic: 'the youngster') – Emma's future husband

Blanik – Prague Castle Constable, Podevin's tutor

Cesta – a Bohemian warrior, a particular crony of Tugumir

Dalimil – chef at Prague castle

Krok – a runaway peasant

Lyudmila – his bride

Maria – their daughter

Father Militus – Wenceslas's chaplain (sent from Rome)

Mikael – Bohemian knight who loans his sword to Emma

Podevin – page, squire and bodyguard to Wenceslas (also his second cousin)

Pribyslava, "Priby" – an abandoned child, adopted by Krok and Lyudmila

Radslav – Duke of Kourim, an old warrior and former rebel, now loyal to Wenceslas

Stanislav Blanik – a younger cousin to Blanik, a warrior in the Bohemian army

Tomas – one of Young Boleslav's companions

Tugumir – Podevin's older half-brother (on their mother's side)

Wenceslas – King (or Duke) of the Bohemians, of the Premyslid line

Saxon

Artur – a captain of the Saxon army

Henry – King of the Saxons, father to

Otto – Prince of the Saxons, later King (marries Anglo-Saxon Princess Matilda)

Welsh

Cadwallader – Welsh outlaw, purported husband for Emma

Hywel Dda – Prince of Dehenbarth (part of Wales)

Morwen – Cadwallader's sister, appointed (briefly) as Emma's chief lady-in-waiting

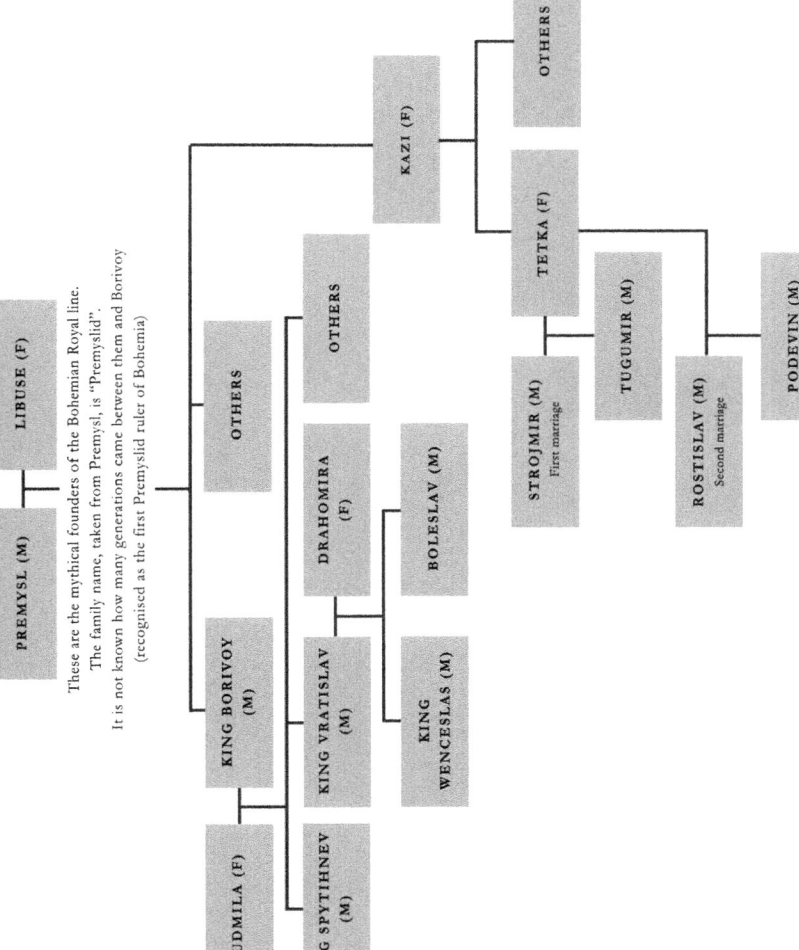

These are the mythical founders of the Bohemian Royal line.
The family name, taken from Premysl, is "Premyslid".
It is not known how many generations came between them and Borivoy
(recognised as the first Premyslid ruler of Bohemia)

PREMYSL (M)

LIBUSE (F)

KAZI (F)

OTHERS

TETKA (F)

STROJMIR (M)
First marriage

TUGUMIR (M)

ROSTISLAV (M)
Second marriage

PODEVIN (M)

OTHERS

KING BORIVOY (M)

OTHERS

DRAHOMIRA (F)

BOLESLAV (M)

KING VRATISLAV (M)

KING WENCESLAS (M)

LUDMILA (F)

KING SPYTIHNEV (M)

Chapter 1
Exile

A.D. 930

Emma listened; still as a wood mouse sensing a barn owl overhead and wide-eyed in the darkness. In her imagination, she scanned the room behind the bed curtains. The wooden walls hung with faded skins and tapestries, the rugs on the floor, the single window facing the courtyard—no parchment in it, certainly no glass, just a heavy curtain of furs to stop the worst of the winds. But the winds had dropped; there was not even a whisper of a breeze outside.

The cold had crept into the bedchamber, behind the curtains separating her from her companions. Had there been light enough, she would have been able to see her breath. She could hear it, fast and shallow—something had panicked her awake. She forced herself to breathe deep and slow. Her aunt had taught her that: 'If you're panicking, you're going to make mistakes.'

However, her aunt, Lady Æthelflæd of the Mercians, was dead now, and Emma's half-brother ruled all of England. King Athelstan preferred his princess-sisters demure; but Emma had been fostered in Mercia, where they were used to women who knew their minds. Lady Æthelflæd had led them in battle, and wielded weapons in her own defence. And it was Emma's weapon-wielding that had brought her here. It wasn't as if she'd killed a person—in fact, by killing that boar, she'd saved a soldier's life! But sneaking out to go on an early morning hunt and coming back covered in blood, even if none of it was hers, was unacceptable. She'd been recalled to Wessex, to the Winchester Court, only to be sent away again almost immediately. Out of King Athelstan's sight. So, here she was, lying in bed, in the old royal burgh of Chippenham, wide awake and listening.

With her breath now under control, it was still too quiet. The flighty young girl who was to sleep on the couch in the room with Emma, what was her name? Mabel? Like the rest of the gaggle of women detailed to 'protect' her, Emma had never met the girl before yesterday—or was it the day before? Either way, this trip to Chippenham had been sprung on her; it was her grandfather's hunting lodge. If she wanted to hunt, despite the king's orders, she could hunt here. But just because she was King Alfred's grandchild, it did not mean she could defy the current king, and Athelstan didn't need her hanging around him. She would dress appropriately and disappear from his sight and, while she was about it, she'd better remember a nunnery was very much an option!

There was still no sound. Despite the cold, Emma reached out and pulled aside the curtain, straining to see Mabel on the couch. Nothing. It was still gloomy, but that lump on the couch wasn't big enough to be a person, and hadn't moved. A lady-in-waiting shouldn't sleep so soundly that she was unaware of her mistress's movements.

'Mabel?' Emma's voice was soft.

Now certain all was not right, Emma flung back the furs covering her slim body and moved on bare feet over to the couch. She was right. Mabel had gone. It was unusual enough that she had only one overnight companion, but for that companion to creep away... Senses fully alert, Emma crossed the room to the window. It had been before she was born, but she had heard the tales of that Christmas, back in 878, when, long before anyone called him 'the Great', her grandfather Alfred had been surprised by a Viking attack. Was the same thing happening now? Emma lifted the curtain over the window, inch by inch, until she could see out. The window looked out onto the courtyard, not outside the walls. Even so, there were too many people. There were horses—no, they were ponies, sturdy Welsh ponies. No good on the plains and fields of southern England but, in the Black mountains of their homeland, they'd leave bigger mounts floundering.

Emma peered out; she had to poke her head out of the window and look left, but what were the gates doing open?

Sound. At long last, a sound! But it came from the corridor outside her room—a room she was in alone and from which there was no escape. She leapt for the door, realising there was no bar across it. As she opened it, she heard the solitary guard say to the men outside: 'Who are you?'

They were his last words as he was chopped down, his unused spear clattering to the ground. Emma was screaming, a full-throated yell as fury overrode fear. The spear lay across the doorway on top of the dead man. His killer, the first of three warriors outside her room, was still grinning as Emma, guided by her reflexes, or her aunt's training, grasped the spear, then turned and thrust it with all her might in the direction of her well-armed assailant. His expression changed to one of surprise as his axe dropped to his feet. He died with the guard's spear through his throat.

Seizing the axe from where it lay by the dead body, more of her aunt's words came to Emma: 'An axe is always the best weapon of war. Forget your pretty swords, and daggers only work at close quarters. Know how to use an axe.' Even as her startled brain registered this as the first time she'd held a full-size battle-axe in anger, Emma started swinging it against its former owner's accomplice. Once the descent started, it was as if it guided itself into the neck of the second warrior, and it was sharp enough that she could pull it away with all but zero resistance. She turned to the third man who, now he was alone, decided he did not want to face a deranged, yelling, armed, daughter of the previous king of England, whose half-brother was the current occupant of the throne. He fled, leaving Emma still yelling murder and, heedless of her own safety, charging towards other sounds of clashing metal, her borrowed axe raised above her head.

She was told afterwards it took a mere five minutes for the chaos to recede. As Emma stood in the middle of the courtyard, holding her borrowed, bloodied axe, chest heaving as the adrenaline left her body, she watched as the invaders scuttled out through the still open gate. The Welsh, she found herself making that assumption, desperate to leave. There were remarkably few bodies; there were ponies, but the noise was getting less. Emma turned as a commotion came from behind her. What now?

Emma's Anglo-Saxon guard stood in the gateway, ushering the last of the invaders out of the stockade. Then came a screech: 'Don't you leave me behind!' Emma's new chief lady-in-waiting, the one who was supposed to give her life in defence of Princess Emma's honour, tore across the courtyard, running straight for one of the riderless animals as two scruffy, dark men turned. The Anglo-Saxons held off as the Welsh paused. Hair flying, bare feet splashing in the mud, but with a woollen cloak clasped to her throat with one hand; the lady-in-waiting was allowed to mount the pony, which she urged into an immediate gallop. Followed by the two men, she fled into the night.

In seconds, the gate was closed behind them. Emma saw Geraint, captain of King Athelstan's bodyguard but currently assigned to her own, issuing orders for a double guard for the rest of the night. Only then did he turn to face her, but Mabel was by her side first.

'Madam, I am so sorry. Morwen ordered me to leave you as soon as you slept. I was told I had to be out of the way—you'd have me killed if I stayed—Morwen would report my misbehaviour to the king and I'd be responsible for my father losing his lands. Madam! You're so cold!'

The last comment penetrated Emma's befuddled brain. That, and the thought, *Who's Morwen?* She was shivering with cold; a silk shift and bare legs on almost frozen ground were not conducive for warmth, so she let herself be wrapped in a cloak. Not her second best, dark blue one, the one that still smelled of her father. Emma looked at Mabel, who could not meet her eye. They both turned and stared at the closed gate. Emma's cloak, a gift from her father, had gone to Wales, around the shoulders of her treacherous lady-in-waiting.

'Your axe, madam?' Geraint held out a strong hand for her stolen weapon.

Startled back to reality, Emma handed over the battle-axe; someone else would have to clean it.

'I'm going to my room, Geraint. I want a brazier lit, and I want an explanation.'

'Madam, I—'

Emma cut off his expostulation. 'You have five minutes. You really expect me to sleep after this?' Emma flung out her arm to encompass the whole courtyard with its overturned barrels, wounded men and cowering servants. She glared at the captain of her bodyguard. 'And, by the way, Geraint, there's a dead body or two in the corridor outside my room.'

Only then did she let Mabel lead her back to that same room, call for lights, wash the mud from her feet and legs, the blood from her arms, and change her now useless silk shift for a warmer linen one and a proper, fur-lined, regal cloak.

Geraint arrived within his allotted five minutes. In the flickering torchlight, for someone who had allowed his fort's defences to be breached, forcing his chief charge to fight for her life, he looked calm. Emma had listened as the bodies outside her room were taken away. She had sent Mabel to check and knew there were now two guards outside her bedroom door. However, she sat in her chair, brown hair scandalously uncovered, and waited. Geraint moved towards the chair next to her.

'You presume too much! Did I say you could sit in my presence?'

He stopped, turned to face her and folded his arms. As if daring her to make anything more of it. She was right, of course she was. But she was also aware Geraint had known her since she was small. She shivered, both from the cold and from the memory of the last hour. Mabel made a move from her corner to grab another cloak for her, but Emma waved her away and returned her attention to the man who should have stopped this from happening.

'Who were they? How did they get so close to me? And why did one of my ladies flee with them—wearing my cloak?' She wanted her bed, but she was getting an explanation first.

'You do know Morwen was sister to that man you killed? A man who had come to claim a wife? That's how the Welsh do it—so I was given to understand.'

Beyond that, Geraint would only insist he was under orders from Athelstan, informed her the stockade had been cleared of all intruders, and that she was safe. Whether the king would be pleased by the outcome of this night's activity, remained to be seen. And, if madam would excuse him, he still had work to do. Emma realised, she might be a princess, but she was not the king, and Geraint was the king's man. Besides, she had no more energy to argue against the half-tale Geraint had told. Mabel was ordered into the bed with her and, against what she thought might happen, she slept.

❧

It was, as Emma found out on her return to court, the last straw for the king. Athelstan's plan, which had been told to her so patiently once it had failed, was to have her carried off, so officially he'd not have to pay a dowry.

'Marry or bury? Was that the plan, dear brother?' Emma's sarcasm was dangerous in front of an angry king, but Emma was of royal blood too, and that blood was up.

The too-late explanations, now offered as if obvious, did nothing to appease her. Clearly, with Emma carried off—willingly or not—the Anglo-Saxon king would have an excellent excuse to mount a punishment expedition into Gwent and thereby expand English territory. If the worst came to the worst, the Welsh rebels, with their chief married to Athelstan's half-sister, could form an alliance with the English and he—King Athelstan—would have a buffer between his lands and those of Hywel Dda, the Prince of Dehenbarth. Even Emma surely knew how dangerous Hywel Dda had become recently?

Everyone, or rather everyone else, had been in on the plan; Chippenham's gates were left open and unguarded, even her bodyguards had pretended to sleep. A few deaths, like the guard at her bedchamber, were acceptable to 'lend verisimilitude' to the 'attack', but no-one important was expected to put themselves in harm's way. Especially not Morwen, the outlaw's sister and his emissary at the English court, who had arranged it all. It was Morwen's job to make sure Emma was in a fit state for her husband—a pity she hadn't drugged the girl! The trouble was, no-one had seen fit to tell 'the girl' about the plans being made for her at the time. Emma's response, repeated frequently, made it clear she was not happy; she was not to be parcelled off, put on the back of someone else's horse, and pitched into marriage because 'you, dear brother, can't be bothered to find me a dowry.'

Her reaction, though perhaps not its extremity, had been anticipated. Forewarned, Cadwallader, the rebel leader, had professed himself to be 'looking forward to meeting such a spirited lady', or so they said back at court. Cadwallader himself, of course, was no longer available to verify or deny the claim. Athelstan, who had never appreciated Emma's spirited nature, was furious at the plan's failure; how could he lead a punitive expedition into Gwent to avenge the kidnap of such a foolish girl when she was here at his court? Couldn't she see that it was all politics? As a girl, she was to accept what her menfolk decided for her. On the other hand, Hywel Dda was not lamenting the loss of his outlaw. In fact, after some huffing and puffing on both sides, there was something of a diplomatic rapprochement between England and Wales, or that bit of it anyway. Emma was told to accept that her cloak was lost. The treaty signed two years ago, with the border set at the River Wye, was reaffirmed, and there was peace—until the next crisis.

That wasn't the end of it for Emma, though. Athelstan had ambitions. Now he was king of all England, he wanted deals abroad too. And now he had an extra bargaining piece, which hadn't gone to Wales, he was going to use it. Emma's elder sister Matilda was tall, blonde, pretty, demure, excellent at embroidery and, at sixteen, decidedly marriageable. She was already going to Saxony. Now, Matilda would be accompanied by Emma; just as tall, dark, of a surly expression, not good as a seamstress, but unfortunately well practised in the martial arts (why had she ever been allowed to spend time with the Lady of the Mercians?), and, at fourteen, needed to find a husband who could control her.

There would be one accompanying troop of bodyguards for their journey across Europe, led by Geraint, and Brother Mark would be their chaplain. Matilda had accepted all this with a simpering smile and a dropped curtsey. Emma hadn't. What, she had asked, was supposed to happen to her, once the Saxon king had decided on Matilda? That was apparently up to the Saxon king. He had plenty of nobles and vassals—Athelstan was sure Emma would be perfectly happy with one of them. She'd fumed, but his mind was made up, and she didn't need telling she was the also-ran. Not even Athelstan had questioned her assessment that King Henry of the Saxons would be choosing the pretty sister for Otto, his son and heir.

The only good thing about the journey was that she, Emma, wasn't seasick and she could ride on horseback—and not sidesaddle either. Matilda had offered to help her improve her embroidery while they both shared the litter, but Emma, through gritted teeth, declined the gambit. She'd ended up having long conversations with Mark instead as he dutifully rode beside her. At least, outside the court, he treated her as if she had a brain! Geraint even managed to mend his bridges with her. Much as he hadn't liked it ('I've never refused a fight before in my life, my lady, you have my oath on that!'), he had been under strict orders at Chippenham not to interfere, but 'if my lady would cast her mind back', as soon as she called for help, he, Geraint, had rallied the troops and it became very hot for the Welsh from that moment on.

Emma had to admit, once she had emerged from her chamber, there had been some serious fighting, and dying, going on in the court-yard, with the Welsh desperate to get away. Also, she had been there later, when Athelstan had berated Geraint, only to find the knight was prepared to give as good as he got. 'My job, as I have always under-stood it to this point, was to protect the king *and his family*, with my life if needs be!' With Emma in the room, what could the king say to that?

The king said nothing at the time, but Emma was never sure if Geraint accompanying them to Saxony was a sign of Athelstan's continuing faith in him, or a punishment. Geraint was never to see England again.

Then there was Saxony and the beauty contest, with one obvious winner. Matilda was looking up under her long lashes at Prince Otto. Her wimple artfully pushed back enough to show her luscious blonde hair, her dress so tight that Emma wondered how her sister was going to be able to eat anything. However, it certainly showed the shape of her bust—prominent—and her waist—tiny. This was not in Brother Mark's brief; it was up to Mabel and the other ladies sent on this trip across Europe to try to persuade Emma into some sort of shape. On the jousting field, there could have been a contest Emma would have enjoyed. But, no. It was not to be.

Chapter 2
Podevin Arrives in Saxony

If the sight was calculated to intimidate, as far as Podevin was concerned, the Saxon king's tactic had worked. King Henry did not need those silent warriors on the wall, standing two deep with their pointed spears glinting in the sun. The stone-faced wall surrounding Augsburg might be over fifty years old, but it still stood in good repair and over three metres high. The wall rose even higher to encompass the gates through which the Bohemians were to enter the Saxon citadel.

Podevin, now he was sixteen, had at last succeeded his father as royal page and bodyguard to King Wenceslas of Bohemia. Tall, taller than the king, and slim, he could wield a sword to deadly effect (though never yet in anger). He'd been page for a long time, serving at the king's table, but it had been a proud moment when he'd been sworn in to take his full place as part of the bodyguard. He was the one to stay closest to the king, to give his life so the king could live.

The late afternoon sun shone down on the line of troops approaching the fortress, the Spring rains having dispersed, leaving a blue sky flecked with pure white fluffy clouds. The Bohemian party had emerged from the trees miles back, thus giving their position away in plenty of time for the Saxons, should they be minded to, to mount a defence of the city, or even to attack the slow-moving party of visitors.

Not, Podevin mused, that they were expecting an attack. Or even for the gates to be closed against them. Wenceslas had kept his peace with Henry, despite what his brother thought of the chicken-livered approach, so Henry had nothing to complain about. Except for their lateness. But Wenceslas had insisted on paying his respects at the shrine dedicated to his grandmother's saints; if it had just been him, or even just him and a few followers, that would have been fine. However, there was a whole troop of Bohemians, an entourage from the Prague court, and there was Captain Artur and his Saxons. By the time all that lot had stopped, they all decided they needed a rest, and, as it was a small shrine, all those who wanted to keep in with Wenceslas had to wait their turn to show how pious they were. Basically, it took too long and, by the end, Captain Artur wasn't hiding his frustration. He was right; they could have done their praying on the way back. Podevin didn't bother ducking into the shrine; he'd keep his pennies in his purse, thank you. Besides, he was kept busy making sure his charge was comfortable.

Now they were nearly at Augsburg, Podevin glanced to his right. Mladenic was on a pony and was still being too hard on her mouth, yanking at the reins every time the poor beast shook her head. With the dusting of freckles either side of the bridge of his nose, and his small round face, Mladenic could have been pleasant if he'd smiled occasionally, but his brattish behaviour did make it difficult for anyone to like him. Mladenic, 'the youngster', wasn't his real name, of course, but everyone called him that behind his back. His real name was Boleslav, like his father. Mladenic was Duke Boleslav's only surviving son and was assumed to be his father's heir.

Podevin knew, none better, that the youngster had not had an easy start in life, but Mladenic was sullen, demanding, and very aware of his dignity. He might be the next-heir-but-one to the Bohemian crown, but that did not mean there was a rush to serve him. Podevin had objected strongly when he'd been told he was to become Mladenic's personal assistant for the duration of the journey.

'You're closest in age. Keep him entertained,' Wenceslas had said, overruling those objections when yet another warrior had been goaded into drawing his sword and threatening to 'demand satisfaction' from the ten-year-old. It could not be a child fighting a fully grown warrior, so there would need to be a champion; as Wenceslas (the child's uncle) could hardly spend his days fighting his own knights, did Podevin (a distant cousin) want to take the role? No, absolutely not. Peace had to be restored by persuading Mladenic to apologise, which he did with ill grace.

'Just keep the brat quiet!' one of the king's bodyguards had muttered to Podevin once they were out of Wenceslas's hearing.

Podevin tried to object, tried to say Mladenic should just be told to obey what the bodyguard said, but was overruled. At sixteen, Podevin considered himself all but a man. Hadn't Wenceslas said, back in Prague, it was about time they thought about a wife for him? And now he was being relegated to looking after a ten-year-old? After coping with the whining for yet another evening at yet another camp at the side of the road, which Mladenic did nothing to help with, Podevin had grabbed Mladenic, hauled him close, and hissed: 'You don't want to be here, and I don't want to be your nursemaid, but we're stuck with it, both of us. So, either do as you're told, little boy, or I'll damn well tie you on that horse and use a leading rein to get you in to see King Henry.'

Shocked silence from Mladenic, apart from a muttered 'wait till I tell Father' had at least given the bodyguard, if not Wenceslas, his wish.

෴

The fortress, with its silent watchers, grew closer. Mladenic became aware of Podevin's look.

'What now?' he said.

'Just relax,' Podevin said, 'and loosen your reins a bit.'

'I don't need orders from you.' Mladenic did the opposite, causing his pony to stop. The lad kicked furiously at the beast's sides to get it going again. Podevin resisted the temptation to roll his eyes.

'Look,' he said, 'you're nervous. We're all nervous—just try not to show it. All right?'

'I'm not nervous! After Father, I'm the next king of Bohemia.'

However, Mladenic finally loosened the reins enough to allow his pony to plod on in time with the rest of the party. His eyes, flickering from the wall to the gates to the open spaces either side of them, betrayed him though. Podevin refrained from pointing out that nothing was guaranteed and he, Podevin, as Wenceslas's second cousin, also had a claim to the Bohemian estate. All right, he was descended from a female line and there was an older half-brother, but there was still a claim.

Wenceslas had been allowed, as the most important guest, to go ahead on his own through the gates, while Duke Radslav, as chief bodyguard, and Captain Artur, as chief Saxon escort, rode two abreast immediately behind. Two big men, Bohemian darkness against Saxon blond; seasoned warriors who had long since sized each other up and hoped wary mutual respect would never have to be tested by a clash of arms.

Following behind, Podevin glanced up at the wall to meet the indifferent gaze of the Saxon guards. They'd remained immobile as the Bohemian retinue approached. So still, it had been difficult to be sure they were men and not statues. Surcoat, mail, iron helmets, pike, sword and dagger. All identical. As King Wenceslas rode through at the head of the column, there had been a thunderous stamping of feet above them, as the second line of men came to life and about-turned so they faced the visiting monarch as he rode towards the meeting with their Saxon overlord. There were more men lined up on either side of the track as the Bohemians and their escort made their way towards the inner wall surrounding the fortified castle. An inner wall that was also topped with armed men.

They rode on, exposed, their troops behind them and unable to do anything if they were attacked. The order of arrival had been arranged long before they came in sight of the city. No more could Wenceslas's bodyguard surround him—the Bohemian duke was to be in the lead, wasn't he? Captain Artur had phrased it as a question, but 'No' was not going to be an acceptable answer.

Captain Artur, blond, bulky and belligerent, had met them at the border. He had troops, at least two for every one Wenceslas had brought. For all there had been appropriate bowing and adherence to the niceties, there had been no argument, no discussion. Wenceslas had even put up with being called duke. This was one of the tactics the Saxons used to put their vassals in their place. Only Henry was king. Everyone else—whatever they were styled in their own lands—was referred to by a lesser title in Saxony. As they had moved through foreign territory, Artur had allowed Wenceslas's immediate party to remain in the middle, surrounded by his Bohemian guard, but the Saxon guard had been before, behind, and to the sides. It was a statement: Bohemia only existed on Saxon sufferance.

For all the formal welcome as they approached the fortress and its great hall, the silence overpowered everything. They halted. Captain Artur pointed the official party to the shut doors of the great hall, the rank-and-file already being led off to their own quarters. Blaze, Podevin's horse, catching the tense mood, pawed the ground. Podevin patted his neck, shushing him. Wenceslas dismounted, his slight sinewy frame making him seem even smaller against Artur's bulk.

'I need to change,' he said, indicting his muddy boots and cloak.

Of course! The shrine had been in a forest, and there hadn't been time to sort out a change of attire from that moment on. The baggage train was only just lumbering its way through the outer gate. Wenceslas looked round. Normally, it would be Podevin's job to get that kind of thing sorted out, but nothing about this trip had been normal. Although he, like everyone else, had now dismounted, Podevin was not about to leave Blaze to trip over his reins and, besides, wasn't he supposed to be caring for Mladenic?

'Captain?' Podevin, using halting German, called to a frowning Artur, who glared at him, but nodded. 'Why don't we do as my lord duke suggests? Once we've stabled our horses?'

At Artur's clicking of his fingers, servants appeared out of nowhere, ready to take their horses. Podevin moved round to Blaze's head, reaching into his pocket for the remains of the lunchtime apple he'd stored there. He allowed Blaze to press his head against his chest and, despite the bit still being in his mouth, let him have his treat.

'Look after him. I'll be checking later,' he said to the man beside him.

The man nodded. 'We know what we're doing,' he replied.

'I'm sure,' Podevin said, 'but Blaze is *my* horse.'

They locked eyes before the man grinned and led Blaze away, leaving Podevin free to sort Mladenic.

'I'm hungry!'

Podevin ignored the words, and took the young man over to his uncle.

❧

Not even getting changed could be accomplished without whining.

'I want my *red* cape!'

For Podevin, who'd had about two seconds to deal with his own muddy boots and change out of his travelling clothes into something more appropriate for a member of the family, while, at the same time, sorting out both Wenceslas and Mladenic, this was not worth a response.

'Duke' Wenceslas was ready. Podevin had thought Mladenic was ready, but Mladenic had thrown off the short cape he'd been given. He stamped on it as it lay on the floor. On the other hand, Wenceslas was at the door. Duke Radslav, with Captain Artur as his shadow, was ready to escort him to the hall.

Wenceslas looked across at Podevin, mouthed 'Deal with it,' and left the room.

Thanks! thought Podevin as he strode across to Mladenic, picked up the dark blue cape he had given the young man only minutes ago, shook it clean of dust and held it out to him.

'I said I wanted the red one!'

'And I told you, the red one isn't there. It hasn't been packed, and you could be the king of Saxony himself, but you can't make things just appear.'

'You should have made sure it was here!'

'I am not your slave!' Podevin said, still holding out the blue cape. 'Besides, I thought you were hungry?' Podevin certainly was—lunch had been hours ago.

The cape was grabbed from his hand, and thrown willy-nilly over Mladenic's shoulders. 'Come on, then!' he said, also heading out of the room, leaving Podevin to choose between staying behind to tidy up, or following behind Wenceslas's nephew like some lackey.

He chose to follow, which was fortunate as Mladenic's pushing and shoving to get to the head of the queue at the door got him nowhere. No group of people can close ranks like aristocrats thinking someone of lesser rank is trying to usurp their place. Podevin was able to reassure them the boy was indeed Wenceslas's nephew and he did have a right to enter the hall—as did Podevin himself, as page and cousin to k–Duke Wenceslas.

On entry, Podevin had to grab Mladenic by the shoulder. They paused and bowed to the throne. Mladenic shook himself free as soon as they'd returned to upright and darted off to the left, where the Bohemians were waiting. Podevin took a closer look. What was Wenceslas doing up there with King Henry? They were seated together and chatting like old friends. More than that, Wenceslas was on Henry's right—the favourable position. Wenceslas had always said he wanted peace; had he achieved it at last?

Chapter 3
Meeting a Husband
A.D. 930

Emma wished now she'd paid more attention when the Bohemian party came through those big double doors into the hall at Augsburg, the Saxon capital. At the time, it had seemed as if a ragtag battalion had tumbled through the ranks of Saxon guards, just to disrupt the party. Not much of a party. Names being called out, people going up to kneel in front of King Henry, then going down the steps backwards—how anyone didn't fall, Emma had no idea. Matilda, not that Emma could blame her, had eyes only for Prince Otto. The heir to a kingdom the size and power of Saxony would be attractive anyway, but he was broad-shouldered, brown-eyed and looked as if he could be a dangerous enemy. Perhaps Athelstan was wise to make an ally of the Saxon kingdom. What no-one understood was why King Henry left his throne and went down to meet Wenceslas, who was only a vassal. He then escorted Duke Wenceslas (let the Bohemians argue about rank if they liked, Emma was quite prepared to take her lead from the Saxons) to sit beside him as he continued to receive homage from other important people.

Emma had watched. Of course she had. The whole thing became the focus of everyone's attention, but when Brother Mark, who was seated beside her, had told her to look carefully because her husband was among that crowd, she'd nearly made a scene of her own. It took some very firm pressure on her arm from Mark's hand to restrain her.

She stayed in her seat. She looked at the young Duke of Bohemia and the rest of his party; the old, grizzled warrior, the puffed-up squire who seemed to be in ineffective charge of a little boy (who appeared to think he was the most important person in the room), and the knights who made up the rest of the retinue.

'Is the duke married?'

'No, my lady.'

'So, it's him, then.'

'Probably not, my lady.'

'Riddles, Mark. Riddles.' She glared at him. He knew she didn't like having to draw answers out of people.

'His plan is to hand his dukedom over to his brother—his brother is married—and go to Rome. He wants to be a priest, so he needs to remain single.'

'You don't give up a throne to become a priest! Or is he really just afraid that, if he gets married and has children, his brothers and nephews will rise up and kill him?'

'Like Athelstan?' Mark paused. 'Wenceslas only has one brother still living. But the brother has a son. I thought Wenceslas was bringing his nephew in his party?' He looked pointedly at the teenager who, having caught the boy, was attempting to shush him.

'Mark? How do you know so much?'

'Simple. In exchange for sending certain information on ahead, I asked for information in return.'

Emma turned to stare at him. 'Certain information. What certain information would that be? Like: who's the pretty one? The compliant one?'

'And which is the one who's already killed one suitor?' Mark's light-brown eyes met her gaze without flinching or embarrassment.

Perhaps it was the privilege of being part of the royal household from before she was born. Perhaps, as he was a monk, normal strictures failed to apply, but Brother Mark was often a law unto himself.

However, he spoke again. 'If one party to a treaty wants information, and you can give it without loss, why not? Also, you can then gain information you might otherwise not obtain. So, it's all to the good, wouldn't you say?' He buried his face in his goblet.

'Did you really tell them I'd killed Cadwallader?'

'They'd heard a garbled version. I corrected them. What did they expect from a princess who had been surprised in her bedchamber by some outlaw determined to carry her off? There might be some parties who would subscribe to such "rough wooing", but I understood the Saxons were not among that number.'

'Otto still chose Matilda.'

'Which means, whatever happens, you have an ally in Otto's court.'

'But?' Emma pointed at the dais, where Henry and Wenceslas were hobnobbing like old friends.

'Just because Henry and Wenceslas behave as brothers, it doesn't mean Otto will be friends with whoever next has the Bohemian crown—or dukedom. Does it?'

It was at the dinner later that night when Emma's future life opened up before her like a chasm. She had almost reconciled herself to marrying the puffed-up page. That was the first thing, his title. Her idea of a page was a little boy. It seemed, in Bohemia, a page could be a grown-up, and a grown-up page not only served his master at table but also was his bodyguard in battle. Her error, and Mark's error too, was in thinking the page was also the nephew. After all, wasn't Podevin (thankfully the page had a name she could just about pronounce!) there in attendance and serving them their supper? Or would have done if Wenceslas hadn't sent him off to get 'the youngster'. For all he was supposed to be there, for all Podevin insisted he had seen his charge into the hall for the meal, Mladenic was not to be found. Emma noted the flash of anger in Podevin's emerald-green eyes as he was sent off. They had not exchanged a single word.

☙

As he made his way out of the hall, Podevin tried to compose himself. What was he supposed to do? Be in two places at once? The two knights he had charged with watching over Mladenic both blamed the other for losing him and regarded his absence as a case of, 'If he wants to miss a meal, then it's his look-out.' Without Wenceslas's specific order, Podevin would have agreed with them, and left it at that. He leaned over to the central plate in front of the knights and grabbed a piece of bread, used it to envelop some nameless meat, crammed the handful into his mouth, and caught Wenceslas's eye. It was not friendly. The Bohemian ruler even gestured to the seat, the empty space, at the top table. Podevin had his orders, so he took his empty belly away from the tables piled high with rich food, the sauces and even the smells of fat dripping from roast pork, and mutton, and beef. The rich colours of the fruit—the dark purple grapes, the red and green apples, the brown nuts ready to be cracked open to reveal the salty smoothness of their creamy, filling, flavoursome kernels.

He could even feel the sinews of his solitary mouthful with his tongue. With an effort, he swallowed, but the result did no more than tell his stomach how empty it was. Even the apple core he'd given Blaze would be welcome now. Podevin made his way back to their quarters, walking past the guards on every door—including those to their own chambers—where he found servants carefully sorting out his, Mladenic's, and Wenceslas's clothes and other equipment.

'Found anything not to your liking?' he said as they paused when they saw who had arrived. He spoke in Czech. Deliberately.

'We're obeying orders, that's all,' came the reply in guttural German.

Podevin nodded. Had the positions been reversed, Wenceslas would have ordered the same careful sifting of what had come into his castle. He switched to German. They might as well know there was no point in holding conversations thinking he couldn't understand.

'I'm looking for the young man, Duke Wenceslas's nephew. Have you seen him?' He included the guards in his question, but the answer was obvious.

Mladenic, although he could have hidden himself away in the garderobe, or possibly under the bed, was not the sort to conceal himself from those he deemed lower rank than his exalted status. So, it was no surprise when all Podevin received in reply was shaking heads.

Podevin stood outside Wenceslas's quarters. Where would a ten-year-old go in an unfamiliar environment? Where would he go if he'd decided to duck out of what was going on in the great hall? Podevin looked round the courtyard. Wooden buildings, most no more than shacks, leaned against the more permanent structures. All ready to re-open in the morning, selling their wares to the castle company or anyone else who had business here. This might be a defensive structure, but it was one that did not expect an attack anytime soon. There were cobbles under his feet, and everywhere was clean—much cleaner than Prague.

Except for the church, which stood in splendid, central isolation, ready for an impending royal wedding, the whole edifice seemed linked. Defenders could get from one place to another without unnecessarily exposing themselves to attacking arrows. He heard a whinny: the stables! Maybe Mladenic had gone there to feed himself and hide away? It was worth a try; he'd have a quick look, and then head back to the feast, whether he'd found his quarry or not. If nothing else, Podevin wanted to eat something before it was too late.

Also, he had said he'd check on Blaze. Podevin set off, the noise and smells guiding him towards the opposite side of the inner courtyard—opposite the hall, that is. Always a difficult decision; where to keep the horses? A knight's most valued possession, a lord's most feared weapon, and the pack animals must also be tended if the lord wanted, or needed, to get his equipment moved. King Henry, it appeared, was often on the move, so there were a lot of horses. Podevin went unchallenged as he entered the stables, but not unwatched. The grooms were gathered outside, eating and drinking. Everyone had food this evening, it seemed, except him. He did think of asking them whether they'd seen Mladenic, but resolutely turned backs, once they'd worked out who he was, dissuaded him.

The stables went on forever. Keeping up a low-volume, but cheerful, monologue so the horses knew he was there, he found Blaze. The black stallion's ears came forward on hearing him and the horse let him approach. He felt Blaze's flank. He'd been rubbed down before being given access to water, hay and even some oats. Blaze nuzzled him.

'Sorry, lad, I've nothing for you. I've had nothing myself!' He really was going to have to stop thinking about his empty, growling stomach—he had a job to do.

A final pat and he turned away. Only then did he notice the food the horses had been given. Thistles in the hay. So many thistles.

'Just a minute, lad,' he said.

A few extra thistles for one horse could be an accident, but he could guess at another mount whose mouth would not want to deal with anything prickly. The pony was in a stall but had her head down. He approached, soft and calm, doing nothing to startle her.

'All right, my lovely. Let's just have a look.'

Once, as he'd said to himself, could be an accident, twice was stupidity, but the whole lot? Podevin charged back outside.

'My God! I hope your orders came from on high! Disrespecting the king's guests might be one thing. I know you saw me! But maltreating the horses. What have they done?'

Surly faces turned to him. Shrugs, and a muttered, 'Who are you?'

'Who's in charge here?' Podevin said in his best barrack-room voice.

'I am. So what?' The man was standing apart, having appeared from round the corner.

'Are all those animals, delicate mouths or not, really meant to eat thistles or starve? What do you think they are, donkeys?'

'No. But their masters are!' That came from the group still sitting down, but the laughter was choked off as their boss glared at them.

'Let me see,' he said, indicating to Podevin that the Bohemian page could precede him back into the stables.

It didn't take long; now his eye was in, he could see the quality—or lack of it—in the feed the horses had been given.

'As I said, we might have offended, but these animals?'

Podevin did not have to raise his voice. Nor did the chief groom. By the time the two of them strolled back outside, the group had broken up and there was a lot of activity. Podevin noted the chief groom had singled out one man—perhaps it was the man who had made the comment about donkeys—and was calmly but fiercely berating him.

Podevin let him finish and watched as the man slunk away.

'Don't worry, your horses will have the best from now on.'

'Thank you,' said Podevin, 'but can you watch the pony? Her rider was hard on her mouth—she might need special attention.'

'Don't tell me, your little lad?'

Podevin nodded. 'Don't know where he is, do you?'

෴

An unused, straw-filled stable. A sulky boy.

'Even telling tales on me to the Saxons! I'll—'

'Tell your father? Of course you will. And I'll tell him you absented yourself from the presentation to King Henry. Unless Wenceslas tells him first.' Podevin hauled Mladenic to his feet and began, not too gently, brushing the straw from him.

Chapter 4
The Husband Revealed

Wenceslas bored Emma senseless with his talk of Christianity but, beyond checking that Mark could still be her chaplain—she needed one friend on her side—she had merely been agreeable, and allowed her thoughts to wander. How old was Wenceslas then? Early twenties? Couldn't have been much older, and certainly she was old enough to marry him instead of the nephew. Wouldn't that make for a stronger alliance with England? Duchess Emma of Bohemia had a nice ring to it. She gave up on that line of thought and started wondering how Wenceslas could be the Duke of Bohemia if his brother—she assumed it was a brother—had sired a son as old as Podevin. If Podevin was to be her husband, hadn't she better save him some food? No-one else appeared to be bothering, and she found she wasn't that hungry herself. She put food in her mouth for politeness' sake whenever Wenceslas reminded her to eat. How was she supposed to cope with Podevin's native tongue?

It wasn't Podevin she had to worry about when he reappeared with the boy. The boy, moreover, kept his head down as he scuttled around the side of the hall to the Bohemians and had to be dragged, no other word for it, towards where she and Duke Wenceslas sat at the top table. As they approached, she could see Podevin's mouth set in a thin line, his hand clamped to the child's shoulder, should the latter wriggle free.

'Ah! There you are, nephew! You took your time!'

Emma still didn't get it. Why should she, as it was Podevin who gave a stiff bow. The little boy merely glared, only moving when he saw there was food on the table.

'Come, come, lad! You can sit with us and greet your intended wife. She's even saved you some food! Where were you hiding? The stables?'

At that, the boy, with straw still attached to his cape, jerked himself free from Podevin and clambered onto the bench next to her. The child grabbed the platter and started stuffing his face. Emma began to rebuke him, but subsided when she realised Wenceslas was still smiling. Indulgent. She glanced at Podevin, who gave the briefest of shrugs, an equally brief bow at Wenceslas's back, and turned away.

'This is your nephew? He's a child! And an ill-mannered one at that!'

'And you were never a child who disobeyed your elders and betters? I assure you, he hasn't killed anyone, at least.' The words were mild, the dark blue eyes steel.

Emma looked round the hall, seeking Brother Mark. He was talking with Podevin, who was trying to grab some food from a dish in the middle of the table as he did his best to answer whatever Mark was saying. Mark looked up and stared straight at her. With a sharp gesture, she indicated the little boy to her left. Mark held his hands out, palms up in a gesture of appeasement. They would talk later, but not now, as King Henry was standing; the meal was over. A clatter as chairs were pulled back and people stood up from benches. Emma saw Podevin wipe his mouth with the back of his hand as he stood—uneaten food still on his platter. The boy next to her was still chomping food down his gullet; she left it to the noble on his other side, she never found out his name, to lift him to his feet.

The man earned a hissed, 'Don't you know who I am?' for his pains.

Emma didn't care. She cared even less when Wenceslas suggested a progression round the great hall to where her future subjects were waiting to greet her and the child.

Mladenic objected. He didn't want to get married. He didn't see why he should marry—and certainly not her, some person who talked funny and was so old she'd probably be dead in a year or two. If Emma waited for a telling off from his uncle, she waited in vain.

However, before she could take matters into her own hands, Mark materialised by her side.

'Be gracious, they know what he's like.' A murmur and a warning.

So, she was gracious. She nodded, smiled and kept silent as Bohemian lords bowed over her hand. The hand soon to be given in marriage to a ten-year-old child, but it was Wenceslas's arm her hand was tucked into as they made their way out of the hall. All the while, her supposed future husband declared himself bored of the whole thing, reminded everyone his father needed to agree before anything could happen, and demanded to know where he could get some proper food. It was Podevin who was told to take the nephew to the kitchens, if he needed food that badly.

'Come on, then!' Mladenic said, leading the way, only to be held back by an old warrior, whom Emma was told afterwards was called Duke Radslav.

'You'll leave after your king, not before!'

'The king's gone, and Uncle Wenny's only a duke!'

'I said, *your* king. And your uncle is King in Bohemia.' The old man leaned down to the boy. 'And you know full well he doesn't like being called "Wenny"!'

'I'll tell my father on you!' But Mladenic stopped struggling and no more was said. Wenceslas was able to proceed peaceably out of the great hall and escort Emma back to her chambers.

❦

Later that night, when they had retired to their shared bedchamber, Matilda turned to Emma.

'Sister, I am sorry.' Emma barely heard the words. It wasn't until Matilda grabbed her that she took note.

'I thought we'd both remain in Saxony! And I wanted to be able to spend time with you!' There were tears in Matilda's blue eyes, and Emma looked away from supervising her packing.

'So, Princess Matilda, what had you understood?' She smiled as she said the words, but she knew her sister had always been adept at knowing only what she wanted to know.

'I knew the king—Athelstan, I mean—wanted me to marry Otto and I was to make myself pleasant to him. I mean, I was the one chosen when it was just one of us coming to Saxony.' Matilda's eyes still pleaded with Emma. 'And for you, it was either come with me or go to a nunnery, like—' She stopped.

There were other sisters who could have been married off, but Edfleda, Elfleda and Ethelfleda were all nuns. While Edfleda was much older than them and had perhaps chosen to take the veil, there were rumours that Elfleda had found an unsuitable lover and her entry into the convent was punishment, but why Ethelfleda was in a nunnery when the girl was but ten, was one of the English court's unasked questions. Three of their father's daughters sacrificed to God? It was indeed a man's world when your half-brother could send you across a continent, or to a convent cell, on a whim. Emma held her arms wide, and Matilda fell into them for a weepy embrace.

'I wanted—' Matilda stopped speaking again.

'Wanted what?' They separated. Matilda moved to the window.

'I don't know. To please everyone? Keep everyone happy?' Matilda gazed out into the darkness before turning her weepy gaze to her younger sister. 'But Mark says we can only look after our own happiness.'

'Full of wisdom is our Mark.'

'But now you're off with a load of barbarians!'

'They can't be that bad if Henry's friends with them!' But it was said more in hope than expectation, now she had met her future husband.

Chapter 5
The Journey to Prague

The feasting was over, the goodbyes had been said, promises of eternal friendship and peace between one and all had been made, and the various groups of people were all heading off in different directions from the castle.

The Bohemians were to be the last to leave. The trumpeters fell silent after tooting all the other groups out of the castle gates. Podevin stayed in his place beside Wenceslas, watching as Prince Otto and his new wife stood with King Henry, all making appropriate diplomatic noises. The flags hung limp in the quiet. The night had been clear and, although the morning held the promise of later heat, Podevin felt the cold air grab at his throat as he breathed in another sigh. He was glad of his riding gloves and his boots. A horse snorted in the silence.

There was a hiatus. The goodbyes between Matilda and Emma were, predictably, going to be drawn out with hugs and tears. Prince Otto had to stand aside for a while. As part of their goodbye ritual, Matilda tugged a ring off her finger; Emma copied her. The rings were exchanged and Emma, after yet another hug, finally turned and walked over to the litter that was waiting for her. She had wanted to ride, but Wenceslas insisted she arrive at Prague Castle appropriately, that is, as a ladylike bride, fit for a Bohemian prince. In the end, it took the intervention of Brother Mark before Emma conceded defeat. The fact that everyone else was riding didn't help. The ladies-in-waiting were riding side-saddle with a mounted soldier as an escort.

The youngest one, a mere slip of a girl, seemed quite content to flirt with the young man who had been ordered to stay by her side. The older ladies seemed less keen on the idea, saying at least one of them should be in the litter with Emma. The princess disagreed.

Matilda and Emma's bodyguard, who had accompanied them all the way from England, had decided what they were doing. Princess Matilda, without thinking it through, or perhaps in a desire to please her new husband, had been inclined to dismiss them all, but Wenceslas pointed out that Emma might need familiar faces around her on her way to the Bohemian capital. Of course, this then caused a slight diplomatic incident as some of the Bohemian men-at-arms were inclined to take this as an insult against their ability to protect their new princess. Wenceslas merely pointed out that, until they got to the Saxon border, Captain Artur and his men would be with them as well. It would make for a large party of Saxons, Anglo-Saxons and Bohemians, but, if the princess felt happier with some familiar faces around her, then who was he to deny her? Podevin hid his grin behind his hand as he saw Emma's expression over the male patronising attitude. Her smiles and nods seemed somewhat forced as she conceded that Geraint, if not the rest of his troop, was a familiar face.

In the end, all the married Anglo-Saxons set out for home from Augsburg; the single men, under the command of Geraint, would accompany Emma; and the decision to go back home or stay would be made in Prague. Matilda, it appeared, required no Anglo-Saxon protection now she was a married woman. Mladenic took no part in this or any other discussion about or involving his future bride; he was too busy studiously ignoring her. That had been another diplomatic incident. Emma had descended from her quarters to be greeted by Wenceslas and Mladenic. As, or so she thought, a gesture of appeasement, she had sunk into her deepest curtsey.

'My lord Wenceslas; my lord Mladenic.'

Her greeting left her lips, and she had dared to rise upright, when the shrieking started.

'She called me a child. A little boy! How dare she make fun of me? I'm not little, I'm not 'the youngster'. You can't make me marry her. She's ugly. She's horrible. I hate her!'

By this time, Mladenic was puce, his fists clenched, and his uncle Wenceslas was trying to placate him by insisting Emma would apologise.

'His name is Boleslav!' Mark, who had done his materialising act again, hissed at her. 'Just do it.'

Emma could see she was the centre of attention, most of it male, and all looking unfriendly, so she sank into a second curtsey in Mladenic's direction.

'I am sorry, my Lord Boleslav, for giving offence. I pray you can forgive my ignorance.'

She kept her head bowed. Nobody had told her Mladenic was a nickname. Her resentment at her predicament built in the silence.

She heard whispers.

Then, 'All right! She can stand. But she had better behave from now on.'

Emma rose to see Mladenic flouncing off across the courtyard towards his pony. After an awkward silence, in an aside to Radslav and Podevin, but barely glancing at Emma, Wenceslas decreed Mladenic's attitude was best ignored and that he would change his mind sooner or later.

☙

Unlike with Otto and Matilda, there had been no ceremony; Emma could go to Prague as the younger Boleslav's prospective bride, but not as his actual wife. Perhaps fearing a scene from Mladenic at the altar, Wenceslas had conceded the point. Podevin wondered if it would have been different if the ten-year-old had not been there, and someone like himself would have been able to stand proxy for the bridegroom. Not that he was looking for that sort of role. Given the princess's reported ability to argue with anyone and everyone to the point of killing them, he preferred to give her a wide berth. Although he was of royal descent and second cousin to Wenceslas, he was not quite sure if his rank would hold any merit with the foreign princess, even if she was alone and hundreds of miles from her home territory.

Podevin watched as Emma, the perfect picture of feminine decorum, climbed into the litter and settled back on the cushions provided. The party moved out, with Wenceslas in the lead and Mladenic by his side. The promotion of Mladenic to the Bohemian's ruler's right-hand side was galling. Podevin narrowed his eyes, but Mladenic did seem to be gentler with his pony; he wasn't tugging on his reins, anyway. Then, with a stomping of feet and harsh commands, Captain Artur and his troop moved out, followed by the Anglo-Saxons, who provided a guard around the litter. Podevin was with Radslav in the rearguard.

'It's past time you mended your fences with Radslav,' Wenceslas had told Podevin earlier. 'If I can forgive him, so can you.'

Podevin had bowed his neck and said nothing. They both knew, for all that Radslav's actions had not been the direct cause of Podevin's father's death—that was a Saxon mace—Podevin still reckoned he was an orphan because of Radslav's tactical decisions.

Thankfully, marching pace is universal and there was no need to hurry. There was also no need to talk. What could he say anyway? 'You got my father killed,' was not a brilliant opener, and the reply could only be, 'It was in battle.' Podevin concentrated on the countryside and the crops in the fields. There was even an occasional vineyard groaning with grapes. Every now and again, Wenceslas would turn and ride back to the litter to check on how Princess Emma was doing. After the third check, however, she decided that she had had enough and was going to draw the curtains and snooze. Mladenic made no effort to communicate with Emma. Podevin noted this, and even forgot himself so much as to venture to point it out to Radslav.

'The boy will grow,' came the reply. 'You don't choose your bride in his station in life. His father should have told him that by now.'

The silence between them descended again, so Podevin was left alone with his thoughts as they plodded on down the road, over hills, through valleys, through forests and meadows, making their slow and steady way back to Prague. Despite the clop of the horses' hooves, despite the tramp of the men's feet kicking up the dust, Podevin could still hear the trill of the birds from the bushes or high up in the blue skies. The oaks and the ashes and the elms were just beginning to lose the leaves; the golden, the red, the yellow, the occasional brown. But there were plenty of green leaves still attached to their branches and twigs catching rays of an only slightly weakened sun. They'd make it back to Prague before the autumn rains. Occasionally, they could hear water as they approached another tinkling brook and, inevitably, it would then be time to rest, as well as keep the supplies of drink as full as possible.

Especially with such a large group, it would not do to pass one flowing brook simply to find the next one had dried out at the end of summer. They had brought plenty of other provisions with them. Henry had been generous with his beers, his cold meats, his flatbreads, and even some early fruits; but still, the men were glad to forage for berries and nuts in the woodlands by the side of the road. At every stop, the women formed a little phalanx around Emma and made sure she was comfortable, well fed, and not bothered by any men. Podevin wasn't too sure whether Emma would have preferred to be able to walk by herself, but she seemed too listless to argue with her chief lady-in-waiting, who had, apparently, known her since she was with her wet nurse.

The first crisis, when it came, was nothing to do with Emma or Mladenic. Mabel was the youngest lady-in-waiting and seemed to regard the whole affair as a bit of adventure, and was quite happy to contemplate not going back home. She had also, despite the language differences, seemed most content with her Bohemian knight as they rode their way through Saxony. How she had slipped away from the rest of the women and, indeed, the rest of the Anglo-Saxon camp after they had stopped for the night, no-one was ever sure. The trouble with travel is that it is tiring, even when all you're doing is sitting on a horse. So, despite being on a lumpy bed, Podevin had slept well. So had everyone else. Including, it seemed, some of those who ought to have been on guard duty in and around the village where they had camped.

Therefore, the second day started with Wenceslas, Radslav, Artur, and Sir Geraint questioning their troops. But if anybody had seen anything, they were keeping very quiet. What was certain was that, if Mabel had been a virgin the previous night, she was no virgin now and her escort had been much closer to her than his orders stipulated. The two of them had spent so much of the night not sleeping, that they had been discovered together 'in a state of undress', long after both should have been about their duties. The unhappy couple were separated while Wenceslas retired to the village hall and considered what to do. Podevin watched Brother Mark go up to him and whisper in his ear.

Wenceslas straightened up, and called Podevin over. 'Would you give the Princess Emma my respects, and ask her to join me here?'

Podevin left the rude village hall and jogged over to the hut where Emma and her other ladies were staying. He hovered in the doorway until Emma noticed him and invited him to step over the threshold.

'King Wenceslas sends his respects, madam, but he would like you to join him in the hall.' He remembered to speak in German.

'Am I to witness the execution, then?'

'We are not that barbaric, madam!' replied Podevin, stung by her assumption.

'You watch your tone, young man,' came the response from the chief lady-in-waiting.

'Peace, Ursula,' said Emma, 'and let us go and see what the King of Bohemia wants.'

Podevin watched as her women stood. He'd only been asked to bring Princess Emma.

'I don't think he's expecting your ladies-in-waiting, madam,' he said.

It may be Wenceslas would not be bothered, but Podevin was hanged if he was going to be seen by his fellow Bohemians as incapable of escorting one female into his master's presence. Emma looked at him.

'I think he wants a private conversation. Brother Mark is there,' Podevin said, only then wondering why it was that Mark had been in Wenceslas's presence.

Podevin felt himself flush as the hazel eyes bored into his soul, but stared back. Then she nodded once.

'Stay here,' she told the ladies and stepped away towards the king's messenger.

They said nothing to each other as they walked the short distance across the village green. At one point, Emma stumbled on a tuft of grass and Podevin instinctively put out a hand to prevent her from falling. Emma grabbed him, and Podevin felt the warmth of her touch but, almost before he'd thought to ask if she was all right, she straightened, nodded at him and resumed her stately pace towards where Wenceslas was waiting.

As soon as they appeared in the doorway, Wenceslas beckoned them to approach.

'I do not normally censure my troops for immoral behaviour, but I understand your lady-in-waiting is from a good family and would normally expect to marry well.'

Emma inclined her head but said nothing. If she was surprised at Wenceslas going straight to the point, she didn't show it.

'I could, to satisfy honour, have Stanislav executed now. But, as your chaplain has informed me, we may have to wait to see if there is a child on the way. Further, there is another solution.'

Another pause. Podevin saw Emma shift her weight from one foot to the other, but her gaze, apart from one brief flicker in Brother Mark's direction, remained steadily on Wenceslas.

'Although Stanislav is not from the highest family in my realm, he is not from the lowest. His cousin is well known to me, so, while there would be no dukedom, there could be a reasonable match.'

'Are you saying that, instead of punishing them, they are to be wed?' Emma raised an eyebrow but did not seem annoyed.

'It is a better solution than an execution or two. And who knows whether their marriage will be punishment or not?' Wenceslas spread his hands.

Podevin looked up in surprise. Was he making a joke?

'I see. Mark?' Emma said.

'King Athelstan is unlikely to travel this way, even if he was inclined to disagree with your plans for young Mabel.'

'My plans?'

'It needs your agreement.' Mark stated the obvious. He had somehow moved close to her other side, so he was able to lower his voice to continue. 'And, while I cannot suggest you lie in your letter to your brother the king, it might be best to leave out certain incidents?'

'Like last night?' said Emma. She raised her voice to address Wenceslas. 'All right. Given the alternative, let them be married. But keep them apart until we get to Prague!'

With that, she swept out of the hall, and returned to her women. The hall emptied until Podevin was left with Brother Mark and Wenceslas.

'Well,' said Wenceslas, 'we'll just have to put Stanislav with the rearguard, I suppose. Podevin, will you go and inform Radslav?'

Podevin left on his mission. Later, he understood Stanislav faced considerable ribbing when he joined the rearguard, but, given the alternative, Stanislav submitted with good grace. All in all, he did not seem too bothered that he was about to get married to someone his parents hadn't even met, much less approved of. As for Mabel, she was to travel with Princess Emma. Quite what they would talk about, Podevin could not guess; he had seen Brother Mark talking to the young lady-in-waiting, trying to make her see the folly of her actions, and then to try to stop her crying.

Despite the interruption caused by the night's events, they made good progress. All too soon, they were at the border, and Captain Artur led his troops away, presumably to deal with any bandits lurking in the forests. The rest of the party pressed onwards into Bohemia. It was pleasant and cool under the shade of the trees. They would have to march some way into the evening to get to the next decent stopping off point, but nobody voiced any objection. Both Anglo-Saxons and Bohemians were determined not to be the first to admit tiredness. By the time Wenceslas decreed they could all stop, Princess Emma had decided she was bored of Mabel's sighs and that the next day would bring different company. Podevin assumed her other ladies-in-waiting would fill the breach.

Chapter 6
Unwilling Conversation

He would never find out if Emma, or Mark, or Wenceslas made the decision. All Podevin knew was he was informed after the fact.

'And what am I supposed to talk to her about?' Hands on hips, Podevin stood in front of Wenceslas.

'I'll have due deference, if you don't mind—you call me "sire", or have you forgotten?'

'I have forgotten nothing, cousin!' Podevin said. 'I sometimes wonder if there are things you have forgotten.'

It was dangerous territory; a ruler could dispose of his lands how he willed. Wenceslas might be older, and he might be the ruler of Bohemia after his father and his uncle before him, but there were limits. He was also family. Second cousin was still family. Wenceslas had dues to pay to Podevin, and promises to keep.

'I hardly think this is the time and place. All you're being—'

'All I'm being asked to do is desert my place again. First, I had to nursemaid Mladenic, now Emma!'

Wenceslas came close, leaning towards Podevin. They were alone, which was why Podevin had dared to push his grievance as far as he had.

'Your place, young man, is where I say it is!'

So much for Podevin's pride at being promoted to the bodyguard.

'After you have listened to Radslav—your favourite!'

'What is it between you and Radslav? He doesn't understand it, *I* don't understand it! And, for what it's worth, *cousin*, both he and

Brother Mark think you might be able to help Emma come to terms with her destiny. Introduce her to our ways. That sort of thing.'

That sort of thing. What did that mean? But Wenceslas had turned away, as was his habit when he was pressed. Short of grabbing him, forcing him to turn around and discuss Podevin's lack of lands, lack of inheritance, lack of status, the talk was over. Besides, it was too late; other voices demanded Wenceslas's attention.

Podevin's lord and master stopped long enough to say, 'You ride beside Princess Emma, this day and every day until we arrive in Prague. And mind you think of things to say. Radslav tells me most of your ride with him was spent in silence.'

Then he was gone.

~

Despite Wenceslas's orders, there was mutually hostile silence as Podevin brought Blaze to a walk beside the litter. Podevin had half-hoped Emma would take one look at him and decide to draw the curtains, so he could justify not saying anything. Wenceslas's court was hardly overrun with women, and what women there were, tended to stick together, so Podevin's experience of conversation with the female of the species was, at best, limited.

'This is ridiculous. Is this my choice? A surly brat, or a sullen teen-ager!'

Podevin looked down at the face glaring up at him. She spoke in German, but he'd already worked out she had no Czech.

'You're supposed to be engaging me in conversation, aren't you?' Emma continued.

'And what topic of conversation would madam like to begin with?'

'"Madam," he says! Dear God!' She flung herself back on her cushions, out of his line of sight.

Up ahead, over the heads of the marching troops, Wenceslas chose that moment to turn his head and look back at Podevin. So the young man sighed, turned towards the litter, and tried the only opening gambit he could think of.

'How would you like to be addressed? And what should I talk about, other than myself?'

The final words had popped unbidden out of his mouth. The last thing he wanted to discuss with a foreigner was his grievances.

'If that's all you have, we'll start there.' But Emma didn't sit up again, so he just had to hope for the best.

'I have been serving Wenceslas since I was seven, and—' He got no further.

'Seven! This country has servants from the age of seven?'

'When their fathers are killed defending the king, and their mothers are already dead, then, yes, the orphan is taken into that king's court and looked after. Maybe it could have been better, but it might have been worse—a lot worse.' He hadn't meant to speak so sharply, or so truthfully, and lapsed into silence again. Great! Now he really had made a mess of it. What would Wenceslas say?

'I'm sorry. I didn't know.' Emma had sat up in the litter. She was busy rearranging her cushions, but still managed to look at him with a disconcertingly direct gaze.

'No reason why you should.' Podevin tossed his head to break eye contact, so she would not see the tears that had started at his unwonted memories. Blaze chose that moment, with a jangling of his bridle, to toss his head as well. 'Easy, boy.' Podevin patted his horse's neck. 'Easy. You're not in trouble, lad. You're fine.'

After another shake of head, neck and shoulders, Blaze settled down.

'Is he yours?'

'Yeah,' Podevin said, patting Blaze's neck again. 'He just doesn't like plodding, do you, boy? You'll need a good, long gallop once we get home.'

Blaze's ears pricked up at the mention of home.

'Find me a horse, and we'll have a race.'

'Sure. Why not?' The words were out of his mouth before he realised why not. 'Assuming the king allows it.'

He could guess the answer. Bohemian ladies never go to battle, so don't ride … He tried to explain, but Emma affected to believe he was afraid of being beaten by her.

'I'd like to see you try,' he muttered.

A mistake; Podevin spent the next ten minutes hearing all about Emma's aunt and her fighting prowess against the Vikings. All he could do was counter with the Bohemian foundation myth, where the prophetess Libuse had to marry before she could be accepted as being a joint ruler with her husband.

'The people demanded a male ruler, and that's what they were given.'

'But she was a prophetess, and she pronounced the laws.'

'Only under Premysl's authority, I'm afraid.'

Why was he 'afraid'? He could see that Emma would find it difficult if she tried to replicate her aunt's authority in Prague, but he hoped she would be able to adapt.

After they stopped for lunch, it was easier for the two of them to re-establish their conversation. Emma's request to ride for the afternoon—she was getting a crick in her neck from having to look up at Podevin, up there on Blaze—was turned down by Wenceslas. She had to learn how to behave as a Bohemian lady, whatever she might have done back in England.

However, once they were underway again, Emma was perfectly happy to hear about Podevin's training with Blanik—once, that is, she had worked out who Blanik was. By now, Podevin was not stupid enough to ask if she knew what a castle constable was, or what he did, but merely contented himself with saying Blanik fulfilled that role in Prague. He tried to describe his former tutor to Emma. Blanik was broad-shouldered, an excellent fighter and general. He was a big man, but not pretty—there had been, so it was said, a childhood illness. And everyone called him Blanik.

'What should I call him?'

It took a moment for Podevin to realise what Emma was getting at. She didn't want to make another mistake like when she had called her betrothed by his nickname.

'Blanik. It's one of our stories, "The Knights of Blanik." People disappear on Blanik Mountain and reappear after a year. No-one gets to know the knights who ask people to do things for them. Those are old tales, and our Blanik never says where he is from. It might be Blanik Mountain. Wenceslas trusts him.' Podevin grinned. It was an old legend and it no doubt suited Blanik to have a bit of mystery around him.

Blanik had risen through the ranks to be in charge of Prague Castle. Now, rather than taking all the lessons, it was Blanik who sorted out who was to be taught what, though he came and watched the sword and axe play often enough. Especially when Mladenic made one of his visits.

'Why when Mladenic comes?'

'Because he cannot be injured. Not even a bruise, and I'm too often the one who has to lose!'

He had given himself away. There were many times he had left the practice ground bruised and battered when he knew it was the young child who should be coping with the blows. It was when someone got under your defence and hurt you that you started taking notice of how to stop them.

'That's ridiculous! Can't you trip him up?'

'Easily, madam, and I'd often love to, but his father would have my head.'

'Surely he's got to learn?'

'Apparently, he's too young for that sort of lesson.'

'But not too young to marry,' said Emma, lowering herself back on her cushions.

There was a pause. Podevin cast about for a new topic of conversation. He settled on the times he'd had to help Wenceslas make bread and wine. As Emma said, these were not seen as kingly pursuits among the Anglo-Saxons.

'I'm not sure they're kingly pursuits here, either, madam,' said Podevin, 'but my lord is used to doing it, and no-one stops him.'

'He doesn't spend all his time doing that sort of thing, though, does he?' asked Emma.

'Oh no, madam,' Podevin hastened to assure her. 'He also fights the occasional battle and duel!'

Here, Podevin glanced back toward Radslav, still leading the rearguard.

'Yes,' murmured Emma. 'I heard about that from Prince Otto. But you're among those who would have preferred Radslav to have lost that duel more permanently?'

It was old news in Bohemia, but the idea that they knew in Saxony, or England, about Duke Radslav's rebellion, startled Podevin.

However, Princess Emma wanted to know, so he revisited the time when he was nine, a new young member of the court, and told her how Wenceslas had led a small troop out to Pristoprim, 'a small village in the foothills towards the south of Bohemia, madam,' challenged Radslav to a duel, and defeated him.

'And then he forgave him, madam.'

'Everything?'

'Yes, madam, everything.' Podevin paused. 'I have to say, in the spirit of Christian charity, there have been no more rebellions.'

'So, it's worked? This forgiveness?'

'It appears so, madam.'

'You're not convinced.'

She was looking at him. Podevin broke eye contact first, unwilling to recall the time when he was seven and his father's bloodied body lay on a battlefield not far from where they were marching now.

Chapter 7
Attacked!

Podevin didn't want to talk about his memories. It was more than half a lifetime ago when he had run through the Bohemians lines, desperately searching, but dreading what he would find. His father still came to him in dreams, but he had shared enough with this girl, who, even if she was nearly the same age as him, he had only known for a few days. He turned the conversation to the countryside and hunting.

'Will I be able to hunt?' The inevitable question.

'Absolutely,' he replied, though he wasn't as sure as his words made out. Like riding, Bohemian ladies and actual hunting didn't usually happen. 'I'll take you if you like and show you the best spots.'

The words were glib, easy to say. For all he knew, Wenceslas, or Blanik, could decide that either Podevin would not take her on a hunt, or Emma would not hunt at all, due to her status as a foreign bride. Unless she would be content to follow on behind on a tame pony and not take part in any chasing or killing. He looked around. He was getting used to being back home, in his own country. He hadn't noticed how strung out they'd become. Blaze had accepted the plodding pace of the pack horses drawing the litter, and the cavalry had not stopped to listen to his childhood tales. It was good country to hunt in, though the woodland wasn't so good for horses.

'I'd like that. It will make a change from travelling like this anyway!'

From his position on Blaze's back, Podevin looked down and grinned at the Anglo-Saxon princess. She smiled back and shrugged.

Flaming arrows landed on the litter, which burst into flames. Chaos broke out. Podevin couldn't see where the arrows had come from. Without thinking, Podevin jumped down from Blaze and grabbed the side of the litter, but Emma was scrabbling around for something, despite the flames.

'Madam, get out of there!'

The Anglo-Saxon warriors were also quick to react; they had dismounted, weapons readied, and, with shields up, they ran to defend their princess. One of the first to arrive hit Blaze with the flat of his sword as the horse, though wild-eyed with the smell of smoke, seemed disinclined to get out of the way.

Screams and shouts filled the air as Emma finally found what she was looking for and leapt out of the blazing litter, sword and dagger in her hands. Podevin had his sword drawn as well. Most of the sound came from the other side of the flames, but then a second group of attackers appeared, even as Wenceslas came riding back with the vanguard, and Radslav and his men came charging up from behind.

'This side!' Podevin yelled as the first bandit reached him.

He ducked under the man's wild swing with a bill-hook, and came up with his sword in an overarm strike that connected between the man's shoulder and neck. The blade went into flesh like an axe striking rotten wood and then jarred as it struck bone. Podevin hadn't time to think as he pulled the blade away and the man fell, his neck three-fourths severed. He could hear screaming as he turned to deal with another attacker, armed with some sort of mace. The hand holding the mace was severed in one blow, which Podevin followed with a straight thrust to his chest, cutting through the padded jerkin. Podevin put his foot onto the dead man's belly and pulled his blade clear. There was another one to deal with.

Someone was getting close to Emma. Podevin turned again, but Emma herself had dealt with him; sword to hack at his right arm, dagger to finish him off. By then, the rest of the Bohemians and Anglo-Saxons had joined in the mêlée. Podevin could hear Wenceslas's shouted orders, while Geraint's bellow added volume as the Anglo-Saxons forced themselves into a group around Podevin and Emma. Screams, more screams and shouts. Constantly turning to check for attackers—there was still space, gaps in the wall of Anglo-Saxons. Podevin yelled at Emma, asking if she was all right.

'Back-to-back!' came the reply.

He realised it made sense. Without a shield, he'd found time to draw his dagger as well. Now, both of them held bloodied weapons in each hand. Who had he cut with his dagger? Emma's back was warm against his as they stood firm; anyone slipping under the still burning litter would have to deal with four blades. But now, everywhere they looked, they faced the backs of red Anglo-Saxon surcoats. Any remaining attacker faced a shield wall and some very determined, fully armed, men.

Quiet. Apart from one person squealing, it was quiet.

They had time to look around. The litter had disappeared in the flames. Horses can be trained to cope with a lot of things, but fire is not one of them. Someone, attacker or defender, but quicker-thinking than most, had cut the beasts free and they had galloped into the forest. It was time to take stock. Two Anglo-Saxons lay dead, taken by arrows in the initial attack. And there were a few walking wounded. The Bohemians had fared better; one dead, and a few flesh wounds to bind up. And just one voice squealing close by as the attackers fled, leaving their dead and wounded behind.

Slowly, as the shield wall broke up into individual warriors, Emma and Podevin moved apart. Embarrassed at having been so close, and in such danger, Podevin reddened.

'I am so sorry, madam,' he stuttered.

'For what? Saving my life?'

'No. No, I didn't mean that. I meant…' What did he mean? That he had killed his first enemy in her defence? That he was glad he had been there? That she was safe? That she knew how to fight?

'Will somebody shut that child up?'

Mladenic. He could have guessed. Podevin didn't know who had called out the order, but he was thankful he didn't have to carry it out. Mladenic was curled up in a ball in a ditch, well away from the fighting, demanding to be taken care of. Needless to say, he was completely uninjured. Now the shield wall had dispersed, the Anglo-Saxons, along with the Bohemians, were on the lookout for any remaining brigands prepared to offer resistance, as well as any wounded who might give up some information. Emma and Podevin stood together in the middle of the road and watched as Radslav went up to Mladenic, dragged him from the ditch and slapped him hard across the face. At least the shock of being hit shut him up for a bit. Emma stood and looked on, disgust written all over her face.

'And you have my full permission to go and tell your father I hit you!' Radslav growled at Mladenic. 'Now see if you can do something useful!'

Mladenic's idea of something useful was to make himself scarce. Podevin knew the child was only ten, and part of him wished he too could run away to hide. It was only now he realised he was starting to shake. A passing Anglo-Saxon warrior laid a heavy hand on his shoulder as if sensing this had been his first skirmish. Podevin straightened his back. He was fine; he had survived.

He stood by Emma as she dealt with Geraint and Wenceslas both enquiring whether she was all right. Of course she was, but there was no way she was travelling in that wreck of a litter for the rest of the journey; she would go on horseback and if they didn't like it, tough! If she was going to have to deal with this sort of welcome, she was going to be in a position where she could deal with it!

Nobody was disposed to argue with her, Podevin least of all. However, before he could voice his support, he had to leave her to the ministrations of her ladies-in-waiting. They, of course, had been kept away from the fighting, guarded by a small detachment of Radslav's men. And, of course, as soon as she had done her duty by her princess, Mabel rushed to find Stanislav, and was much more concerned about the minor wound to his arm than about Princess Emma nearly being burnt to death.

'The sooner the two of them are married, the better it will be for us all,' was Emma's only comment.

Then there was the clearing up. Weapons to be cleaned before they were sheathed. The litter was useless, but there were some items that might have survived the fire. The horses would need rounding up—if they could be found. Parties of troops were sent out to try and track them down. Podevin was torn between helping Emma and finding

Blaze; his dilemma was solved when he heard a familiar neigh behind him. A grinning Anglo-Saxon, perhaps the same one who had sent the horse on his way, handed over the reins, then loped off to do his duty elsewhere.

∾

They all heard it at pretty much the same time. Unlike the attack they had just endured, this was disciplined. This was horses moving at a canter. They could not tell how many, but the troops must be confident, approaching like this, with no attempt at disguise, no effort at being quiet. There was no time to form much more than a makeshift defence. The Anglo-Saxon shield wall that had done so well just now was pressed into lining up across the track, archers placed either side of them, and the mounted Bohemians in front with Wenceslas, ready to sell their lives dearly. Other men were quickly posted off to either side and even to the rear in case the noise of the approaching troop was covering more furtive movements from other directions. Radslav was muttering curses; he'd have led a charge at the enemy without a second thought.

The few walking wounded, huddled behind the lines, looked to their weapons as well. No-one spoke. Emma and Podevin were confined with the wounded in the centre. Podevin still held Blaze's reins. If the worst happened, he was to get Emma and himself on the horse and ride for Augsburg. Emma's ladies-in-waiting and Brother Mark were moving among the wounded, tending them as best they could while they awaited the outcome of the latest threat.

'Get me a horse.'

'What?' Podevin was too surprised to be polite.

'A horse.' Emma was looking at him as if he was being particularly stupid.

Which, of course, he was. Emma could ride. If she was ahead of him, he could still fend off the attackers so she had a better chance of getting away. He handed over Blaze's reins.

'Wait here.'

He dashed to the side of the road—the rescued horses were now tethered to sturdy branches. He looked up and down the line. Something

Emma could ride, but what? These were war horses, destriers. And those that were not, were pack horses, only good for plodding along.

'Hurry up. Or I'll take yours!'

It would have to be a destrier, and he hoped she could manage the beast. He led it back to Emma. She took one look, almost flung Blaze's reins at him, and vaulted into the saddle.

'Madam!'

'This is hardly the time for side-saddle, Ursula!'

Podevin grinned and mounted up. Now they could see Wenceslas at the head of his mounted troops as the other cavalry came round the bend in the road. He drew his sword.

'Madam,' said Podevin, 'I will die before they get to you.'

'Thanks for the sentiment, but let's stay alive, shall we? Your job will be to get me back to Saxony. If they really don't want me here...'

'I'm sorry. We all have bandits.'

'But we don't all have bandits who can call on cavalry.'

In other circumstances, it could have been a small attempt at a joke, but Emma was grim, her eyes red-rimmed. Podevin did not know what to say, what to do. This whole attack had all the hallmarks of something more organised, more official, than a few bandits taking a chance opportunity.

'We ride as soon as they strike the first blow. If they get past Wenceslas, Geraint will hold them for as long as he can.' Emma's words were low, but they were clear enough.

Podevin's admiration grew at her self-control. He glanced ahead at the few, the very few Anglo-Saxons. A shield wall would block a bandit or an outlaw, but an armoured knight?

'Are you sure?' he said. 'We could go now.'

Emma's horse pawed the ground. She checked it with an easy twitch of the reins. Despite himself, Podevin was impressed. Usually only fully trained knights rode war horses. His thoughts were interrupted by Wenceslas's laugh.

Laughing? What was going on? Podevin raised himself in his stirrups. And then, he too relaxed.

'It's Blanik. He's come from Prague. Reinforcements.' He tried to explain. 'They're on our side.' Podevin sheathed his sword.

Indeed, they were. There was meeting and greeting going on. Geraint stood his troops down. Emma and Podevin shared a glance. Then a giggle. Then both of them were laughing. The relief, the joy of being alive. She reached out her hand across the tiny gap between the two horses. Podevin took it. It only lasted seconds, but Podevin remembered the warmth of her hand in his for a very long time.

Chapter 8
After the Attack

It was Blanik who organised the meal. Soldiers who have been in a fight need feeding up afterwards. It was Blanik who took them to a clearing so they could camp. It was Blanik who sent out mounted troops to round up the rest of the horses that had bolted, who organised the double guard duty, and who made friends with Geraint. It was Blanik who heard from Emma how Podevin had saved her life, and it was Blanik who heard from Podevin how Emma had saved his!

Emma had found herself looking at Blanik's pock-marked and scared face. Only Podevin's hissed, 'Don't look!' reminded her of her manners. At the time, she couldn't work out how the Bohemians did not also stare at the big man, but time accustomed her to him. In the end, she barely noticed.

While all this was going on, it was Radslav who questioned the prisoners—those wounded bandits who had not made their escape. Podevin ignored the screams. They did not last long. They were only peasants, probably outlaws, paid by someone to disrupt the march home. No-one with any real knowledge would have thought they could have succeeded against trained knights. Podevin's mind skittered away from the fact that the bandits had so nearly succeeded with their plan. That is, if the plan was to kill Emma.

She found him after dark. He was sitting, squatting rather, by the campfire, roasting a piece of beef. It was more for something to do than because he was hungry.

'Can't sleep?' she asked, speaking in German.

'Can you?' he replied in the same language.

'Soon, perhaps.' She paused. 'Your meat's burning.'

He pulled it from the fire, looked at it. Offered it to her, but she shook her head. He looked at it again. And tossed it aside.

'A trying day,' she said.

'More for you than me, I suppose,' he replied. Then, because he had to say it to someone: 'I killed men today.'

'They would have killed you, or me, if you hadn't.'

'That's what I tell myself. But they always say, the first time—you remember it.'

'Yes. You do.' Emma looked into the fire.

'Today wasn't your first?'

She shook her head. 'I've been in fights.'

'But…'

'I'm a woman?' She was smiling.

He grinned, shrugged.

'When the men aren't there, and you're attacked, you have a choice. Allow yourself to be captured, or fight. I chose to fight.' It was her turn to shrug.

She pulled her cloak around herself and moved closer to the fire. Podevin found himself standing by her side.

'How old were you?'

'It wasn't that long ago.'

'And they got in?'

'Yes. They call it a "rough wooing". Kidnap your intended, spend the night with her. She can only marry you, or go to a nunnery. Or die.' Emma paused. 'He didn't expect a spear in his throat, his side-kick killed with an axe. The rest of them decided to call it a day, and my brother, bless him, decided to send me here.'

She looked around. Podevin noticed her shivering. He began to unbuckle his cloak.

'Here. You're cold.'

She nodded, but refused the cloak. 'Your king will notice, as will my intended husband.'

'Oh, Wenceslas is asleep. So's Mladenic.'

'Then he'll need you awake and alert in the morning.'

'I'd rather—'

But she turned and stopped his words by putting a finger on his lips. Then she hugged him, fiercely, tightly. And, for an everlasting moment, he hugged her back. She released him. Stepped back. Looked him in the eye. In the flickering, dying light of the flames, he could see her eyes were moist with unshed tears. He blinked. His own eyes had watered, but that must be because some stray ash or smoke had risen from the fire.

'We very rarely get to do what we'd rather do. Anyway, Brother Mark will be having words if we're seen.'

'You're afraid of a monk?'

She paused to consider the question. 'No, I don't think afraid is the right word. It's more the case that he's known me since I was an infant, and he's very difficult to lie to.' She turned away. 'Goodnight, Podevin.'

'Goodnight, madam.' He watched her return to her part of the camp. He went back to where he knew his place should be.

Podevin slept, as usual, at his master's feet on the dry ground. It was a troubled sleep; he dreamt of his father, and of Emma.

❧

In the morning, Mladenic told everyone who would listen, and many who would not, that he'd had an uncomfortable evening and night, but nobody was disposed to let him off from his chores. For once, he had to go to the stream to fill water skins, had to help sort things out, had to help strike camp, had to help make sure the wounded were comfortable. Podevin could see he resented it but, at the time, nobody, not even Wenceslas, cared. For Wenceslas had heard the attack on Emma had been set up by his brother, Mladenic's father. Duke Boleslav had decided, whatever Wenceslas might have said, that he was lining Emma up to be his queen. The ruffians, it appeared, had been gathered from castle dungeons and other unsavoury places, been promised freedom if they could kidnap, or kill, the Anglo-Saxon princess and, if in so doing, they managed to kill Wenceslas as well, they'd get lands and rewards beyond their wildest dreams. If they failed, well, the consequences were obvious.

Blanik had only found out two days ago that this was the plan. Boleslav had turned up unannounced at Prague Castle and done his best to pooh-pooh any thought of an attack. As for the idea of marching out to meet this supposed threat, that was just silly! Blanik had gone anyway, arguing that Boleslav had arrived with so many of his own troops that Prague Castle was hardly undefended, and if, say, there had been no attack, then he, Blanik, was just meeting the king on the road. He had managed to gather enough troops to make a decent company, then force-marched them along the route to Saxony. However, neither he, nor Boleslav, had counted on an Anglo-Saxon bodyguard supplementing the Bohemian troops.

'But why do they want Princess Emma kidnapped?' asked the king.

'I don't know. To show your incompetence? If you can't defend one princess, how can you be trusted to defend the kingdom? Besides, it looks to me as if they wanted Princess Emma killed! Once you have heirs, Boleslav's chances of getting to the throne are shot out the window, aren't they?'

'Blanik.' Wenceslas's voice was cold. 'You make too free. I do not intend to wed. Emma, as decided with King Henry, will marry the young Boleslav—and the boy will grow. Kings need to be more than warriors. Princess Emma will be happy in our court. I have not been killed, nor has the princess. And there will be peace once Bohemia is ready for me to go to Rome. Now, let us all try to live together in harmony. We have still to get to Prague.'

Hands clenched into fists, Blanik turned away. He shared a glance with Podevin on his way out of the hut. They both knew Wenceslas had not answered Blanik's points. Those bandits had come too close! The king went back to his breakfast. Podevin ducked out of the hut, to find Blanik just outside the doorway.

'The idiot's going to get us all killed—whether or not he gets himself done in first. And, for the sake of all that's holy, don't go getting feelings for the girl yourself!'

Podevin opened his mouth to respond to his tutor but was cut off.

'You were seen with her last night.'

With that, Blanik strode away, yelling at anyone and everyone to get a move on.

∽

There weren't enough horses to go round, despite the search through the forest, even if the Anglo-Saxon bodyguard went on foot—a suggestion they didn't take kindly to. The bandits were blamed; why run when you can steal a horse and ride? But the Bohemian party still had to have enough mounted troops, in case of further attack. The wounded had to be cared for. And the princess, it was accepted, could not be expected to travel in the burnt-out litter, even if it could be repaired in time.

Podevin let Wenceslas, Radslav and Blanik sort it out. He was too busy fetching and carrying supplies. He knew it was not Blanik's suggestion, but Emma was to ride beside him. Due to the lack of horses, there was brief consideration of the idea that Emma would ride behind Podevin on Blaze. However, for the person not in the saddle but riding bare-back behind it, the riding could hardly be comfortable. In an emergency, two could flee danger on one horse but, for a long ride to Prague, the Anglo-Saxon princess made it clear she would have her own mount. As she had shown her mettle on the back of a war horse during the recent events, her elders gave way. Her ladies had to make do with pack horses.

Pack horses don't canter, gallop or trot. They walk, and their walking pace is an amble. Even with soldiers at their heads encouraging them to pick up the pace, they amble. At the first stopping point, Radslav decreed that leading reins must be found and each animal tethered to a faster horse. It was incongruous and the ladies-in-waiting were inclined to grumble until Emma turned and glared at them. After a moment, Emma looked again.

'Podevin?'

'Yes, madam?'

'Whose horse is Mabel's mount attached to?'

It was Podevin's turn to take a second look.

'I believe that's Stanislav's mount, your highness.' He was ready to intervene on Emma's behalf until he noticed the amused glint in her eye. 'Do we say events conspired against us, madam?'

It was awkward, and he was feeling his way. The two lovebirds had clearly disobeyed an express command, but that command had been issued before yesterday's attack. Emma was still looking in Mabel's direction. Podevin saw the flush on Mabel's cheek as she dropped her gaze to the ground. Emma allowed herself a rueful grin.

'She knows I know. That will do. Besides, we need to get on. And Podevin?'

'Madam?'

'Less of this "madam" formality when we're alone.'

Despite himself, Podevin grinned, then nudged Blaze's sides with his heels so they could move into their allotted place. After yesterday, and the knowledge of who had planned the attempt on Emma's life, they could not be sure about when, or whether, another attempt might be made. Therefore, Emma was to be kept in the middle of the party. The idea, hence Radslav's agitation at their current slow progress, was to get to Prague within the day and confront Boleslav.

As Blanik's news was now common knowledge, Mladenic also knew of the wicked accusation against his father. As far as he was concerned, Blanik must be the traitor and must have set up the attack in order to make himself the hero when he rode to the rescue. Of course, if his father wanted Emma, Mladenic thought he could have her. He, the younger Boleslav, had better things to do than get married. It had been explained to him, patiently, that he had no choice in the matter; neither of getting married, nor whom he would marry. His father or, more to the point, his uncle, would decide.

'If Uncle Wenny can choose not to get married, why can't I?'

'Because you're not the king,' pointed out Radslav, not for the first time.

Chapter 9
Reaching Prague

'How long could I put off this wedding?' the intended bride asked Podevin that afternoon, during one of the last changes of the guard.

A brief halt had been called, as the horses were getting tired, and the men could not be asked to keep marching all day without breaks. Blaze was cropping the grass. Podevin had dismounted and loosened Blaze's girth, while Emma dealt with her own horse. There'd be a bridle to clean, especially the bit but, just now, Podevin had other things on his mind. Like Emma's question, and the realisation that he didn't have an answer. They would soon be coming in sight of Prague Castle and Podevin could only suspect the reality of arrival was concentrating her mind.

A small mounted troop had been sent on ahead with the message that all was well; the king was returning home, and he was bringing the Anglo-Saxon bride for his nephew. Quite whether Boleslav senior would agree that all was well was open to doubt, but he would, Podevin was sure, be at his diplomatic best. Mladenic, with all danger past, seemed anxious to get his story in first and rode ahead without waiting for any order to mount up. But Wenceslas sent Blanik to remind him that no-one—no-one—riding with the king, preceded the king into his own castle.

Once the young Boleslav was put in his place—back in the rearguard—they were ordered to mount up. Podevin retightened Blaze's girth.

'Last part of the journey, my lad, then you can rest.'

He had offered to do the same for Emma's mount but, in one of her many changes of mood, she seemed to regard it as an insulting suggestion that she could not deal with her horse herself. Which, of course, she could, very competently. They mounted, and she repeated her question.

'Mladenic was born when his father was fourteen,' said Podevin. 'The wedding was a bit hasty…' He trailed off.

He had been going to say something stupid about it being the first event he could recall after he arrived at court following his father's death. He covered up by telling Emma that Boleslav had tired of his wife and had her sent away and, although Boleslav had sired plenty of children, not all of them had been acknowledged and, of those who were, all the survivors except Mladenic were girls. The second he finished, he realised he had not been reassuring. What if Wenceslas decided Boleslav senior would be the better husband for Emma? A divorce and re-betrothal could be arranged—not for the first time in royal families. If that happened, what were the chances Boleslav would also tire of Emma and put her in a nunnery as well? Podevin tried to rein in his thoughts.

'I could end up waiting five years, or five minutes?' Emma said.

'Yes, I'm sorry. It depends on the king.'

Podevin sighed, his diplomacy exhausted as they approached the last rise and the castle came into sight. Less than a week ago, he would not have been bothered at the idea of escorting a foreign princess back to Prague. But now, with his escort duties coming to an end, he felt an indescribable sadness rising in his chest. It was absurd, but he felt the prick of tears behind his eyelids and a desperate urge to reach across the gap between them and hold on to Emma for ever and ever. He'd only known her for what? Four days? Five? She could never, ever, be his. It didn't matter that, over this last ride, Emma's beauty had shone forth; the way her hazel eyes sparkled when she laughed, the beautiful smile and a mouth (Podevin didn't need Blanik telling him he shouldn't think this) just made for kissing. She was a royal bride and would have to accept her fate, though Podevin imagined they would find it a problem if they expected her to just sit inside sewing.

Podevin pointed. 'There it is, madam. Prague Castle.'

Emma said, 'I've told you, when we are alone, I am Emma and you are Podevin. Understand? So, none of this is "madam" business, unless we are in court.'

'Yes, madam,' said Podevin, but he had his tongue in his cheek and earned a playful glare as Emma raised her hand as if to slap him. She lowered it again so she had two hands on her reins.

'Podevin?' The tone was new. For once, Emma sounded unsure of herself.

'Yes?'

'I'm going to need friends inside there. And I don't mean my women. Will you? Can you?'

If he could have done, Podevin would have stopped his horse. He twisted himself around in the saddle so he could look at Emma. She was only fourteen. Suddenly, that seemed very young to be on her own in a new country. Podevin was going home; Emma was going to a strange place, already betrothed to someone who didn't want her. And, moreover, a potential father-in-law who had been prepared, like that Welsh idiot she'd told him about, to try to take hold of her by force. Or kill her.

'Emma,' he said quietly, 'as long as we both live, I am your servant, and your friend.'

There was no time for anything else. They were approaching the gates. Emma had to compose herself and be a princess. Podevin had to be a mere Bohemian page, simply escorting a bride to her new home.

Boleslav senior was in his best finery, and superbly well behaved, bowing over Emma's hand and personally escorting her, with her ladies in fluttering attendance, to her quarters. He graciously allowed Geraint and Brother Mark to come along as well. Mladenic was allowed to go off with his friends and tell his tales of the dangerous journey. Wenceslas seemed happy enough to let his younger brother take on the role of host. However, Podevin did see the king looking on as his brother disappeared. Wenceslas's eyes were narrowed and, for once, he appeared worried.

Podevin saw no more; he was detailed to make sure the Anglo-Saxon troops were quartered comfortably, and all Emma's belongings, except of course those that had been lost in the litter, were to be taken up to her quarters. Quite how he overlooked her items in Blaze's saddlebags, he couldn't say. If Brother Mark guessed it was deliberate, he said nothing when Podevin came up to present the comb and the jewelled garnet rings to her, with his profuse apologies. Emma was surrounded by her ladies, and Boleslav seemed to have left a guard behind to match Geraint's presence. This other guard was someone whom Podevin did not recognise and so he had to assume the report would not go to Wenceslas, at least not at first. Just as the guard would do well to assume the king would be made aware of his presence at Emma's quarters, as soon as Podevin finished his duties and went back to the king.

At least Podevin was waved in and was able to present the items to Emma. She nodded at him and carried on discussing her affairs with her ladies. The reaction, given they were in public, was only to be expected, but Podevin kicked at every loose pebble in the courtyard after he'd left her. Dammit! Why couldn't he be the one marrying her? They could go and live at Budec Castle, his rightful family home, even if Wenceslas hadn't given it to him yet. Emma didn't need to be a queen, did she? Or they could somehow get rid of Boleslav and Mladenic—that was it! Podevin nearly failed to see Blanik, who was crossing the courtyard at the double, heading for Wenceslas's quarters. He saw Podevin and beckoned him over. Inside, they came upon a row.

'If you think I'm going to admit for one second that I organised an ambush, or that our darling mother had anything to do with it, you can think again. I am perfectly happy with my position, my son's position, and, as far as that goes, you have all obviously made up your tales to show my son in a bad light. And you—' Here, Boleslav turned as Blanik and Podevin entered the room. He pointed at Blanik. '—cannot be a good tutor. If you cannot train him to fight. I will remove him and get him trained myself.'

'Blanik seems to have done reasonably well in training Podevin,' Wenceslas said. 'After all, it was Podevin who saved the princess's life.'

'I am positive that, if my son had been a little older, he would have done the same.'

'But your son was there, or rather, he was running to hide.' This was Radslav.

'He's only ten!' Boleslav paused. 'So, you're all agreed on these lies and misrepresentations? And yet you still want him,' Boleslav addressed Wenceslas, 'to marry this woman who is five years older than him?'

'Four years,' said Wenceslas. 'And I'm happy for her to stay here until we decide your son is old enough for the wedding to take place.'

Blanik and Podevin were still standing in the doorway listening, but Boleslav had had enough.

'I'm not entertaining any more of this rubbish!' he said as he turned his back to them and made his way to the door.

'Oh, brother,' said Wenceslas. Boleslav paused but did not turn round. 'Next time you decide to send a group of ruffians against me and want to pretend that they are Saxons, at least train them to speak German.'

'Maybe I should just rip their tongues out,' muttered Boleslav. 'And yours too, Blanik.' He pushed his way out, leaving the room silent and, on Podevin's part, apprehensive.

'I don't suppose our mother is going to say a lot different,' mused Wenceslas.

'Sire,' began Blanik.

Wenceslas held up his hand. 'No, Blanik. I am not getting married. Once my brother or his son can be trusted to be good rulers of Bohemia, I am off to Rome. I will have no arguments, and no more talk of me getting married. Is that understood?'

Podevin never knew what prompted it, especially after what the king had just said. Perhaps it was the tiredness of a new warrior, bloodied in his first battle. Perhaps it was the culmination of years of hopes held in check as he had watched others take what was his. His father had died defending the king, and Budec Castle had been given to Podevin's half-brother, who had no right to it. Perhaps he was fed up, or, for the first time, had met a girl he could be fond of. But, without thinking, Podevin spoke.

'If you don't want to marry her, why can't I? I have royal blood and I'm more likely to rule this land as you want it ruled. Far more likely

than Boleslav, father or son! Can't you see it? They want you dead—
and us too, no doubt! And Emma and I are of an age! You can give me
my castle and lands, and we'll go and live there!'

'Enough! I said, enough!' Wenceslas glared as Podevin opened his
mouth again. 'Is this what you all think? Blanik? And Radslav—you're
hardly on the page's side, are you?'

Silence. That would be pushing it, Podevin thought. Radslav? On
my side?

'So, my enemies are closer than I thought,' Wenceslas said, but the
typical wry smile was back on his face, as if he expected nothing less.

'Sire! We are not your enemies!' Blanik said.

'You presume on your position to give me unwarranted advice.
Advice that goes against my known wishes.'

'Sire! Cousin! If you want your rule to continue after you have gone,
you need—' Podevin's words were stopped by a raised royal hand.

'My brother is my heir. And his son after him. King Henry expects
the Princess Emma to be married into the ruling family of Bohemia.'

'Which she would still be, if she married me.' Podevin's words were
no more than a low growl that Wenceslas could pretend not to have
heard, but he chose to answer anyway.

'You, Podevin, are my page and my bodyguard. Your half-brother
has your father's castle and, as it is near the border and he is a proven
warrior, that is for the best. Understood? Emma will marry the young
Boleslav as soon as the time is right. And, as soon as I can see that my
brother knows how to rule this land, he will have this land as its ruler.
That is my fixed intention. And I hope you all understand that, or I
will be looking for new advisors. And not amongst my junior second
cousins.'

Silence. The other three in the room looked at each other. They
bowed and begged leave to depart.

They understood, but they didn't like it. Podevin, the king's second
cousin—that is, one with enough royal blood to be a problem to a
usurper, but with no realistic prospect of succeeding to the throne—
didn't really know what he wanted. With Wenceslas married to Emma,
he'd at least see her, but what would Wenceslas be like as a husband if
he was constantly wanting to go to Rome to be a priest? What would

Boleslav be like once Emma had any sons of her own to rule Bohemia after Wenceslas? On the other hand, if Emma was to wait five years for Mladenic to grow up… A lot could happen in five years. He had promised to be her friend and servant, but could he even tell Wenceslas that? He was Wenceslas's page, not Emma's; but Emma needed a friend. And friends tell friends what they know.

Podevin needed to keep his wits about him. There would be a feast in Prague Castle's great hall that night, a welcome home feast. If he didn't see Emma before, he would see her there. He would have to tell her about Boleslav's denial of the raid. It was interesting, unless he had missed that bit, that Boleslav had not said anything about marrying Emma himself.

According to Wenceslas, that had not come under discussion. But Duke Boleslav insisted that Emma, as his future daughter-in-law, would come to live in his castle, under his protection. Emma, and her entourage, did not even get time to unpack. There was no time for any conversation.

Chapter 10
Christmas

A.D. 930

The Christmas season that year could hardly be described as normal. Firstly, there was Emma's flight from Stara Boleslav—the city that was Duke Boleslav's centre of power in the east of Bohemia. She, and the rest of her Anglo-Saxons, galloped up to Prague Castle gates just after dark, five days before the festivities. Blanik had to rush to the gates, order them to be opened, get word to Wenceslas, and close the gates before the second, pursuing party galloped up the hill.

Geraint, in full battle mode, had his troops dismounted and forming a shield wall inside the gate before Wenceslas and Podevin dashed to the courtyard. Blanik, catching the mood, was ordering his guards to the walls, ready to repel attackers. The second party stopped in front of the now shut and barred gates. There was silence. Emma, who appeared to be wearing hunting attire, dismounted and approached Wenceslas. She curtseyed but, before she could speak, there was a hammering on the gates.

'Open up! Open in the name of Boleslav, Duke of Bohemia, whose servant you are sheltering against the laws of the land. Open up and deliver those you are sheltering as our prisoners.'

'Servant? He thinks I'm his servant.' Emma was back upright.

'Go up there, Podevin,' said Wenceslas, pointing to the passageway at the top of the gates, 'and parley with them. And no, Blanik, you are not to give the Princess Emma a battle axe, nor even a sword.'

Podevin saw Blanik shrug an apology towards Emma, who had been in the act of appropriating a weapon from one of the guards. It seemed, this time, history was not to repeat itself. He mounted the steps to the wall, feeling very exposed until he realised Blanik had sent two crossbow archers with him. Podevin moved into a gap lit by torchlight. He could be seen, but anyone outside could see that, either side of him, were men ready with crossbow bolts.

'Most unfriendly, my lord,' called the voice from below. 'We have raised no weapons against you.'

'I will stand these men down when I can see you dismounted and without your weapons. You and your men.'

The other man's features were masked by the night, so Podevin could not tell how his demand was taken. He could only wait for action. It was a long enough wait. He could hear there was a conversation going on behind him between Emma and Wenceslas; Emma furious, Wenceslas placatory. As if trying to keep the peace between the Anglo-Saxons and his brother's forces was a matter of words.

Podevin's attention was drawn back to the men outside the gates. They had dismounted and were removing their sword belts. He nodded at the men, who put up their weapons.

'Don't go too far,' he said. 'I might need you yet.'

'So,' said the voice from outside the gate, 'may we enter and claim our prisoner?'

Podevin was about to refuse or, at the minimum, demand an explanation, when Wenceslas called up, 'Let them in.'

It was his command voice, and loud enough for it to be heard on the other side of the gate. The leader, if that was who he was, had already started to re-buckle his sword belt and was preparing to mount his horse.

'If you want to enter, you will enter one at a time. You will lead your horses. And you will be disarmed as soon as you have entered.' Podevin projected his voice into the distance, where the rest of the party was but shadows.

Then he turned to face Wenceslas's glare. A glare that resolved into a resigned nod as both Emma and Blanik clearly approved of Podevin's strategy.

There were twenty of them. All knights and all well-armed. Just opening the gate to that lot, would have been inviting a bloodbath, had they come charging in, determined to carry off Emma.

∽

It was all a misunderstanding. Of course Boleslav didn't regard the Princess Emma as a servant. And absolutely his knights had overstated the case when they used the term 'prisoner'. She was an honoured guest. She had been permitted to continue with any and all the lady-like activities Stara Boleslav could offer. And if his own visits to her rooms had not been welcome, all she needed to do was to say so. He was only visiting her in her quarters as his son was yet too unformed to appreciate that the lady might become starved of company, might prefer to get to know her prospective groom and husband. He had no desire, no wish to alarm the lady—by passing his arm around her, he was doing no more than showing his desire for friendship. No more. And he stated that on his honour.

All this and more, much more, had Duke Boleslav stated on his own arrival. An arrival made with much pomp and fanfare, two days later. Two days, during which Podevin and Blanik had been kept busy sorting out extra provisions, extra accommodation, and extra vigilance. It was clear there was no love lost between the Anglo-Saxon bodyguard and Boleslav's knights. In the end, it was decided Emma and her ladies would be guarded by Geraint and his men, and Boleslav's knights would remain out of the way—on pain of having their weapons broken.

Podevin was kept away as well. As far as her ladies were concerned, what Emma had suffered over the past months was unendurable. She could not possibly be expected to converse with any other men. She had made her case to the king and that was the end of it.

Podevin had more than enough on his plate to press for an audience. He could only hope Wenceslas would not give in to his brother, or Emma would indeed be a prisoner. There was also the party from Budec, headed up by Podevin's own half-brother, to be polite to...

❧

Except for the service in St Vitus's Church, where everyone had squeezed in to hear Father Militus extolling the virtues of poverty, chastity and obedience, Christmas Day was spent in the great hall. There was feasting, entertaining, and music playing all day in the gallery. Remarkably, there were no disputes. Even Duke Boleslav was on his best behaviour. His son, so it was said, was spending Christmas quietly back at Stara.

Normally St Stephen's Day, the day after Christmas, just like the day after any major feast, is a day to spend quietly, a day to recover from sore heads and even sorer stomachs. So, why was Podevin standing at an open window with Wenceslas breathing down his neck for 'a name, Podevin. Any name'?

The trouble had started when Brother Mark had crashed into the great hall, looking for Wenceslas's chaplain. Militus had failed to turn up to the chapel to lead the service.

'You address me as "Father". I decide when I say the office; and you, Brother Mark, should remember I am the priest.' Father Militus, Wenceslas's priest, not long arrived from Rome, had squinted at his interrogator and resumed his contemplation of his breakfast.

It was fair to say the priest's long face was greyer than usual, with a hint of green underneath the pallor.

'So? You've taken holy orders, have you not? The daily offices are a requirement, are they not? As priest, you are to set an example, are you not?' Mark was not in a forgiving mood and strode towards the priest. 'And nightly fasts cannot be broken until Mass is said.'

The priest's meal clattered to the floor. Father Militus was on his feet. The sudden movement was a mistake. He swayed and grabbed the table.

Brother Mark did not let up. 'I wonder how long you will keep your position if you get too inebriated to stand—much less able to elevate the host and blood of our Lord.'

'I'm sure our heavenly Lord will forgive a little over-indulgence on his earthly birthday.'

A dutiful titter of appreciation greeted this sally from King Wenceslas. Podevin, from his position standing at the king's side, offered up a silent prayer of thanks; the quieter life was today, the better.

'A feast day is no honour to God if some overindulge whilst others starve.' The monk had everyone's attention now.

He left the priest and wandered to the back of the hall, where, up some steps, a small window overlooked the wooden palisade surrounding the castle. The forest, in the distance, gleamed clean and bright like a winter jewel.

'Shall we take that man out there? Hardly overindulged?' The monk pointed out of the window and looked back at the king.

Which was where Podevin came in. He had to be Wenceslas's eyes and ears. Except he, of course, had no idea who this peasant was. Why should he? Never mind that it was a blizzard out there and the man wasn't even close by. He had squinted. He had stared. Then he had jumped when he found the king had come up behind them—Mark hadn't moved, he'd just gone quiet—and wanted his answer.

So, in his way, had Wenceslas. Podevin turned back to his master. 'That's Olaf, sire. He's a, uh, forester. He lives by Perun's fountain.' He gave the old name of the only spring he knew, one of many that eventually fed into the Vtlava as it flowed round Prague on its way to the sea. Duty done, Podevin smiled at Brother Mark, and bowed towards Emma. But the monk was not finished.

'Then you'll know just where to go, when you take his gifts, won't you?' Mark said.

Podevin's throat closed. His objection was forestalled by the king. 'Better go down to the kitchens, hadn't you? Meat, drink and firewood. We'll wait here. Oh, and Podevin…'

'Sire?'

'Isn't it Saint Agnes's fountain? We did give orders about those pagan names, didn't we?'

Podevin bowed, and left the hall, fuming.

෴

Kitchens don't exactly get a day off. But they do expect not to be so rushed off their feet the day after a major feast. And when it is *after* a meal time *after* a feast—even more so. Therefore, Podevin had a lot of explaining to do, and a lot of incredulity to overcome, when he turned up requiring more meat, drink and firewood.

Firstly, there was the fact that the great hall was already well stocked with firewood for the whole day. Secondly, there was the fact that the kitchen staff knew Wenceslas and his men (and women) had not eaten nor drunk the supplies which had been taken in earlier. Including the small beer.

'For a peasant? For a peasant! You're taking the king's food to a peasant?' Dalimil had his pride. He'd been turning out feasts fit for a king for ten years now, and never before had he been told to send meat, drink and firewood off to a peasant. So, Podevin had to explain how the Anglo-Saxon monk—yes, he was a foreigner and so, according to Dalimil, not to be trusted—had burst in on the midmorning ease and quietness.

Meat, small beer—the stuff that had been brewed twice, so it was practically water (and, no, Dalimil was not wasting wine on a peasant)—and pine logs had been found. Podevin realised he'd been too long when Blanik came looking for him. However, as there were now two of them to carry the stuff back to the great hall, it all helped.

'Your orders have been carried out, sire,' Blanik said on their return.

Wenceslas looked up and saw the little party gathered at the door.

'So they have.' He paused and raised his voice. 'All that remains is to get these provisions to Olaf. Any volunteers?'

The hall remained silent, unsure. After all, knights and dukes carried swords and battle-axes, not beer and logs. They rode horses, especially in this weather, to keep their fine clothes from getting muddy and wet. Surely, sending a servant was the obvious thing to do. They weren't volunteering for that sort of job. Podevin looked around. He turned his attention back to Wenceslas and saw that the king was smiling to himself.

'Well, I'll have to do it myself, then. Blanik, you're in charge.'

As soon as he spoke, there were cries of 'Sire!' and 'Allow me!' but Wenceslas ignored them all and joined Podevin and Blanik at the door. He looked at the basket of logs, put the meat on top, told Podevin to pick it up, and picked up the cask of beer himself. They walked out of the hall, not hearing any following footsteps.

Chapter 11
In the Snow

Podevin had been out in snow before. Of course he had, but it had always been as part of the hunt, or as a fun time before the end of the day. He could even remember being out with his father throwing snowballs before—he stopped himself from thinking along those lines. It didn't help; it never helped. But now he was out in the snow, ruining his new leather boots, lugging the best of the kitchen's remaining meat down the hill, and no doubt up the other side, for a peasant.

Oh, sure, the king was with him. And the king was carrying the beer. Something kings didn't normally do, but Podevin had the logs and the meat to balance in a bulky basket, while keeping his footing on the snowy hillside.

The king was making easy work of the drifts. Podevin could hear the beer sloshing around in the small cask on Wenceslas's shoulder. The king had his head down, eyes slitted against the daggered wind. Podevin lumbered after him, trying to hurry and trying not to fall over.

He was halfway down the slope before his first slip. He landed hard on his bottom, still holding the basket of logs. The venison jumped; the partridges fell out of the basket and splattered into the slush. Podevin muttered as he stood up, collected his provisions, and started off again, ignoring the noises behind him. If the guards wanted to laugh at his misfortune, why not let them? It was typical, he thought, that Wenceslas hadn't even noticed.

The second time Podevin fell, Wenceslas was a good ten yards ahead of him. This time, Podevin slipped on the snow-covered ice just the other side of the stream at the bottom of the hill. In order to save himself from further damage, he had to let go of the basket, which inevitably landed upside-down in a drift.

'Oi!' Too tired to think, too upset to be polite, he shouted at his master.

Not that the master in question was in any great condition to object, or to hear, apparently. Podevin scrabbled to get the basket upright before the logs picked up too much moisture from the snow.

'Oi!' This time, the shout had the desired effect, in that Wenceslas looked back. But someone else had also heard.

'You know, even in this wind, you're much too easy to follow.'

'Emma!' Too surprised to be formal and, realising he was pleased to see the smile on her face, a face surrounded by a fur-lined cloak, he blurted out the first thought in his head. 'But what are you doing out here?'

'Running away!' she said, making him stare at her in shock. She giggled. 'Or maybe helping you. Come on!' She bent to help restore the logs and meat to the basket.

'But your ladies? Boleslav?' he said, also putting logs back where they should be.

'My ladies, if they're doing anything, are watching us.' Emma turned and waved at the castle wall. There was no response Podevin could see.

'But?' He pushed for the whole story.

'I wanted to see what was going to happen with my own eyes. By the time I had my cloak, you'd gone. I snuck out the gate before they closed it. I thought I wasn't going to catch up, until you slipped … twice!'

Podevin looked at her. He knew that glint in her eye. 'If my falling over has served to give your highness pleasure, I am gratified, madam!'

'So you should be.'

'But, so you know, I've got a wet bottom!'

'*I* didn't slip!' The conversation was getting silly.

On another occasion, Podevin would have grabbed some snow for a fight, but they had to stop the verbal sparring. Wenceslas had rounded up the peasant and brought him over to join the party. The king stared at Emma, who met his gaze without flinching. A royal shrug and Wenceslas turned his attention back to the peasant.

'Right, you—Olaf, isn't it? We need some help here,' the king said.

The man looked blank but was awake enough to realise he was being addressed, so nodded.

'Yes, sir.'

Podevin opened his mouth, to correct the 'sir' to a 'sire' or 'my lord,' but a frown from Wenceslas made him shut it again.

'Right, Olaf, why don't you put your bundle in there.' Wenceslas pointed at the basket of logs. 'Podevin here will carry the meat, I'll carry the drink and Emma … will carry herself. How's that?'

Olaf presumably thought the question rhetorical because, while he put his bundle into the basket with alacrity, he didn't venture any comment. Indeed, he stood, holding the basket, looking from king to princess to page and back again.

'Right, Olaf, lead on,' Wenceslas said.

'Sir?'

'This is all for you.' Wenceslas was patience personified. 'We are bringing it to your home. So, you'd better take us there, hadn't you?'

'Oh, right. Yes. Your honour. Um. Er. This way.' The man grabbed the basket and stumbled his way back towards the forest.

Wenceslas followed, leaving Podevin and Emma to follow as best they could. The page stole a look back at the castle, now squat and imposing on the opposite slope, but no doubt full of piercing eyes, some friendly, others not, watching what had been going on.

'Keep up, Podevin; use my footprints, if you like, to guide you. Emma—you had better bring up the rear. And help Podevin if he drops any more food!'

With a mental shrug, a patient grin at Wenceslas's dig at his clumsiness, a lighter load, and Wenceslas's body providing some shelter from the icy wind, Podevin followed the two men towards the forest, with Emma walking beside him whenever the path allowed.

Now he didn't have to carry the basket as well as the meat, he made better progress. He still slipped a little on the way into the forest but, once past the first line of trees, the ice hadn't penetrated. Neither had the snow, except for the clearings, so it was simply muddy going. Olaf knew his way and, for the most part, king, princess and page grew no muckier—from the ankle up—than they had been when the peasant joined them. The forest wasn't even as gloomy as Podevin had expected. Yes, he had to get used to the lack of direct sunlight but, even in winter, there was dappled daylight in the clearings and between trees. No, they wouldn't want to canter their war horses through here, but even the king's night-black stallion could have found a way through, if he was going at walking pace.

It was still cold enough for Podevin to be glad of his cloak, and the exercise was warm enough for him to be glad that there was no conversation he had to take part in. He tried to say something to Emma on a couple of occasions, but she just shook her head at his opening gambits, pointing at Wenceslas. As she wasn't carrying anything, she was able to look around as they trudged along, often enough in single file. Podevin was careful to keep to Wenceslas's footprints; once or twice, there was a splash as their route took them across a boggy patch of ground, and Podevin still hoped he could dry out his boots before he needed them again.

Finally, they made it to some huts, decrepit-looking dwellings they seemed to Podevin. Even with his minimal experience, he could see that none of them had been maintained properly. But there was a fence to keep the wildlife out and a gate. Olaf had some difficulty with the gate—getting it open more than just enough to squeeze through was a problem. In the end, Wenceslas told the man that enough was enough and sidled his way through the gap. Emma and Podevin followed, with the gate closing as soon as Podevin, the last one through, had squeezed his way into the enclosure.

Chapter 12
The Peasant's Child

In the days when King Borivoy, Wenceslas's grandfather, had ruled, the forests by the river Vltava had been a safe place to live. Homesteads had been built, clearings enlarged, and people had gone about the daily grind of sowing where the soil was deep and living off the forest for the rest of the year. But, as is the way with all things, Borivoy died and his successors had other issues on their minds than the safety, or the lives, of a few peasants living in the royal forests. Homes were abandoned, fences left to rot, and the forest started to claim back its own. Occasionally, the process would be reversed when new people, who needed a place to live, would enter a clearing and decide that these huts would do for them.

In the biggest hut, which managed to be both smoky and draughty, neither Podevin nor Emma forgot that first afternoon listening to Lyudmila as she sat and told her tale. At first, Podevin was prepared to be bored; after all, what could a peasant girl know about recounting stories? However, as Lyudmila spoke about being seven months pregnant and aware she could no longer flee from town to town, village to village at a moment's notice, she knew she had to find somewhere to stay that was out of sight, Podevin forgot his discomfort, the dampness of his clothes, and became lost in the tale. Whether Lyudmila would have made the same decision to stop in this collection of huts if she had known how close Prague and its castle were, is unlikely. But her man, Krok, which they discovered was Olaf's actual name, although he would not admit it, was also exhausted with running away. His injuries were as healed as they were going to get, and he could see they could scavenge enough to start making the place, one of the huts anyway, habitable.

Their first night had been terrifying. The fire had kept the wolves at bay, but when, through exhaustion, they had let the fire die and a boar had come into the camp in the early dawn light—Emma gasped in sympathy, only relaxing when she heard Krok had killed it. Half-starved as they were, Lyudmila told them she hadn't cared about the hot blood spurting onto her chest. Or that one of the tusks had so nearly gored her leg before Krok's third stab had stopped it. And, despite being peasants and banned from such meat, they'd eaten it. Here, Lyudmila glanced at Wenceslas, but he waved away their crime. For the peasant couple, having so much meat available meant they had the energy to rebuild the boundary fence; after that, the wolves could howl, they could prowl, but they could not get at them. Eventually, the boar was nothing but bones and skin. They kept the skin and buried the bones. As winter set in, they'd been content with smaller game, knowing every kill deepened their guilt, but what could they do? Returning to Budec was no option. Maybe if they were able to stay hidden for a year, they could claim freedom, if Krok could get work in another village.

Lyudmila skipped over the details of how she became pregnant by the lord of Budec, Tugumir—who expected his rights from all his peasant women and took them. For their different reasons, both Podevin and Emma grew indignant, and then angry, as Lyudmila continued speaking in her low, calm voice. Podevin, unsurprised at his half-brother's behaviour, could only simmer in his discontent. Emma, however, could see parallels to her own treatment; had she not been offered first to a Welsh outlaw and then to a Bohemian boy? Two tears seeped from her eyes and down her cheeks as Lyudmila told them how, as soon as she started to show, Tugumir had cast her out. He had his thugs beat up Krok for daring to argue against the injustice of it all. Two castaways, lost, but unable to travel farther. Unable to travel at all for two months as Krok's injuries, broken bones and all, needed time to heal. But they had managed to steal away. In the time since their flight, Tugumir's henchmen had relaxed their guard.

After all, Lyudmila was just another peasant girl, only there to be used and cast aside.

Krok and Lyudmila knew they had to leave Budec, or live as slaves. While Wenceslas had been visiting Saxony, the two had stolen away at night. No directions. No idea where they were going, and no friends to help them. They had found this place, as they had said, and tried to make it a home. In the bitter winter, Lyudmila's waters had broken. In Budec, her mother would have helped and the other women would have known what to do. All she could do here was send Krok away so he didn't hear her screams. He had come back with one small rabbit, just as Maria's head was starting to appear.

Lyudmila had always been told men were useless when it came to childbirth, and could not handle pain like a woman. Yet, here he was, crouching between her opened legs, ignoring the blood, easing her daughter into the world. He had worked on the land; he had seen cows and sheep and pigs and horses deliver. Babies are smaller than foals. She had not known whether to laugh or cry when he said that. In the end, despite the exhaustion, she supposed she did both, before screaming again with the afterbirth.

Krok must have melted snow by the bucketload, but their daughter—she'd been so relieved—he'd held her as if she was his own. He'd even chosen the name. Maria was cleaned and so, very gently, was she.

There had been more snow and then more freezing temperatures in the night. She had insisted she would be all right. He needed to check all the home-made traps. The boar-skin was needed for Maria, so he had set off with nothing for a cloak. He would keep moving, he had said. There was enough rabbit stew for now, but Lyudmila didn't want to think about what would happen if Krok came back with nothing.

However, Krok hadn't come back with nothing. He had come back with a feast; with firewood, with beer, and with a nobleman who could only just hide his horror at their living conditions, and two youngsters who couldn't.

Podevin was horrified. He knew Prague could not measure up to Augsburg, but it was brilliant compared with this! Walls of mud, and holes everywhere—when had this set of dwellings last been cared for?

The rough outer fence was the best kept part of the whole establishment. The two smaller huts were so tumble-down, they looked more like half-walls forgotten in a clearing, just waiting for the forest to reclaim the ground they'd been built on. There had been an attempt to repair the walls and roof of the main building, but there was clearly work still to do. Those bits of bracken could not possibly be waterproof, could they?

Krok bustled about in the dusky, smoky midden they dared to call home.

'I'm terribly sorry, sir,' he said, 'but Lyudmila has only just given birth.'

'Which is why you were out in the freezing snow?' queried Wenceslas. 'Oh, don't worry,' he said as Krok glanced furtively at the bundle of sticks and the half-hidden rabbit. 'I know what you have in there, and I'm not planning to worry about it. After all, what would I say to Brother Mark, if I came all the way out here with provisions, and then hanged you for finding something for yourself?'

Krok looked at Wenceslas but said nothing. Podevin wondered whether the peasant had any idea who had come visiting. He supposed they took seriously the idea that Wenceslas could indeed have them killed, but then any noble could have any peasant killed and nobody would say anything; it was the way of the world.

Maria stirred in her sleep and started to grizzle. Her mother tried to stand. Instantly, with what Podevin assumed could only be female instinct, Emma jumped up and told the peasant girl she should be lying down, or possibly sitting—as she had been while she told her tale. But not standing. Emma picked up the little bundle and brought the baby to her mother.

As Lyudmila had told her tale, Krok sought to ease the tension of the situation by encouraging the visitors to sit. Podevin looked around for some chairs or even a bench. But there was nothing. Wenceslas pulled a polite smile and, tucking his cloak underneath him, sat gingerly on the log Krok provided. After a pause, Podevin followed suit but, without a full-length cloak, he was a bit more concerned about splinters; though the logs had at least been smoothed off and had been in the smoky house long enough for the sap to have dried up. However, there was still the dampness from his falls in the snow. He tried to ignore it.

Krok moved across to Lyudmila and had an urgent whispered conversation with her. Emma came to sit on the upended log next to Podevin, who gathered from the silence that the baby was asleep again. Leastways, the woman was able to sit up holding the child. Her husband helped her so her back was supported. She turned her head and looked at them.

'So, you're not here to hand us over to Tugumir?'

Wenceslas stared at her for a long moment. 'Why should we want to do that?'

'We're his property.' The woman shrugged. 'We were hoping to be able to live free here. Out of the way. Not harming anyone. But no doubt Tugumir said we're deserving of death.' She indicated the sleeping baby in her arms. 'And I don't suppose he'd care what happened to her.'

Wenceslas looked from the man to the woman. He looked down at his hands. He looked up again. 'You gave yourself to him?'

'I had no choice!' Lyudmila cried out. Then she turned her head away. 'I was simply there out in the fields when he rode by and demanded his due. I was to be married.' As if that was all the explanation needed, she stopped.

'And you?' Wenceslas said to the man, 'What's your part in this?'

'We're cousins,' came the short reply. 'My grandfather and her grandmother were brother and sister. There have been too many deaths in our family and, before he died, her father gave me responsibility to look after Lyudmila.' He looked down. 'I was too late.'

'Show them,' Lyudmila said. 'Go on!' she added as Krok hesitated.

Krok turned around and hauled the shirt off his back. Podevin didn't want to look, but stared. The man's muscular back was crisscrossed with scars. He heard Emma's gasp, her hand up by her mouth.

'It still hurts him, you know,' said Lyudmila. 'He can't do as much. We had to get away or die.'

Krok put his shirt back on and sat by Lyudmila. They looked at the king, waiting for judgement.

'I want a word with Tugumir. Back in England—' Whatever Emma was going to say was cut short when Wenceslas held up a hand.

'In England, you have bad masters as well as good ones. As in all countries.' Having secured her silence, he relapsed into his own quietness.

Podevin stole a glance at his king. The dying fire gave one last crack, ending the silence that had stretched to breaking point, and a few timid sparks ventured out to the edge of the brushwood. Krok turned and stamped the embers out.

'Why not build the fire up, and put some meat in the pot?' said Wenceslas. Krok looked back at him. 'Go on,' said the king. 'Tugumir will not harm you—and certainly not while you're on my land.'

'Your land?' breathed Lyudmila.

Podevin started. They really did not know who had brought them this largesse? Everyone knew who the king was! But Wenceslas smiled and stood up.

'I could insist that you bow, but I won't. I am Wenceslas. And when I say …' Here, the king started pacing, Podevin could see he had a peculiar half-smile on his face. He was planning something. 'And when I say,' he repeated, 'Tugumir won't harm you, I assure you he won't. And if I say you have your freedom, then my clerks will draw up the documents and Tugumir will affix his seal. For good measure, so will I. You two—sorry, three—will be able to live here unmolested. Besides, I obviously need a forester.'

During this speech, Lyudmila's face had registered scorn, disbelief and finally open-mouthed joy. She started to move. Emma prevented her, insisting her husband move to the fire and deal with it.

Podevin asked the obvious question. 'Surely Lyudmila could do that?' He meant sort out the meal.

'She's just had a baby! You really expect her to be up and about?' Emma turned back to the mother and told her not to move for a week.

Chapter 13
Promises, Promises

Wenceslas did not seem to notice the argument. He was too busy wandering around, looking at the hovel.

'Given the means, Krok could turn this place into a decent home,' Emma muttered under her breath to Podevin.

He would never have imagined doing women's work, but Krok seemed used to standing over the cooking pot. The king also went over and peered in. But it was not a long look—perhaps the smell reminded Wenceslas he had been a little too free with the wine yesterday, but he was still smiling when he left Krok to deal with the food.

Podevin could see it would be a little while before anything was ready. Anyway, Emma was cooing again and had the bundle in her arms, which she was holding out to him. Podevin glanced down and realised that Maria was awake. She was staring at him with wide-open deep blue eyes. One tiny hand had wriggled free of the cloths. Without thinking, Podevin offered his little finger, and stroked the tiny palm with it.

'Now you've met your niece. How does it feel?' Emma was looking at him, demanding an answer he did not know how to give.

Maria was his niece, his brother's child, a relation. He stood. He straightened his back. For want of something better to do, he rubbed his backside; it was a relief not to be sitting on such a hard stool.

'Well?' Emma said.

'I don't know how it feels. We…I…need to do all we can to help. But I can't exactly be happy about how she came to be, nor what my half-brother did to her mother, can I?'

'I take it you don't get on with Tugumir?' Emma's wry comment was unnecessary, she knew the answer.

Podevin nodded. His head was beginning to hurt, not from the effects of alcohol, but from trying to sort out what had been going on—today was meant to be quiet, wasn't it? A day when nothing happened. Not a day when he acquired a niece, had a fracas break out in the great hall between two men who were both supposed to be Christians, and found himself reunited with Emma. As he watched, lost in thought, she passed his niece back to her mother.

Wenceslas had moved over to the doorway and was contemplating the half-light. He turned.

'It seems we'll need your purse, Podevin.'

'Sire?' Podevin was puzzled.

Wenceslas carried no coin on him, as suited a ruler, so Podevin always had the purse on his belt.

'Yes. Now Krok and Lyudmila are joining society, their taxes must be paid, including those for giving birth.'

Podevin hastily untied the purse from his belt and put it into the king's hand. Without looking into it, Wenceslas handed the whole purse over to the astonished peasant, 'For all your obligations to the exchequer.'

Podevin gaped, before recovering himself. If Wenceslas wanted to give his money away, it was not Podevin's place to object. He did hope, however, that Wenceslas would explain the loss of funds to Blanik when they arrived back at Prague Castle.

Krok opened the purse. He looked in it, gasped, and rushed over to his wife, showing her the coins nestling inside the leather pouch. Lyudmila burst into tears but, encumbered by her child, could do nothing more than gabble her thanks.

'All right! All right!' said Wenceslas.

'But why are you being so kind to us?' Lyudmila asked. 'I don't understand. We now have food and drink and fuel—and even money to go to the market. And a place to live, and freedom.' Maria's mother, like Podevin, had reached the limit of her understanding.

The king leaned against the doorpost, taking in the hovel with his gaze. 'I'm doing what I should have done years ago. I have let too many people get away with the idea that this kingdom is run as if God did not exist. Things need to change, and I see no reason why they shouldn't start with you.'

Podevin wondered what Tugumir would say about it. Even if he did not make a fuss in Prague Castle about the loss of two of his peasants, Podevin could not see him forgetting about it.

The stew was bubbling away merrily in the pot; the smell wafting towards Podevin's nose was rich and meaty, and it reminded Podevin of home. He hadn't thought of home for a long time, but his father had told him his mother insisted that meat was not just for roasting. However, it seemed Wenceslas was not interested in partaking of what the peasants were offering; he had not 'brought all this food to gorge himself.' There was, after all, plenty still to eat at the castle. Podevin, with his younger stomach—and one that happened not to have overindulged in alcohol the previous day—would have sampled a snack. Emma went quiet, so he could not tell what her thoughts were. Whether they ate, or not, Krok would not have to go hunting for a while. Maybe he could focus on some repairs to the walls and roof. Wenceslas, still being polite and kind, insisted they needed to take their leave.

Krok escorted them out and heaved the security fence closed behind them. As the only one knowing the pathway, the new father had to leave his family behind for a little while until the visitors could see their way out of the forest on their own. Once he had been assured they could find their own way back, he turned and, within seconds, he was lost to sight.

The holly and the ivy with their dark green foliage, their poisonous berries glistening under the weak winter sun remained immobile as Podevin and Emma started forwards. However, with a muttered, 'Wait,' Wenceslas turned aside. Podevin didn't have to wait long. He barely had time to form the question on his lips as to why the king was in no hurry to get back to the castle when he had been in such a hurry to leave the peasants' hovel. A couple of coughs and Wenceslas was heaving up the remains of the food he had been idly ingesting in the great hall a short while ago. Normally, Podevin would have produced a bowl of water and a wet cloth to smooth his master's brow but, here, there was just muddy slush and nothing to use as a bowl. Podevin took the easy option and obeyed the order to wait. The heaving degenerated into dry coughing.

Once silence was restored, Podevin hazarded a couple of paces towards his master to see what was going on. Wenceslas had his right arm out, leaning against the rough bark of an oak tree, while his left hand was kneading his stomach and he was bending forwards far enough to keep his feet and his cloak from being splashed. He looked up and smiled ruefully at Podevin.

'Perhaps I shouldn't have had so much wine yesterday,' he said as he moved away from the mess. 'One of us might just have to get some water from the stream.'

He paused, stopped, looked, as if for the first time, at Emma, and said, 'And, until we get to the stream, perhaps our Anglo-Saxon friend can tell us why she came with us on our journey in the cold and snow today.'

Wenceslas indicated Emma should carry on walking and speaking, if she could 'cope with doing both.'

Emma shrugged. 'Perhaps I was fed up with doing nothing, just because I am a woman.' Seeing that Wenceslas wanted her to say more, she continued, 'I knew life was going to be different here, but I was raised in a royal household and I was raised to play my part in the running of that household. And that part involves more than sitting in a solar—where it is too hot when the sun shines through the window, and too cold when it doesn't—doing embroidery and sewing. I could not even ride out to watch, much less take part in, a hunt. Oh, and trying to think of ways to entertain a child who finds everything suggested to him "boring" on principle.'

To Podevin, it sounded like a prepared speech, but Wenceslas replied anyway.

'Doesn't that child have his lessons and training? I did say Mladenic could join us in Prague, and train under Blanik.'

'Yes, sire,' Podevin interrupted, 'but I was told Duke Boleslav was finding someone better for him than Blanik to train him.'

'He's finding someone more afraid of him than Blanik—that's quite different.' Emma said, only for Wenceslas to rebuke her.

'Careful, my lady, that is my brother you are referring to.'

'My lord. Sire,' Podevin had to interrupt again, 'you do know he is being called "Boleslav the Cruel" behind his back, don't you? If no-one dares speak truth to him, especially about his son, then what does that say about the future of Bohemia?'

'My brother knows, the sooner he can assure me he will govern himself and this country in a Christian manner, the sooner he will get to govern this country.'

'And if he doesn't?' said Emma, but she was met with silence. So she continued on to a different topic. 'Is Tugumir to be deprived of his castle and lands? Podevin could replace him.'

'Tugumir is a proven warrior.' Wenceslas held up his right hand to prevent interruptions. 'But he will be punished. However, I need Podevin with me at court—as my eyes and ears. It has not passed unnoticed that he has developed good relations with many people in the castle, whether in the kitchens or the stables.'

'Fine! But my father—' Podevin noticed they had all stopped. Perhaps both he and Emma had realised they wouldn't get another chance to talk as freely as this with the Bohemian monarch.

'Will be very pleased with you,' he said. He turned to Emma. 'As for my brother, I will talk to him. It was always assumed by Saxony that your alliance with my family would proceed sooner, not later.'

Emma bristled. 'Mladenic behaves as a spoilt brat and, because of his father, gets away with it!'

'Firstly, his name is Boleslav, like his father. Secondly, he will grow. I am sure he will make you a good husband. You have not one, not two, but three countries relying on that; Bohemia, Saxony and England. While we might have accepted your reluctance to return east, you must be aware I cannot keep you in Prague for ever.'

Wenceslas's little speech silenced Emma. Podevin sought to refocus the conversation.

'So, how much of all that stuff are you actually going to do for them, sire?' he asked, nodding back into the forest and the little family they had left there.

'All of it, Podevin. All of it,' came the mock-stern reply. 'Oh, regarding our talk just now, I do hope neither of you will ever make so free in your conversation with your lord and master again. Let's get on, shall we?'

Within moments, the chastened page and princess emerged from the edge of the forest onto the open banks of snow. Wenceslas heeded a suggestion from Podevin to scoop up a handful of snow and rub it over his face. The duties of a page did indeed include helping the king to kneel beside the stream so he could swallow several ice-cold mouthfuls of water. Podevin hoped the king found it refreshing.

At least the wind had dropped, so they didn't have to battle that as they clambered up the bank towards the castle gates. Thankfully, the guards didn't mess around; as they approached, the gates swung open and they could enter.

꙰

They could enter but there were none of the usual shouts of greeting. Podevin usually exchanged a smile or a nod with the guards, who knew him well, but eye contact was avoided and they made their way inside the castle without any conversation.

Podevin could see that Wenceslas was troubled. He was used to the idea that the king's more Christian activities were not approved of by a large section of the court, but mutterings, if mutterings there were, were kept very low-key indeed. All right, what they had been doing today was unusual; it was certainly unusual for a monarch, but would people not have been curious? Would they not have wanted to know what happened?

They had started to cross the courtyard when the door to the great hall opened and Blanik stepped out. As did Emma's chief lady-in-waiting.

'Sire,' Blanik said without preamble, 'you have been the subject of great debate. The principal point at issue is whether a monarch who is pushed around by a mere monk can really be trusted to rule.'

In the meantime, Ursula, all plump matronly indignation at the folly of her young charge, was berating Emma for going 'on a foolish errand without appropriate company' and 'coming back all cold and muddy'. Despite Emma's protests and Podevin's attempts to assist her, she was borne off to her quarters to change and be warmed up against any chills she might have caught. Thus leaving the men free to discuss what had been going on while they had been out of the castle.

'And people are taking sides?' Wenceslas asked, not breaking his stride towards his rooms.

Blanik accompanied him and Podevin as he made his report.

'Very few are openly against what you have done, sire. Most of those who think Brother Mark is in the wrong, have been careful to speak theoretically. But Father Militus is clearly unimpressed with the Anglo-Saxon monk—the feeling is mutual, by the way—and, need I say, your brother has made it clear he would not have behaved as you have?'

'I see,' said Wenceslas. 'And are they all still inside?'

'Most of them, sire,' said Blanik.

'At least I'm feeling well enough to face them,' muttered Wenceslas. 'Come on, Podevin,' he added as they mounted the steps to the king's quarters. 'First, we need new footwear. I don't know about you, my page, but my feet are frozen! Blanik, arm yourself and wait for us.'

Podevin grimaced. He'd have to wear his old boots for the rest of the day, but at least they were comfortable. Wenceslas could put on his fur-lined soft boots. They were only ankle high but would suffice. The brazier was alight and the manservant waiting. He took the muddy boots and promised to have them clean and dry by morning.

Wenceslas left his heavy cloak behind in his quarters. The great hall was always well heated. His seat was near the fire. Blanik was waiting just inside the door. He inclined his head as they passed him.

Chapter 14
Disputes

'Brother Mark,' said Wenceslas as they entered the hall, 'I can inform you that your instructions have been carried out to the letter.'

'Sire,' replied the monk, 'I was not aware that I had stipulated instructions. I merely took the liberty of reminding you of your Christian duty. It was others who mentioned your coronation oath. Which is something I have been stating repeatedly since you left.'

In the silence, Podevin accompanied his king as Wenceslas moved towards his throne. The priest and the heir were, of course, the most obvious antagonists in the hall but there were others. Podevin had been surprised not to see Tugumir in the thick of the argument but, as he took up his position behind the throne, waiting to see what Wenceslas would say, he saw his half-brother skulking in the shadows. Listening. Waiting to see which way the argument would flow, waiting to see when it would be the best time to declare himself one way or the other.

Wenceslas eased himself back in his throne, but Podevin could see the king was watchful behind half-closed eyelids. He leaned forwards to whisper in his master's ear.

'Tugumir's here, which is where I want him,' Wenceslas muttered before Podevin could say a word. 'Get me a drink, if you'd be so kind.'

Podevin bowed and went to do Wenceslas's bidding. The silence was like cold treacle, slowing everything, including thought. Even Blanik was watchful. Normally, he would have said something loyal, asked about the trip, checked whether the peasant was all right, but he was leaning against the door post, making sure no-one went in or out.

'Well, my fine loyal colleagues,' said Wenceslas at last, as Podevin presented him with his flagon of wine, 'you may be interested to know that our loyal friend "Olaf" has now a much better chance of surviving this harsh winter. We will be going out to see him again and, when we cannot, we will be sending emissaries—people we know we can trust to ensure that his home and his family are well cared for. However, there are a few things we need to clear up first, and we will be consulting with some of you, like Brother Mark, as to how best to do it.'

Wenceslas was interrupted by Father Militus.

'My lord,' said the priest, 'forgive me but, if I may make so bold, it is surely me, your confessor, and not some imported monk, who should be guiding you in any change of policy.'

'Or, for that matter, the royal council. Kings don't have peasants for friends,' put in Boleslav.

'Ah, yes, my royal brother,' said Wenceslas, dealing with the second interruption first, 'I was fully intending to consult you. As for you, Father, I would suggest that you be a little careful about your use of the word "imported". Are you not yourself imported from Rome?'

There was a pause. Podevin waited to see who, if anyone, was going to take their objection further, now the king was back. No-one said a word.

'You may all go. When I say I will consult, I mean I will do so if and when I need to. And I will decide with whom, and when,' said Wenceslas. 'So leave us, all of you, apart from Blanik, Podevin—oh, and you, Tugumir. I want a special word with you.' The king looked over his shoulder at Tugumir's skulking place when he made this last comment.

If the knight was surprised at being caught out, or embarrassed, there was nothing to see, no blush or downcast look that Podevin could discern, by the time Tugumir had walked to the high table. Throughout the hall, there was a scraping of benches and chairs against the floor as people stood. Podevin noted the glance between Tugumir and Boleslav. Boleslav, like everyone else who had been told to leave, bowed and retreated out of the door past Blanik. Father Militus bowed at least twice. His smirk of triumph as Brother Mark also prepared to leave was, to Podevin's eyes, nauseating. However, this did not go unnoticed by Wenceslas, who sipped his wine and waited until Brother Mark neared the door.

'Brother Mark?'

The monk turned and faced Wenceslas across the length of the hall. 'Sire?'

'As she accompanied us, be so good as to ask your lady to join me here—and return with her, if you please.'

Brother Mark inclined his head and exited. Father Militus, who had stopped his progress out of the hall as soon as Wenceslas spoke, stormed off. No doubt he was heading to his chapel to pray fervently for humility and patience in dealing with his young king, and for divine inspiration to guide that same king in the governance of his country.

Once again, silence reigned in the hall. This time, there were fewer people to break it.

'Sit,' said Wenceslas. 'Go on. Sit.'

Tugumir tucked himself down at the end of the table, out of Wenceslas's direct line of sight. Podevin took the place beside his master. Blanik wandered down the table, choosing his seat opposite Tugumir.

Wenceslas shifted in his chair, turning so he could face Tugumir.

'Tugumir, I am about to free those peasants that I went out to see this afternoon. And you will affix your seal to the documents as a witness.'

Podevin's half-brother was clearly puzzled; this was a role for clerks, after all, but he muttered something that could be taken for agreement. However, Wenceslas hadn't finished.

'You see, my friend, if it hadn't been for your actions nine months ago, these people would not be in the predicament they are now.'

Tugumir made to shrug but hesitated as the king's words sunk in. Podevin watched, intrigued. He would not have considered Tugumir to be remotely interested in the peasantry unless he needed something from them. Like his taxes. On the other hand, all knights should look after their people, should they not?

'Have you heard of *droit de seigneur*, Tugumir?'

Despite what had been said in the forest, a small hope began to rise in Podevin's breast; this was the man who had been gifted his father's castle a dozen years ago, though Podevin and he only shared a mother. He saw Blanik had his head cupped in his right hand, watching, making no comment but listening hard. Wenceslas, his eyes still slits, his voice sharp with anger, spoke again.

'You see, Tugumir, our peasant was out looking for both food and fuel so that his cousin—who is younger even than Podevin here—would neither starve nor freeze to death. It appears they are runaways and can only expect death if they dare to return to their homes.'

There was a pause, which Tugumir did nothing to fill.

'So, Tugumir; *droit de seigneur*?'

Even Podevin could hear the impatience in Wenceslas's voice.

Tugumir shifted on his seat. The door of the great hall creaked open.

'Sire,' he said, 'there are ladies present.'

'There is now one lady present,' came the reply, 'but I fail to see why my question cannot be answered.'

For the first time in his life, Podevin saw Tugumir redden with embarrassment. The knight coughed twice as he prepared to speak.

'It is simply an old custom, sire, that when a woman of inferior status wishes to get married, she spends time with her lord.'

'She spends time—only time?'

'It is assumed, sire, that...' Tugumir paused, searching for the right combination of words.

Princess Emma and Brother Mark came to the table and sat down.

Tugumir began again. 'It is assumed that her fertility will be checked—to make sure the marriage will be fruitful.'

'I see,' said Wenceslas. 'And how often have you exercised this right?'

'Sire.' Tugumir stood. 'What I do on *my* land is *my* business.'

'It is only your business while you obey the laws I lay down,' Wenceslas said. 'And, whether or not you obey those laws, I have every right to ask any question I choose, and to expect answers.'

'It is an ancient custom, sire.'

'Not a nice one, if you simply pluck the girls from your fields and expect them to comply with your springtime wishes. There is a child out there, and you are the father.'

Tugumir shrugged.

'One of many, is she?' Wenceslas was relentless.

'Sire, you would not understand. You cannot be kind to peasants.'

Wenceslas interrupted him. 'Whether I "understand" or not is irrelevant. You took advantage of a young girl for your own pleasure.' There was the briefest of pauses. Then: 'How much is in your purse?'

'What!'

'You heard. Either hand it over, or I'll get Blanik to cut it off your belt.'

Tugumir glared down the table at his king. His hand moved to his sword. Blanik, never taking his eyes off Tugumir, pushed his seat back and stood up. He placed his battle axe on the table between them, but not so close to Tugumir that the younger man would ever reach it if it came to a fight. Blanik was too experienced a fighter for such an elementary error. His opponent glared at him, then at the king, for a long moment. At last, Tugumir reached for his purse, flung it down on the table, where it landed between Wenceslas and Blanik, and stormed out. Or tried to.

'Guards! Arrest him!'

Tugumir stopped.

'Is that how you treat your king? Duels have been fought for less in the past, as you are aware.' The threat in the king's voice was obvious.

Tugumir licked his lips, but sanity prevailed.

'I crave your majesty's pardon. I will, of course, amend my behaviour, and will gladly attend you when you grant these—people—their freedom.'

'Very well. You may leave us.'

Wenceslas waited until the guards shut the door behind the disgruntled knight.

'Podevin,' he said, 'would you mind decanting it for us?'

Podevin emptied the purse onto the table and counted. 'It's nearly one hundred crowns, sire.'

'A lot to be carrying on his person,' muttered Blanik.

'But more than enough to set our friends up in their new life. Blanik, I want the charters drawn up as soon as possible to give them the land and the right to make their living off the forest. Including hunting deer.' Blanik made to interrupt at that, but subsided. Wenceslas had one more stipulation. 'I want it made clear that all their taxes have been paid up.'

'Sire?' Podevin had to speak up.

Wenceslas turned to him, indicating he could speak.

'Sire,' he repeated, 'we have already given them a purse.' He pointed at the gap on his belt where the king's purse had hung until recently.

'Ah! So we did.'

'And you did say it was for their taxes, sire.'

'What are you suggesting, Podevin? That I go to ask for it back?'

'Why not, sire, keep back enough to replenish your purse, and leave the rest for the couple in the forest?'

'Don't forget Maria, Podevin. Don't forget Maria.' The king paused, but Podevin's hopes were to be dashed. 'No. This is Tugumir's fine. Any knight who abuses a woman will, from now on, pay the same. As for my purse, I choose to be generous. We will send Brother Mark to explain. After all, if it wasn't for him, none of this would have happened.'

Podevin looked at Mark, who inclined his head, accepting his commission.

Breaking the mood, Blanik reached for the purse. Wenceslas put his hand over Blanik's.

'My friend, make sure they get this money.'

Blanik nodded. 'I'll get the clerks to draw up the charter in the morning.'

Until then, the princess had sat quietly, watching the drama. Now, she leaned forwards, looked Wenceslas straight in the eye, and spoke.

'Sire. Your brother, despite what he said to you about giving me space, saw fit to visit me just now. Brother Mark discovered him in attendance when you sent him to find me. He "forgave" me my "flight" to Prague, said if I preferred it here, I could stay—his son could always visit. However, there was another issue he wished to address.' Emma paused, took a breath, and carried on. 'Duke Boleslav is of the opinion you would probably get away with being kind to this peasant but, if you tried to be kind to the whole peasantry, you would face revolt.'

'Expected you to pass on the warning, did he?' said Wenceslas, amused by his brother's serpentine methods of making his point when he wasn't even in the room.

'Yes, but Brother Mark ventured to disagree, saying the peasants would work better if they were treated well.'

Brother Mark looked down at the table. Podevin thought that he had not expected his conversation to be repeated in front of Wenceslas. Blanik shot a sideways glance at the Anglo-Saxon princess and a more direct look at his king.

'Maybe they would work better, eh, Blanik?' said Wenceslas.

Blanik was bold enough to keep eye contact. 'Yes,' he said, 'that would be my thought. Though there were those who thought your being kind to a single peasant simply showed your softness to the peasantry in a general way, so maybe they won't be too surprised at whatever you choose to do.'

Wenceslas nodded, and allowed Blanik to leave to attend to his many duties in the castle. Then the king stood up and wandered over to the window. The same window he and Podevin had looked out from earlier in the day to see the peasant gathering his sticks and, as they now knew, checking his traps. He climbed the steps and pulled aside the heavy cloth that covered it, allowing an even colder draught to enter the hall. Darkness had fully descended as the short winter's day had drawn to its close. Out of the window, there would be nothing but shadows, nothing but the wind and the occasional curse of the guards as they kept station on the wall. If the clouds cleared, they would see stars, and that would be their only commonality with the peasant family. They too could look up at the same sky. Wenceslas stood there, looking out but saying nothing. Then he returned to the high table, letting the cloth fall back into place over the window.

'Tomorrow,' he said, 'I'm going to need to consult with the exchequer. I need to understand better all this process about taxation. We need to make things fairer—whatever the cost. And Brother,' he looked at Mark, 'we need to pray.'

He was looking at Mark and talking religion, but it felt to Podevin like a declaration of war. They all left the great hall.

Chapter 15
Friendship

'You can't blame the king!' Brother Mark said.

'Why not? If he hadn't pushed us together, a lot of this wouldn't have happened!' Emma replied, still furious.

'Are you saying you only liked him because Wenceslas took a hand in it?'

It was unanswerable, and Emma knew it. She'd known it that time they had been attacked on the road from Saxony; she'd known it that first Christmas in Prague; she'd known it through the years that followed before Boleslav staged his coup; and she knew it now during this conversation between her and Mark, when there was no hope of any further contact between her and Podevin.

The epilogue to that first Christmas, when Maria was born in a hovel in the forest, occurred when Wenceslas and Blanik left St Vitus's Chapel after the Epiphany Mass to find Duke Boleslav with his sword to Podevin's throat.

'When you kill a rat in its nest, you don't leave the young to grow up to bite your children!'

'Brother! That young man—that unarmed young man—is under my protection. I say he lives!'

'And I say, once you no longer live …' Whatever Boleslav had been going to say, he thought better of it.

Blanik, moving as quietly as he ever did, had retrieved his battle axe from the weapons store outside the chapel and stood holding it. Boleslav sheathed his sword.

Wenceslas spoke. 'I think, brother, you will leave today. Before there are any more disputes. Blanik will supervise your departure.'

'I'm taking the Anglo-Saxon wench with me!'

'I think not. Your son needs to grow up a bit before his marriage,' Wenceslas said.

'Then you'll keep her from that cur!' That cur, having risen to his feet and brushed himself down, made a move towards the weapons— Blanik's wasn't the only battle axe left behind before the service started—but Boleslav chose to misinterpret the gesture. 'See! He wants to defend her from me!'

'From you, brother?' Wenceslas could also misinterpret if he so chose. 'From you? But you're already a husband. Have you annulled your marriage? Because, if not, and if you violate the Princess Emma, I will not stand in the way of Athelstan and Henry when they seek your life!'

'You'd let them invade your lands!'

Boleslav opened both arms as if to encompass the whole of Bohemia, but Wenceslas folded his arms across his chest and waited. As ever, it was the younger brother who gave way. Wenceslas let him walk a few paces.

'Oh, brother!' he said. Boleslav stopped, but did not turn. Wenceslas continued, 'I think I will make Podevin our guest's especial guardian. I'm sure he can make himself useful.'

As far as the court was concerned, back at the start of the year of Our Lord 931, it was presented as a pragmatic solution to the problem of Duke Boleslav and his apparent desire to be close to Emma whenever he could. If she was with Podevin, learning Czech or any other aspect of court etiquette, then she would not have time to fritter away dancing attendance on her future father-in-law, would she? The fact that it did nothing to help positive relations between the king's brother and his second cousin was another problem. One Wenceslas chose to ignore.

Having decided that Emma would stay in Prague until her wedding and that it was now Podevin's duty to be Emma's guide and companion, Wenceslas was blind and deaf to Mark and Blanik's objections. If Podevin and Emma were 'of an age', then they would make excellent companions. If a young man and a young woman are constantly in each other's company and that very circumstance 'gives rise to talk', then that is good, for 'how is she to learn the language if they don't talk?'

'We mean gossip, sire—that this is more than a friendship,' Blanik clarified.

'We don't listen to gossip. And she is betrothed, so let her be faithful to that.'

'But the young people themselves! Their own feelings for each other may easily be aroused!' Brother Mark came as close as he dared to saying what he feared.

'Feelings? Why should feelings come into it? They both have their duty.' If the king chose to be so blind, Mark and Blanik could do no more than keep watch as best they could.

The two young people were told to pray for self-control, reminded that friendship was all they could enjoy, and left to obey the king's commands. Emma, as the one whose behaviour was under more scrutiny, was never able to work out over the next three years whether she preferred the times the two of them were together more or less on their own, or whether it was better to be part of a larger group.

When it was just the two of them, or as close to it being the two of them as court etiquette would allow, they would try to talk. However, was she allowed to link arms with him or not as they wandered, say, in the gardens? If she did link her arm with his, would someone who saw them report it to Boleslav? If she didn't and they kept their distance, would that distance be reported as a falling-out between her and Podevin, thereby offending Wenceslas?

When they did walk in the gardens, Podevin would have to confess he did not know the names of the plants, nor what disease each herb was supposed to cure. So, either they had to pursue the conversation by roping in Mark, or the head gardener, which stopped the conversation being just the two of them, or there was a horrible pause while they both tried to find a safe topic to discuss. Could they discuss what Podevin would do if he was given his castle? Could they discuss what Emma wanted to do if she could ever slip the leash of her ladies-in-waiting? And what could they do? In Bohemia, women did not take an active part in the hunt but, after much pleading, Emma was allowed to accompany the menfolk—provided she avoided being around at any killing.

Emma was allowed on a destrier. The first time, she and Podevin broke away from the main body following the hunt. Blaze needed a gallop too. They only went a short distance and back—they did come straight back—but they faced fury on their return.

With their flushed faces and heaving chests, who knew what they had been up to? Their protestations went for nothing. Their offers to show where they had been, to demonstrate that they had hardly had time to dismount, much less abandon their horses, were ignored. Emma was demoted to a palfrey—a tame, timid pony. When she followed the hunt ever after, her ladies and her bodyguard went too.

One of the very few times Emma was able to slip her leash was when she and Podevin were taken on a visit to the peasant family in the forest. Once Wenceslas had sealed all the forms, and Tugumir had dutifully witnessed them to say Krok and Lyudmila were no longer his vassals, Krok had become the king's forester, and Mark had taken on the responsibility of ensuring the peasant family lived unmolested in their new home. Podevin surmised Mark simply wanted to ensure Tugumir never located the huts in the forest. Emma had other concerns: How was little Maria getting on? What did their place look like now? Could they make a decent living from it? Therefore, when Mark suggested a trip out on one of the first warm days in the spring, Emma was happy to go along with the idea. A grudging permission was granted, on the understanding that Mark was in charge.

They were barely out of sight of the castle when Emma spoke up.

'I'm told you don't want Tugumir knowing where these peasants live? So why are we going there on the most easily trackable animal of all?'

'So whoever's following us can track us easily,' said Mark, guiding his horse northeast as soon as they'd crossed the stream at the bottom of the hill.

Emma looked at him, exchanged a look and grinned. Podevin tried to see what was funny, but failed. Emma looked at him, mouthed, 'Think about it,' and returned to conversing with Mark as the monk led them on another change of direction as they went deeper into the woods. From all he could remember, this was not the way to the hovel, but he was trained as a warrior, not a tracker. Emma muttered something to Mark, and he replied. Then Podevin spoke up.

'Will someone please tell me what is going on here—you two speaking Anglo-Saxon to each other isn't helping.'

'But I thought we were supposed to be teaching each other our languages!' said Emma, switching to German, which was still better than her Czech.

'Yeah but how can I practise? I can't spend all my time with Geraint and his mob, can I? Talking of that lot, where are they?'

'They were told you and I were sufficient for today's outing. We are only visiting a family, and not an important one, after all.' Mark, now speaking heavily accented Czech, led them to a clearing.

At the far side, he rode his horse down a muddy track and then, at a spot where the pathway became a bit drier, he dismounted and signalled for the other two to do the same.

'Where are the weapons?' Emma hissed, staring back the way they had come.

'But, madam, you know I am a man of peace,' Mark said. He then held his hands up in mock surrender as his princess turned on him. 'We couldn't say anything! We don't even know if we can trust your ladies—especially the Bohemian ones who have recently joined you—but we are sure you are being followed.'

'But why set it up like this?' Podevin asked as he at last saw what had been going on.

'Do you really think Duke Boleslav would risk taking on the whole troop under Sir Geraint? This way, we just might flush one or two out.'

'So, we're just going to hide here and see what happens?' said Podevin.

'Unless you have a better idea? We do want them to talk.'

'What are we going to do? Ask them nicely to tell us what they're up to?'

'Don't be ridiculous, Podevin,' said Emma who, although she had taken no part in the conversation, had not taken her eyes off the track. 'Shh!'

Chapter 16
A Life Lesson

Whoever was coming down the track had already dismounted; perhaps he had become suspicious. They heard him slip in the mud, and curse. Podevin drew his dagger and felt Mark's hand on his shoulder. Mark shook his head and, for good measure, wagged a finger at him. With a shrug, Podevin replaced the dagger in its sheath. Mark stood and stepped onto the path.

'Well, my friend, a nice day for a walk in the woods, isn't it?'

The man started at Mark's words, but he was not startled enough to forget to draw his sword.

'Not very friendly,' said Mark. 'You're not proposing to hurt anyone, are you?'

'You keep back! You're supposed to be visiting the renegades!'

'And how do you know that? And what do you mean, "renegades"? Come on. Our plan was to find some people granted their freedom by the king, so who is calling them renegades?'

Despite the fact the new arrival was the armed man, he was the one retreating as Mark stepped forwards with his questions. Emma followed him, leading her horse, indicating that Podevin had better make sure Mark's horse wasn't lost or left behind. That was a good idea, of course, but it meant both Podevin's hands were occupied and he couldn't draw a blade, even if he had a decent one to use against their adversary's sword.

'I do think you'd better put up your sword. It won't help you, you know,' said Mark.

'I could kill all three of you and the king would know nothing!' However, he made no movement to turn word into action.

'The king would know very quickly because your head would be delivered to him—by me!' Blanik's voice came from a little way back, his body hidden by a bend in the track.

The newcomer looked left and right, as if an escape route would magically appear; a nice hard, rideable track perhaps—but nothing happened.

'You can raise your sword against us and die. Or you can admit you've been caught and start talking.' This was still Mark, being reasonable.

Behind the man, emerging into full view, came Blanik, Geraint, and several Anglo-Saxon warriors.

'I won't talk!'

It was a last throw of the dice and they all knew it. Like with the brigands on the road, there were always ways to make a man talk. The only question was what shape he would be in after he had told his inquisitors all they wanted to know.

Mark held out his hand. The man placed his sword, hilt first, into it.

'If you satisfy my lady, and me, as to your orders and intentions, you will be allowed to live with no harm coming to you,' Mark said. 'If you don't, I'm afraid the constable of Prague Castle has a rather uncomfortable dungeon waiting for you, and some friends who will make sure every scrap of information is pulled from you. Your choice.'

'Look! I can't be seen to have said anything or Boleslav will do worse to me than he can.' The man gestured at Blanik. 'I have a wife, a family!'

Mark looked at Emma, at Blanik. There was a mutual shrug.

'Let's all make ourselves comfortable, shall we—in the clearing? I don't think Boleslav will be waiting for us there, will he?'

They had to endure a load of self-pity. Karol—they could not keep referring to him as 'the man'—lived simply on Boleslav's land but had extended family in Prague, which was why he had been chosen. His uncle could get him into the castle guard here. Karol hesitated but gave the names. His job was to make sure he sent off all the information about Podevin and Emma he could. If he could ensure there was enough to have Podevin killed, that would please Tugumir, and Boleslav. Tugumir? Yes, Podevin's half-brother was in Boleslav's camp now; there were rumours he had been promised more land, more castles. However, Duke Boleslav wanted Emma; she was to provide heirs for the Bohemian crown—and he was not bothered if it was through his loins or those of his son. As for spying on Emma, Karol even let slip he was not alone, or did not think he was.

'I don't even know who else is a spy, so I have to send all my information—you see, my family!'

It turned out, the ignorance wasn't quite true. As Karol didn't ride back and forth to Stara Boleslav, he must give his information to someone. So, who was that person? At this point, Mark decided Emma and Podevin had heard enough; it would be Blanik's job to hunt down Karol's contacts. Wenceslas would have to be informed, and no doubt he would be the final arbiter of what happened to Karol, and any other spies, discovered in Prague.

Mark detached the saddlebags from the horses. Yes, these were supplies for the family in the forest, but no, they weren't going to ride there, just in case there were others who wanted to track down the so-called 'renegades'. Podevin was strong, wasn't he? Surely, he could carry some medicines and supplies? With the memory of his wintertime visit in his mind, Podevin gritted his teeth and slung the saddlebags over his shoulder and prepared to leave the clearing. He followed Mark and Emma as they took their leave, for the second time that morning, of Blanik and Sir Geraint.

They plodded for a good five minutes. Podevin did not even bother listening to Mark and Emma's idle chatter. If he tried, they would probably only switch to Anglo-Saxon anyway.

'You can stop sulking, you know, and grow up! If my lady can accept the need for discretion, so can you.'

Despite carrying a couple of saddlebags himself, Mark did not even slow down. Podevin got the impression Emma was smirking at him.

'I'm the king's page. I'm supposed to know what is going on.'

'You're the king's servant. You're supposed to do as you're told.'

'But that's the point, isn't it? I was told nothing!'

Mark stopped. 'Two points, Podevin. One, you could, or even should, have guessed some of what has been going on. And two, there's a very good reason why—especially as you obviously had guessed nothing—you weren't told!'

'How could I guess?'

'You know what Boleslav is like. You know what his son is like. And you know what Wenceslas is like. So, when Boleslav suggests certain ladies become part of Princess Emma's court, Wenceslas agrees. Now, Podevin, are those ladies likely to be loyal to Emma, to Wenceslas, or to Boleslav?'

Podevin decided the question was not worthy of an answer, so stood silent. He shifted the weight of the saddlebags on his shoulders.

'And what do you and Emma discuss? You might think it court tittle-tattle, but somehow Boleslav has been very well informed about life in Prague. Oh, it hasn't mattered much, but we'd rather it stopped. You see, Podevin, information doesn't always travel only one way. You remember Mabel?'

How could he forget the flighty inconsequential thing so determined to catch a man that all other considerations, moral and otherwise, had disappeared? Her flying visit to Prague to show off her newborn had put all Emma's ladies in a tizz, and he'd been happy to give Emma's quarters a miss that day, finding other things to do.

'You should have attended. Maybe you, rather than Emma, could have brought the news.'

'What news?'

'The obvious!' said Mark.

'Boleslav is putting, or wants to put, the worst possible construction on our friendship!' said Emma, hands on hips, giving him her imperial glare for his stupidity.

'Well, if that's the situation, why are we in the middle of the forest with just a monk for company?'

The 'just a monk' raised his eyebrows, but said nothing, leaving it to Emma to explain.

'We were checking if we were being followed.'

'Then we should have been quiet—even I know that!'

'Look down, Podevin.'

'What am I looking at?'

'Our tracks.'

'There's nothing there!'

Mark crouched down and pointed. He pointed at the indentations in the leaf litter, at the marks in the mud, at the snapped twig in the middle of the path. He pointed behind them, and ahead of them. Puzzled, Podevin looked at him, but he merely grunted and stood up. Emma had her hand over her mouth, trying to stop her giggling as he worked it out. He peered ahead of them.

'Are you trying to tell me we've been walking around in circles?'

It was all right for Emma. She was, yet again, just carrying herself. Mark was used to carrying stuff. He, Podevin, had saddlebags from two horses, thank you very much, and it was not the first time he had been fetching and carrying for peasants! He drew in his breath, but suddenly thought of Mladenic—did he really want to behave like a brat? All right. He could take a joke.

'Can I assume from our conversation, our noise in the middle of this wood, that we are not being followed?' he said.

'I think so.'

'You only "think", Mark?' Podevin, for the first time, began to relax.

Yes, he'd been a stupid fool—and he needed to grow up. However, an apologetic shrug in Mark's direction and a shamefaced grin was all he could manage. Mark appeared to accept it as he treated Podevin's comment with possibly more seriousness than it deserved.

'It is, I suppose, possible for a scout to have retired to the centre of the circle we've been traversing and be merely watching us from afar. Possible, but unlikely. Mabel's information was useful,' he continued, changing the subject, 'but she isn't going to be free to come back and forth. Stanislav,' Mark glanced at Podevin, but the page nodded to show he knew Mabel's husband, 'for all he's related to Blanik, also has family under Boleslav's control. They have to be careful.'

'Haven't we all. Does this mean Emma and I shouldn't…?'

'Wenceslas hasn't changed his orders, has he? In fact, he's even more determined you two should spend time together—how dare his brother cast aspersions!'

'Cast what?'

'Try to say your friendship isn't anything other than friendship.'

Podevin could feel Mark's penetrating gaze as he said the words and, despite himself, he blushed. Dammit! He couldn't help it if he liked Emma. And she was much too good for the likes of Mladenic.

'All right, stop getting embarrassed, the pair of you. But I'm afraid Blanik and I will be keeping our eye on you. Lives, as we know, are in danger.' Mark paused. 'So, come on, let's get this stuff to Krok and his family, and allow Emma to coo over Maria!'

Chapter 17
A Fight

The thought that someone wants you dead, and is watching you from afar, does concentrate the mind. Despite the reorganisation of Emma's ladies, and certain guards no longer being around, Blanik and Mark could not be absolutely certain they had all Boleslav's spies under lock and key—or observation. Podevin continued to spend his time, under Wenceslas's orders, with Emma. Walking arm-in-arm, now they had been told it was allowed, was as close as they got and they stayed well within the bounds of propriety in company. Unless Emma's wish to take part in more aggressive pastimes counted as stretching propriety to breaking point. Blanik was also worried; he supervised the training in arms.

'So, madam, you are here to watch? Perhaps, if you stood over there, I am sure you will be able to see what goes on…' He faltered as Emma didn't move.

'She's here to take part, sir,' Podevin said. 'She says she needs the practice.'

'Can you explain to her that we don't train girls here?' Blanik tried to draw Podevin to one side, but it was Emma who replied.

'If you can explain to her why you think she should have waited to be roasted in her litter and not defend her own life from your bandits?' Emma said.

Podevin glanced at her, then grinned at Blanik.

'Maybe you should find out how good she is?' he said.

Blanik sighed and picked up a sword—blunted for training, but still able to deliver a painful bruise. He essayed a couple of passes in Emma's direction, thinking to warn her off. But she stepped forward under his defences and would have stabbed him full in the stomach with her own practice sword if he hadn't leapt backwards, all but falling over as he landed. She came at him, still swinging the sword. Metal clashed against metal as Emma vented the frustration of the last few days against Blanik. It took all his skill and expertise to keep her at bay. Only his superior strength gained him the upper hand. In the end, he gave no ground, no quarter due to her age or sex. Blanik had to win as he was fighting in front of his class. A full body check while their swords clashed finally pushed her to the ground. She lost her grip on her sword. As she rolled away, somehow drawing her dagger while she did so, ready to stand and face him again, Blanik pulled back and held up his sword in a salute.

'Dagger against sword won't work, my princess, and no, Podevin, you are not tossing another sword in her direction.' Blanik could see out of the corner of his eye that Podevin was holding another practice weapon, ready to throw it for Emma to catch.

They could both see, as could the rest of the lads, that Blanik was puffed. It had been a hard fight. Emma, watching Blanik all the while, stood up.

'I practise, yes? Not watch "over there",' she said.

Blanik looked round. Podevin might not have tossed the sword to her, but he had not put it away either. The tutor scratched his face with his free hand. He went to where Emma's sword lay on the grass, picked it up, walked past Podevin and put it with the other weapons.

'All right. You practise. You practise with Podevin. And you help teach the younger ones. And Podevin comes with me to explain to the king when he asks what we think we're doing.'

It worked. Prague Castle became used to seeing Emma and Podevin slugging it out every time they got frustrated over language, over fate, over the way life had drawn them together but put limits on how close that togetherness could become.

The king did not demand an explanation but merely commented, 'I hope she doesn't think we are proposing to send her to war.'

Podevin bit his lip, saving his riposte until he was alone with Blanik.

'If Emma ever had to lead us into war, there's at least one group of squires who'd follow her into battle without being asked twice!'

At first, they'd been inclined to mock her Anglo-Saxon accent and frequent need to speak in German to make her point when her Czech failed, but actions speak louder than words. Not one of them had ever come close to hitting her, even when she took on two of them at once. She would explain what she had done to defeat them, then she would show them what to do.

However, when Mladenic visited, late that summer, it didn't go well. Mladenic was meant to have instruction from Blanik, to see how he had come on in his training since he had been under his father's tuition. Podevin was to be Mladenic's opponent. Because Podevin went to the training ground, Emma went too.

'Don't forget, I win!' Mladenic called out, his high voice carrying in the breeze.

For once, Emma had been prevailed upon to sit the session out—it would not do for her to beat her future husband and, besides, he would not know what to do if he faced her.

At his words, Podevin smiled, teeth clenched. Emma could see the muscles tightening in his jaw. Mladenic rushed at him, sword swinging—he blocked it with ease, but she saw Podevin made no move to follow through with his own thrust. Mladenic turned, making the fundamental mistake of showing his back to his opponent, but that opponent waited until their swords clashed. Podevin could have forced Mladenic's sword down and then simply brought his own sword up to the younger fighter's throat. He forced the sword down, but then stepped away. Emma saw his distaste; she felt it in her own breast. If nothing else, how was Mladenic to learn how to fight if he was given no chance to learn from his mistakes? She knew, oh, how she knew, if you were the weaker one in the fight, you used guile, you ducked, you weaved, you did not pit your strength against someone older, stronger, more experienced. She could tell Podevin was hating this; there was another clash of arms and Podevin all but threw his sword away.

'Aha! You're useless!' Mladenic rushed in, sword still flailing, and began to beat it against Podevin. 'Take that! And that! And that!'

'Sir! Sir! Young Boleslav!' Blanik was hollering as Podevin had to go down and curl up under the blows. 'Your opponent is unarmed! That is not how to behave!'

Blanik had to go right up to Mladenic and shake him. Emma had risen from her seat and was also running to the training ground.

'I win! I win! The rules say I do what I like!'

Emma stooped, picked up Podevin's training sword. 'Then fight me!'

Blanik shook his head. Podevin groaned and looked at her. She saw the blood coming from a split lip, then turned to face Mladenic.

'Oh, all right!'

He rushed at her, as he had done with Podevin, but she stood her ground, blocked his blow, and tripped him as his momentum carried him past her. He lost his grip on his sword. He went to get it, but she was there, standing on it.

'Now, what do I do? Do I hit you like you hit him?' She didn't dare say Podevin's name, in case she let slip how annoyed she was. However, she poked Mladenic with the blunted end of the blade, enough to hurt, enough to bruise.

'Madam. Perhaps you will restore his sword to him? Another pass? Let him know he was merely unlucky?' She had never heard Blanik so obsequious.

'If I restore his sword, it'll be to teach him a lesson.'

'You give it to me now!' Mladenic yelled.

'I give up,' she said, and turned away, walking over towards Podevin, who had been left on his own and was holding his side.

A scrabbling sound and a yell of 'I'll get you!' made her turn to find Mladenic charging at her, his sword raised over his head. He was bringing it down as if to cleave her head in two—which it would have done as she was wearing no helmet—but she used her own sword to change the direction of the blow so the blade thudded into the ground. This time, there was no hesitation; before he could recover, she used the flat of her blade against his shoulder—hard. As hard as she could and, as he still stood there in shock, she swung it against the other shoulder.

'I beat you, and it wasn't luck. You need to learn how to fight.'

She turned her back on his opening mouth and the tears starting in his eyes. She went to Podevin and guided him back to the benches, where she and her ladies checked him for bruises and broken ribs; plenty of the former, but none, God be praised, of the latter. Mladenic yelled. Mladenic screamed. Mladenic demanded vengeance. Blanik stood over him while he sat on the ground demanding this, ordering that, but no-one came. No-one killed Emma nor Podevin, and no-one sacked Blanik.

There was an audience with the king in the great hall, which Mladenic refused to attend. He was busy packing to go home. Emma insisted on Podevin not being used as target practice by 'that boy'; she also insisted on 'that boy' taking proper lessons in the art of war if he ever came back.

'If he can't take it, he shouldn't give it out. No Saxon will roll over and allow himself to be beaten like that.'

'And the Magyars certainly won't—which is what he's more likely to get in the east,' said Blanik.

'Are you saying his father's been too soft on him?' said Wenceslas.

'Yes,' said Emma, before Podevin and Blanik could get in with their equivocations, 'Nobody should be suffering bruising or broken bones just to let a child think he knows more about fighting than he actually does. At the moment, he'd only be a danger to his own side.'

'Blanik?'

'Yes, sire. The princess speaks the truth. The child cannot learn if his mistakes are always covered up.'

'Leaving me with the problem of dealing with his father.' Wenceslas rose from his seat and gestured at the two younger people. 'You may go. Podevin—get those wounds treated. And if you are getting them treated by Anglo-Saxon ladies, make sure Brother Mark is also in attendance.'

Podevin bowed; Emma curtseyed. Mark would be there, but they could still talk, couldn't they?

Chapter 18
The Groom Arrives
A.D. 934

Emma never told Podevin how much self-control it took not to order her women to leave him alone so she could deal with his bruises herself. They had stripped him to the waist. Not a spare bit of flesh on him. Plenty of well-defined muscles, though. And a lot of unnecessary smoothing of skin around his ribcage and across his back to check and recheck there were no more bruises. How she would have loved to do that herself, but she had to sit apart and watch, and pretend to be indifferent. She supposed she ought to be grateful Mark was there, going back and forth with his pots and potions. Lots of heavy breathing from Beatrice and Hilde, and Podevin in the centre of it. She could not even get close until her ladies had redressed him.

There was one advantage to all this fuss over Podevin. None of them were there, down in the courtyard, for Mladenic's departure. No doubt, as far as the Boleslav clan were concerned, Podevin and Emma should have been there, grovelling at his feet, hoping for his mercy, thanking him for his generosity in allowing them to live after they had insulted him. Not that his rush home helped him. For once, even his uncle had been compelled to see his brattish behaviour for what it was. Wenceslas had to conclude that either he changed his mind over who Emma's husband was to be, or that husband had to grow up, and fast. The number of unofficial prayers sent up by Emma and Podevin that he would choose the former option was clearly outmatched by the official prayers spouted by Father Militus in chapel that 'young Boleslav' would soon become a proper husband for 'our Anglo-Saxon guest'.

On that day, however, Wenceslas sent a messenger, and the messenger carried what might diplomatically be called a strong note. This time, not even Boleslav senior could help. He could, and did, continue to refuse to allow his son to live permanently in Prague and be taught by Blanik, but he was compelled to ensure his son was being taught proper swordcraft, so it could be shown that his son would be a help, not a hindrance, to his own side. It was, according to rumour, threatened that his battle-hardened uncle would be the one to test him—and the whole of Bohemia knew that not even Duke Radslav had been able to stand up to Wenceslas. Also, manners became part of Mladenic's required curriculum: *If it cannot be expected for the young man to fall in love with his intended bride, it is our desire and commandment that he shall approach her with the appropriate and required courtesies at all times.*

'Having been on the receiving end of the father's flattery, I'm not sure if the son's rudeness isn't easier. It is, at least, more of an honest expression of his feelings,' was Emma's comment when Mark relayed the content of Wenceslas's missive to her.

'It might be honest, but is it accurate?' Mark said, causing both Podevin and Emma to turn to look at him. 'Think about it,' he continued, 'the poor lad's how old? Eleven? We make fun of his nickname, but he is just a boy. A mere youngster. Yes, my lady, we all know what you were up to at eleven, gearing yourself up for battle and all, but what chance has the young Boleslav had? A father who constantly demands that he behaves as if he's more grown-up than he is, to be tougher than he is. While, at the same time, not giving him the opportunity to grow up at his own pace. And he has an uncle who produces a proper grown-up woman for a wife but who also, in his own way, expects grown-up behaviour from a mere child! No wonder all that child can do is express anger—it's about the only feeling, the only emotion, left to him. Perhaps a little understanding on our part might help.'

For all she might have been, at the time anyway, prepared to consider Mark's outburst, 'the child' was miles away, suffering whatever educational regime his father might have prepared for him. He was not seen in Prague for two and a half years. Not, that is, until he arrived as a bridegroom for his wedding in the late spring of A.D. 934.

ॐ

Emma could not shake the feeling they were all keeping something from her. Snatches of conversation that stopped as soon as she was noticed by the flighty ladies who surrounded her these days was one thing, but the sudden acquiescence when she wanted to join the hunting parties, or join Podevin on the practice ground, was another. After Mladenic's disastrous, and now half-forgotten, visit, every request went all the way up to Wenceslas with the objections piling up on the way, and she would have to wait with bated breath, wondering what excuse would wind its way back down the chain of command. Usually, the watchword was 'caution' regarding Emma's friendship with any member of the opposite sex. Therefore, her requests were frequently declined on the most spurious of grounds: a potential rain shower could ruin her chances of being outside for a walk in the garden, much less a hunt. On receiving a 'no', the decision then whether to accept or fight it would depend on what she could find out about Wenceslas's mood—the more distracted the better—if he could not be bothered, she could get her way.

That spring, however, he had been too distracted even to say 'no' in the first place. As far as she knew, there had been no special urgency in any correspondence between Bohemia and England, nor between Bohemia and Saxony (where Matilda was settling down to married life very well, thank you). There had been, as far as she knew, nothing special in any messages going back and forth between Wenceslas and his brother. It was true Podevin was not always available, as he had his duties with the king. Now the new tax system was in place, Wenceslas was getting back into his old ways of baking bread and making wine, going out on progressions, or official visits, to see his subjects *in situ*. The idea that she, Emma, could accompany the king and his entourage was squashed. She could make her progressions once she was married, should her husband and father-in-law wish it. Not even her plea that she was already here in Bohemia, so might as well meet her future subjects, changed Wenceslas's mind. The English princess could occupy herself in and around Prague Castle, but she could not be seen to be doing anything useful—not in terms of running the kingdom, anyway.

It was May. Even the ground had decided to start warming up and drying out. As the king seemed to have relaxed the rules and Podevin was free, the two of them had engaged in some pretty fierce combat. She had managed to trip him and land on him before he could think about getting up. That was the trouble of fighting someone you knew; they knew your tricks, your attacks, your strengths and weaknesses as well as you knew theirs. She was straddling him, both on the ground, but Podevin was on his back and she was on his chest, holding a practice dagger to his throat.

'Do you yield, page!'

'Not your page, my lady!' he puffed.

'Madam!' Ursula came into view, all ruffled feathers and indignation. 'I shall have to speak to the king about this! You'll catch your death, rolling around on the ground!'

But Emma was into her game and continued demanding Podevin should yield as he was wriggling under her.

'Madam! That really is most unladylike! What would your future husband say?'

'He's not here,' she said. Adding, 'Thank God!' in a more muted tone for Podevin's ears only.

Podevin duly grinned and stopped wriggling, so they both caught Ursula's next words:'He'll be here tomorrow, though, won't he? In all his finery.'

'What! Why?'

'For your wedding, of course! Why do you think I told you to be ready to have your gown fitted?'

Emma had not been listening. If she had, she might have reminded Ursula it was not her place to tell her what to do. Besides, a new visitor to Prague, a new diplomatic initiative, a new…whatever tended to mean Emma had to be dressed in a new gown so she could be shown off as Mladenic's future wife and the hope of the kingdom. At the inevitable banquet, she would be seated next to the important visitor who, depending on temperament, would ignore her as a woman (who therefore would know nothing about politics) or, as she was female, try to flirt with her. She learned to sit and smile with both types and gather as much information as she could by earwigging on other conversations.

Other conversations had not covered Mladenic's imminent arrival in Prague. Emma was hustled away, leaving Podevin to tidy everything up and vent his fury on Blanik. The last thing she heard, before she had to give all her attention to her upcoming dress fitting, was the castle constable denying he knew anything about what was going on.

What a way to remember a friend. Podevin's last words in her hearing while she was an unmarried woman were him swearing and blaspheming at his tutor. Podevin had been blindsided too. As Ursula tried oh-so-carefully to explain, they all knew both she and Podevin were anti-Mladenic so, if she had been 'aware of the immediacy of her wedding', the two of them might have tried planning 'something desperate', as it was obvious 'there was considerable, er, attraction between the two of them'.

'Why, madam, just look at the way the two of you were behaving when I came to get you! You have grass stains all over your leggings!'

'That's why we wear them, Ursula. Or would you prefer me to practise in this sort of outfit?' Emma gestured at her new dress.

'I very much doubt your husband will want you practising any war games once you are under his protection, madam. Now, let us see if this fits properly.'

There was a pause. Emma allowed herself to be fussed over until she caught sight of herself in the mirror.

'Why is this cut so low? All I have to do is jig up and down,' she suited actions to the words, 'and Father Militus will have a heart attack!'

Beatrice grabbed at the material, tugging it back over her nipple, but Emma had not finished. 'Anything I have worn before has covered my breasts completely, and now I'm supposed to be somebody's strumpet! No! Get me out of it!'

'It's the king's command, madam!' said Ursula.

'Right, I'm off to see the king!' Emma pushed her ladies aside and made for the door, 'See what he says—he's the one pushing propriety! And this is what I have to wear in his precious chapel!'

'Madam! Please!' came from behind her as the women gathered thoughts, skirts and tried to catch her up, but their words were echoed by Mark, who came out of nowhere to block her passage. She skidded to a halt.

'Ursula, you had better stay,' Mark said. 'The rest of you, leave us!'

'Not Ursula!' Emma said, still furious. 'Beatrice. You stay.'

Knowing better than to argue with Emma in this mood, the ladies filed out; the Bohemians avoided her gaze. Emma held the dress closed over her breasts. Ursula would have tried to impose herself, but at least Beatrice was a loyal Anglo-Saxon and could be relied on to keep quiet. Mark pointed to the chairs by the fire. It might be warm outside, but the chill inside meant fires were still needed. Beatrice retired; she knew she had to be present, but Mark expected to be able to talk without being overheard.

'Emma. Madam. You knew this day was going to come. You, like your sister, were sent abroad for a purpose and, yes, your sister has done very well out of the situation. How well you do out of yours could be down to your attitude now.' He paused. 'I think that dress does need alteration.' He stood and grabbed a cloak, handing it to her to put around her shoulders. 'The court has been negotiating your wedding ever since Mladenic left here over two years ago.'

He paused again. Emma could see he was picking his words with care.

'The king was coming round to the idea that, if your wedding did not take place with the young Boleslav soon, then he would have to appease Athelstan and Henry of Saxony by allowing his brother to annul his marriage, disinherit Mladenic, and marry you himself. Which Boleslav do you prefer? Because, madam, that is, or that was, your choice. Wenceslas is remaining single, and…a second cousin only hangs onto his life as long as he doesn't make trouble.'

'Marrying me would be trouble, would it?' Emma stood up and, clasping the cloak around her, moved to the window, passing Beatrice on the way.

The lady-in-waiting's eyes were all sympathy, but they both knew neither of them could change anything.

'Oh, my little lady. Of course it would. And you know it. Where could you go? What could you do? We know Duke Boleslav was unhappy about you seeing Podevin at all. Remember those spies? That's why we were always worried about the two of you,' Mark said.

'You mean, in another world...'

'I mean precisely that, but we're living in this world.' Mark stood and came to join her. 'You have to marry and produce heirs. At least they say he's a young man now, rather than a mere boy.'

'How long have you known?'

His silence gave it away. Emma let the cloak fall from her shoulders.

'Call my women,' she said to Beatrice. 'This gown needs to fit me.'

It was Brother Mark who answered, 'It was the king's orders, Emma.'

'Hadn't you better call me "madam", or "my lady" from now on?'

'Yes, madam. As you wish. But the king insisted.'

It was too much for Emma. If she'd only known how much she sounded like her aunt when, her face closed, her eyes venomous, she hissed, 'Since when has that stopped you in the past, counsellor? Go! Just get out.'

Beatrice had not moved, but now, at a gesture from Emma, she went to the door and held it open for Mark to leave. Emma's rigid back brooked no more confidences. As soon as Mark had shuffled away, Beatrice made to follow him, but Emma called her back.

'Give me a minute. Dammit, I need a cloth for my eyes.'

Emma had turned from the fire, and Beatrice rushed to her side. Tears from the bride was not something she wanted the Bohemian ladies to see. They went into the inner room where a bowl stood on a side table with a jug of water. Beatrice splashed some water into the bowl. Emma scooped it up with her own hands and splashed her face, making sure she washed her eyes. Beatrice took the cloth and dabbed her lady's face dry.

'And you, did you know?'

'No, my lady. But...but Ursula was most insistent we all went over to...to interrupt your time with Podevin. And, out of all of us, she has always been the most friendly with the new ladies-in-waiting, and—' Beatrice stopped, but Emma raised her eyebrow and waited. 'And I saw her talking with Brother Mark the other day—normally, she hasn't got much time for him.'

'Thank you, Beatrice. But now we have to sort this dress.'

'We can put a bodice underneath it. That'll help, while still—'

'Showing my shape?' Emma finished. 'Yes, all right. Get them in.'

Chapter 19
Wedding Night

The wedding was awful. The groom's scrupulous politeness deceived no-one, except the king, who wanted to be deceived. Even the fact that the groom did not glance at Emma's breasts won approval. Wenceslas was delighted with Mladenic's behaviour; how he could bow over a woman's proffered hand and offer the lightest of kisses. He was delighted by how Mladenic had 'shot up since we saw you last'. Indeed, he was now taller than his uncle. He had grown up all right, but had hardly filled out; like his three companions, he was extremely slim with, as far as anyone could see under all the fine, brightly coloured clothing (dark greens, reds and purples predominating—all very expensive), no breadth to him. For all he was reputed to be a fine swordsman now, Emma did not see how he could have spent any time wielding any weightier weapon.

Her only view of Podevin was seeing him standing beside Wenceslas, as Father Militus droned his way through the marriage service. Sir Geraint stood in for Emma's half-brother, the king of England, and gave her away to her Bohemian groom at the appropriate moment.

Until the evening, Emma thought the worst moment was when Father Militus decided he would give a homily, a sermon, about conjugal bliss. It took a while, not helped by the fact she was not listening, for Emma to work out what the priest was on about. He was saying that a husband had to know his wife and it was the wife's job to 'allow herself to be known by her husband and keep herself pure in mind, even if she could no longer be pure in body, as that is only possible in the state of bliss achieved by the blessed Virgin Mother of our Lord, and she shall be saved by the bringing forth of many sons!'

'What the hell does he know about married life?' The comment came from behind her.

Beatrice was immediately shushed by Ursula, but it brought a flicker of light relief to Emma's mind. Father Militus was something of an austere loner, much more ready to find fault than give praise; and he had never given any indication that he knew, or wanted to know, anything about any woman, including princesses. However, the convoluted message was clear enough: Emma's job from now on was, as she could no longer get to heaven by being a virgin, to be a mother.

The wedding breakfast was long, full of speeches, and Emma's jaw ached from having to smile and smile and smile at platitudes and innuendo. It was long, but she did not have to do or say anything herself. Speeches were made by men, who talked about her, at her, over her. Was she really just a package for a womb?

However, minute by minute, the thought of it robbing her appetite, closer and closer came the moment she must be prepared for—the bedding. Her deflowering had to be witnessed. Her bedroom, previously so closely guarded against intruders, especially male ones, was to be open to king and courtier while her husband 'had his way with her'. This time, there was no option but to accept the nightdress which all but exposed her breasts. At least there was a screen at the back of her bed chamber where she could change—closing the door even for this was not permitted. While she was being divested of her wedding clothes and the nightdress eased over her head, she could hear the mutterings and murmurings of the watchers.

'For God's sake, remember to cry out when he does it,' said Ursula, keeping her voice low, so as not to be heard by the gathering around her mistress's bed. As there were also Bohemian ladies, she spoke in Anglo-Saxon.

Emma glared at her erstwhile chief lady-in-waiting, replying in the same language. 'And if he doesn't hurt me?'

'Then pretend he has!'

'Pretend blood as well?' She knew the fables, and she knew from her aunt what was expected.

'If it's your first time, you will bleed. Just make sure you bleed onto the sheets.'

'I'm sure it will be fine, madam.' Beatrice leaned in, putting a warm hand on Emma's naked shoulder.

Emma looked up at her; she caught Beatrice's brief wink but, her mind was full of her aunt's warning that she had been too active; it might be she would not bleed, despite never having known a man.

'Ursula, you were with me in Mercia. Did you not hear my aunt?'

'Your aunt is dead, my lady, and she has no sway out here.'

'But she is right. Whatever he does, or doesn't do, I may not bleed.'

'Madam,' Ursula hissed, 'if you don't bleed, your life, and your precious friend, who's come to watch by the way, his life is forfeit too. The king has attested to your virginity. You get to that bed and prove it!'

'Ursula! That will do! Remember who you serve!' Beatrice's shock almost overcame the need to speak in whispers.

'Why don't you go and make sure the bed is prepared?' Emma said, and turned away from Ursula. Who, instead of moving, started talking about knowing Emma since the princess was in her swaddling clothes.

Emma stood. 'That does not give you the right to offend me. Do as you are told!'

It took ten seconds, ten seconds of staring, before Ursula dropped her gaze and left to check the bed.

'Madam, we must put you to bed soon.' Beatrice spoke halting Czech, so Emma knew she was including the other ladies in the discussion.

To Emma, these ladies changed so often, at Wenceslas's, or Boleslav's, whim, that she never had time to learn their names, or their characters, but at least they escorted her with due decorum as she walked the few metres to her bed, which had been folded down for her by the waiting Ursula.

How do you climb into bed decorously, especially when it is that bit too high for you to sit on it while keeping your feet (cold, because they have been naked for several minutes now) on the floor? In the end, she placed one knee on the bed, followed by her bottom and her right hand on the pillow to make sure she did not take a tumble. Then she sorted herself into the bed while Beatrice and the other ladies pulled the covers over her legs. They arranged the pillows behind her so she, as befits a princess receiving courtiers, could sit upright.

She looked around at her audience. Only Wenceslas was sitting; the rest, even Duke Boleslav, stood. Boleslav leered, making no secret of where he was looking. Wenceslas looked anywhere except where she was. Podevin was by the king's side, blushing as she caught his gaze; he too was transfixed by her breasts. *Keep looking, why don't you! My face is still here. I thought you were my friend. I've had breasts ever since you first saw me.* In her fury, she almost missed the commotion at the entrance to the chamber.

Mladenic, accompanied by his three companions, entered. His nightshirt left his white, skinny, hairy legs exposed. The groom paused, as if taking in the room full of people. It gave Beatrice time to lean over towards Emma. Emma pushed her hand, the one Beatrice had held half a second ago, under the pillow to release the knife she had just been given. She did her best to resume her expectant expression.

By this time, Mladenic's companions, all still dressed in their flowery finery, had brought him to the bed, yanked the covers back and let him climb in. He too sat with the bedcovers over his legs and in silence. Then he snapped his fingers at his friends and pointed at the bedposts.

Tittering, the boys started undoing the curtains and drawing them around the bed. Emma breathed a sigh of relief. Maybe there was going to be privacy after all. However, she heard no sounds of anyone leaving.

'Go to it, my son!' shouted Boleslav, making Emma jump.

'Yes, the sooner the better,' said Wenceslas.

Now Emma heard nervous movement around the bed as the rest of the witnesses tried to adjust to the scenario.

Inside the bed, all was quiet tension. Mladenic had not even looked at Emma; for all her internalised complaints about the male gaze half a minute ago, she'd have given a lot for some male reaction to her all-but-naked body. She half-turned towards him, allowing the thin material of her nightdress to expose even more of her upper body.

'Well, husband?' she said in an effort to encourage him.

He moved at last. She rolled onto her back, expecting him to climb on her, pull her nightdress up, get her naked. She expected any or all of that. Instead, he rolled towards her and grabbed her throat with his right hand, while he leaned on his elbow.

'Not so clever now you haven't got a sword,' he said.

Emma was stunned. Was he going to kill her here and now, on their wedding night and in front of all the witnesses? Was he still, after all this time, so upset she had bested him in a practice fight? He was hurting her, but she could still breathe.

'Go ahead, big boy. Kill me, and then see what your uncle does.'

The pressure increased, but she just stared at him, while her hand reached under the pillow until it grasped the knife Beatrice had so thoughtfully given her. Then, with one lightning move, she brought it out and placed it under his jaw, right beside his jugular vein. His eyes widened. He snatched his hand away, but made no other move.

'I didn't mean it!' The squeak was more pathetic than the threats.

She kept the pressure on his neck with the blade as she raised herself up and he was forced to lie back. In a parody of her game with Podevin, only a day ago, she straddled her husband with a blade in her hand. She leaned close so she could hiss in his ear.

'You don't ever do that again! From now on, you keep your filthy hands from my neck. You didn't want to marry me, and I sure as hell didn't want to marry you. But that's as may be; you have a job to do—so get on with it.'

'I can't!' Another terrified squeak.

'Why not?' A thought. 'You do know what men and women do together, don't you?'

A nod.

'Well, we just do that.'

'I can't. No-one's ever shown me.'

She took the blade away from his neck but stayed straddling him. 'No-one has shown me either, but I know what happens.' She cast around, trying to think. 'When we came back from Saxony, you knew what Mabel and Stanislav were doing, didn't you?'

'A kiss and a cuddle? I was ten!' he exclaimed when he saw her expression. 'I used to ask what was going on when my father went off with yet another woman, but no-one dared tell me.'

Emma rolled off her husband and closed her eyes. What was she supposed to do now?

'What's going on in there? We're all waiting, you know. Shall I take those curtains down?'

Emma jerked her eyes open in time to see the terror on her new husband's face at the sound of his father's voice.

'For God's sake. Get on top of me.' she hissed.

He did as he was told, but it was clumsy, painful as he had no regard for where he put knees or elbows, so it was easy to cry out. There was no point in trying to pull her nightgown up. He just lay there, panting, wild-eyed.

'All right, you can get off now.'

She would wait until he was asleep to prick herself with the knife. Tomorrow was another day. Mladenic—she still thought of him as 'the youngster'—heaved himself off her and retreated to his side of the bed, pulling the covers up over himself, leaving her to do the same on her side of the bed. She heard the undiplomatic scramble for the doors, even as hands reached for the curtains to open them up so the watchers' last image would be of the sated couple lying side by side in the bed, ignoring each other. Wenceslas led the way out. Emma's ladies, not all of them, but some, were to remain in an outer chamber along with Mladenic's companions. In the morning, it was their job to inspect the sheets.

೮೨

Despite the reported success of the wedding night—blood on the sheets taken as proof positive that not only was Emma a virgin before that night, but also that young Boleslav had done his job in taking that virginity—as the weeks turned into months, it became clear there was no child. Despite the desire for a grandchild expressed by Boleslav senior, and the threat to come to the chamber himself to watch his son perform, Emma slept alone.

Her apartment at Stara was bigger and better than her rooms in Prague, but the chances of getting out were limited. She was given a pony to follow the hunt, but that only after she had made a fuss. There were progressions, but Emma did not accompany her husband and father-in-law. Mladenic was always in the company of his tittering companions, and avoided her when possible. When avoidance was not possible, he took to disparaging her, while Duke Boleslav continued to complain about her lack of pregnancy.

In the end, after another banquet when Boleslav senior, having drunk enough wine to put another man under the table, told her she was a failure and asked where was his grandson, she exploded. If she was to get pregnant, then wasn't her husband required to do his duty by her? Her husband, if the duke didn't know, had not visited her in her chamber since they had come to Stara and, if her father-in-law expected a pregnancy and a child, what was she supposed to do, take matters into her own hands?

In the shocked silence, she, followed by her ladies, all except Ursula, left the hall. Ursula arrived later but refused to say what had happened in those minutes she had stayed by the duke's side, whispering into his ear.

'Don't you worry, madam. It will all be sorted. The trouble is, the young man needs a bit of experience, that's all.'

The smile on Ursula's face, and her disappearance overnight, only to emerge tired and late the next morning, gave the game away. Someone had finally shown Mladenic what to do.

It still took him a week to appear in her rooms, a full fortnight after her menstruation, and he kept his eyes closed throughout the whole exercise. If his men were not in attendance, then Ursula was, or at least she was close by, appearing as soon as Mladenic had departed and instructing Emma to place a cushion under her bottom and stay lying on her back.

One way or another, it worked. By the end of August, in the year of our Lord 935, a full fifteen months after her wedding, it was clear Emma was pregnant.

❧

It was only as he grew older, that Podevin began to appreciate some people were never going to be content. They would always look to grab more for themselves. As a youth, while he was perhaps over-ready to believe the worst of some people, like his half-brother, the fact that Tugumir had secured a castle and lands but wanted more, a lot more, did not register. Podevin always assumed, when he was given his rightful inheritance, Tugumir would get something else as compensation, though to be honest, he never got as far as thinking what it might be. It was the same with Duke Radslav—though he never really worked Radslav out—Podevin always thought the way the Duke of Kourim managed to jump ship at just the right time was suspicious. And of course, Boleslav, brother to the king, heir to the throne and just waiting until Wenceslas disappeared over the mountains to Rome…

All Podevin could do was monitor the petty discontents that disrupted castle life. Wenceslas's reforms had been enacted—at least as far as the royal estates were concerned. The exchequer was not in such a healthy position that those sent to collect revenue from ducal lands, or receive it as it rolled through the gates of Prague Castle, could afford to send it back if more money came from the peasantry than it should, and thereby less from the landed farmers, merchants, and nobility. Podevin grew aware of conversations stopping as he approached the treasury, the over-hasty assurances given to Wenceslas from the same quarter, and the eye-rolling behind official backs as the new tax laws were (supposedly) enforced.

Podevin also found the kitchens and stables becoming quieter. He was still able to take part in some gossip, as Dalimil shared another platter with him; and he could always discuss any slight worries about Blaze at the stables. However, afterwards, he began to wonder if he hadn't given more information than he was given in return. Of course, there were slip-ups; apparently, Boleslav's kitchens had been rebuilt in stone and even the kitchen boy had money to spend. Boleslav's stable attendants had also been given new livery to go with their new quarters. However, what worried Podevin was the way in which he was being looked out for—not in the sense of being looked after, but in the 'Podevin's coming!' warning little boys in the schoolroom issue to each other when the class prefect, or head boy appears in view. Yes, of course he would take any concerns to Wenceslas, that was his job, but it had always been his job and everyone knew that.

Chapter 20
The Absence of Emma

A.D. 935

The problem was, these days, Wenceslas was too busy to do anything other than receive official reports, checking items off yet another list. Podevin went to Blanik. Blanik sat Podevin down and looked him in the eyes, the most serious expression on his face. Emma was pregnant. Did Podevin know what that meant? It meant she was a proper wife who loved her husband. Podevin needed to remember that, and stop dreaming about—

'How the hell do you know what I'm dreaming!' The stool he'd been sitting on clattered against the far wall. 'I know what pregnant means! Damn you to hell, Blanik. Do you think I've wandered about this castle, the stables, the farmsteads all my life with my eyes closed! For your information, I have not laid sight on, nor heard from, the Princess Emma since she left here over a year ago. When Wenceslas went to visit her, he carefully did not take me, as you well know!'

Podevin was shouting now, pointing his finger at his tutor, who was slowly getting to his feet.

'And another thing,' Podevin continued, 'if you're all so god-damned worried about me pining for Emma, why hasn't our high-and-mighty king found me a wife and some lands to help me forget? Hey! What am I supposed to do? To be? "Eyes and ears?" How does that work when what I report is ignored? Come on, answer me.'

'When you give me a second, I'll remind you I could demand satisfaction for that little outburst—' Blanik began.

Podevin's sword was out of its scabbard in a second.

'Why don't you? Perhaps you can work out whether or not you taught me well.'

'Your eagerness for news rather gave you away.' A new voice came from the doorway, and Blanik turned his reaching for his sword into a bow with his arm crossed in front of him. The king waved his hand in greeting before turning to Podevin to continue his speech. 'And you could not hide your pleasure at her discomfort in not giving my brother his grandson.'

'I was not pleased at her discomfort!' But he put his sword away at the king's entrance and sketched his own bow.

Unlike Blanik, Podevin was not officially greeted, so could only remain erect and stiff, while the king wandered around Blanik's office. It was at times like these Podevin wished he had more clout in court, more ability to be heard.

He waited, fuming, while Blanik told Wenceslas about what he, Podevin, had heard, and not heard, in the kitchens and stables. Then, as Podevin was about to interject, Blanik went on to say that he, Blanik, had been hearing from the east that the road between Stara and Tetin was being worn out by the passage of horses' hooves, 'and neither your brother's messages from Stara to Tetin, nor your mother's from Tetin to Stara, are coming via Prague, sire.'

Prague was the obvious overnight stopping-off point in the journey, as any cursory look at a map would tell anyone.

'Are you, nonetheless, aware of the contents of these messages, Blanik?' the king asked.

'No, sire, but we can guess.'

'And what would those guesses be?'

'They are plotting to take over the kingdom, and return it to its pagan ways...sire.'

'But my brother knows the kingdom is his as soon as I depart for Rome! My only conditions are that he keeps the Christian religion and runs the country on Christian lines—as I am doing!'

'He's not likely to make his own bread and wine, is he?' Podevin was weary of standing, being ignored and, at that moment, did not care if his unasked-for comment brought him a rebuke. 'Blanik's telling you about plots going on outside this castle; I'm trying to get you to listen to what is—or, all right, isn't—being said inside the castle. What are you going to do, actually do, about it?'

'Find new advisers, comes to mind,' said the king.

'Ones who are deaf and blind, do you mean? And, oh, yes, before you say it, I do presume on my "familial relationship" with you, sire! It would be nice if we all slept in our beds safely, but with these plots, these rumours, people are starting to get jittery!'

'Really? Are you feeling "jittery", Blanik?' Wenceslas smiled at Podevin's outburst, and hadn't even looked at Blanik.

Not until he became aware of the silence; that Blanik had failed to reply to a direct question from his monarch. The mood shifted; the king spared Blanik a long, considered look, but there was no reply. Wenceslas sighed and paced the room.

'I have always said my brother was my heir. All he had to do was wait until I put Bohemia in order. That has been understood ever since I decided I was going to Rome.'

Wenceslas paused, Podevin opened his mouth but Blanik shook his head; even if they'd heard this before, it was clear the king was not in listening mode.

Wenceslas continued. 'I have made, and kept, peace with Saxony. I have done all I can to keep the Magyars from raiding. And I have compensated all those whose lands were affected by those raids! I have set up a new, fairer taxation system, and I have introduced the true faith. What more could I have done?'

'Do you really want an answer to that, sire?' said Podevin.

'Oh, you'll be all right, Podevin. You're Boleslav's cousin as well as mine.'

Podevin closed his eyes at that. After the incident with the spies, and his complete separation from Emma, he very much doubted Duke Boleslav wanted a second cousin alive who might hold any affection in his daughter-in-law's heart. And, of course, there was always that time just outside the chapel when Boleslav had drawn his sword on him! Wenceslas used to be more astute, like when he faced up to Radslav in that duel, and before that, when he routed the Saxon troops under Prince Otto. But now it was as if everything could be made perfect just by wishing!

The king was speaking again. 'If you are so sure there is a plot, that something must be done, let us go to Stara and hold talks with our brother. Going there gives us the advantage of being able to see what is, and what is not, being done there.'

'Sire?'

'You can't!'

'You'll get yourself killed.'

Podevin and Blanik spoke over each other, seeing the plan for the madness it was. Unless he took regiments of troops with him, who could guard him day and night; unless he insisted on having his own attendants at all times—and no-one, not even his brother, was allowed to approach unsupervised by Blanik, or possibly someone like Radslav—would this madcap scheme possibly work. And Wenceslas would need to have lots of people with him to look over the defences of Stara, people who could mingle within and check out all parts of Boleslav's domains—from the kitchens to the stables, to the guards on the walls. Only then, might it be possible. All this flashed through Podevin's mind in an instant. He was sure, despite their disagreement of moments ago, it was in Blanik's mind as well. A progression like that would take some organising. It could be done, Podevin was sure; he'd organised others—not on such a scale, but…

'There's no need, you know. We aren't at war. Just a small bodyguard for the road, and we can set out tomorrow—or the day after. Give you a chance to supervise my packing, Podevin, and for a message to get to my brother. We don't want to surprise him, do we?' Wenceslas dismissed their concerns, reiterating that his brother was his heir, so what was the problem? Besides, Podevin would come with him.

'What! But you've kept me apart from—everyone in the east—for over a year.' Podevin's finish was lame, and he knew it.

'As she is now a proper wife and about to be a mother, I see no reason why you should not see her. I think I can trust you to behave properly, just as you did before.'

Yes, yes! Just as before, decorous decorum in front of her women, Wenceslas's court and Boleslav's spies. What would it be like now she was a married woman? All bowing over proffered hands, polite, mean-ingless conversation at the banquet table (assuming he was allowed to sit at the table, rather than spend his time serving Wenceslas). Frankly, he'd rather not go within forty leagues of Stara, but what he wanted was not being considered here, was it?

'I'd better go and tell the bodyguard,' Podevin said into the renewed silence once Wenceslas had left.

Blanik resumed his seat and sighed. Podevin realised the man looked exhausted.

'There's something you're not telling me.'

'We thought it best. What was done, was done, and couldn't be changed.' Blanik pulled a chain from under his jerkin and took it, as if it cost him the last of his energy, from around his neck. He held it out to Podevin.

'Take it.' He pointed to the chest at the far side of the room. 'You'll find what you're looking for in there.'

The key was stiff in the lock, but it delayed him for no more than a few seconds. The chest was full, as these chests often are, of parchments. Official correspondence of the sort Podevin had always been told didn't concern him. He had thought, for a wild second, he would be looking for information about Budec, but it was the letter on top with his name on that caught his eye. That and the fact the seal was broken.

'Shut up and listen!' Blanik spoke before Podevin was off his knees, the precious parchment in his hand. 'We thought, at the time, we were doing the right thing. And I still say, had everything worked out, it was the right thing. Her warnings unnecessary, and no point in getting your hopes up—they'd have to be dashed anyway.'

Podevin turned the parchment over in his hands. Blanik watched him as he opened it up, looked at the name at the bottom—a name that brought a broken smile to his face.

My dear squire and sparring partner,

Mark has said he will deliver this to Prague for me and I trust it finds you well. I am left here at my desk, scribing my official reports to my half-brother in England and my sister in Saxony. It appears Matilda is doing well in her role. Thankfully, the doctors are still telling my father-by-marriage to be patient, but I fear such a virtue is running thin with him. I miss the hunts we went on together, the mock battles we fought and even your attempts to teach me the names of your garden plants! I wonder if you recall the Anglo-Saxon I taught you? Perhaps you should reply in that language so I can check your grammar? I have much to say but my time has run out and Mark is anxious to be away.

With fondest wishes,

Emma

Podevin checked the parchment. It showed no sign, other than the seal being broken, of being tampered with. There was no piece, as far as he could tell, that had been cut off. There was nothing there to get Emma into trouble, unless asking for him to reply was the problem.

'This, Blanik, says everything and nothing. So why did you and Brother Mark—I assume it was the two of you—decide I should not see it?'

Blanik shifted in his chair. 'We had our orders.'

'Wenceslas decided no communication between us, after all he did to practically push us together!' Incredulity overcame Podevin, but a bigger shock followed.

'Not Wenceslas. Duke Boleslav.' Blanik, for the first time ever, failed to meet Podevin's eye.

Podevin strode over to his tutor's desk, stood in front of it, and waved the parchment in front of his nose.

'And since when do you and Mark obey the king's brother instead of your king?'

'Ever since it kept you and your precious princess alive! Don't you realise how dangerous this is?' Blanik stood. 'If this had been found in Stara, what would have happened to Princess Emma? To you? Do you think Wenceslas would have stood in Boleslav's way?'

'If Boleslav had proof? No. But I don't think Wenceslas would have winked at an assassination.'

'That letter's proof enough you two were too close, "dear squire"!'

'"My dearly beloved and trusty servant." Doesn't that go on so many of your official letters? Does this really read like a,' Podevin paused, reaching for the correct term, 'a letter a beloved would send to her betrothed?'

'Possibly not, but what would your Anglo-Saxon reply have said?'

'It would have told her what Wenceslas was up to, what we knew about Boleslav's plotting. The whole point would have been a line of communication to the heart of Boleslav's dukedom! And, if you're worried about not being able to read Anglo-Saxon, can I point out who was going to be the courier? Brother Mark. Has he forgotten his own language?'

'We were keeping the pair of you safe. Time apart and you could both get used to your new situations.'

'What new situation?' Podevin hissed. 'Does Emma have the husband she deserves? Do I have a wife—whether deserved or not? No! On both counts! All right! Emma's pregnant—at last! But we know Boleslav is still plotting and God knows when Wenceslas will actually give him Bohemia because I don't! Yes! I grew fond of Emma. And yes, while I'm being honest here, I think she grew fond of me! Given Mladenic repeatedly said "no" to a wedding, why not put the two of us together? Does she really want the whole of Bohemia?'

'Hold it! Do you mean to tell me you two discussed this between yourselves?'

'Why not? Do you think we spent all our time saying, "this is a rose," "this is a tulip"?'

'But you didn't tell us! We thought you were just trying to…' Blanik stopped in exasperation.

'Set up a love affair?'

A sudden thought, unbidden: lying next to Emma on the bank underneath the castle walls. It must have been summer. What were they laughing about? It didn't matter, they were laughing, no cares in the world! But her ladies were just a few yards away, the guards still patrolled the walls. In his mind, Podevin remembered Radslav there, peering at them from the ramparts. 'It's all right for some! Others of us have work to do!' before he disappeared again. Oh, yes, they could be friends, but too closely watched to be anything else.

'Look!' Blanik was trying to explain. 'If we'd let this go on, and then you were caught, what would have happened? If Emma thinks she's closely guarded now, it would be as nothing, assuming Boleslav let her live. And you would be dead, and so would anyone who knew any Anglo-Saxon, Emma's ladies-in-waiting, her bodyguard.' A pause. 'And it would not be an easy death, either!'

So, he had not thought of the possibility of death—the death of others, the death of those who would have had no choice but be caught up in their incomplete, unformed plans.

But, 'Don't you think we might have been able to make the decision about that? Don't you think we were old enough to hear your objections? And what does Emma think?'

In the end, Blanik apologised, but Podevin accepted he would, in all probability, have rushed ahead with whatever half-formed plan he could come up with. They both knew Wenceslas's plan would be a disaster, and could only hope they could survive the fallout. What they did not realise was how much of a disaster was awaiting them all.

Chapter 21
At Stara Boleslav

A.D. 935

It had been obvious for days. Discontent throbbed behind every conversation, contaminated Boleslav's courtiers' lungs with every breath, and the very walls seemed to drip with it. Boleslav had always been their mother's favourite, and was impatient for power. He worshipped the old gods, resisted all Wenceslas's plans and, with his mother's connivance, plotted.

'He's my brother. What can I do?' had been the eternal response to Podevin's repeated demands of the king for action.

Others had tried, including Princess Emma. Only last night, she had all but forced the king to listen to her news. She lived here now, in the east, where Boleslav had his power base, and where all those who resented Wenceslas's new taxes gathered around the younger brother as flies on rotting meat.

While Duke Boleslav remained in the east, and his brother in Prague, his brother thought he was containable, his plots mere gossip. Of course, Blanik, on the morning they set out, had again begged the king to take a large retinue with him. But that, said Wenceslas, would intimidate his brother. Blanik, and his advice, was left behind, and a small detachment accompanied the king and his page on the journey east.

Boleslav's new stone-built castle was set on a hilltop outside the town. The outer, surrounding curtain wall was, like at Augsburg, a good three metres high. High enough for an archer standing on the walkway at its top to pierce the king's heart or throat as he waited for the gates to open. The idea that Duke Boleslav did not know about his brother's visit was nonsensical, and it was preposterous they had to wait again when they approached the inner bailey.

'Welcome to Stara Boleslav!' was the duke's greeting when they eventually made it into the courtyard.

All Podevin could see, left, right and centre, was armed troops. Hundreds of them. However, Wenceslas demanded that courtesies were to be maintained, and Boleslav was nothing if not courteous. The rooms found for Wenceslas were well prepared—so he had been expected—and Podevin could not fault them. There had been rumours of forced labour and extra taxes to pay for the project, and, yes, the result looked good, but Podevin did not relax. The outer rooms were cleared of Boleslav's men; Wenceslas's guard would remain here. Podevin did his best to ensure if he wasn't by the king's side himself, then one of the twenty men they'd brought with them took his place.

Also, Podevin had to worry about seeing Emma.

'I only saw your letter three days ago!' he hissed while refilling her goblet of wine at the first feast.

'Talk to Mark,' she hissed back, sipping the wine, but turning away.

For all his pagan beliefs, Boleslav kept a Christian chapel as well, but no resident priest. Father Militus had accompanied Wenceslas. Podevin merely waited after mass, allowing the priest to accompany Wenceslas outside and progress to the great hall for yet another discussion.

'Shouldn't you be earwigging on the talks between the brothers?' Mark appeared from behind a pillar.

'What's the point? One's so serpentine he'll say anything in the moment, ready to go back on it when it suits; and the other's stuffed his head with so much religious gobbledegook he doesn't care to listen to me anymore,' Podevin said, not bothering to lower his voice.

'You do know his choice is Rome or death—and he'll have to make that choice soon?'

'And what about those he leaves behind here?'

Mark turned and looked at him. 'I'd find other protectors, if I were them.' He paused. 'Wenceslas has walked into a trap. Boleslav allowed Blanik to find out about the messages between him and Queen Drahomira. He told them to gallop by Prague in full view. The only reason the trap hasn't already been sprung is that Boleslav doesn't believe his brother would have been so stupid to come here on his own.'

Podevin opened his mouth to mention the bodyguard.

'Your bodyguard? Against how many troops living here? Come on, Podevin!'

'We've got to get him out of here! If he takes the bodyguard with him to Rome, then at least the rest of us have a choice…' He faltered as Mark shook his head.

'Get him back to Prague—tonight, if possible. You'll need surprise on your side. This coup is well planned. You can't get to Rome via Tetin, not without a fight. And Blanik's on the black list, too.'

'What black list? How do you know all this?'

A new voice interrupted them. 'The black list is the list of all those who must die, whether Bohemia is given to Boleslav or taken by him. And he knows some of it because I've told him what my husband has told me.'

Recognising the voice, Podevin spun round to see Emma seated by the chapel wall. She was smiling.

'How are you, Podevin? You do realise I have yet to decide whether to forgive you for not realising there was a letter to find, but it seems our elders only had one thought on their collective minds.'

'Madam, I cannot tell you often enough!' Brother Mark protested. 'But I really don't think your words would have helped when so many others have failed.'

'They might have helped fill the cart until its axle broke, don't you think?'

Podevin smiled as Emma used an old saying he'd heard in the kitchen. After all, she might have been right.

However, Mark wasn't done. 'But at what cost? Putting others at risk without asking them is not politic. Boleslav lashes out when he's angry. But we have to say goodbye to Podevin. You are here for your confession, so, shall we begin?'

Podevin found himself outside the chapel before he had time to think, and barely time to sketch a bow as a farewell to Emma. He wanted so much to talk with her himself, to explain about her letter. Though why, if it was so dangerous, had Mark brought it to Prague and Blanik kept it? Did they think it could be used in some way against her and for their benefit? He brought himself up short; all this talk of plots was infecting his brain. Emma's women were waiting a few steps away, ready to escort their lady to wherever she was going next. Podevin acknowledged them with a wave and was about to pass on back to Wenceslas's quarters. Plot or no plot, he knew his place.

However, there was someone else waiting. A member of the bodyguard detached himself from the ladies and moved to intercept Podevin.

'Luca! What are you doing here? You're meant to be with the king! What's going on?'

Luca didn't even have his sword and was completely unarmoured, wearing only his linen shirt, and not even a padded jerkin.

'We've been stood down. All of us. Told to enjoy the hospitality on offer. Though I don't think Wenceslas quite meant what Boleslav meant!' Luca looked meaningfully across the courtyard.

Podevin followed his gaze. Two men in Wenceslas's livery were seated there; both had drinks to hand, and a woman sat on each lap, snuggling close and showing more flesh than the king would deem suitable.

'May the Lord and the Saints protect us!' Podevin breathed, before turning back to Luca. 'What's been going on?'

'A letter from his mummy,' Luca said, ignoring protocol.

'What did it say?'

'That there was no plot against Wenceslas that she would be part of. She was sure Boleslav would wait until Wenceslas was ready to go to Rome and she hoped he—Wenceslas—would also visit her at Tetin before he went south.'

'No plot because his mother says so!' A thought stopped Podevin. 'How did she know to send her letter here? Why didn't it go to Prague?'

Luca didn't know, but he had another message. 'The king's compliments, but could the Princess Emma attend to him in his quarters as soon as she has finished in the chapel. The king says you can tell her.'

Could he? What was he supposed to do? Wait here? Join the ladies-in-waiting? Luca, having given his messages, wandered off to join the drinkers and their women. Podevin sighed. He did not fancy listening to women's chatter, but there was a bench at the side of the chapel, and it was in the sun. Podevin sat and closed his eyes.

For all of two seconds. The chapel door opened and both of them came out. Emma headed off towards her ladies.

'Madam! I have a message! From King Wenceslas!' Podevin scrambled to his feet.

Emma stopped, but her ladies didn't. They surrounded her, ready to bear her off as if Podevin hadn't spoken.

One spoke. 'You know what the duke has said, especially about him! I really hope the duke does not find out about him being in there!'

Podevin did not recognise the speaker. Not an Anglo-Saxon, that was certain. They might be in Stara, but Wenceslas was still king, wasn't he? And if Wenceslas wanted his page to deliver a message to the Princess Emma, then the message would be delivered.

'Madam!' he called again.

'What's the message?' Mark had joined him by the bench. Emma, after a further hesitation, gave in to the ladies' entreaties and moved off. 'Sorry, Podevin, but you are considered extremely suspect here. If you value your life, if you value *her* life, you won't be seen with her—ever. The one plus side of there being no child in the first year of her marriage was that we could say with absolute certainty you and she had not...' Mark's words faded away, letting Podevin complete the thought.

'But the king wants to see her in his quarters! As soon as she's finished in the chapel.'

'I will let her know.'

Mark didn't move. Emma was out of sight. Podevin did not move either.

'And what am I supposed to tell the king?'

'That she, Princess Emma, will attend him, with her chaplain, once she has completed her penance.'

'I'm not sure—' began Podevin.

'Or do you want her ladies to join her? We took enough of a risk in there,' Mark nodded towards the chapel, 'and, I can assure you, if Boleslav doesn't know now you were in there too, he will very soon. We can only trust Hilde, Beatrice and Ursula. The rest owe their allegiance to Boleslav—and don't you forget it! Off you go.'

Hilde being the third Anglo-Saxon lady-in-waiting, sent out from England as Mabel's replacement after the flighty young lady had married her Bohemian knight.

Every conversation, every event, was making Podevin more nervous, more on edge. He was just a visitor—they'd go back to Prague soon, wouldn't they?—but how did Emma cope with this, day in and day out? He trudged back to Wenceslas's rooms.

᧢

He looked tired, Emma thought. There was a worry line in the middle of Podevin's forehead, and he was mouthing 'sorry' at her. With him standing behind Wenceslas as she approached the Bohemian ruler, he could do that; but all she could do in response was try to flick a sympathetic glance in his direction. It was now too late. Being angry with Mark and, by implication, Blanik, for making sure there was no, repeat no, communication between the two of them about anything…what was the point?

Emma knew. Oh, she knew all too well that Boleslav had been plotting, fomenting rebellion. Their mother, Drahomira, had told him she was sure he'd make a better ruler, a more traditional ruler, than Wenceslas, but did that mean she would countenance killing her eldest son?

Drahomira was hedging her bets. Emma had heard all about the letter. A letter which 'cast all aspersions aside', according to Wenceslas.

'The very idea that my own family would go so far. The very idea—I understand that includes you, my dear niece—that those around me would encourage me in that belief! My own brother!'

'But, sire, he has his messengers, his spies even, in all parts of your kingdom! They are reporting back all the time. And they're building discontent.'

'Oh, Emma. My kingdom is at peace. The people are producing more food. For the first time since I came to the throne, I've been able to stand down half my troops!'

'And a lot of them are now taking their pay from Boleslav.' Podevin opened his mouth for the first time.

'Really? You might be my cousin, but I am getting tired of your... The way you insist on putting the worst possible interpretation on everything. Enough!' Wenceslas held up the inevitable hand to prevent any more words. 'I called Emma here so she can tell me all about how she's settling in to her new life.'

Emma had to sit next to Wenceslas and dredge up all the silly gossip her ladies gabbled about. She gritted her teeth as Wenceslas made it clear he did not think she could possibly know anything about Boleslav, about plots (that didn't exist anyway), or even about Saxony—never mind the letters that passed between her and Matilda. It was all what services she attended ('talk to Mark about that'), her embroidery and other work 'in anticipation of the little one' ('talk to Beatrice'), and maybe she was allowed to have a say in the nursery for the little chap? (No. Boleslav wanted the child wet-nursed from its birth, somewhere else in the kingdom. Emma's job was to produce the infant—nothing else.) When she, using as much diplomacy as she could, managed to get the point across, Wenceslas's eyebrows shot up.

'Really! That is archaic. Very old-fashioned! I must have a word with my brother.'

Across the room, Mark and Podevin, locked in their own conversation, looked across at them. Had Emma finally persuaded Wenceslas to take some action?

It took the combined efforts of the three of them to persuade Wenceslas that Boleslav would only see this intervention as interference in how he, Boleslav, wanted to run his family. While it was not what Emma wanted, having other people raise royal children away from court was not unknown. What Wenceslas ought to be dealing with was potential rebellion.

They had been there before. Not even a private conversation between Mark and Wenceslas—they prayed together, while Emma and Podevin were allowed to have their own conversation—changed the king's mind.

They started off very formal; at least, Podevin did. 'Madam' this and 'madam' that. Emma was married, and she was carrying young Boleslav's child. There was no going back. The letter was mentioned. Podevin should have realised Emma would write. Emma could have suspected Mark would not deliver the letter—rather than assuming Podevin had failed to reply and didn't care anymore.

In protecting Wenceslas, they had common cause. At least she understood, if her husband didn't, that killing Wenceslas could destabilise the whole kingdom and invite both the Magyars from the east and the Saxons from the west, to invade. Conversation stalled. It was time to eat. Another celebratory meal, another costume for Boleslav. This time, the king having escorted her into the hall, Emma was seated next to Wenceslas. Podevin was kept busy serving them both.

જો

Positioning some of the king's own guards around the king's bedchamber, Podevin had managed partly to countermand the king's order not to be protected. Did he think God's angels would stand guard over him? Podevin's desire to be part of that guard was thwarted when Wenceslas ordered him to escort Emma back to her quarters in the new tower near the new chapel. Emma had made a token protest, but now she was pregnant, it seemed she was considered too delicate even to walk across a castle courtyard by herself. In deference to Boleslav's suspicions, and his spies, there was no conversation, not even linked arms, and the bows and nodded adieu occurred at the first door of her outer chamber.

With the curfew ever closer (though why, if there were no plots, no risks to anyone's life and limb, was a curfew required?), Podevin had just enough time to visit the castle kitchens on his own behalf. Serving at table meant he'd gone hungry. At least the staff were friendly, and he could, for a few minutes, relax.

Chapter 22
Wenceslas's Last Night

Podevin was tucking into his bread and meat when Mladenic turned up.

'Well, well, well, if it isn't the page boy. So, what's your master doing at the moment? No,' Mladenic held up his hand just like his uncle, as if Podevin was about to interrupt him, which he wasn't, 'let me guess—he's having a prayer time!'

Mladenic picked up a leg of a bird, possibly a swan, from the size. He tore off a couple of mouthfuls with his teeth and tossed the rest to the dogs. A fight broke out. He watched. Then went over and kicked out at the animals until yelps replaced growls.

'Perhaps these curs should be fed, or have their throats cut.'

There was no reply. The kitchen crew were silent. So was Podevin, but he carried on eating. Perhaps it was the prospect of fatherhood that gave Mladenic some sort of spurious confidence, or maybe he was growing up; but Podevin didn't think he liked this new version any more than the old. Mladenic wandered up and down the kitchen, picking up food and utensils, looking at them, putting them down again. He even went over to the fire and kicked out at that, his leather boot connecting with a large log that unsettled the whole blaze and showered sparks into the air. Podevin saw the kitchen staff tense, watching until every last spark had either gone out or returned to the ground without doing any damage.

'Tell you what, Podevin. You come with me. There's going to be a nice little show starting soon over in our chapel. You'll like it.'

'I'm not sure I can—'

'Wenceslas has dismissed you, hasn't he? He doesn't need you any more tonight, does he? Actually, he won't need you; he's off to bed. After his prayer time!'

Podevin didn't respond, alert to Mladenic's knowledge of what was going on. How did he know what Wenceslas had ordered? Why was there another chapel service? And without the king?

'Well?' Then, as Podevin failed to move, 'I'm ordering you to come.'

Again, the kitchen servants kept quiet, the men and women who had been happy to chat with him a few minutes ago now doing their best to indicate by gesture they thought Podevin had better do as he was told. Podevin dipped the last of his bread into the sauce and stuffed it in his mouth. He grabbed the last bit of meat and did the same. He gulped the beer.

He'd run out of time. Mladenic was already at the door.

The chill of the autumn evening made Podevin wish he had brought his cloak, but the younger man had already set off. He did not go to the front of the chapel but round the side. He kept going, even when Podevin tried to call out and ask what was going on.

'This is where the priest, when we have one, goes in.' Mladenic smirked as they found an open door.

'Won't he be cross if he finds us coming in this way?' said Podevin, trying to humour the young Boleslav. Mladenic's strange excitement was troubling him.

'Oh no. We're not going to be seeing any priests. Someone else is in charge of this service.'

No king and no priest. Podevin was torn between curiosity and the thought he ought to inform someone. But, by the time he had fumbled his way to any decision, they had climbed the few steps and were inside a small room. The priest's robes hung in one corner, a little table held a Bible, and there was a bench and a wooden shutter over a gap in the wall. Mladenic went straight over to the bench, lifted the shutter and put it back on its hook, so it stayed open. Despite himself, and in response to Mladenic's urgent gesture, Podevin went over and sat down on the bench. Through the opening, they could see into the chapel. Four braziers had been brought in and were alight. The smoke was rising up, giving off a rather heady stench.

'What's that smell?' asked Podevin.

A shrug was the only reply. Mladenic was leaning forward, but only so far. Just enough to see without being seen.

'Are we supposed to be here?'

This did bring a response. 'Shut up. And if you get us into trouble, I'm not going to help you.'

Podevin rose. He was tired and getting fed up with the pantomime. 'Then I'll go.'

Mladenic's dagger was out and pricking Podevin's tunic. 'You'll stay and see what a proper service is about.'

'Put that away.'

The two of them glared at each other. Podevin knew he could best this youth in any sort of fight. But there was resentment and defiance in those narrow-set eyes, and Mladenic was the one with the unsheathed dagger.

'All right. I'll stay. For a bit,' he said. Mladenic put up his dagger. 'But answer me this,' Podevin said, 'why aren't you down there?'

'Because I'm not old enough to be initiated. All right?'

Podevin glanced at his companion. His head was held high, looking down his snub nose at Podevin. As an attempt at hauteur, it failed, but, remembering Mark's words to him and Emma, Podevin tried to feel pity for Duke Boleslav's eldest child and only son. Mladenic might now be, what? Fifteen? And a potential father. But the lad's attention, now he felt he had Podevin's obedience, returned to the chapel.

In the gloom, Podevin could see several cloaked figures wandering around. One had a head-dress, complete with antlers. The dank light made it difficult to see any detail. The chapel door opened, another cloaked figure entered. All the other cloaked figures turned to it, nodding, bowing.

'He's here,' whispered Mladenic. 'Now they'll begin.'

One of the figures, the one with the antlers, approached the altar, which was covered in a blood-red cloth. The figure, muttering incantations, seemed to be flicking something onto it.

'What's going on?' hissed Podevin. This was nothing like any service he had been to in his life.

'Shh! Just watch and you'll find out,' came the reply.

Then the figure went behind the altar and raised her flabby arms. Her arms? A woman priest? What was this? Podevin could not understand; he needed to get help. Would Mark still be around? He began to recognise the guttural 'ch', the growling 'g'; this woman was speaking Anglo-Saxon! He had heard enough of it when he was trying to teach Czech to Emma. What little of her language he had picked up then, he had forgotten since Emma left, but the woman's antlers, or the hood they were attached to, had slipped back. Podevin recognised Emma's lady-in-waiting. The older one, Ursula? The one who was supposed to be ill. She hadn't been at Emma's quarters when he took her back, and that had been the excuse Beatrice had given her mistress.

'Bring forth the sacrifice!' Anglo-Saxon incantations over, the woman switched to Czech.

A figure was brought forward, held by two others, presumably strong men. The figure's shoulders were shaking.

'Has she been chosen? Does she come willingly?'

'She has been chosen. She comes willingly.' A chorused reply.

The fact she was held rather suggested to Podevin that she, whoever she was, had not had any choice in the matter.

'Let us see her!'

A third cloaked figure stepped up behind the girl, reached round her neck and fiddled with the front of her cloak. She struggled but was held firm, and the cloak was removed. She was naked. She was facing the altar. Even from this distance, Podevin could see she was terrified. A long pause. Podevin watched as the lady-in-waiting looked the girl up and down.

'Let us all see her.'

The two men, still grabbing hold of the girl's arms, turned her round. She tried to resist but was hit for her pains.

'What the hell is going on?' Podevin hissed, ready to back away.

'Oh, hell is right,' said Mladenic. His eyes were shining, his breath shallow and fast. 'This is what Mass should be like. It's fun! And you're going nowhere. I've still got my dagger!'

The braziers crackled. The light flickered. Mladenic licked his lips.

'Can't we do anything? This is barbaric!'

'Shut up, can't you?'

'Does she satisfy you?' The voice came from behind the altar.

'Yes!' A single voice.

'Then prepare her!'

Without further ceremony, the girl was lifted up; four men now, one for each limb. She was spread-eagled across the altar. Her chest rose and fell rapidly. The priestess placed her hands on the girl's naked stomach, kneading it.

'Oh, yes! She is well chosen! Oh, king! Come forth and claim your own!'

King? Podevin could not believe it. How could he? But of course, even in the gloom, Podevin could make out the shorter, darker form of Boleslav advancing to the altar. As he approached, the girl raised her head. Her eyes opened wide and she began to struggle, but the four men held her tight. Podevin turned away, wanting to be sick. Mladenic was transfixed.

They heard Boleslav chuckle. 'Oh, yes. You'll be good for me!'

Podevin heard the girl's scream—quickly stifled. He rose from the bench.

'Where are you going?'

Mladenic, dagger in hand, leapt after him, but Podevin parried the thrust and caught him on the side of his head. The dagger thudded into the wooden floor.

'You hit me! You'll pay for that!'

But Podevin had pulled the dagger out of the floor.

'You came for me. Under your rules, I can kill you. Any time. But you're not worth it.' Podevin turned.

In the distance, he heard Boleslav grunting. He didn't look back and moved to the stairs.

'At least we know how to have fun.' Mladenic had not moved.

'Is that girl having fun?' Podevin's voice was low, intense.

He could hear other grunts from downstairs. He didn't want to guess, and didn't want to know, what was happening.

'She's a peasant. What do you expect? Her parents were well paid. And tomorrow, you die too.'

'Then why bring me here and warn me?'

'Your last chance. Join us. Or kill Wenceslas yourself.'

Podevin needed no thinking time. The bile rose in his throat. He dropped Mladenic's dagger as he turned, letting it clatter to the floor. He had his own if there was any further trouble but, by the time Mladenic could reclaim his weapon, Podevin had made his way down the stairs and out into the cool evening air.

He made it over to the outer wall before he vomited. Had Mladenic chosen to follow him, Podevin would then have been an easy target, but he was unmolested. As he recovered, he wiped his mouth on his sleeve. Wenceslas! He must get back. He must warn him.

Podevin turned, and then checked. Someone else was moving by the chapel. Had Mladenic summoned up the courage to face him? But the shadow was too big for Mladenic. Podevin took a step backwards and slipped in his own vomit. He stumbled and all but fell; the wall steadied him at the price of a grazed knuckle.

'Be quiet, can't you?' came a voice, and Podevin relaxed.

'Mark! What are you doing here?'

'I could ask the same of you. You should be at your master's side! Are you all right?' Brother Mark had reached Podevin, who was still bent over, nursing his knuckles, his mind addled, and still standing in vomit.

'Come on,' said Mark in a different voice. 'Let's get you where you can clean up.'

Podevin found himself being led to Emma's quarters. This time he was the one being escorted. They stopped by a bucket of water—in all buildings, including castles, even stone ones, fire is an ever-present danger. Podevin splashed water over his face and dipped his foot carefully in the bucket to wash the worst off his boot. They mounted the stairs. Given he had just been told he should be at his master's side, Podevin was surprised to find himself heading in this direction. He was even more surprised to find Emma still up.

'Have you found her?' she asked as Mark appeared. Then: 'Podevin, what are you doing here?'

'One question at a time, please, madam,' said Mark, pointing Podevin to a bench. 'I'll get him a drink. He's had a bit of a shock.'

'I'm fine,' said Podevin, 'and if the "her" you were looking for is Ursula, I know exactly where she is—or was.'

A beaker was thrust into his hands.

'Drink,' came the order from Mark, 'but only a sip at a time. It will soothe your stomach. And help you sleep.'

'I can't sleep; I need to report.'

'Report what? The king's in bed by now. And what has actually happened?'

'It sounds like you know,' Podevin said, but Mark shrugged.

'You'd better tell us what you know first.'

So Podevin relived the past half-hour.

'He told you to go with him?' Emma asked as Podevin told his tale.

'He knew Wenceslas had dismissed me for the night. I'd gone to the kitchens.'

'And he knew where to find you?'

Podevin thought before speaking. 'He didn't seem surprised I was there...and he hadn't come for food.'

Brother Mark raised his hands briefly. 'Our enemies are in our own households.'

Emma nodded. She was clearly interested that Boleslav was keeping his son at arm's length from the rite, but Mladenic was clearly aware of his father's plans. The only question was when, not if, they put their plan into operation. Podevin yawned. That drink! What was in it? He needed his bed. The discussion moved to Ursula.

'Her family has served mine since my grandfather's time.' Emma sounded weary. 'Perhaps she even thinks this will help.'

'It's obvious. If you ignore the probable reaction from Saxony at the death of an ally.' Podevin roused himself.

'What do you mean?'

'With Wenceslas out of the way, you'll be queen-in-waiting after Boleslav.' He yawned a second time.

'Not this way. Don't you realise curses have a habit of coming home to roost? And she did curse Wenceslas, didn't she?'

'I couldn't tell the words, but it didn't sound like anything you taught me.' Podevin yawned again.

'Bed,' ordered Emma. 'There's a spare pallet in Mark's room.' She raised herself to her full height as Podevin tried to protest. 'You won't be any use to Wenceslas if they attack tonight. There are guards, aren't there?'

Podevin yawned yet again. Barely able to keep his eyes open, he followed Brother Mark into a side room, down a corridor, turned a corner; Podevin was getting lost.

'Where are we going?'

'To my quarters. You don't think they'd let any man, even a monk, sleep anywhere near the wife of an heir to the kingdom?'

Even as he said this, and it sort of made sense in Podevin's befuddled mind, Mark opened a door, and, at last, Podevin was shown where he could lie down. He stumbled into bed.

Chapter 23
Disaster!

Podevin awoke to the sound of Brother Mark crashing through the door into their room.

'Come on!' he said. 'Or she'll go out there alone!' Then, as Podevin just lay there gawping at him, Mark grabbed the bed coverings and pulled them off him. 'Move!'

Podevin stumbled upright, grabbing at the clothes he'd discarded before sleep overtook him last night. Shouts and screams from outside filtered into his befuddled brain, but, before he could say anything, Mark was hustling him towards Emma's rooms.

'Shouldn't we get Geraint?' Podevin said, thinking Emma's bodyguard might be a better idea than his dagger and Brother Mark's prayers. He was overruled. Emma's ladies were to stay, while the two of them went with Emma to see what was going on. They left. No guards outside the door? Surely there would be guards to protect Emma? Again, Podevin was hustled on, down the steps, to the horror that awaited them in the half-light of dawn.

'No!' Podevin began to say, before Brother Mark clamped his hand, none-too-gently, over his mouth, turning the shout into an ineffective mumble.

Podevin's eyes weren't covered, though, as he gazed, aghast, at the scene before them. Duke Boleslav's knights rushed in with sword and axe raised, adrenaline pumping, felling King Wenceslas as he tried to enter the chapel. Podevin struggled to escape so he could dash to the king's side, but Mark dragged him behind the wooden steps they'd just rushed down, as they'd accompanied Princess Emma in her own headlong, heedless race towards trouble.

The king's body, broken and bloody, lay on the ground, stabbed and hacked at a dozen times, the side of his head a mess of blood and bone, his right ear severed. And even the knights, evidence of their crime dripping from sword and axe, were standing around as if they could not believe what they had done.

'He attacked me! You're all witnesses to that! He attacked me!' Boleslav screamed.

'By God's teeth—another lie!' But Mark didn't have to stop any more mouths. Emma's words were no more than a breath.

Nobody looked their way; their hiding place was in early morning shadow. Podevin pushed Mark's hand away from his mouth.

'I should have been there. I should have died first!'

'And then what?' Brother Mark hissed into his ear. 'Wenceslas would still have died. He had no sword. And what do you have, apart from a dagger? Have you counted them?'

For a monk, Mark could be infuriating at times.

Even as they kept out of sight, they could hear fights from over by Wenceslas's quarters. They discovered later that Wenceslas's knights, rather than trying to defend a doorway, or even a stairway, had rushed outside, were outnumbered and slaughtered. Over the noise of the fight, one of Boleslav's knights was banging on the chapel door. The same door that had remained locked against Wenceslas's frantic pounding, was it only a minute ago? Podevin recognised an enemy, his enemy. His enemy and his older half-brother.

'Tugumir.' Podevin's vengeful thoughts were interrupted as the chapel door creaked open and Father Militus's white face peered out.

'It is done, then?'

'Yes, priest,' said Tugumir, 'you can claim your reward.'

At that, Father Militus stepped forward, and Tugumir drove his sword into the man's belly to the hilt, striking upwards. With all that had happened, Podevin was surprised to find himself almost admiring the cleanness of the kill. Someone else did admire the killing. Beetle-browed, with no gap between his eyebrows above a flattened nose, and a scarred cheek, a nearby warrior clapped his hand on Tugumir's shoulder in approval. He got a grin in response.

'Thanks, Cesta,' Tugumir said to his friend, before turning his attention back to the dead priest, 'Yes, Father, your reward—as for all good Christians—is in heaven,' Tugumir tugged his sword out of the body.

'Right,' said Boleslav, who had stood back while others did the killing for him. 'For all he was useless, he was my brother. So, get his body into the chapel where it can be cleaned up.'

Four of the assassins picked the body up, showing it more reverence in death than they had in life, and carried it inside the chapel where, Podevin presumed, a bier had been readied for the corpse. Boleslav didn't watch but turned to the rest of his allies.

'I don't want a single one of his guards left alive. Not one—you hear me?' He turned to a new arrival. 'Late to the party again, are we? Where is she?'

The three watchers saw it was Boleslav junior, Emma's husband and, now, after his father, heir to the Bohemian crown.

'My lady isn't in her chamber, Father. No-one knows where she is.'

'You mean you couldn't make them tell you? No royal ever goes anywhere without someone knowing. Find her!'

The last words came out as a roar, and Mladenic prepared to do just that, but Emma, with a flat hand gesture at the other two to remain in hiding, stood up. She sidestepped Podevin's attempt to grab her, to stop her giving herself away; she walked round the stairway and into view. As befitted a queen-in-waiting, she took her time crossing the stone-covered yard, stopping just before the first pool of blood.

'This royal does, if she so chooses.' She looked around, noting the faces of all those in front of her. Not even Boleslav senior met her gaze. 'So, you couldn't even finish him off by yourself?' The contempt dripped from her.

'You be careful, my girl, or you could be next.'

Avoiding the puddle of blood, Emma stepped well within range of his swinging sword. Opening her cloak, she tugged at her flimsy nightdress. The material came apart.

'Go on, then. Destroy me and your grandson. I'm sure you can find another way to secure the succession.'

There was a pause. Podevin and Mark held their breaths, Mark still preventing Podevin from moving or speaking. The paralysed knights looked to Boleslav for instruction. He turned his back on his daughter-in-law and pointed at Father Militus's body with his sword.

'You see, my dear,' Boleslav glanced back over his shoulder in Emma's direction, 'not even his own priest would defend him in the end.' He paused. 'You can cover yourself up. My son won't be interested in you in your condition.'

Emma looked at her husband. The younger Boleslav would not meet her gaze. His sword, like his father's, was clean. The fights in the other parts of the castle seemed to be over as an early morning silence descended, broken only by the far-off cawing of some crows; perhaps they scented a feast.

Emma slowly, ostentatiously, drew her covers about herself. As she did so, the four knights, having done what they were told to do with Wenceslas's body, returned to the courtyard, uncertain as to what to do next.

There was a pause. It was Emma, her voice calm, authoritative, who broke the silence: 'Get rid of that treacherous priest. I will see to the king.'

The men looked from Emma to Boleslav. He acquiesced with a half-shrug, so, after cleaning their weapons, two of them dragged the priest's body away. The rest of the assassins followed the grim procession.

'I suppose you'll want to lay him out in there, all nice and tidy,' Boleslav said, pointing at the open door of the chapel. 'Go ahead. I'm sure your women will help you. Come, my son, we have things to do.'

With that, he turned on his heel. Then he stopped, turned back, and said, 'By the bye, my dear, I think you'll find I am king now. You'd better get used to it.'

He walked away. His son still hesitated.

'I had nothing to do with it,' he said to Emma. 'Nothing.'

'But you did nothing to prevent it,' his wife replied. 'Nothing.'

At a further shout from his father, young Boleslav trotted off, leaving Emma alone. Podevin and Mark emerged from hiding.

Mark followed Emma into the chapel and walked up to the bier, but Podevin hovered in the doorway, unable to get closer to that mangled body. He had been Wenceslas's page. And his bodyguard. It had been his responsibility to keep Wenceslas safe. He was supposed to guard the king with his life! Lost in his thoughts, he almost didn't hear Emma.

'Go and get my women.'

'All of them?'

'All of them. Especially Ursula.'

Suddenly, despite everything, Podevin's stomach gurgled. He realised he'd had nothing to eat since yesterday evening.

'And get some food inside you,' Emma said.

'What about you, madam?' The response was automatic.

'Just some flat bread and a small drink, more for the child's sake than mine.'

Podevin turned to go, but Mark's voice stopped him. 'Send the food with the women. You stay in Emma's quarters until I come for you.'

'Huh?'

'You're a target, lad. You think they want you to live? Didn't you hear Boleslav say not one of you was to be left alive? We have to get you out of here.'

Podevin opened his mouth to argue but, realising the truth of Mark's words, nodded. By staying here, he would be a danger to Mark and Emma. As he left, he glanced back. He saw that she had sunk to her knees by the body, talking to the dead king as if he could respond.

'Why? Why couldn't you listen?'

Mark was beside her. Podevin hoped he would be able to offer more than empty words of comfort. Either way, Wenceslas would never listen to anyone again, and it would be Podevin's job to avenge his death.

❧

Podevin delivered his message and endured the clucking, as the women demanded to know exactly what their lady might need. His news was no surprise—they had hardly been sitting there with their ears covered and eyes closed—but they were worried enough about what the assassination might mean for them. Although Emma's entourage was mixed, the agreement that the Anglo-Saxons among them could stay had been brokered by Wenceslas, not his brother, and none of them viewed a return journey to England after years in Bohemia with any sort of pleasure. It was the Anglo-Saxon ladies who'd been with her last night, and it was perhaps fortunate that no Bohemians had yet turned up for their duties. All Podevin could suggest to Hilde, Beatrice and Ursula was they made sure they served Emma as best they could—their lady was unlikely to argue for them to remain at her court if she was disappointed in them, was she? Most of the time, he was glaring at Ursula. Ursula, the chief lady-in-waiting, who had been with Emma since she was in swaddling clothes. Who now looked and acted like a plump, motherly matron. Hilde and Beatrice rushed to get everything ready. Ursula stood apart, not expressing shock or even surprise.

'Your lady expressly requested your presence, Ursula.'

'Oh, I think I have a job here first.'

'Like what?'

'Making sure the king is safe from his enemies.' She approached Podevin. 'Boleslav won't want you. And once she realises what's good for her, my lady won't want you either.' She leaned closer, and Podevin moved away from her rancid breath, but Ursula followed him as he retreated. 'King Boleslav, the new king, needs me. He doesn't need you. You're going to *die.*'

She grabbed at her belt, a dagger appearing in her right hand as she leapt at Podevin, her face contorted. Then she gasped and crumpled to the floor, Podevin's own dagger in her stomach. His reaction had been the learned instinct of a trained warrior: strike first, strike hard; go for the enemy, not the weapon; and, if there were any questions, ask them later. He knew, none better, there had been questions to be asked and now it was too late. He looked up at Beatrice and Hilde's shocked faces, wide-eyed in horror. Mark stood in the doorway; Podevin glanced at him. Somehow, he was not surprised to see Emma's chaplain there as a witness to his killing one of Emma's ladies-in-waiting.

'It's not my time to die. It's not my time…' But Ursula's eyes dulled, and she was still.

Podevin retrieved his dagger, cleaned it on the woman's clothes. Only now, he noted that her blade had blood on it as well. His sleeve was red.

'The castle's being searched for you and anyone else deemed sympathetic to Wenceslas,' Mark said. 'Tugumir's baying for your blood. Or the rest of it!'

The speech was unnecessary; they could hear bellowed orders from outside and the red patch on his sleeve was growing. With Podevin dead, Tugumir would be the unopposed custodian of Budec Castle. Podevin knew he would fight his half-brother for it, but not today. Brother Mark opened the door into the corridor towards the small room where, minutes ago, Podevin had slept. Once in the room, Mark firmly but gently bound Podevin's wound. All the noise came from outside as Mark picked up a straw mattress and indicated that Podevin should wedge himself between the floor and the wall in the far corner. Perhaps it was because of the shock of killing a woman, even in self-defence. Perhaps he was still in shock from the morning's other events, but Podevin did as he was told. The mattress was placed diagonally across him, as close as Mark dared, and Podevin felt something fall across his feet, one of Mark's old habits or a cloak? Podevin didn't dare look. Then Mark's footsteps faded as he returned to the main room, leaving Podevin to his thoughts.

Chapter 24
Plans

Wenceslas was dead. So was his bodyguard, and so was one of her ladies-in-waiting. Podevin had been hidden away. Emma didn't dare ask Mark where; the less she knew, the better. But there was one thing she had to know. She pointed at Ursula's body.

'Explain,' she said.

'I was too late. It was her or him.' Mark gave the briefest of brief reports. 'As we guessed, Ursula knew about the plot against the king. It seems she thought to make good on the command to kill Podevin as well. He was quicker.'

A peremptory knock on the door was followed by a shout of, 'Open up!'

'I see. A dagger! Give me a dagger!'

Apart from a horrified 'Madam!' from one of the women, no-one did or said anything. The silence was so complete, the repeated bangs on the door made Mark jump. Emma had to grab a knife from a side table herself. A fruit knife, but it would have to do. She nodded at Beatrice to open the door.

'Excuse us, my lady, but we heard a report of a disturbance…' The man's voice trailed off, his soldiers peering into her rooms, then entering on his command.

'She attacked me. I had to defend myself,' Emma said, her women agreeing with her in a babble of voices.

'We'll have to tell the king about this.'

'Do. I am sure your master knows more about why she should attack me than he's told you.' Emma tried to sound bored, as if she killed her ladies on a regular basis. 'And tell him I want Geraint here, and the rest of my bodyguard.'

There was a pause, then the captain, or whatever he was, said, 'Geraint is just outside. He's been demanding access to your quarters for some while, but the king felt it better we saw to the current emergency first.' Another pause. 'So, while we are here, madam, we need to check the room. Wenceslas's page has gone missing. The king wants him found, and you were seen with a male servant earlier. He was wearing a cloak.'

'Like that one—though I fail to see how Hilde could be confused for a man.' Emma was amazed how clear her thinking was.

There was a pause as Hilde faced the soldiers, her busty shape emphasising her gender. Emma heard a titter, instantly smothered.

'Look,' Emma said, hoping she sounded calmer than she felt. 'My servants are here with me. But hadn't you better report what's happened? You could help by taking the body away and sending me my bodyguard.'

However, the captain was made of stern stuff; either that or he was more afraid of the new king than the new king's daughter-in-law. He had been told to conduct a search, and that was what would happen.

Saying no more than, 'If you must. My bedchamber's over there.' Emma could do no more.

The search was quick, but appeared thorough to Emma. Mark accompanied the captain to his own quarters—they had to be searched as well. The captain returned and seemed satisfied with his search, but there was more to say.

'The king will no doubt wish to speak with you, madam.'

'I have no doubt of that myself.' Emma paused. 'And you may inform the king that I wish to speak with him about whom his heir will be. He told Ursula there was some doubt.'

Emma did not know whether that last statement was true or false but, if being the wife and mother of heirs to the kingdom was all she was going to be allowed to do, she was going to find out what was going on! She still had a brother who was king of England, and a sister who was queen of Saxony. Even Boleslav would have to think twice about that.

'Yes, madam, I will go and inform him at once.' The captain bowed.

'Do. You can also tell your master that I did not get the time I expected to lay out King Wenceslas in the chapel.'

The captain did no more than repeat that he would inform the king of Emma's requests. Ursula's body was taken away. Geraint entered and began to apologise, but they had found themselves outnumbered and under guard, and thought it best to await the outcome, before trying to lead a fight so they could get to her quarters.

'No need to apologise. You did right. I should have insisted you were here last night. We must get used to the new situation.'

'Shall I put a guard on the door, madam? Alongside the duke's man?'

'So, we have a guard on our door, do we?'

'Perhaps, madam, your husband's inability to find you has triggered Boleslav's change of heart.' Mark's voice held a note of amusement—trust him to find something funny in the midst of all this mess, Emma thought.

'All right,' she said. 'Let's have a guard. Just to show them they'll have trouble if they try anything. And Geraint.'

'Madam?'

'You'd better call him "king" from now on—to his face, at least.'

Geraint had turned and was on his way to the door as Emma called him back. 'If anything does happen to me,' she said, 'you're free to stay or go back home as each of you see fit.'

Before Geraint could act on his orders, more boots thudded up the stairs. This time, it was only a summons for Emma to go to Boleslav.

'Inform *King* Boleslav that I shall be there presently,' Emma said.

≈

Silence. All Podevin could do was wait. Then the door to his little room was pushed open, steps moved unerringly to his hiding place, and the mattress was pulled aside; it was Mark.

'Thank goodness that's over,' said Podevin.

'First, shut up. And second, it's only just started,' hissed Mark. He crouched down beside Podevin. 'In case you haven't worked it out, there's a price on your head. You're the only member of Wenceslas's party still at large in this castle. The rest are either dead or escaped.'

'How many dead?' whispered Podevin.

'Every single one that you'd put in Wenceslas's quarters. And most of the rest.'

Podevin glared at Mark; he did not need reminding of his responsibility. However, Mark had said 'most'.

'Who got out, then?'

'Luca's wounded but gone. Jan and Brok escaped with their skins whole. Boleslav told his guards to open the gate at the normal time. Probably, he wanted to pretend everything was the same as yesterday.'

'How do you know all this? How do they know I didn't go with them?'

'Your horse is still in its stable and they can count! As for how do I know? I asked! At least Emma's household isn't under threat—yet— but you are! Do you really need reminding there were rumours about you and Emma, rumours the new king is more than ready to believe! So, if she is caught sheltering you…' Mark let the thought hang in the air. 'You have to leave here as soon as possible.'

'But it's broad daylight!'

'And you think it's going to be easier at night?'

'It won't be so easy to recognise me. Once I'm past the gate, I'll be fine.'

'To go where?'

'I could join Blanik.'

They were still talking in whispers, but Podevin caught the look on Brother Mark's face.

'Blanik will have enough trouble keeping his skin whole, won't he? We know Prague was not exactly entirely in favour of Wenceslas. And most people will go the way the wind blows.' Mark sounded so sad that Podevin almost forgot his own predicament.

'What are you going to do?'

'Serve my God and my lady, as always. We need to pray.'

For all he had attended many services with Wenceslas, Podevin was never sure how open God's ears were. It wasn't as if God had listened when Podevin was pleading for his father's life; and it didn't seem as though God had listened to all those prayers to keep Wenceslas safe either. But if Brother Mark wanted to pray, then Podevin could kneel and listen, and say his Amens.

They prayed where they were. Kneeling on the hard floor. Podevin let Mark do the talking, but he could not help his tears. He was tired. He had seen death. He had thought he would see this death, and had tried, with many others, to stop it. It had been no use. Then the thought came to him; he had killed a woman. No matter that she had wanted to kill him. And now Mark was praying for forgiveness for him!

'Amen.'

Podevin repeated the word, not knowing if he meant it.

'Let's have a look at that arm.'

It was painful, peeling his sleeve back from where Ursula's knife had sliced into him. The wound opened up again, but Mark was not bothered by that. He cut some clean cloths, knelt by the patient, and rebound Podevin's arm.

'No point in leaving your blood all over the floor.' Brother Mark looked at him, stood, and said, 'Get some sleep. You look like you need it.'

'With everyone looking for me?'

'They've looked, if you remember, and didn't find you. So, for the moment, you're safe.'

Podevin returned to the mattress, lay down on top of it and closed his eyes. Despite his sense of failure, and the thought of all of those knights who'd died defending a king who was already dead, he must have dropped off, because he was woken by Mark on Emma's return.

They went through to Emma's rooms. Mark overrode Podevin's objections by pointing out the only guards were Anglo-Saxon. While Podevin had slept Boleslav had decided he needed his troops by his side. Also, the Bohemian ladies had, at Emma's suggestion, been given leave to see to their own families 'in these strange times'. The new king had approved her request.

Despite getting her way about her ladies-in-waiting, Emma was unhappy. 'Whatever he is, Mark, Boleslav's not stupid. Having to tell him I changed my mind and went back to my quarters to get the herbs for the laying out, rather than expect my ladies to know what to do…well, it wasn't easy. Then, despite what he said out there earlier about me seeing to Wenceslas's body, I was told I wasn't to worry as his mother was seeing to it. I thought she was in Tetin.'

'She was.' Mark's voice was as calm as ever.

'Mark, we need to know more about what's going on. A lot more. Too much has taken us by surprise. And now he's in charge, Boleslav keeps changing his mind!'

'What you need now, though, is food and drink. Then we can think,' replied Mark, being practical.

Podevin realised, despite his orders from Emma earlier, none of them had eaten.

It didn't take long for the food to arrive. Kitchens, Podevin supposed, knew they had to produce food, whatever else was going on. Once the castle servants had gone, Podevin joined Emma, Mark and the ladies in the main room. Perhaps Mark was right, again. With bellies full of meat and sweetmeats, it allowed time for thought. The castle was quiet. A pit was being dug outside the curtain wall for a mass burial. Emma wanted to see Boleslav's mother so they could discuss what to do about a funeral for her eldest son.

'Why does Drahomira want to have anything to do with this? She was always on Boleslav's side,' Podevin said.

Mark shrugged. 'Perhaps her letter did say what she believed, or wanted to believe? Maybe the shock of what's happened made her realise she's made a mistake, or maybe she just wants to atone for encouraging Boleslav?'

'But if she's already here, she must have known about the plans, and when Boleslav was going to strike!' Podevin pointed out.

'Or was she on her way to stop it?' Brother Mark put another option to them. It was Emma who went to the nub of the matter.

'We don't know anything! Is she here?'

No-one knew.

Chapter 25
In Disguise

Emma, her ladies and Mark left Podevin alone again while they went to the chapel. They were soon back; it seemed the new king had changed his mind again.

Emma brought him up-to-date. 'Wenceslas is being buried in Prague. Drahomira's in charge. And we are required to travel to Prague as well. My son is to be born there.'

The old queen's arrival, scheduled for the next day, answered one of their earlier questions. Podevin thought it was about time he introduced some calm.

'If that's the case, we've plenty of time,' he said, thinking of the months ahead before Emma gave birth.

A wry smile crossed Emma's face. The ladies glanced at one another. 'Hardly. We are to set out this afternoon.' Emma caught his eye. He felt he'd missed something, for, despite the circumstances, there was a spark of amusement.

'You've made a deal?' he said.

'I'm beginning to learn that life is one deal after another, but, fortunately for me, Boleslav seems strangely wedded to the idea of having Anglo-Saxon blood in the royal line of Bohemia. He will be announcing my husband as his heir at the same time as announcing he's taking over after his brother's "unfortunate demise". And with my husband as his heir, my son follows after. And if that involves a journey to Prague starting this afternoon, then my entire household goes with me, doesn't it?'

'Just a minute,' Podevin said. 'Something isn't right here. As far as Boleslav is concerned, Ursula—Anglo-Saxon Ursula—tried to kill you; yet he's prepared to only have Anglo-Saxons around you? I know that's good for me, but what is the plan?'

'The plan is, we've enough time to get organised before Boleslav's escort arrives. They're not here now because they're too busy elsewhere,' Emma said. 'If you're going to get out with your skin whole, you are just going to have to dress up and do as you're told!'

By this time, Hilde and Beatrice were giggling. Podevin looked at Emma; Mark seemed to be in on the joke as well. Realisation dawned.

'I am escaping from Boleslav's castle as one of your *ladies*?'

'Well, most people don't know Ursula is no longer with us and, if they do, then I have simply replaced her with a new lady. You might be a bit tall, but I'm sure we can kit you out. Or can you think of a better plan?' Emma asked, also trying not to laugh.

Podevin racked his brains. He could pretend to be one of Geraint's men!

'Hardly. How many people do you want to know we're trying to get you out of here? Besides, how's your Anglo-Saxon?' That was Mark.

'I can be one of his knights—or Wenceslas's—dress me in their clothes!'

'Since when did we start digging up bodies only an hour after they'd been buried? And you'd still be showing your face—a face everyone's looking for.' Emma again, getting annoyed.

'All right! Just leave me here. I'll get out at night!'

'With the castle under curfew? It's not been lifted, you know.' Mark, also unhappy at his obstinacy.

Podevin accepted defeat. He'd be skulking out of Stara Boleslav, dressed as a woman. Hilde and Beatrice were kept running around. In the end, it was an old dress of Emma's that fitted best. The worst challenge was finding something to go under the bodice to give him a proper, feminine shape. Podevin had never realised what women did to keep themselves, well, uncomfortable, but all he could do was stand there and move as he was told. Then Mark pointed out Podevin needed to be shaved; not many women, certainly not many twenty-year-old women, had a beard. By this time, Podevin was almost beyond caring. All those months and years when he'd been desperate for his beard to start growing! Next, Emma decided Podevin's lips and cheeks needed reddening, the rest of his face and head being hidden by a borrowed wimple. She applied it herself as, by that stage, the departure time was approaching and everything needed to be packed and ready.

He could feel her breath on his skin as she worked silently, deftly.

'I thought you said you were no good at women's stuff,' he said as she moved from his lips to his cheeks.

She stopped, and he thought the small joke had fallen flat.

'I have to practise looking good for my husband.' She half-smiled at him. 'Don't I?'

'You don't have to try—'

'Hush, we're not alone.'

'But they can't hear us.'

'You forget your place, Podevin.' He missed the wry smile.

'My place has been taken from me. And I might be dead by tomorrow.'

She stopped what she was doing. She looked deep into his eyes. 'What you don't know is that, before the end of the feast, Wenceslas asked me to look after you, and I will; but for both our sakes, also think about others. We too could be dead tomorrow for helping you. Boleslav might talk about my use in Bohemia's continued alliance with Saxony, but he might easily decide I'm dispensable and take the risk my brother won't be able to take any action.'

A pause.

'I'm sorry. I won't forget what you've done, but if I am to die today—especially dressed like this,' Podevin indicated his new bosom and borrowed attire, 'then I will die with your name on my lips.'

She put her hand over his. 'You needn't be melodramatic either.'

A cough from behind them broke the moment.

'Madam?' It was Beatrice, the new senior lady-in-waiting now Ursula had met her untimely end. 'Are we ready?'

Emma stood up; Podevin did the same, glancing at Beatrice. Emma stepped away from him and looked at him critically.

'I think you'll just about do. What do you reckon, Beatrice?'

Unlike a Bohemian lady, who'd have known better than to be cheeky in her mistress's presence, Beatrice didn't trouble keeping the grin from her face. 'He'd better behave as a woman, is all I say, my lady.'

'We'll just have to make sure he does. He'll travel with me. A name. We need a name.'

'If I might suggest, my lady?' Brother Mark had also reappeared, having done his minimal packing.

Emma nodded at him to continue.

'Matilda.'

Beatrice gasped. Emma looked at Mark, frowning.

'It makes sense,' Mark argued. 'We can't use Ursula, can we? And your sister's name may come more readily to you than any other...' Mark let the silence draw out, while Emma thought.

'It's a risk—'

'The whole plan is a risk, madam,' Mark said.

Emma nodded again. 'There isn't much time. Matilda it is.'

Never was Podevin more grateful for a well-practised routine. Emma was clearly used to moving house, or castle. Beatrice and Hilde knew what should go into which trunk. Brother Mark, who travelled light, also seemed to know more than Podevin would have thought possible about his mistress's household effects. Podevin was kept out of the way as servants went backwards and forwards, carrying heavy boxes, trunks or tapestries. Boleslav had given orders that Emma was to travel in a litter. Podevin was horrified to hear Emma protesting about this with the Bohemian captain detailed to accompany them.

'I wouldn't worry. She's more subtle than you suppose,' said Brother Mark. 'Do I need to explain? You know, I know, she always prefers to ride on horseback so, if she didn't object, it might occur to Boleslav to wonder why when the report gets back to him.'

Podevin still thought it was a risky strategy, but it worked even better than he might have supposed, as Emma was able to insist—given that she was being treated this way as she was with child—on having a companion with her in the litter. Podevin, or Matilda, was to be that companion.

He nearly spoiled the whole thing before they had even started. Taking his usual stride in his usual boots, as they hadn't managed to find any female shoes to fit him, he managed to catch the inside hem of the dress. It took both Hilde and Beatrice to stop him stumbling.

'Short strides, you fool!' Hilde hissed. 'And clasp your hands in front of you. You're supposed to be demure.'

'Yeah, so keep your eyes down as well,' added Beatrice.

It was all very well them getting cross with him, but they'd had a whole lifetime to learn how to behave; he'd had less than half an hour to get used to the dress.

'And for God's sake, don't get discovered or we're all dead,' Brother Mark said in passing.

Tempted to snap back that he knew all about the risks they were taking, Podevin took a deep breath. Up until now, secure in Emma's rooms and in her presence, he had allowed his mind to shy away from the reality of death. Not just his; discovery would be fatal for Emma, Mark, and maybe the ladies-in-waiting too. Emma might trust Geraint and his men, but could he? Now Emma had gone on ahead and was processing down the steps to the waiting train of carts and packhorses, acknowledging the Anglo-Saxon men-at-arms. It was too late to ask questions. Like, what if any of those men felt they owed more loyalty to Boleslav than to Emma's orders to shelter him?

Podevin swallowed and, in silence, with Brother Mark keeping up the rear, they followed each other down the steps. A litter is a cumbersome thing to clamber into, even when steps are provided. Emma went first. Podevin let Hilde and Beatrice fuss around her while he tried to remember what Emma had done.

'Just hitch your dress up, but not too much, so you don't trip over it! And don't show those boots!' That was Brother Mark.

Podevin was about to retort, but then he remembered that the monk's habit probably acted the same way as a dress. He grabbed the front of the dress, scrambled up the steps and half stepped, half fell into the litter. Hilde and Beatrice scuttled round. Brother Mark yelled at the servants to remove the steps, and Emma grabbed a cushion and placed it over Podevin's feet. After a chaotic thirty seconds, Podevin and Emma were reclining on cushions at each end of the litter, facing each other. Podevin would be travelling backwards to Prague.

'We're quite all right,' said Emma, waving Hilde and Beatrice away.

She exchanged a glance with Brother Mark as he left to mount his horse. It should have been the companion's job to draw the curtains, but Emma did it, hissing that Podevin's hairy arm would give them away. He just lay there, keeping his hands clasped in his lap and his eyes down. He heard the shouted orders, the stamp of the guards' feet, and they lurched forwards. Podevin and Emma grasped the sides of the litter.

'And the men wonder why I prefer riding,' muttered Emma. She sank back against the cushions as the pack horses settled into their steady walk. Emma smiled at him as they went through the gates. 'Once you're moving, it isn't so bad. You get the bruises from the stopping and starting—especially when you don't get any warning.'

'I'll try and remember, madam,' said Podevin, matching Emma's tone.

It was going to be a slow journey. There were guards tramp, tramp, tramping either side of the litter. No doubt they'd be lost in their own thoughts, on the lookout for attacks from outside, bandits or such-like. There would not be much in the way of talk either; the guards might not be listening, but even they would react if they heard a male voice inside the litter.

As he became used to the gentle sway and the shade inside his novel mode of transport, Podevin studied the young woman opposite him. Her hands were resting across her barely swollen belly; it was months yet before her time. Her hazel eyes were closed, her russet brown hair hidden away, her face a little drawn—he had known her in happier days. And there had been that moment, that desire when he had thought he could be the one who would marry her and it would be his child in her belly. Foolish of him, of course; his bloodline was generations away from the throne. Back then, he had thought Wenceslas would fulfil his promise and give him back his father's castle and lands and send his half-brother packing. He had once dreamt what he and Emma could have achieved together. Now dreams had turned to dust; Wenceslas was dead; he had a price on his head; and Emma was hitched, for better or worse, to the son of the new king of Bohemia.

Emma had closed her eyes. For want of anything better to do, and knowing nothing of Emma's own observations of the worry lines on his face, Podevin did the same.

Chapter 26
Escape

A.D. 935

'You're snoring!'

Emma's foot was prodding his side, and Podevin jerked awake. The horses were plodding along, but Podevin had no idea where they were. The curtains might be great for privacy, but they made the inside of the litter dark and stuffy. He reached for the curtain, remembering in time to check with Emma. A glance, and her nod was enough. The breeze wafted through, freshening the air. Podevin blinked in the unaccustomed light. There were woods on either side of them, but the road, pitted as it was, kept to the clearings.

'At least we're not likely to be attacked this time.'

The words were barely out of his mouth when the procession halted. They stared at each other, listening hard. Silence. Then someone approached the litter.

'We're stopping for refreshments, my lady,' Brother Mark said, drawing his horse up by the side of the litter. 'Do you two need assistance in dismounting?'

A soldier darted up with a step so they could exit the litter. Getting out was easier than getting in; Podevin shuffled himself across until he was sitting on the edge of the litter, then levered himself onto the step, and down to the ground.

Once they had both left the litter, it was taken away so the horses could also rest for a while. They looked around and saw Mark talking with the Bohemian captain, passing the time of day.

The soldiers from both nations went about their business. A food stop was nothing unusual for those used to going on campaign, and they would not be sure of their welcome, or lack of it, if they imposed themselves on a village or town. Podevin started to wander off.

'Matilda!' hissed Emma.

It took a moment, but Podevin remembered that was his assigned name.

'You wait. You're a lady!' Thankfully, Brother Mark approached.

'The captain insists we refresh ourselves quickly. There may still be those who are loyal to Wenceslas lurking around the place.' Mark paused to share a glance with Emma.

'You mean there's a fight-back?' Podevin exclaimed.

'Shh!' duetted Emma and Mark.

'Unless you can speak like my sister, keep your mouth shut,' continued Emma.

'Yes, all right!' muttered Podevin, remembering Queen Matilda, like Emma, was Anglo-Saxon so would no doubt use that language with her sister. 'But there's something else I can't do like a woman.' He paused as the others looked blank. 'I need to, you know, go!'

Enlightenment dawned on both of them. Then Mark frowned. 'I don't think you should talk about that sort of thing here.'

'Oh, Mark!' exclaimed Emma. 'What is he supposed to do? Wet himself? Besides,' she leaned towards her confessor, 'we all need to piss—even princesses!'

Podevin was getting uncomfortable with all this standing around. And, after being cramped up in the litter, he wanted to stretch, and he would have if Hilde had not hissed, '*Not* very ladylike!' at him.

'Ladies do not stretch with their arms up to the heavens. If they really need to stretch, arms are kept by their sides and muscles tensed.'

Podevin tried it; he could feel the tension in his shoulder muscles, but it wasn't the same. Not that he could do a lot about it, with so many soldiers around, the lady-stretch would have to do until they were hidden by the bushes and trees at the edge of the clearing. Guards had to check the area before the ladies were allowed to move. Podevin set off, but he had only gone a couple of strides before he was checked.

'What the hell do you think you're doing?' hissed Hilde. 'Don't you listen to anything? *Small* steps. And we go together, following my lady!'

Emma was already picking her way across the closely cropped grass towards the forest. As her three ladies caught up to follow behind, without turning her head, she was heard to mutter, 'One of you seems to be doing her best to get us all killed.'

Podevin pretended to be watching where he was putting his feet, trying not to catch the hem of his skirt with his boots, but he could feel the furious red flush on his face. Nothing more was said until they were far enough amongst the trees to be out of sight of the villagers.

'Let's hope Mark can just keep the rest of them away for a minute or two,' said Beatrice. 'We don't need any guards poking around here, however well behaved they might be.' Emma was already hitching up her skirts. Podevin turned his back.

'Haven't you ever seen a woman go before?' Hilde smirked.

No, he had not, but he wasn't about to admit his ignorance. If he couldn't go very soon, there would be an accident! He heard the Bohemian captain saying something to Mark.

'All right, Beatrice, that's enough,' Emma said, 'You needn't turn around, Podevin, but why don't you just use that tree in front of you?'

Podevin was already grabbing at the cloth between his legs as he took the four strides necessary to reach the tree. Never was there such relief. For those moments, he didn't care what the three voices behind him were whispering and giggling about. For those moments, he would not even have cared if there had been a guard around, but reality intruded quickly enough. Hilde had just squatted over the same spot when chaos erupted.

'One of those women's a fake!'

'You've been seen!'

He didn't know which one of the ladies stated the obvious. He was too busy fighting for his life. The guard had no pike or sword, but both had their daggers. Podevin was impeded by his woman's wimple, and the dress. Thankfully, the guard, despite his cry, had been the more surprised of the two of them, and even now was weakening. Podevin's dagger was bloodied. He freed his arm and plunged it into the man's chest. It was over. He stood, panting hard. What now?

'How many more, Podevin? Did he have to die?' Emma said, despair written all over her face.

'But he saw!'

Then Mark came crashing through the undergrowth. On a horse. Soldiers were converging from all sides; the pregnant wife of the new heir must be protected at all costs. The horse reared in front of Podevin, and Mark fell to the ground.

'Get on it!' he gasped. 'Ride to Prague, but stay in the woods.'

Before he could think, Podevin had mounted and was riding away, through the trees, dodging branches, keeping low over its neck in case an arrow or spear came his way.

'Help! Kidnap!'

The shrieks followed him. Kidnap? Then his brain, even as he ducked and weaved through the wood, began to make sense of the women's cries. That was going to be the story? Matilda had been kidnapped. Fine by him. If he could only get away and keep his hide whole until he had avenged Wenceslas, he would be happy.

The shouts receded. He reined the horse in, took it off the road into the woods, and back to where he could see what was happening. There was clearly an argument going on. However, there was no-one chasing after him. Despite Emma's gesticulations, they were going to Prague. At least Emma was riding now. Podevin turned his horse. He'd stay out of sight and hope Mark found him and brought him some proper clothes soon.

❧

"You're being hunted high and low, Matilda!"

Despite his vigilance, Brother Mark had surprised Podevin. It was all very well, but he'd had to wait all night, all the next day, and all the next night out here, while the rest of them had been comfortably tucked up in their beds.

'Comfortable!' Mark snorted on hearing Podevin's complaints. 'With the new king demanding to know what's been going on?'

Mark was furious. So furious he couldn't keep still. Podevin, on the other hand, had to sit and take it.

'You do realise your very existence puts Emma in danger! The king's demanding to know why one of Emma's ladies should be kidnapped? And how did the kidnappers get so close? Why was there only one guard accompanying them? What about the rumour you had escaped with them, a man disguising himself and hiding among them? And it's hardly comfortable when Boleslav insists that Emma *will* have sufficient ladies for her station, whom he will appoint. It is extremely fortunate, young man,' Mark was all but spitting in Podevin's face, 'that Emma was able to suggest to the new king how lucky she was that Matilda was able to pretend to be a princess and was kidnapped in her place!'

'Who the hell's Matilda?' Podevin blurted. He was so sunk in his misery and hunger for the moment, he'd forgotten his own name.

'You!' Mark turned away, exasperated. 'Think, man! How my lady kept her head, I don't know—she had just arrived in Prague with a guard dead and a lady missing.' Mark paused, turned and faced Podevin.

'My lady has lied for you, put her life on the line for you, sent me on errands for you. At the moment, I'm sure I don't know why! And get those on!' A bundle of clothes was thrust at him. 'Clothes first, food later.'

'How did you find me?'

'I knew you'd not be out of sight of the castle, and this spot is where you first met Krok. Perhaps you were hoping he'd set his trap and you might dine on rabbit?'

Podevin paused in his dressing; how had Mark known? But there'd been no trap and no rabbit. He was starving. The horse could feed on grass and drink from the stream. After that first night, he had not known what to do with the animal. In the end, he pointed it in the direction of Prague Castle. Then he realised the clothes he was putting on were more suited to a peasant than a knight. He paused, looking at the shabby jerkin.

'Just put it on.'

'But if I'm going to Saxony?'

'You're not.'

'But—'

'Put it on, sit down and eat. And, when I've finished tidying up here, you're going to listen to me.'

While Podevin devoured the bread and meat, Mark gathered up 'Matilda's' clothing, reached into his bag, brought out a knife, and started tearing at the dress, the undergarments, everything. Then a small, stoppered bottle came out. Mark unstopped it and poured the contents carefully over the dress, wimple and even splashed the undergarments. It was blood. He saw Podevin watching him.

'It's mine.'

'What?' His words were muffled by the bread.

'The blood. It's mine. So we can cover up your disappearance. You're lucky those guards didn't get a good look at you. We've already found the horse the kidnapper rode.' Mark narrowed his eyes at Podevin, who shrugged; what else could he do? 'If we can now find a woman's bloodied clothes and solve a mystery for King Boleslav, we can hope he forgets the whole thing. After all, what's a lady-in-waiting? Or a guard, for that matter?'

Podevin felt Mark's gaze on him. Now what? So, there'd been a guard—he'd had to kill him. Like he'd had to kill Ursula in Emma's chambers, however many days ago it was now.

'You've killed two people. Neither was killed in battle. I can accept Ursula struck first, but would it have been so difficult to disarm her? We might have discovered much from questioning her.'

'Or you might not, given she was operating under Boleslav's orders.'

'And the guard?'

'Was a guard, an ordinary foot soldier! You didn't seriously expect me to reason with him? He was going to shout his head off!'

'So, you killed him. Why not knock him out?'

'Look, Mark, he had seen me in such a way that it was obvious I was no woman. What would you have me do? Allow him to arrest, or kill, me? I had to do something!'

Podevin had had enough of this inquisition, and he was fed up with Mark's temper. He looked at the equipment Mark had brought. 'Where's my sword?'

'Not here. Two points: where you're going, you won't be able to get away with killing, so you had better learn to think first; and two, we're hoping once "Matilda" is dead,' Mark held up the bloodied garments, 'they won't worry about who it was who attached herself, or himself, to Emma's party.'

Mark busied himself for a while, then said, 'You have enough food?' Podevin nodded.

'Right, I shouldn't be too long.' With that, Mark melted away. He didn't return until the sun was high in the sky.

'Where've you been?'

'I needed to make sure I didn't attract suspicion. So, I have some supplies for the sick I've to attend, whom I met while looking for Matilda. Unfortunately, people don't stop being sick just because there has been a change of king.'

Podevin peered into the bag Mark had put down. 'Who's sick?'

'No-one, I hope. I can always replace herbs.'

Podevin looked again at the dried leaves. 'What are they?'

'Mint, camomile, and apple. They work well as infusions in boiling water. The camomile is good for an upset tummy, helps keep you calm. Either way, you can't do any harm.'

'I can't?'

'You're staying, remember?'

'Hang on, I told you. I'm going to Saxony!'

'And then do what? Plot vengeance?'

That had been exactly what was on Podevin's mind, but he thought better of confirming Mark's guess.

'So, what's your plan, then? And does Emma know?' Podevin said.

'Her idea, actually—and it's a good one. Come on.'

They forced their way out of the thicket, and Mark turned to plunge deeper into the forest, following paths Podevin began to recognise.

'You're not taking me to those peasants!'

Mark did not break stride, forcing Podevin to catch up to continue his protest, but any further words were forestalled.

'Yes. I am taking you to those peasants. They're one of the very few families still loyal to Wenceslas; they won't ask too many questions and they'll be happy to feed you. Which is more than we can be sure of in Saxony. Do you really think Henry will invade on your say-so? And who would he put on the throne if he did? You? Or one of his own relations?'

Mark didn't have to say any more. Podevin got the point. Emma was in enough trouble, according to what Mark had said, on his behalf. If she now wanted him to live with some peasants for a while, then so be it. Podevin squared his shoulders and the two of them marched along for a while.

'How is—how is Emma?'

'That had better be Princess Emma, or my lady, from now on.' Then, with a smile, Mark relented. 'She's fine, though she's had to grow up faster than I'd like. We can be grateful Boleslav is too busy to chase up on the death of a guard and the Matilda that rode away as a kidnap victim. I think they were more worried about the horse anyway.'

'It's a fine horse!' Podevin said. Then, in an effort to change the subject, 'Did you know Ursula followed the old gods?'

'Not until recently.'

Was it really only three nights ago—in the chapel at Stara Boleslav— that all this had started? Podevin found his mind contemplating his change of fortune.

Chapter 27
With the Peasants

'Have you been listening to anything I've been saying?'

Podevin stumbled over a tree root and snapped back to the present at Mark's tone.

'Daydreaming of Emma again? Don't you understand? All that is lost to you. There is no chance of a counter rebellion. Who'd lead it? You? Even Tugumir, as your mother's firstborn, has a better claim to the throne than you. Boleslav was—is—Wenceslas's designated heir. And you, my friend, have a price on your head. Not even Emma can do anything about that. Her role is to produce the next generation of heirs. While her father-in-law battles his supposed enemies, Mladenic's going to have to learn how to rule.'

The last comment was muttered so quietly, that Podevin almost didn't catch it.

'Mladenic rule Bohemia?'

'He is the heir.' Mark's face was grim as he turned and darted down another woodland pathway.

The peasant family asked loads of questions. Despite having met Podevin before, the six-year-old girl hid behind her mother's skirts. Of course, they were mainly worried about how the new king would change the tax system to affect them, or if Tugumir would be allowed to come after them. Mark did his best to reassure them; Boleslav was too busy, and he was sure Tugumir was as well, to worry about a couple of runaway peasants. After all, the new king was fully engaged going round saying that everything was the same as before, except that the crown rested on a different head. Besides which, Tugumir was not here; he'd been sent to Tetin, where Queen Drahomira, Wenceslas and Boleslav's mother, had fled after dealing with Wenceslas's body. The task was to return the old queen to Prague.

'Oh, he'll be pleased,' grunted Podevin. 'Tugumir on escort duties.'

It was only later that Podevin found out why the old queen had fled. Somehow, Drahomira had discovered Boleslav wanted her dead. Whether it was because she had wept over Wenceslas's body, changed her mind about the coup (when it was too late), or because Boleslav just wanted to be rid of a co-conspirator, and a fellow pagan one at that, Podevin never knew.

Nor was he bothered. He had, he reckoned, enough problems considering this hovel a sanctuary. Mark was still talking with Krok.

'But you'll have to teach him a lot before he can be remotely useful to you.'

Podevin glared at Mark, who was grinning at him.

'He knows absolutely nothing about being a forester. Weapons of war, yes. Court etiquette, yes. Appropriate deference to princesses, maybe. But living off the land, definitely no.'

'I've done lots of hunting,' said Podevin.

'On horseback,' was the crushing response.

They did not have horses here. Riding down a deer, or a boar, spear in hand, was out of the question. Podevin began to realise how different life was going to be, and he did not know when or whether this different life would end. He did not know when or whether he would be useful, or wanted, again. He must have groaned, or sighed, or something, because Mark suddenly stopped saying whatever he was saying to Krok and gestured to Podevin to accompany him outside.

'You need to change your attitude. It shows us exactly why we're right to put you here. Who would expect you to be living with peasants?' Mark paused. 'It never crossed your mind. Right?'

Podevin nodded.

'So that means we're hoping it won't cross anybody else's mind either. So, if—when—they come looking, they won't look here. Do you get it now?' Podevin nodded again, but he avoided Marks's gaze.

'Right,' Mark said, 'I'm going to leave you. I don't know when you'll be able to come back. I'll do my best to get messages to you. Just do *your* best to learn how to be a forester. All right?'

Podevin nodded, the bravado dropping from him like rain from a springtime leaf. Two days ago he'd had clothes, boots (best, second best, day-to-day), possessions, and now he had a borrowed jerkin over the old clothes he stood up in and one pair of boots. Didn't a soldier always make the best of it? Hadn't he survived when his father was killed? He squared his shoulders and went back to join Krok and his family.

✌

Podevin's concerns over the next weeks became much more basic than manners at table, or who had an empty goblet, or making sure he was dressed correctly to be seen on horseback—there was no horse to be seen on and, if there had been, it would have been turned into meat in very short order. The boots he had worn down to the forest soon had tide-marks of mud and damp. It was the season of plenty; even little Maria was doing her bit to fill the storehouse under the hut. The child was out picking berries and fruits, coming home with scratched hands and arms her mother barely had time to tend before more tasks claimed both their attention. Podevin felt he was back to being seven again, trying to learn how to be a page, only there were no clear rules; no-one said what was a male, or a female, role. They all mucked in: salting meat, setting traps, finding kindling and logs, cutting down trees, checking the roof after the first autumn rains—there could be no suggestion now of any help coming from the castle. And every-body looked for food. The crops, such as they were, had been brought in and the grain stored in dry pits under the floor.

Podevin did not know how to hunt—not this way. He was used to galloping over the ground in full cry after the deer or the boar; armed with spear and dagger, not stalking through the undergrowth looking for tracks and lying in wait. The first time out was a disaster.

There was a pit. He was told it had taken a week to prepare; the natural hollow had been scraped out and enlarged and was now covered with light branches and bracken. The idea was to get a deer to walk over it and break through. Then it could be killed. Podevin had talked about bows and arrows and stalking; even Geraint's men knew how to do that. However, it was pointed out that he had no bow or arrow, and Krok's shoulder was not all it might have been, so could Podevin please do as he was asked? Only when a deer was caught could Krok be sure of a clean kill. There was no point in stalking one, only to have an arrow fall short. Podevin was hiding by the side of the path, ready to force the animal to choose the correct route.

'Provided you stay still enough not to scare it away before it gets anywhere near.'

'It'll smell us.'

'Which is why we're downwind. Don't they teach you anything up at the castle?'

Podevin could think of no reply to this. They had servants to flush the game out of cover; it had not been his role to work out what they did or why. Besides, he still had to be careful not to be seen.

'Cheer up! You don't smell like one of those pomaded lords anymore!' was Krok's parting shot as he left to circle round the deer. At least he would be keeping warm by being on the move.

Podevin sat and thought about bathing; here, there was either the cold, cold river, or a small bowl to try to clean yourself in. He could not work out how they managed it—and he wasn't about to ask!

Podevin sighed and settled down to wait. Waiting was boring. Before, on a proper hunt, they could chat with each other while the servants flushed out the game. Now, any movement, any noise, startled the birds, and, no doubt, all the wildlife too. Dusk arrived—a little earlier in the woods than out on the sun-drenched fields, and the temperature dropped. Podevin shivered, and then froze. At last! A beast was making its way down the track. Snuffling, and grubbing the soil, the massive boar passed within a couple of feet. Then it paused and turned towards him in his bramble hideout. He looked up into the small eyes. The tusks eased closer; the beast snorted.

Podevin yelled and broke cover. He screamed his defiance as the boar startled. Then the animal charged and Podevin was, somehow, running down the track, trying to make headway. Then the pit! It was there. Podevin jumped. He landed. The boar was behind him, charging! Snorting! And falling into the pit. Podevin ran for his life, not looking back. He ran until a massive oak barred his way, and he had swung himself into the branches before he noticed his bleeding hands, or his torn jerkin. Then he heard Krok bounding towards the pit. Using his wooden staff as a third leg, he could move surprisingly fast.

He had the energy to shout at Podevin, 'You bloody idiot! What you do that for!'

The beast was in the pit, but the pit had no stakes in the bottom, so the boar was still very much alive and struggling to get out. Krok jabbed at it with his staff, keeping it in there. Above the sounds of the boar, Podevin heard the birds squawking their fright at the evening's disturbance. He turned his head, his heart still pounding. Krok, minus his ever-present staff, had changed tactics and was limping round the edge of the pit, an arrow ready in his bow.

'Get your knife! Come here! Distract it!'

Pride awoke. If Krok could be down on the ground, facing the animal, then he could too. He was a warrior, wasn't he? He was supposed to be used to this, not squalling like a child. Podevin clambered down and ran towards the animal. He waved his blade, wishing it was at the end of a lance, but, as the beast turned towards him, Krok finally loosed an arrow, then another, into the beast's side. Without the power a trained archer could put behind an arrow, the boar still lived, but it was thrashing more feebly. Krok put down his bow, picked up the axe he had left with Podevin, and clambered into the pit, wincing. The beast still had the strength to turn to attack, but Krok struck out with his axe, straight between the beast's eyes. Blood and gore splattered out and Krok flung himself out of the way as the beast collapsed. Finally, the wood went quiet. Krok stood up in the pit and reached for his staff.

'And what the hell did you run for?'

'It was about to get me!'

'Don't they teach you to leave boar alone?'

'No. We hunt them all the time.'

'On horseback! And in big groups! And even then, you get injuries, don't you?'

Silence.

'Don't you?'

A nod. Then: 'And deaths. I'm sorry.'

'No harm done. Except to my ankle.'

'Oh.'

'Help me out, then!'

Podevin sheathed his knife, and went up to Krok, holding out his hand.

'Not like that. Grab my wrist.' Podevin did so. 'Now I can grab yours, and it's easier to pull me out.'

With Krok limping more than usual, and the light fading, the beast had to be left in the pit. Podevin worked under Krok's direction, started to cover it up as best he could for the morning. But they were interrupted.

'You two can be heard a mile away!'

'Good.' Krok smiled at his wife. 'At least you knew where to find us.'

'That and you telling me where you'd be.' Then she noticed his limp. 'Tell me.'

The two of them went off for a brief chat, leaving Podevin, burning with shame, by the boar.

Krok and Lyudmila came back to the pit. There was no way Krok could handle, much less lift, the boar. In the end, they decided to do it in stages. First, to heave the boar out of the pit, Podevin had to get down beside the animal and try to lever it out, with Lyudmila pulling and Krok directing.

'Even with one ankle gone, I can do better than that!'

'Then why don't you?' Podevin snapped, and clambered out from beside the dead animal.

'Where d'you think you're going?' That was Lyudmila at her most assertive.

'Home.'

'Our home or yours?' Podevin turned as she approached. 'You need to get some things straight in your head,' she hissed. 'You are an incompetent, arrogant brat. You might have served a king, but, by God, you expect everyone else to serve you! And what do you think is going to happen if you leave that boar here? Think you can get some castle servants to sort it?'

Podevin broke eye contact. Krok was back in the pit. Whether he was wincing because of his ankle, or the weight of their kill, Podevin could not tell, but, in unspoken agreement, he and Lyudmila walked back to the pit.

This time, with both Podevin and Lyudmila pulling, and with Krok able to get his shoulder under the beast's side, they rolled it out onto the path.

Then it became more familiar to Podevin. They tied the beast's legs. Using Krok's axe, Lyudmila felled a sapling and stripped off the minor branches. She passed the crudely fashioned pole between the boar's legs.

'Right,' she said, 'I hope you're feeling strong.'

'Me?' said Podevin.

She stood and pointed at the other end of the pole. Podevin didn't argue. He bent and picked it up.

In complete darkness, they set off. Krok limped ahead. The boar, heavy, and getting heavier with each step, swung side to side as it dangled from the pole, but Podevin said nothing. Lyudmila had the other end. At least she was in front and knew where she was going.

By the time they arrived back home and staggered through the opening in the hawthorn fence, Maria had fed the ducks, pigs and goats. The little girl ran to meet them.

'Why the hell,' Podevin gasped, 'didn't you just kill one of those?' He pointed at the pigs' enclosure.

Still clasping his daughter to him, Krok turned.

'One, we went for deer, which we are allowed, and not boar. Two, we don't kill our own animals until we have to. And three, we need extra, as there is an extra mouth to feed. Any more questions?'

There were no more questions.

There was also no point in trying to do any more with the carcass that night. There was stew for supper, there were injuries to bind. Podevin nursed his own bruises and sore shoulder from where the sapling had rubbed through his clothes. He accepted his food from Maria, but retired early to brood. And dream of how life used to be.

Chapter 28
Lessons Learned

An understanding talk with Emma would have been such a relief for Podevin the next day. For he found out he knew nothing about butchering boars. In a hunt from the castle, others had always dealt with the kill once it had been made, and he certainly did not spend time in the castle kitchens preparing meals. His place was in the great hall, by the king's side. Nor could he be useful in plugging any holes in the hedge. He had been sent to look, but found none. Maria found half a dozen and pointed them out to him without a word, before going back to help her mother deal with the boar. He knew they would need salt, but he could hardly volunteer to go to Prague to get any. Krok was laid up, but refused to give him any jobs.

'Can you find your way back to the pit? Can you re-cover it?'

He didn't even have the sharpness of hearing to know someone was coming down the track towards the huts. He did notice Lyudmila's tension but, by the time he heard the footfall on the fallen leaves, she had relaxed again. Maria was sent to meet the visitor.

Brother Mark was welcomed in and taken to see Krok. Podevin stayed outside, out of the way. He heard the murmur of conversation—a sharp intake of breath as, he presumed, a bandage was removed—and relieved laughter. Conversation resumed. Podevin carried on walking around the enclosure, barely noticing as ducks scuttled out of his way.

'Well?'

Podevin jumped. He had not heard Mark come up beside him.

'Well, what?'

'How are you doing in your new home?'

'You mean, how am I doing as an extra mouth to feed in their home?'

'As bad as that, eh?'

Podevin swung round to face Mark. 'Yes, it's every bit as bad as that! Are there no knights who could have taken me in? No nobles supporting Wenceslas? Nobody of the right background—'

Mark had never struck Podevin before, but the slap both ended the diatribe and brought tears to Podevin's eyes. He put his hand to his cheek.

'We will walk.' Mark led the way out of the enclosure.

Silence. Except a wood is never silent, once you are attuned to it. Birds never stop chirruping. Pigeons can even be heard in flight, the way their wings beat the air, and walkers can hear their own feet scuffing their way through the leaf litter. Podevin even became aware of Mark's steady, regular breathing.

'Where are we?' Mark asked.

Startled out of his reverie, Podevin looked around. He knew the way to and from Krok and Lyudmila's place—provided he started at Prague Castle. Apart from that…

'If we keep going another few hundred yards, we'll join the main path, the road that leads to Saxony. There are some who might have given you succour who have travelled that path. But they are those who have no castles to lose, or have already lost them. Those still with castles, land, property, are coming to terms with the new regime. Besides,' Mark had stopped walking, 'at the risk of repeating myself, anyone who is suspected of being too close to the former king, is also suspected of harbouring those who might be on the wanted list. Hiding you in a castle would not be clever—even if those are the only skills you have.'

Podevin opened his mouth, but Mark forestalled him. 'So far, until yesterday, you were able to treat it all as a bit of a game. You'd won every fight you'd been in. Perhaps that enabled you to forget how serious the situation is. But yesterday, reality bit back. And I thank God for that.'

'But I could have been killed!'

'Any day that goes by, you could be killed.'

'Then give me a sword or battle-axe and let me face the enemy!'

'Oh, I'm sure you'll face them, but not yet.' A pause. Then: 'Why did I bring you here?'

Another shrug. Then Mark grabbed him, one hand to each shoulder. Podevin winced; his shoulder hadn't recovered from carrying the boar, but Mark was shaking him.

'I haven't time for this! Don't you realise there'll be war!'

'What war? Who with?'

'Saxony! Or the Magyars.' Mark glared at Podevin's bemusement. 'Boleslav's stopped paying tribute to Saxony, and told his people to follow hunted game across the borders in the east.'

Podevin winced; the Magyars, famous horsemen and bowmen, would not take kindly to finding Boleslav's minions on their land. He shook his head. 'Who would tell me? I don't live in Prague anymore.'

'Wake up! We had it all wrong. We thought Boleslav would want to keep everyone outside our borders sweet so he could consolidate his power in Bohemia. It seems he's taken the opposite line. He wants a war as quickly as possible, so everyone will unite behind him in battle.'

'I suppose the quickest way to rouse Henry would be to deny him his money. And pinching the Magyars' game won't amuse them either.'

'Yes, but you need to become a forester. You need to be able not just to look like a peasant, but to think like one. You may never be a knight. We hope you will, but we don't know.'

Podevin caught one word. 'We?'

'Yes. We. Though what she'll think when I tell her about yesterday, I don't know.'

'You'll tell her?'

'Of course.'

There was a pause. Mark made no effort to fill it.

'Oh.' Podevin looked into the middle distance, trying to ignore the sinking feeling in the pit of his stomach. 'I've made a mess of it, haven't I?'

'You made a mistake. So? We all do.'

Podevin raised his eyebrows at the idea of a mistake-ridden Mark, but didn't interrupt.

'One of the advantages of getting old is that you can forget the mistakes of your youth, or cover them up better, as those who know about them die off. But we're not talking about me. This is about you, and keeping you alive until you can be useful.'

'As a peasant?'

'As a knight who can pass for a peasant—or an archer—preferably both.'

'I need a bow.'

'You've got one.'

Of course, Podevin had not even looked at what Mark had been carrying when he arrived.

'Will Emma employ me?'

'She'd employ you tomorrow if it wouldn't get you both killed.' Mark indicated that they should keep walking towards the road to Saxony.

'You need to know this road. You need to know who and what travels along it, and you need to know this forest so well, you can disappear into it at will and not be caught.'

'But Boleslav has his own scouts and spies.'

'That's as may be, but we need someone we can trust.'

'You need what?'

'Someone loyal to Emma, who will give her the truth—even when it isn't what she wants to hear.'

'Why?'

'For the moment, Mladenic has been put in charge of Prague and its environs, while the king goes to the border.' Mark paused and looked at Podevin.

'I know what "environs" means.' He stopped walking as Mark stayed silent. 'We're in the environs of Prague, the surrounding area,' he said.

'And he expects it to be properly defended.'

'But Mladenic—'

'Isn't up to the task. But Emma's a woman, so can't possibly be left in charge in her own right, can she?'

Podevin assumed Mark didn't need him to answer that question. They came to the road. After peering up and down to check no-one was around, Mark stepped out of cover. He bent. Then, still crouched, he beckoned. Podevin came up, but Mark put his arm out and stopped him going any farther. He pointed at the ground.

'When did it last rain?'

Podevin thought. 'Last night sometime. Didn't hear it.'

'So you manage to sleep well. Tired after carrying that boar, were you?'

The tone was light, so Podevin let it pass. Mark knew he would never have let anyone get at Wenceslas over his sleeping body. He knew how to sleep lightly, but he had never had to sleep lightly because it might rain. Podevin peered at what Mark had found.

'Tracks,' Podevin said.

'Go on.'

'Horse.'

'Cantering down this road towards Saxony just after daybreak. Before the carter came by with his wares to sell in Prague.'

'What?'

'The fore and hind hoof marks aren't together, as they would be in walking or trotting, but not individually spaced out as in a gallop. The cart wheels have crossed the hoof print just down there, so the horse came by earlier. The cart wheels really sink into the mud, so it was heavy. And no,' Mark said as he stood up, 'I can't tell you the colour of the horse... Unless.'

He wandered down the road for a bit. It curved round to the right. Podevin followed.

'A nice chestnut.' He passed some horsehair to Podevin. 'They must have passed here. He reined the horse in at the bend and kept to the side.'

'And you expect me to learn all that?'

'And more. We need to know everything you can tell us. Come on, we'll go back now.'

But Podevin just stood there. 'Mark?' The monk turned. 'You knew the horse had been here, didn't you?'

'No. I did see the cart come into town, but not the rider going out. But I've learned enough. I can find out whose horse is missing.'

With that, Podevin had to be content.

There was not much conversation on the way back to the huts. Mark insisted that Podevin guide them, and, what's more, walk ahead of the monk. The third time Mark simply stopped, and silently waited until Podevin worked out that he wasn't behind him, he lost his temper.

'If you're so clever, you lead the way, as you know this forest so well!'

'Over the past days, I've had much less opportunity than you to find my way about the forest,' Mark said.

Podevin clenched his fists. His jaw was tight, painfully tight; but he said nothing.

'But all you have to do is follow your tracks, or know which direction you must go. We came north to find the road to Saxony, so we must go south on our way back.'

'South. North. Whatever.'

'Where's the sun?'

Podevin frowned at the stupidity of the question. Even in the dappled light of the woods, the sun's rays were causing them both to squint.

'Exactly,' said Mark.

Silence.

'It's getting on for the middle of the day, so the sun is in the south. We need to go this way. Besides, there's where you nearly stepped into that puddle.'

Even Podevin could see the wodge of mud gouged up by his slipping heel. They plodded on in silence. Then, another fork in the path.

Mark stopped. 'Well?'

Podevin looked. The ground was dry. Both paths went sort of south.

'I don't know! I. Just. Don't. Know. All right?'

And then, at last, the tears came. He felt himself taken in a strong embrace. They moved aside into the wood a few paces. They sat on an old log. Mark kept his arms about his protégé until the storm passed, and the tears dissolved into hiccoughs.

'Does Emma still like me?'

If Mark was surprised by the question, he didn't show it.

'Yes,' he said. 'Yes, she does.'

'Bet she wouldn't be impressed by this display.'

'Oh, she'd cope with an admission of failure, but not the refusal to do anything about it.'

Podevin looked up sharply, but Mark was gazing at nothing.

'You don't approve.' Statement.

'There are lots of things I could disapprove of, but friendship isn't one of them.' Podevin opened his mouth to interrupt, but Mark continued. 'I disapprove of sending a young girl across the sea to be picked over like a brood mare. I disapprove of her having to grow up long before her time. I disapprove of her being married off to a young boy who has no notion of how to treat a woman. But I also have to disapprove of her looking for love outside her marriage, don't I?'

At those last two words, Mark turned and looked at Podevin. 'But then,' he said, 'would she have risked her life for a mere servant?'

'I would hope,' said Podevin, picking his words with care, 'the lady I loved would do just that.'

'And what about you?'

'I hope,' Podevin again chose his words before he spoke, 'the person she cares for would learn all the skills he needed to be of use to her.' Podevin stood. 'Come on. Show me.'

Back at the fork in the track, Mark pointed out the bent grasses and snapped twigs that marked their earlier passage. Podevin crouched down.

'How do you know that was us and not a passing deer?'

'Good question. We're just clumsier and heavier. It's more likely to be us, and there is no similar spoor, no tracks, on the other path. Come on.'

His point made, Mark was happy enough to walk beside him on their way back to the huts. Besides, he had more to say to Podevin. He needed to reiterate that Podevin was going to be needed once war broke out. Mark could see no way King Henry would stand for tribute not being paid. Or Otto for that matter—it seemed Henry was ill and thought likely to die soon. Had they known there was potential trouble in Saxony, they might have been more on guard against Boleslav in Prague, but then, given Wenceslas's behaviour—almost as if he wanted to be a martyr—however much they had guarded him, it would probably have ended badly. Hadn't Wenceslas gone to that chapel alone and unarmed?

Back to the present, the better a tracker Podevin became, the better a scout he would be. People who tracked tended to be better at hiding themselves.

'Which can be useful at times.'

'You mean, if I need to get to the castle.'

'You wouldn't get that far, but you might need to get to the edge of the woods and leave a sign. But that's for another day, after Emma's child is born.'

'She hasn't already retired for the birth? It's months yet, surely?'

'She'll leave it as long as possible, if I know her, but Boleslav is all traditional about women's roles. I fear it will take a crisis to change his mind.'

'Oh dear, Emma won't like that.'

'Princess Emma.'

'No, Mark, "Emma". Unless we are in court, which is unlikely. And sooner or later, I'll forget at…' Podevin gestured towards the huts that were just visible through the trees, 'home, so they might as well know.'

Mark sighed. 'Yes, they might as well.' He changed the subject. 'And you'll let Krok teach you?'

'I'll have to after yesterday's display!' Then Podevin sobered. 'Will he be all right?'

'Provided he rests that foot for a couple of days, he'll be fine. Or as fine as he'll ever be.'

When they returned, they found Maria was scattering corn for the ducks. Krok was sitting outside the main hut, basking in the heat of the day, his leg stretched out in front of him, up on a log. He put his hand up to shield his eyes from the sun as monk and former page pushed their way in through the gate.

'So, you're back.'

'Yes. We're back,' said Mark. 'And I must return to the castle, or they'll be wondering where I've got to.'

'And I suppose we don't really want them to come looking.' Krok paused. 'But you'll have something to eat before you go. I can't see that lot up the hill saving food for you.'

'There's always the kitchen,' said Mark. 'But thank you. I will stay. For a bit.'

Fearing there would be a recount of his failure to identify horse tracks, Podevin thought Mark should visit the castle kitchens if he missed his meal. However, Mark relaxed into genial guest mode—chiding Krok every time the host made to get up. He complemented Lyudmila and Maria on the food and glossed over Podevin's unknown illegality of hunting boar. They did laugh at Podevin's role in that hunt, but Podevin managed to smile. Yes, he had come a cropper, but he would learn. Besides, boars were dangerous creatures. Podevin hoped he would learn quickly. Mark became serious. Boleslav's defiance to his overlord was obvious provocation. Emma had sent a letter to her sister, but it was thought unlikely anything would change…

They all went silent at that point. The crackle of the fire was the only accompaniment to their thoughts.

'You're out of the way here. The main routes are out there.' Mark waved his arm in the direction he and Podevin had taken earlier. 'If they're sensible, they'll avoid the woods where they can.'

'It's not an army marching through I'm worried about. It's when they have to live off the land,' said Krok.

'Then they'll raid the farms, not the forests,' was Mark's optimistic reply.

Podevin wondered. It was all very well; he knew Mark hadn't been a monk all his life, but it would only take one foraging party to discover this little homestead in the forest, for all of them to be homeless, or worse.

All too soon, it was time for Mark to go. He stood and thanked the womenfolk. Krok was banned from walking him to the gate, so Podevin performed that duty.

'You don't really think we'll escape the war here, do you?'

'His knights are just thinking how they'll make money from ransomed opponents. And they don't think about death—only peasants die in battle.'

Podevin glanced across at the monk. It was unusual for him to sound so cynical.

'I don't forget my father.'

Mark nodded. He, too, had heard the tale. Perhaps he had heard many like it. Other people had lost their fathers in battle. They walked in silence for a while.

'Is it going to be dangerous? What'll Emma want me to do?' Podevin asked.

'It's going to be dangerous for you to show your face anywhere you're known for a long time yet.'

On that note, apart from the conventional words of farewell, they parted. Mark to carry on being counsellor and confessor to Princess Emma, and Podevin to learn how to be a forester and tracker.

Chapter 29
Forester

A.D. 936

When he looked back, Podevin realised he enjoyed that year. He even let his beard regrow. Of course, he missed Wenceslas and his funny ways. What king made bread or crushed grapes for wine? He missed the chats, the desire to serve the people—all theory, until Mark sent the two of them, plus Emma, out in the snow that St Stephen's day! But, safe in their forest hideaway, Podevin and Krok could go out and track their game. They could never quite forget the politics, the brotherly hatred that had led to death and the destruction of the carefully built peace between Bohemia and Saxony. They kept out of the way as heralds cantered back and forth. They watched farther back in the winter trees as parties of peasants were sent out, whipped by overseers, to clear the roads and widen the verges. Not wide enough, Krok thought—an archer could still kill a man from a spot hidden in the trees—but deep enough to give decent warning of sword or axe-wielding bandits. Speaking of archery, Podevin had to practise that too—swordplay, or cavalry fighting, was not an option for a forester—he learnt to kill a rabbit with one arrow. He could fell a deer too, but, after his early adventure, he left boar alone.

He also left Prague alone. In the early days, it was Krok who went to the edge of the forest to hand over the information they gathered. But as that first autumn wore on into winter, and Krok's old injuries meant he started stiffening up, Podevin took over. Mark or, very occasionally, once she had been safely delivered of a son, Emma would venture out on a hunt—correction, Emma would be allowed to follow a hunt from a safe distance and with her ladies in close attendance. And that, according to Mark, was only because the spring weather was warm enough. Podevin would watch as they picked their careful way through the castle gates and out into the dangerous countryside. No faster than walking pace, the little party, including a whole bunch of guards, would approach the terrifying forest before Emma reined in her pony.

'Just give me a few minutes, will you? Or do you think the Spirit of the Forest is going to carry me off?'

She walked her pony to the place where Wenceslas had first seen Krok. Podevin would be out of sight, either back in the bushes, or up a tree, ready to give his report. The chestnut gelding was riding out on a weekly basis, but not always on the road to Saxony—there were other paths to other borders.

Then: 'How are you? Really?' he'd say.

'My son has been sent to a wet nurse. My husband ignores me, and my father-in-law thinks I am unladylike because I use my brain! Apart from that, I'm fine.'

'Sorry,' said Podevin.

'It was a stupid question.' But she smiled as she said it. 'Mark and Radslav are working on Boleslav, but it's slow going.'

'Radslav's there?'

'When he's not skirmishing with the Magyars. Yes. Why do you ask?'

'No reason.' But there was a reason. Emma did not need reminding how Radslav had caused his father's death.

Of course, Mark, when it was his turn to collect Podevin's report, did not see things the same way. 'One day, you'll be glad you know Duke Radslav—he's braver and more loyal than you think.'

The subject was closed; never mind what Podevin thought. So, while Mark was once again pretending to gather herbs, Podevin questioned him about the situation with Saxony. There was, as yet, no war.

'What's Henry playing at?'

'Dying. So, Otto's making sure he gets the throne with no arguments. But, rest assured, he'll deal with Boleslav soon enough. And no amount of fortifying the frontier on our side will stop him,' Mark said.

'I suppose everyone's dealing with the crops and so forth.'

'True.'

'Look, we report this stuff; who we think is going here, and who there. Is it any good? Are we helping?'

'We?'

'Well, if it's me or Krok watching the road, someone still has to sort out the home and the food. I mean, we're grateful when you bring us food from the castle kitchens, but there are four of us. And at least one of us is growing fast!'

'Be careful, lad, you're starting to sound fond of your niece!'

Podevin grinned back at Mark. 'She's teaching me about what foods to forage for and when.'

At that, Mark snorted with laughter, before sobering.

'To answer your question, even if all you do is confirm what we know, that helps. Something is going on—there always is in Boleslav's court—but we've heard nothing from his mother since she fled from Tugumir, and the king isn't talking about it. What he is talking about is his penance for not stopping Wenceslas from being killed.'

'Boleslav's turned Christian?' Podevin was incredulous.

'Boleslav's learned the Pope in Rome has allies. Allies with real armies, who wouldn't say no to invading Bohemia. Two enemies are enough, even for our new king. No, Boleslav's merely looked at the way the wind is blowing. So, the knights who performed the deed for him have been banished from court.'

'So, Tugumir's at Budec?'

'Or Tetin. We're not sure.'

'Queen Drahomira's place? But didn't you just say she fled?'

'She went abroad, yes. Look, Emma's no favourite of the Queen Mother. It sounds ridiculous, but your Emma needs Boleslav to stay on the throne.'

'And Mladenic after him, I suppose.'

'If Boleslav isn't on the throne and his son after him, they're dead. And so, if Queen Drahomira has any say, is Emma. Give her half a chance and Emma would lead the army herself!' Mark said.

'Or she could write to her sister. Pursue peace that way.'

'Not altogether sure her letters are getting to the right hands, or even as far as the border.'

'Funny you should say that, Mark.' Podevin paused as realisation struck. 'You remember I told Emma two days ago about the overnight camp in the forest? When your rider could have made it to the border before dark?' He drew a piece of scorched parchment from inside his jerkin. 'We went back yesterday, found this in the fire.'

Mark looked at it. 'Why didn't you hand it over before?'

'We didn't have it, then. If you want the road watched, and the rest of the forest, all the time, you'd need an army. As I said, there is a home to run. Anyway,' Podevin carried on over Mark's attempt to speak, 'I was up a tree and it was Emma I was talking to. And you told me to remember she's being watched.'

Mark held up a hand, placatory. 'I'll get it back to her. We thought we could trust an emissary to hand over a sisterly letter…'

'Boleslav wants his war, doesn't he? If he can get it while Otto is off balance, then all the better for him,' Podevin said.

'Still thinking like a royal servant, then?'

'Oh, come on, Mark. Not many foresters get this sort of dual role. And you can't stop me wondering what's going on, given you tell me as little as you can get away with.'

Mark stood, but he was smiling. 'No, I'm not cross. I do understand it's not easy for you. But it isn't easy for us either. Boleslav is not the sort of person you can go up to and have a casual chat about affairs of state.'

Podevin smiled too. 'If I remember, his brother was awkward about things like that as well. Especially once he'd made his mind up.'

On that note, they parted.

When he was not watching the road, and even sometimes when he was, Podevin realised he still had much to learn about living off the land and in the forest. Over that previous winter, for example, he learned the importance of keeping his sleeping quarters clean and dry—how to build up the layers of dried bracken and straw so there was plenty between him and the ground—not so much because of the wet, or the bugs, but because of the way the cold leached the life from you if you let it. He learned how to build, and tend, a fire. How to place it not too near a tree trunk but to have the smoke drift and dissipate through the canopy so an unfriendly observer could not tell where the fire was—or, hopefully, once Podevin had replaced the turf he'd dug up to create the hollow for the fire, the unfriendly observer would be unable to tell there was a fire in the first place.

Tracking was a constant lesson. It was that spring, over half a year after he arrived in the forest, before Krok allowed him out on his own. He shot his first deer after tracking it for over two hours. At first he'd thought it was a three-legged beast, but no, the front near foot was being put down, but only just, barely leaving a mark.

He shot the deer, and bore it back in triumph, slung over his shoulders. It was Krok who worked out the significance of the snare round its foot. They were not the only people in the forest, but this was new; the first sign of people in the forest who did not know how to survive. If nothing else, you looked after your traps so you could use them again.

'Tomorrow, we go back to where you found those tracks,' Krok said, 'and find out where it came from.'

Podevin nodded. Lyudmila looked up. This was the sort of mistake she and Krok could have made when they first fled Tugumir's wrath. Were those times coming again?

Chapter 30
Friend or Foe?

'Any closer and I'll kill you!'

It was a short blade, lashed to a branch. As a spear, it would hardly be effective against a half-trained foot soldier, but Podevin held his peace. He also held his ground. The young man barred his way to the hut, but there were no other guards. Krok and Podevin had circled the place twice. Information gleaned from tracks seemed to suggest only two people going in and out. Given time, the shack might be made waterproof with a decent thatch, but there was no fence and very little evidence of stores. Podevin reckoned one pair of eyes was peering at him through the gaps in the shack's walls. But the youth was still standing there and had to be dealt with.

'What's your name?' Podevin watched the boy's eyes darting all over the place but, despite the frantic vigilance, he had not noticed Krok, who would now be on the other side of the hut, the fire inside masking any slight noise he might make.

'Who wants to know?' A jab with the makeshift spear.

'I do.'

'From them, are you?' Another jab. A bit closer this time.

'Unless you tell me who they are, I've no idea. Where have you come from?'

The boy took a step forward, another jab. Too close. Podevin feinted left, moved right, left arm up to block the wavering branch, grabbed and pulled. The peasant, too stupid to let go of what had already been lost, stumbled forward, straight onto Podevin's dagger.

Or he would have, if Podevin had drawn it. As it was, he let the boy fall to the ground and twisted the branch out of his fevered grip. Podevin put the blunt end of the branch against the boy's chest and leant down.

'Now, who are you, where are you from, and what are you doing here? Or do you prefer me to use the other end of this pole?'

There was no time for an answer. Podevin heard a charging scream as a woman erupted from the shack, flinging a cooking pot at his head, forcing him to duck. She ran towards him, swinging what looked like a spoon. Reacting instinctively, Podevin removed the branch from the young man's chest and, before the lad could move, Podevin's foot was on his throat. Holding the branch under his arm—properly, like a lance—Podevin pointed the makeshift blade at the woman. She stopped and threw her ladle. It missed.

'You get off my son!' She made to grab the spear, but Podevin jerked it towards her hand. A cut, no more, but she moved back, holding her hand to her mouth.

'I'll get off your son when I have some explanations.'

She kept glaring. Her son was trying to get out from under Podevin's foot but, with every struggle, Podevin increased the pressure.

'Look,' he said, 'I can keep this up indefinitely. You aren't going to get any nearer. And he will choke long before he gets to his feet. Besides, my friend is already inside your hut.' Unlike the woman, Podevin had seen Krok sneak round the side of the hut to the entrance.

At that, the woman faced defeat. 'In that case, he'll kill my husband and daughter. Just do it quickly. And kill us too.'

Her chest started heaving as the tears finally gathered and spilled down her face. She stood there, looking at Podevin. He put up the branch. Took his foot off the young man's throat.

'Go to her.' Then, as the young man just lay there: 'Move!'

He let them hug, busying himself with removing the short blade from the branch.

'No-one is killing anyone today. We came to try and help.' Podevin looked up as Krok reappeared, beckoning him.

It was a sorry state inside the shack. An older man lay on a make-shift heather bed. A young girl lay beside him. The man was in no condition to move; the girl tried to sit, but the movement clearly caused her pain. The story was simply told: a peasant family, unable to pay their increased taxes, was forced off their meagre landholding after first suffering a beating. The father's leg had been broken and was now festering; the daughter had flung herself on her father to try to protect him as he lay on the ground and had a wound on her back. Their home had been thoroughly searched, their few pennies confiscated, and the building torched. The cooking pot had been salvaged later. The party of knights had departed, threatening to return for the rest of the money or the family would be sold into slavery.

'Who's your lord?'

'What does it matter?'

'It doesn't, but we'd still like to know.'

'Tugumir.' The word was spat out.

Podevin sighed. 'So you've come from Budec?'

'Tetin.' Podevin hoped his shock didn't show.

So his half-brother had been given Drahomira's estates. Was that a sop from Boleslav to make up for being banished from court? That was a question for Mark; here, there were other issues.

'But why come to Prague?'

'We thought we might find some help.'

'Not in the forest, you won't.'

'We thought, if we had some meat or something to sell...' The youth hung his head.

'That didn't work, did it?' Podevin reached into his pocket and brought out the snare. 'The deer simply walked off with it.'

'And you stole the deer.' The mother's narrowed eyes daggered venom at him, but Podevin just nodded.

'You'd better build up your fire. We've brought some venison.'

'But we can't have venison. We're peasants.' If the youth was trying to stand on his dignity, it failed.

The father still had not moved, but the daughter looked up, her eyes pleading.

'We're foresters,' Krok said. 'We have Wenceslas's dispensation.'

'But Boleslav's king now.' The woman made no move towards the ash-filled scrape in the ground in the middle of the hut.

'We won't tell him if you don't.' Podevin looked around for the cooking pot. Remembered it was outside, as was the meat. 'Why don't you,' he looked at the woman, 'start the fire, while I get everything for you.'

And, he thought, take a quick scout around, just in case there was anyone else. Besides, he wanted to get away from the sweet, sickly smell that was pervading the hut. All too soon, he would have to return to the hut. It was not as if the cooking pot was hard to find and he could not claim to have forgotten where he'd put his pack.

⁓

The able-bodied ate outside, Podevin and Krok talking in low voices. They both knew that the wounds were infected; they both knew only one person who could help. They both knew the risks of going to find that person.

'But we can't just leave them to die,' said Podevin for the third time.

'Yes, and we can't just have you walking into Prague Castle and being killed!' Krok countered.

'I don't intend to. Look,' he murmured under his breath, 'we can't leave them here or you'll be spending all your time teaching them how to survive in the forest. They can't move unless the two in there are better.' He jerked his thumb back at the hut. 'What do you suggest?' Podevin did not mention the alternative to them getting better, an alternative only too possible, even if they did manage to get help.

Krok sighed. 'We'll talk to Lyudmila.' He stood.

Podevin grinned to himself. He could not see Lyudmila refusing to get help. The only question would be how, and he had an idea.

They left the supplies with the family and promised to be back within a day or two—even if a visit to Prague was theoretically out of the question, they could not let these people starve. As they took their leave, Krok led them away north. Podevin followed, saying nothing until they were out of earshot.

'Wrong way, Krok.' He kept his voice low.

'I know. Listen.'

A twig snapped. A puddle splashed. There was even a stifled curse.

'I don't think we're trusted.' Krok smiled and picked up speed.

Relying on his staff, he moved quickly but silently over a short distance. They turned back and forth for ten more minutes. Krok led them back to the broken-down hut, where they stopped to listen before making their way home—again indirectly, stopping to listen until they were sure all they could hear was birdsong and the breeze in the trees. Last year's leaves occasionally rustling.

Chapter 31
Back to Prague

Never was a pole so laden with meat; butchered pigeons, quail, rabbits, and pheasants, all tied together as, leaving the others behind, Podevin and Lyudmila marched up to Prague. Podevin had been banned from removing his beard.

'Surely, the point is no-one recognises you?'

There were always sellers on the streets and byways of any town, and this, too, was true of Prague. In Wenceslas's day, there had even been markets in the castle courtyard. Lyudmila thought they still existed.

'Boleslav's not going to pass up the chance to make a penny or two in taxes, is he?'

There was a tollbooth just inside the city gates. They tried to walk past.

'And where d'you think you're going?'

'To sell meat in the market,' Lyudmila spat back at the questioner.

'Licence?' The man in the tollbooth held out a grubby hand.

'Since when have we needed a licence to sell our own meat?' Podevin felt it was about time he asserted himself. Dressed in Krok's old clothes, with Krok's hood over his head, he prayed he would not be recognised.

The tollbooth keeper looked at him and then back at Lyudmila. 'No licence? So, you'll pay for one, won't you?'

'How can we pay for one before we've made any money?' she said.

'Not my problem. Two crowns.'

'What!'

'And something for supper for me and my friends.'

Podevin looked round. Two guards had come up behind them. He was unsure, but they looked very like the men who had watched them come through the gate. With the pole balanced across his shoulder, he could do nothing as they started prodding the meat. Besides, there were too many people around.

'All right,' Lyudmila capitulated.

They could both see they did not need to draw any more attention to themselves. She opened the purse on her belt and slapped the coins down in front of the bureaucrat as the guards unsheathed their daggers.

'And a pheasant, I think,' he said as he pulled a piece of parchment towards himself and started scribbling on it.

'Hey, you don't need that much!'

'We have families.' The guards shrugged, and wandered away with their haul of three rabbits apiece.

'Names?' The bored voice from the booth cut across any more objections. 'Come on, I need your names or the licence isn't valid.'

'Lyudmila and Krok.' Lyudmila sounded defeated.

The tax collector scribbled some more and pushed the piece of parchment towards her. She snatched it up and moved away, pushing her way past the people wandering in and out of the gate.

Podevin let her move a few steps down the street before muttering, 'Can I have a look?'

'No.' She turned towards the castle.

'But it might not be written properly.'

'Of course it's not written properly! Just because I can't read doesn't mean I'm completely stupid!' she hissed.

Podevin opened his mouth. Closed it. No, Lyudmila was not stupid. He rehearsed the plan in his mind. Get into Prague as if they had meat to sell. Get to the castle kitchens, hand over the meat and ask for Mark. Lyudmila spoke again, pointing at the mass of people.

'This way, it's easier to get lost in the crowds.'

They turned a corner, and Lyudmila pulled him into a doorway. Podevin heaved the pole from his shoulder and set it down, letting the meat rest on his foot, keeping it clear of the street's refuse. Lyudmila peered out, looking through into the castle courtyard. Podevin looked about, thought he saw a way through the crowd, and nudged Lyudmila. She nodded and, with a 'come on' gesture, moved back onto the road and marched up to the courtyard entrance.

'Licence?'

Another booth. Another bureaucrat. Lyudmila fished in her purse and produced the scrap of parchment.

'Here you are. We bought it at the booth by the gate.'

'I don't care where you got it; it isn't the right licence.'

'But you haven't even looked at it!' Lyudmila screeched.

The man in the booth crumpled the parchment with one hand and dropped it onto the floor. 'I know what a licence looks like, and this isn't it. Three crowns.'

'Give me my license back! That cost two crowns!' Lyudmila was getting hysterical.

Podevin tried to shush her. They were gathering a crowd.

'Guards!' called the man in the booth.

But the guards were already running, pushing their way through, scattering the crowd, which immediately fell back.

But then they stopped. Lyudmila also stopped.

'And what's going on here?' A voice of authority, a voice used to being answered.

A voice Podevin knew. He met Brother Mark's eyes. Read the slight surprise, and the warning.

'We're just poor peasants, sir,' he said, 'trying to sell our meat so we can buy bread and provisions. We were stopped on our way in—we needed a licence, they said—two crowns and some of our meat. We had to pay, sir. And then we came here, and he,' Podevin pointed at the man in the booth, who had stopped looking so cocky, 'said our licence wasn't a licence, and we had to pay three crowns!'

'Oh, come now! You're not going to believe these peasants, are you? They try anything. Here you are.' The man bent down and retrieved the parchment. 'Even you can see that isn't a license to sell meat.'

Mark took the parchment. Looked at it. 'No. It's not a license. But it does say that anyone reading this can "fleece these two idiots".'

'We all know a licence costs half a crown. There was no mention of three crowns.' The man stepped out of his booth, confident he would get away with his lies.

'Yes, there was, sir. We both heard it, and so did—' Podevin looked around, but, as he expected, all the potential witnesses had disappeared back into the general scrum of the courtyard. Even the guards had retreated until they were sure which way this was going to go.

Mark was still holding the piece of parchment. 'I need to have a word with someone. Hradak, isn't it?'

'I'm sure that's not necessary, sir. This can all be sorted, sir. I just need the correct fee…' Without waiting, the man darted back to his booth and another, rectangular piece of parchment appeared. 'And then, I just need the names…'

'Right,' said Mark as he started looking along Podevin's pole. 'This will do.'

A fat rabbit landed on the tax collector's desk. He looked up.

'Payment in kind,' said Mark, 'on my authority. Or do you wish me to ask Duke Radslav to attend to sort out this little fracas? I do know that rabbit is worth more than half a crown. Not three crowns perhaps, but enough for a proper, *permanent* licence.'

He held the man's gaze. The man returned to his writing. Podevin gave the names. The man finished writing, blotted the parchment with sand. Poured the excess off and tried to hand it straight to Podevin and Lyudmila. Mark intervened.

'Seal it,' he said, handing it back.

They waited in silence. Under Mark's gaze, the seal was affixed.

With the precious parchment, they left.

'Payment in kind?' said Podevin.

Mark smiled. 'If you're really here to sell this stuff, I would be very surprised. And after that performance, Lyudmila, you need a drink.'

Lyudmila smiled. 'I had to do something to get your attention, didn't I?' Podevin shook his head; all that hysteria had just been an act. He should have known. Brother Mark turned towards the castle kitchens. Podevin hesitated, looked at the depleted stock of meat he was carrying.

'Yes, you're right. Give me the pole.' Mark carried it as if it was just a twig. 'Wait here.'

Now they were inside the castle courtyard and could sit, Podevin, overcome with memories, looked around his former home. There was the chapel on its own, still the only stone-built structure. The great hall opposite the entrance they had just come through, complete with guards; to the right, the king's quarters…but he must stop. One thing had changed: there was more bustle, more stalls, more buying and selling than Podevin remembered. Or was that because he had never gone down to the courtyard on market days? He never needed to in the days when everything was provided for him. He also, even at the times when Wenceslas was changing the tax system, did not recall any talk of licences and people having to pay for them. His thoughts were interrupted by Mark, who had been gone no more than two minutes. When he reappeared, he was balancing a pitcher of small beer, some bread and broth on a tray. The pole had disappeared.

'They always need meat in there. And firewood, come to that. You need bread. And something else.' A statement. Not a question.

Mark settled himself down on the bench opposite them. Podevin had his back to the castle wall. Just a kindly monk, giving two peasants a meal. They sat on the bench, basking. Lyudmila could still do with feeling a little warmer, as the air had been distinctly chilly when they had set out.

'I haven't long,' said Mark, once they'd finished. 'Emma's already aware of the affray She likes to know what's going on. Boleslav just wants her pregnant again.'

No doubt the new king wanted to secure the succession. Podevin hoped Emma was happier now she could feel she was at the centre of things. However, they were not here to talk about Emma.

Before Mark could object that Podevin's actions were the direct opposite of what he had been told to do when he went to stay in the forest, he launched into his tale and ended by pointing out that Krok was in no condition to come so, 'this "incompetent, arrogant brat" had to come—as we couldn't send Lyudmila by herself.' Lyudmila looked up at him as he quoted her words from last September back at him. Podevin shrugged. 'You were right. I hope you're less right now.'

'Did you see the injuries?' Mark homed in on the vital matter at hand.

Podevin shook his head. 'But they stank. Sorry, but I couldn't wait to get out of the place. Pine logs would never cover that smell.'

Mark nodded. 'I'll be out tomorrow. I'll tell Emma you asked after her.'

Podevin glanced at Lyudmila. She smiled and made a shooing gesture at him. Mark had already stood up. Podevin moved off with Mark.

'There isn't a day I don't think about her, you know. When am I going to be needed?'

'Aren't you being needed today? Especially as we know what's been happening to her letters to Saxony?' Enigmatic as ever, Mark smiled at him. 'Come on, I'll escort you to the city gate.'

Mark gestured to Lyudmila to join them and turned back to the kitchens as the door opened. A servant appeared, carrying a basket full of bread and jars of honey and some cabbages. The basket was handed over to Mark, who handed it to Lyudmila.

'A fair exchange, I think,' said Mark. 'And it goes with the story you told on your way in.'

They wandered across the castle courtyard. Podevin did not look up at any windows, much as he wanted to. Giving himself away now would be particularly stupid. They passed the booth.

'Yes, that's it. Half a crown.' The voice was officiously loud.

Mark grinned. 'He'll be very honest…for a day or two.'

And they walked down the street towards the city wall and their exit to the countryside and home.

Chapter 32
Adopting Priby

'He's dead, and I'm dying!'

The girl clung to the cold, stinking body of her father, her tear-stained face barely registering their presence, even after they'd forced the door open.

'If you're able to talk to us, you're not dead yet.' Lyudmila moved briskly to the bed and sat down by the girl.

She detached her from her father's body and examined her back. The girl winced and bit her lip. She had already learned not to cry aloud. The bandages oozed pus. Mark set his medicine bag down on a log, balancing it carefully. Podevin stood near the doorway. Anything to avoid the fetid smell.

The silence was the first warning. Podevin had left the other two, had circled the hut, checking everything before daring to enter. No makeshift spears this time. No spear carrier either. He and his mother had gone, taking the cooking pot and the provisions with them. There were just the two on the bed.

Mark joined Lyudmila. He checked the man over, then turned to the weeping girl.

'Podevin, we'll need that stretcher,' Mark said. 'Put it over there.' He indicated a dry patch of the dirt floor.

Podevin retreated outside, taking as many gulps of fresh air as he could, and retrieved the stretcher he had carried all the way from home, built with the father in mind, so clearly capable of holding the girl. He'd even made Krok lie on it, while he and Lyudmila lifted it. Their plans had assumed the whole family would be here.

He returned to the hovel to find Lyudmila still bending over the girl. 'We're taking you back with us, Pribyslava, and you're going to get better. Podevin's got a stretcher for you made of deer skins. And we'll have new, clean clothes for you. And a cloak to cover you for the journey.'

Mark and Lyudmila, impervious to the smell—or just not showing their reaction—bent over the girl and murmured. Soon, she was allowing them to carry her over to the stretcher and remove the bandages from her torso.

'As I thought.' Mark reached into his bag. A simple pot stoppered with green leaves. 'Now, lie still.'

Lyudmila stroked the girl's matted hair with one hand while the other clasped the girl's undersized hand.

'It won't hurt, will it?' she asked.

'It's done,' Mark replied. 'No, you need to lie still.'

'But what about Daddy?'

'Daddy's dead, sweetheart. Brother Mark is praying for him now.'

Mark paused long enough to beckon Podevin over to join him.

'I don't know whether the poison from the gangrene killed him or the fever. Was he sweating when you saw him?'

Podevin shook his head. 'Not that I noticed. He just lay there. Didn't say a word.'

Mark nodded. 'If there was no fever, Pribyslava has a better chance. Come on.'

'But what are we doing with him?'

'We're going to burn him. A Viking burial but on land.' As Podevin turned to gape at him, Mark grew impatient. 'We haven't time to bury him and this way at least the poison will be burnt out of the air! You and Krok will have to return when it is safe to bury the bones.'

What Podevin was gawping at was the idea of Mark using a pagan ceremony! Oh, he had heard enough of Mark's tales of his native Northumbria and its history, and Odin and all that. However, there was little time to think, as they busied themselves with starting a fire and using the rushes and bracken to help it build. Lyudmila kept up a low commentary to Pribyslava as they worked, but the girl just lay on the stretcher, immobile, watchful.

Their work done, Mark and Podevin stepped over to the stretcher and, after Podevin's 'One, two, three,' lifted it.

Podevin heard Mark say, 'There's really nothing to her!' as they ducked through the door and left the shack to burn.

The forest canopy would disperse the smoke—if anyone was watching—but, at ground level, there was no hope of masking the fact that people had been here. After all, only people would burn a hut to the ground.

However, they could disguise their own tracks. After they had gone a hundred yards, Lyudmila went back with a branch, while Mark and Podevin waited. They did not put the stretcher down.

'Can I see?'

'Pardon?'

'I want to see!' Pribyslava was struggling to look back at the broken hut. Never much of a home, but it was her father's body in there.

Mark glanced at Podevin, and they manoeuvred the stretcher so that the girl could see the shack, now well alight. She stared, silent, but the tears ran down her face and dripped, unheeded, onto the deerskin.

Walking backwards, Lyudmila returned. She opened her mouth to object at Pribyslava watching the blaze, but merely flung the dusty, muddy branch away as far as she could into the bushes and, without obscuring the little girl's view, approached the stretcher.

'Loved him, did you?'

A nod. Then a quiet, 'Can we go?'

Mark and Podevin trudged along, Mark leading the way unerringly back to where Krok and Maria were waiting.

Podevin attracted Lyudmila's attention. 'She's coming in with us, I take it.' He nodded at the girl on the stretcher.

'Are you making the decisions now?' was the reply. 'Does Krok get a say?'

'Of course Krok gets a say! But can't we guess what he'll say about this?'

'I'm teasing, Podevin. No, we can't leave her on her own, especially not while she needs care.'

Lyudmila drew ahead and picked up the girl's hand. She started talking with the lass. Podevin could not help but overhear the conversation. Priby—that was what her father called her—was tired. She had slept very little since her mother and Sven had left them to go to Saxony with all the remaining food.

'She closed the door so the wolves wouldn't get in.'

One glance at Lyudmila's tightly closed mouth told Podevin all he needed to know about her reaction to the girl's words. He had a sudden vision of what they might have found and was thankful the wolves hadn't hunted in that part of the forest last night. He concentrated on the conversation. The mother had been determined that Sven should not become a spear carrier in Tugumir's war band. Sven was a 'peace-loving boy' who 'needed a chance in life.' Lyudmila had heard all about the home-made spear and the threats that greeted him and Krok on their first visit. The boy was untrained but, for all Podevin knew, maybe he had a trade he could ply in Saxony, if he could learn the language.

Podevin's attention reverted to the stretcher. Even if she had been convinced her daughter was dying, Podevin could not imagine Lyudmila walking out on Maria while she was still breathing—but it appeared Sven was also delicate and could not be exposed to infection. Priby, perhaps because she had not known anything else, accepted what her mother had said. However, she did not let go of Lyudmila's hand.

Back home, they laid Priby down while Maria fussed around her new sister. Mark drew Lyudmila aside but close enough so Podevin could hear.

'Look after her. I'll be back as soon as, and as often as, I can. If she can keep it down, broth with lots of meat in it. And if any of those maggots pupate, get them out of the wound and kill them—we don't want the next generation living off your winter supplies!'

Then Mark removed the cover from the wound, and Podevin saw the festering, pulsating mess. Maria came over, fascinated. Priby lay still. Perhaps it was fantasy, or maybe he was getting used to it, but the smell did seem a bit less disgusting as the maggots moved in the wound. Pretending nonchalance, Podevin moved aside to let Maria approach closer. Mark was peering at the wound but making no move to interfere.

'What are you doing?' Maria asked.

'Cleaning the wound with bluebottle fly maggots. You see,' Mark went into full teacher mode, 'they only eat the rotten flesh. Once we only have clean flesh, we can get them out and let it heal properly. So Priby can get better. Do you want to help?'

Enthusiastic nods as Maria asked more questions. Podevin moved away and began a conversation with Krok about the traps and snares they had set. There was yet another mouth to feed and, though Mark had turned up very early that morning with more bread, venison and beer, they had to wait for the crops to grow and last winter's stores were not going to keep forever. Podevin was part of this now. With Krok failing, it was going to be up to him to make sure there was enough food for all of them.

'We could see if we could get another boar,' Krok mused but, apart from a brief smile as he shook his head, Podevin refused to rise to the bait. Besides, the joke was getting old.

'You could always teach him how to fish.' Lyudmila had joined them, leaving the cooking pot to simmer by itself for a few moments.

'Trees don't grow on water,' Krok replied.

'Yes, but now we know he can pass unrecognised, don't we? Besides, it won't do him any harm to do a bit of paddling,' Lyudmila said. 'And if Mark's going to be a regular visitor, we'd better have fish ready for him on church fast days.'

Podevin's mind flicked back to Prague Castle, in the days when he could watch as the kitchen staff dashed out to the Vltava to check the fish weirs, bringing back the wicker baskets full of bream and perch and trout. Back then, he had never thought he would be undertaking the activity himself. But now, a mental shrug; it was a case of whatever it took to keep body and soul together. Not that he was sure he would ever regard fish as a favourite meal—it was just so fiddly getting all those small bones separated from the flesh and, by the time you'd done that, the meal was cold.

'Right, let's have a look at you, Krok.' Mark had come over from the stretcher.

Podevin glanced across at where the two girls were giggling together, Maria now kneeling by Priby's head so they could hold eye contact. He even thought he heard talk of a hair-washing session. Krok heaved himself to his feet and began to wander away, like he usually did when Mark wanted a word with him. Podevin had always assumed, especially after the first few times when he'd been not-so-politely told by Mark to stay where he was, that they went off to discuss him, what he needed to learn next. He stood aside to let the two men go.

'No,' Lyudmila said. 'I don't know about you two, and I don't really care, but I'm done with secrets.'

The three men looked at her. She had left the girls by the beds and was sitting at the table.

'Podevin already knows some of what Tugumir did to both of us. Isn't it about time he knew the rest?'

There was a pause. Mark looked at Krok. 'It's your decision.'

Krok lowered himself onto his seat next to Lyudmila. He looked at his wife, who, with tears in her eyes, took his hand.

'I'm sorry, my love,' she said. 'When it was just the three of us, and when Maria was small, and you were better than you are now, it was easier. And we didn't have to pretend, not really. Not to each other, anyway.' She fell silent. She had now captured both his hands and was wetting them with silent tear drops.

Lyudmila finally spoke again. 'My betrothed tried to stop Tugumir…'

'But Krok…' Podevin began.

'Krok's my cousin. They did enough to him. Gelded him like the horses he was supposed to be learning how to train for the plough.'

'But you married him anyway?' This was Mark.

'He'd looked after me. Got me away from there. Couldn't stop me being pregnant. And he's looked after Maria as if she was his own.' She stopped and looked at the two girls, wrapped in their chatter. Then she looked straight at Podevin. 'So now you know why Maria's the only one.'

Podevin flushed.

'You know, Lyudmila, I don't think he's even thought about it,' Mark said.

Lyudmila turned to look at him. Podevin blushed again. Lyudmila paused, glanced at Krok. Krok shrugged, but Podevin could see the smile on his tired face. Then Lyudmila laughed. And laughed. Podevin just stared at her. It wasn't fair!

'Oh, dear!' Lyudmila said. 'Your face!'

Mark was grinning too. Then he leaned over. 'Perhaps I underestimated you. Maybe your love for Emma is purer than I thought. My apologies.'

Podevin shrugged and grinned back at Mark, and at Lyudmila, who was still giggling. Podevin could not help but giggle too.

Lyudmila left Krok, came over to Podevin and hugged him. 'Oh, dear. And I was so worried you'd think we were abnormal or something.'

'Or something. Definitely "or something",' said Podevin.

Krok coughed. Lyudmila went back to him and the couple embraced. Podevin looked away and would have gone outside if Mark had not laid his hand on Podevin's arm and shaken his head. Mark folded his arms inside his sleeves and waited for Krok to speak.

'I don't want Maria to know I'm not her father. She can know the proper story of how we came here; but she's been the only chance I've had to be a dad, and I'd like her to think I did my best.'

Then, gently, he pushed Lyudmila away, turned and, with an effort, he pulled his tunic over his head. The scars Podevin had seen all those years ago, when he had come bearing gifts, when Maria was but a day old, were still there, but what was it that he just had not noticed then? There were also the dents in Krok's back where it looked like the flesh had been torn away. There was the obvious fact that one shoulder was lower than the other, and there was the wincing as Mark touched him. Podevin began cursing himself. So obsessed with his own worries, he had accepted the cursory explanation of Krok's wounds without a second thought.

'And your legs?' murmured Mark.

'What d'you think? I need the staff more than ever.'

'I have some valerian root to help you sleep.'

'I need to be alert, in case...'

'You'll take it!' Podevin and Lyudmila spoke as one.

Both girls looked up from their chatter. A hiss of steam from over by the fire interrupted the silence.

'The pot's about to boil over,' said Mark, as the everyday imposed itself on the extraordinary conversation.

As Lyudmila scrambled to rescue the meal, Krok reached for his tunic, but Podevin was quicker.

'You helped me. Now it's my turn.' Krok allowed him to assist.

'He's dying, Podevin.' Mark said the obvious. 'By degrees. I'll do what I can to ease the pain, but you'll have to take over here.' Mark moved Podevin out of Krok's hearing. 'His beating damaged his insides too—beyond my skill, I fear—and his broken bones haven't set properly. He's done well to get this far.'

Podevin looked back at his teacher but, if Krok had not heard, he had guessed Mark's words.

'Will I see next winter out?' Krok asked.

It was not a worried voice, he just wanted to know, but Mark could only shrug. If he avoided the winter diseases, looked after himself, then he had a reasonable chance. Mark was concerned. If Priby became feverish, then she would be more likely to infect Krok than any of the others—did Krok want Mark to see if anyone else would look after the girl?

Krok didn't. Krok wouldn't think of it. After all, if he made it through the next winter, there was always the one after that, wasn't there?

'Mum, Priby needs to…you know!'

'Well, that's a good sign!' said Mark. 'You'll just need to cover the wound so nothing else gets in, then take her outside.'

Frantic activity as Priby was raised to her feet for the first time since she had left her father. Shakily, and leaning on Maria, with Lyudmila in attendance, they made their way outside.

Once they had gone, Mark turned to Podevin and Krok.

'Do you have a cesspit?' Their puzzled stares gave him the answer. 'Just use the forest, do you? Never mind; only towns need cesspits. And the sick. Priby will need help. Make sure what she does today is well covered up. For tomorrow, we'll need a bench.' Mark found one so he could show them. 'Cut a hole in it so she can sit and do her

.ıess. Have a hole in the ground beneath, a deep one. Make sure ʎou cover up her business. Every time. Don't spread the infection.'

'My job for the afternoon,' said Podevin, forestalling Krok.

It was one of the older, lighter benches that Podevin was directed to hack a hole into.

'And mind how you go about it; I've no mind to be pulling splinters out of anyone's backside!' Lyudmila turned back to feeding Priby, little and often was Mark's instruction.

He had left but would return in two days to check if any fever was starting. Podevin dealt with the bench. Soon enough, when Krok was fit enough to teach him, he'd learn how to fish. Krok, staff in hand, was out tending his snares, his daughter with him for the afternoon. They'd promised to be back so Maria could help with Priby's hair.

Chapter 33
Prague Castle

Emma flung down her embroidery. If they really hoped she was pregnant again, after last night, let them hope! Besides, it took a lot longer than a few hours in bed for morning sickness to kick in, so why should she be forced to sit inside doing work she was no good at, especially when she was surrounded by people who could do it a lot better? Hilde placed her own work on the table, bent down and collected Emma's piece from where it had landed between them. She sighed and began unpicking Emma's work.

Brother Mark was not here. For all his wisdom, his usefulness to everyone (was it a week ago she had heard all about Priby?), his spiritual direction, he had no idea how a woman's body works. Did he really also think morning sickness started straightaway? And the king, with all his experience of getting women with child, ought to know better. Besides, the morning sickness had passed last time. Yes, it had been a horrible few weeks, but it had been worse having to endure her ladies' clucking. The 'there, there's. The 'how are "we" feeling today?' The fact that, no, they 'couldn't possibly' leave her alone; a princess should not be holding her own sick bowl, should she?

'You do know, madam, these are the duke's orders. You must rest.'

'So, whose ladies-in-waiting are you? Mine or his?'

Silence. Fearful glances between the Bohemians. Hilde and Beatrice had been able to hold her gaze. Her brain told her Ursula had been there as well at the start of her first pregnancy, but her mind refused to visualise her presence. However, she had always known, whatever they said, that the Bohemian ladies were dependent on Boleslav's permission to serve her, and he still changed them as often as the wind changed direction, so she had barely time to register their existence before they were replaced. The Bohemian way of naming people after their heroes did not help. She could have sworn there had been two Lyudmilas and three Libuses but, no matter how much she might have only wanted Hilde and Beatrice with her, they could not be present all the time with no sleep or food, so sometimes she had to be left with their Bohemian stand-ins, the ones who owed their places at court to the king, not his daughter-in-law.

That first pregnancy, that first dose of morning sickness, she had cried, she had screamed with frustration, but mostly, she had been sick. Until the vomiting stopped. There had been the upset of Wenceslas's assassination, and the events of the removal to Prague, but her child had been born and removed to suck on a wet nurse's nipple. He would be brought to court at the new king's pleasure, and Emma was reminded of her duty. Which was to produce heirs—plural. So, she had better get on with it. It had been months since she gave birth, and there was no new pregnancy. Her father-in-law was commenting on the fact every time he saw her. It was all she could do not to hit him. As it was, she risked a huge row by reminding him (not that he needed telling, with the number of bastards he was siring) it took two to make a baby. So, last night, there had been a visit. A right royal visit, but it was a brief visit. This morning, her brow was not fevered, so did not require wiping with a cold, damp cloth. Whether she sat here, or rode fifty miles, or hiked up a mountain, the child inside her, if there was a child inside her, was staying or not as God willed. Just because the king was worried, it did not mean everyone else had to be, and she very much doubted the king was as worried as he made out.

She closed her eyes as she thought back to last night. Evening. There had been yet another discussion between father and son. The father wanting to know where his next grandson was, and the son objecting, as he always had, to the wife that Wenceslas had chosen for him. Wenceslas was dead. His father interrupted with violence and threats. The son had a month to get his wife with child or the king would find another way to secure the throne for the next generations.

Emma was too valuable to kill; no point in annoying England as well as Saxony. Her husband wasn't so important. The king had tired of his wife (again) and was between favourites. The dreaded option hung in the air: would Boleslav really try to impregnate his own daughter-in-law?

It was only because the thought of having to endure the amorous attentions of the king was more repulsive than his son's ignorance and terror, that she had made herself as agreeable as she could.

He walked in, pale legs visible under his nightgown. She loosened her hair and let it hang over her shoulders and down her back. She had chosen the flimsiest gown she possessed. She had made sure there was rouge on her cheeks and lips and sat waiting.

'Husband.' She'd risked looking up at him. He had not held her gaze, glancing rather over at the pomaded youths who had accompanied him and raising his eyebrows. They dutifully tittered into scented handkerchiefs.

'Your, er, ladies, can leave us.'

'And your, er, gentlemen?'

They could, of course, have merely retired behind the covers of the four-poster bed, but she was beggared if his friends were to watch while her women were sent packing. Besides, it was all too easy to mock him.

Nobody moved. Emma did not lower her gaze. The younger Boleslav failed to demand she should.

'All right!' he said, breaking the tension. 'Everyone out!'

The youths made an ostentatious display of courtesy in guiding the women out of Emma's quarters, bowing to one, suggesting a walk along the starlit battlements to another. At least Hilde and Beatrice wouldn't go far. They would be just in the hall, pacing.

The door was pulled to. Emma went over to it, passing close by her husband, who made no move to caress, or even touch, her body. She checked the door was closed. She turned, leaned against it, pushing her breasts against the fabric of her gown. Nothing. He was less than two metres away, and nothing.

'Shall I disrobe, my lord?' She even moved her hand to the clasp by her neck.

'What? No. There's no need. Just go to bed.'

'Very well.' She crossed the floor and clambered onto the bed.

The covers had been turned down by her assiduous ladies, hoping rather than assuming there would be a fun night ahead. Her husband followed and lay down beside her.

More silence.

'Well? Husband, will you not…' She could not finish the sentence.

What was she going to have to do? But then he moved. Saying nothing, he tugged her gown upwards, exposing her to her waist. His own gown was similarly pulled up. He rolled on top of her. His elbow landed on her ribs, forcing the air from her lungs. She bit her lip, saying nothing. He was fumbling between her legs with his fingers. She closed her eyes, opened her legs as best she could, trying to get her right leg under his body so he could then at least enter her. At last, he took his hand away and was pumping back and forth. She risked opening her eyes to find he was looking to the side, muttering something: Jack? Jacks? Then, with an 'at last,' it was over.

He rolled off her, off the bed and stood. She had felt no pleasure; it had all been over before it had begun.

'You can get up. I'm about to call them back. They're holding my cloak for me.'

The fury sat just under her ribcage, jostling for first position in her thoughts with the memory of that elbow on her ribs, but she obeyed. She let the gown fall into place and walked over to the window—not that there was anything to see outside. If the light behind her meant a guard had a thrill from seeing a princess in her nightgown, then she was happy to give him that thrill. Someone should get some pleasure out of this night. Her husband's companions reappeared, as did Hilde and Beatrice. The ladies took one look and stood aside, knowing better than to approach.

'Well, I hope we hear happy news soon, my dear.'

Before she could turn round, he was gone. Perhaps that was for the best; she had run out of pleasing words. For the second time that evening, Emma closed her eyes. Hilde and Beatrice were guiding her back to the bed. She understood. For all it was probably too late, given that she had already stood, Emma lay on her back, the bolster under her hips, anything to encourage his seed to get to her womb and plant itself there.

'Just give it time, madam.' Beatrice was trying to be comforting, but there were no words that could do that.

The following morning, at breakfast, her husband had gone back to ignoring her, and the king, already full of knowledge about last night's successful visit, was doing his best to confine her to her quarters. With her embroidery. Emma glanced at Hilde, still unpicking her mistress's work.

'Where's Brother Mark?' Emma said.

'In the chancellery, madam. With the king.' It was one of the new ladies-in-waiting, a Bohemian, who replied.

Emma pursed her lips and walked over to the window. *See Boleslav! See Mark! I'm walking, not waddling like some demented duck!* But the words remained unspoken as she gazed at a clear sky, at a forest covered with every shade of green. The forest, which sat at the bottom of the hill, less than a mile away from the castle walls. The forest that was full of game—and Podevin.

At that moment, she no longer cared what Brother Mark said about duty and calling. She knew she was fed up of Mark being able to visit Podevin, and coming back to tell her how well he was doing—he had even let slip about how Podevin had 'filled out' recently with all the physical activity he was doing in the forest. Her own rare visits to the forest had been stopped 'for her own safety'. Podevin was expanding his skills. Someday soon, he'd be at the brook, the one that flowed through the forest, learning how to make a fish weir.

Emma made her decision. 'I'm going hunting. Get Geraint.'

'Madam!' The same Bohemian girl lowered her eyes and blushed as Emma gazed at her. The girl rose.

'No,' said Emma. 'Hilde, you go.'

At least Hilde wouldn't divert via the chancellery to inform the king.

'Beatrice! My hunting clothes! Now!'

Chapter 34
By the Side of the Stream

As she had been told, Mark was not in his dispensary, but Emma knew enough to tell Hilde what to collect. She told herself, if it was God's will, she and Podevin would meet. If not, they would not, no matter how long she searched for him. Thankfully, Podevin had been making so much noise, her appearance at just the right spot was an easy task. She knew no-one would approve of this. But who, other than her horse, was going to be a witness to her meeting up with a friend she had not seen properly for months? Those frantic, now terminated, conversations at the forest's edge didn't count. She bent and touched the ground. It was warm; the trees were still bright green despite the year turning towards autumn. They would be screened from anyone peeking from across the river—though, in a few more weeks, the colour of the leaves would change again, signalling the descent towards another winter of life indoors while she bred the next generation of Bohemian princes. A life of cold draughts and even colder looks from those who preferred her to have never existed.

She tugged at her belt, letting it fall to the ground, telling herself it would only get in the way when she hugged Podevin. She had a brief half-second to wonder what he would make of her dressed like this, in a male hunter's costume, trousers and a baggy top. Her cap had come off in their mad gallop down the slope from the castle. Yes, that was deliberate, too. Only Geraint would have let her get away with it.

'I need some time alone,' she had told him, when he caught up with her.

He studied her face. Like Hilde and Beatrice, he knew much of what she had to put up with, but he still paused, looking at her. She was about to tell him she was not going to be crossed on this—being sociable, making polite chit-chat, even in her own language, was not on her current agenda.

'Two parties, madam. Both thinking you are with the other. And both keen to beat the other in bringing more game back to the castle kitchens. But you'd better stay with me until we are out of sight of the castle.'

He had given her what she wanted, though she could lay claim to no more than an hour of solitude, if that. They rode together until the castle was well hidden by trees and brushwood and she could forget its existence.

They had flushed out a hind. Geraint had gone charging off with his men. She had let them go and made for the river. Mark had not told her where Krok would bring Podevin for his fishing lessons. So, it was mere chance that led her to hear Podevin and find the right spot. She had retreated that first time she saw them, but only to find a place to tie her horse where it could feed. She crept back to her viewing spot. She stood there, gazing, noticing his muscles, the way he moved, wondering if he had ever held anyone in those strong arms. She even admired the way he concentrated so hard on his task, forgiving him for not noticing her, even as Krok noticed and started to make his frantic gestures—as if she would allow Podevin to escape now!

❧

The fishing expedition went well—even if it was chilly stripping off and getting into the water. Someone should have told the river gods it was still summer. Podevin reckoned Krok enjoyed seeing him having to do all the work, banging the stakes into the soft mud whilst waist-deep in rushing water. Podevin hadn't thought how much the brook's flow would pull at him as he stepped into deeper water. He felt the mud and gravel squish through his toes as he carried yet another stake into the stream. Krok sat on the bank, guarding the wattle screens and the rest of the wooden stakes.

'How many more of these? This water's freezing!'

'We're nearly ready for the baskets. Just make sure everything's tied together nicely. Have you used the knots I showed you?'

'Yes,' Podevin said, keeping his teeth clenched so they wouldn't chatter. Krok had better hand over that sacking as soon as he emerged from the water. The knots were fine. The basket was just there, beside Krok.

'Just throw it! I'm not coming out only to go back in!'

The basket, with its twines already attached, splashed down just within reach. Podevin found himself at full stretch getting the basket in place. For the lower twine, he had to duck under the water. At least his clothes were dry, waiting for him on the bank. It was done. Fish for Friday, unless they had all scarpered from this stretch of river.

He stood up and shook the water out of his ears. Or tried to. He could not hear much. No birdsong. He could see Krok gesturing at him. A final headshake and the water escaped, running down his cheek and into his beard.

'What?'

'Just get some clothes on.'

'Not till I'm dry.'

'Or you could come to this side of the river.' A female voice.

Podevin froze, and not because of the water temperature. 'I fear, madam, you have me at a disadvantage.'

There she was. On the opposite bank. And he didn't dare face her.

'You've filled out since I saw you last.'

Podevin just stood there, his hands clasped between his legs, making no move. 'I had clothes on then,' he squeaked, managing to turn his head to look in her direction.

'But they didn't suit you. Besides, I've brought some herbs from Mark. Someone's going to have to get them.' He still hesitated. 'All right,' she said. 'I'll leave my cloak here and turn my back. Then will you come and talk to me?'

It was put as a request. Krok groaned. There was nothing either of them could do but let Podevin obey. He reached the opposite side, used the reeds and a convenient branch to pull himself out of the water and disappeared from Krok's sight.

❧

Covered by her cloak, he was there. She turned to face him. There was a sound in her throat, a gasp, a sigh, she opened her arms, and he was holding her. She buried her face in his naked shoulder and let the tears flow. Thank God he said nothing and let her sob.

'I'm sorry,' she said at last, loosening her grip. Unbidden, her hands crept under the cloak, which, all by itself, slipped to the ground.

'What for?' he asked.

His hand reached her side and pulled her close, the side where, only last night, Mladenic had dug in his elbow. She winced. He removed his hand in an instant.

'You're hurt.' A statement, no point in denial.

She reached for his hand, pulled up her shirt, placed it on her bruise. She left his hand there, where it was warm, moving up and down over the bruise like a wave lapping a shore. She looked into his eyes as his hand began exploring further, their gaze only breaking as she pulled the shirt over her head. She flung it aside, standing straight as she showed her upper body to him; both of his hands exploring her breasts, her back, her sides, but somehow never aggravating that bruise. She heard nothing but their breathing, hers getting deeper and sharper as her body responded to the smooth, gentle touch of his work-roughened hands.

Then he broke contact. Her eyes opened wide in surprise, but he reached down for her cloak. He spread it out on the ground, turned back to her and, kneeling before her, her hand on his strong shoulder for precarious balance, he tugged her boots from her feet. They sat on the cloak and she could not say how, but, gentle, insistent, he pulled her down until they were lying next to each other, his right hand roaming her upper body, fascinated by her breasts, as his left arm was under her, supporting her. Unasked, she lifted her hips, pushing the riding trousers down below her knees; his hand followed, covering her thigh, going round her knee and returning up the inside of her leg. He started to rub, gently, over her belly, she pushed his hand lower, guiding his fingers to find the spot.

'Just there.'

There was no time to think of anything else, no time to worry about being caught, no time to consider last night. There was just now. There was just him. There was pleasure seeping out from her core; her hips were moving on their own. She shoved her arm, her leg under his body, demanding him on top. For a clumsy few seconds, they battled as they readied themselves, then he was inside her, and he was the one whose breath was rasping as, eyes open in wonder, he gazed at her as he moved between her legs.

'Ah! Yes!'

Was that her voice? Her hands reaching down to his buttocks, digging her nails into his flesh as she pulled him into her? Could she, even as she shuddered, feel him thrusting inside her as he grinned his agreement? Did she wrap her arms around him, pulling him down on top of her, so she could feel his weight on her as he lay gasping out his love?

It could not have been more than a few seconds, but it felt an age as they lay there, exhausted and exhilarated by what they had done. Podevin rolled away and glanced at her breasts as her chest heaved. But as he reached out a hand, they both heard it.

'Madam? Are you here?'

'I thought you were alone!' Podevin scrambled to his feet as Emma grabbed her trousers and tugged them up over her waist.

'I was! Don't just stand there,' she hissed.

She could hear the approach. Not Geraint's voice; it must be the other party. She grabbed at the shirt, but he held it away.

'I can help!'

At least Podevin remembered what to do; he had dressed Wenceslas often enough. Her leggings were yanked up to her waist. Then her boots; she had to sit as he pulled them over her feet. Then he turned for her shirt. This time, she grabbed it and pulled it over her own head, terrified she would lose control again if he came too close. The hunting party must be getting near. Podevin lifted her cloak, shook it and tossed it to her. She caught it.

A sudden memory. 'The herbs!'

Podevin grabbed at the bundle, discarded in their passion. Her horse decided to neigh, giving away their position completely.

'Now, go!'

Instead, in two strides, he was holding her unresisting body. His kiss bruised her lips, his tongue explored her mouth, her hands on his shoulders were powerless to push him away until he decided to release her. Then, having spoken no words, he disappeared. She heard splashing.

'I'm here,' she called. The words came out as a croak through swollen lips. Fixing her cloak, noting it was still grubby, she knew her lie. 'I fell off my horse.'

At this, her guard appeared, all concerned for her welfare. The bruise on her side became useful. She insisted on remounting her steed.

'If you don't get back on straight away, you'll never overcome your fear.'

She asked them what they had caught, chattering away, only realising later, she never chattered. None of the guard would ever say anything. None of them saw Podevin or heard him get to the other side of the river. She thought any smell of her on him would be washed away by the water and was sad.

∾

Of course, Mark guessed. No, not a guess. He took one look at her and he knew. He forced her to confession. However, even after he had given her a penance, he was furious. But she matched him with defiance, despite having so recently been on her knees. She sat beside Mark, telling him in scrupulous detail about the previous night, reminding him that, back in England, she could have divorced Mladenic—she still could not face calling him Boleslav. As far as she was concerned, he still was a youngster, a child, a boy—for his lack of interest or ability to please her.

'You're not in England! You are a princess of Bohemia. You are to provide the royal family of Bohemia with heirs!'

'Without the participation of my husband? How does that work? Another immaculate conception, like Jesus?'

'Don't take the Lord's name in vain.'

'Don't be so bloody sanctimonious! You know Boleslav's heir is more interested in his pretty male companions than he's ever likely to be in me.'

'I know no such thing. Besides, I don't think it's true.'

'What?' Emma was shocked out of her rant more by Mark's tone than his words.

'Has he ever had a chance to learn how to behave normally around women?' Mark stopped as Emma jumped to her feet.

'Here we go again! "Think about it from his point of view." Well, I'm sick of having to think about it from his point of view! Why can't other people think about things from my point of view for once—especially him! But no. It's got to be all about him, hasn't it? All about pandering to him and his little ways. Putting up with his little companions, his snide comments, his oft-stated wish I wasn't around. Who cares about me? About what I want, what I need?'

'Enough!' Mark was standing too. 'If you can't see you're surrounded by friends—'

'Friends like you? Telling me off every time I put a toe over some imaginary line! In this place, I am surrounded by enemies, Mark, not friends. The king, his son, his court—would any of them lift a finger if I was in any sort of danger?' She paused, but not for long. 'Well? The answer's no, Mark. For once, just once, I took some comfort where I could find it. Comfort you, Brother, would know nothing about.'

The chapel was small but not so small she could not pace up and down in the silence while Mark resumed his seat. Emma's footsteps echoed. She stopped by the door but didn't leave.

'I know a lot more than you think, madam. All I would advise, my lady, is a certain change—in attitude, if nothing else—if you value your life. And I will say this about your husband, whether you want to listen or not.' Emma stayed by the door, but she did turn her head to look at him. 'The king's son has had to grow up knowing it's only the fact of his birth that secures his position. Does he want the crown? I'm guessing here, but I think his answer would be no. What happens if he says so? He will be killed. And so, in all probability, would you. Not even the Pope in Rome would sanction you being married off to the father after you'd been wed to the son. Yes, I have seen him looking at you as no father-in-law should. So, you deal with the husband you have, or would you prefer to be kept waiting while the king carries on his wicked way, produces a son, who'd be twenty years your junior, not four, for you to wed.'

'All right!' Emma returned to her seat next to her confessor. 'I'll think about it. But Boleslav, if you recall, was blaming *me* for not being pregnant.'

'Looking elsewhere than your husband to solve that problem isn't going to help you keep your head on your shoulders. And I don't see the English king doing anything to help you if there is a whiff of scandal about you.'

'But there can be a whole heap of scandal about the king of Bohemia and no-one is bothered?'

Mark sighed. 'I didn't say it was fair. I am merely trying to point out how precarious your position is. Especially now.'

Emma looked at him. 'Why especially now?'

Mark stood, reached inside his sleeve, and extracted a piece of parchment. He held it out to her. Looking in puzzlement at his solemn face, she took it, looked at the contents. Looked again, read it closely.

'Why? How?'

'Blanik,' Mark said. Then, noting her puzzled face, 'Prague's castle constable under Wenceslas.'

'I thought he was dead!'

Mark shook his head. 'Escaped. To Saxony. Works for Otto. But sent this to me with the Saxon courier.'

'Otto wouldn't want to tell us this! Chaos here would be exactly what he wants.'

'Otto is new to the Saxon throne. He has enough trouble keeping his own nobles in check to risk being compelled to invade here.'

'But Boleslav's doing his best to wage war with him!'

'Aye, but he can't now, can he? Not when he's dealing with the Magyars raiding his lands in the east.'

'Why didn't I hear of this? From you, if no-one else.'

'I think, over the last day or so, we were all taken up with domestic issues.'

'Well, even if there is a child in my belly, I'm not sick yet. And someone else is raising the child I've already had. What are we going to do?' She waved the parchment. 'This is rumour—we need proof.'

The prospect of real danger, real enemies, refocused her mind.

'It's centred around Budec.'

'Podevin's family place—so I'll send him.'

'With respect, madam, you won't.'

'But who else is there? What would you have me do, send Geraint?'

'Not what I said, was it? You, I said, would not be doing the sending.' Mark waited in silence for her to catch up with his meaning.

Emma understood at last. 'I'm really not to see him—ever?'

'Forever is a long time, but I don't think you should go to the forest for a while.' Mark led the way to the chapel door. 'And now I had better plan to see a certain family in the forest. Tomorrow is too soon—we're being watched. But soon, it'll have to be soon.'

'Be gentle with him. For my sake.'

'As much as I can be, my princess. But he, just like you, has to understand there can be no repeat.'

'And this?' She gestured with the parchment.

'It'll mean risking his life.' Mark's words made Emma pause.

A moment ago, it was agony to think she wouldn't see him again. Now she had to contemplate sending him to his death.

'Then say I ask him, I do not command.' She handed the parchment back to him, for the first time wishing the day's events in the forest undone.

Chapter 35
A Job for Podevin

They were not expecting him, after the delivery of the supplies from Emma. But, two days later, Mark arrived to check on Priby. He congratulated Lyudmila on her progress, who referred him to Maria for looking after the wound so well. He heard out Priby's complaints about having to eat lying on her tummy but pointed out it really was the best way to get better. The smell had disappeared. The fact that Priby had strength to complain was a good sign, according to Mark. She was in the warm. She was being fed. She was being kept clean, and she was, though Mark insisted this was not definite, getting better. There was always the danger of fever but, in his experience, if it had not arrived by now…

Mark examined Krok and could not be so optimistic. Krok could limp on for many years yet, but he was never going to be better than he was and, unless he kept someone by him to do all the heavy work, then the years Krok had left were likely to be fewer than otherwise. Krok nodded.

'No more tree felling.' He smiled. It was another job for his apprentice to learn.

Then Mark turned to Podevin. 'Outside.'

Podevin raised his eyes to heaven, but he followed the monk until they were out of earshot from the rest.

'And what did you think you were doing?'

'Fishing. Under Krok's instructions,' replied Podevin.

'You know what I mean.'

'Yes.' There was silence.

'You two are playing a dangerous game. You know that.'

'But she was bringing stuff from you, so you must have known.'

Podevin was cut off from speaking as Mark swung round to face him. 'Yes! I found out too late she was going hunting. If I'd been asked, if I'd been there when her lady-in-waiting came to my dispensary, I'd have said not to. For what I'd hope were obvious reasons. You two are as bad as each other. Do you both want to be killed? If there is one whiff of scandal—a mere rumour would do it. She's not coming here again.'

'She hasn't been here.'

'Don't try to be clever, Podevin. You know what I mean. She's not coming to the forest, and she's not seeing you again. She has to stay alive. And so do you. Besides,' his tone changed, 'we need you.'

'There's a job for me?' Podevin's voice rose to a childish squeak.

'Yes, there is.' Mark paused. The silence lengthened.

'Well? Tell me then!'

'It's to do with Tugumir.'

'She wants me to kill him!'

'No!' The word exploded from Mark like an arrow from an over-strung bow. 'But we do need information.' Another pause. 'You see, Podevin, we've known for ages that Boleslav feels guilty about killing his brother. So, he's taking it out on those who helped him. They're not being rewarded, as they think they should have been. Far from it. So it looks like they're plotting. You know Tugumir was sent after Queen Drahomira?'

Podevin nodded.

'She isn't dead.'

'I know. You told me. Like you told me he's banished from court. But my half-brother holds her lands and you're saying he's still plotting, as if that's not enough reward for killing Wenceslas?' Podevin stopped, amazed at Tugumir's greed, or was it stupidity? 'So,' he said, 'where's Drahomira?'

'As you know, she isn't in Bohemia.'

'But she is in Saxony?' A question, but somehow Podevin was certain.

'More than possible. And we think it's more than possible that Tugumir is in touch with her to get revenge on Boleslav.'

'I want revenge on Tugumir, so send me after him.'

'That isn't how it works! If I thought you still wanted to kill him, I wouldn't have agreed to sending you. Here!' Mark held out the message he'd shown Emma. He let Podevin read it and grasp the implications, before continuing. 'This is only part of it. We need to expose this plot, make a deal with Saxony and fight off the Magyars.'

'Hang on,' said Podevin as a thought struck, 'Drahomira was no friend of Wenceslas—she wanted Boleslav on the throne—why would she want him off it now?'

'It's amazing what being pursued for your life can make you feel about the pursuers,' was the reply.

Podevin thought it through. 'But who would she put on the throne instead?'

'We think it might be Tugumir himself—as her consort or as her daughter's consort.' Mark paused. 'You knew there's a sister? A widow young enough to bear children?' Mark didn't need to spell it out any further.

'If you think I'm going to live under Tugumir as Duke of Bohemia! Or king. And if he kills Emma…'

'All right! All right!' Mark held up his hands. 'We guessed you'd feel this way, but you have to keep calm—all thoughts of revenge must be banished. Do I have your word on that? If you can't give it, we'll find someone else.'

'Vengeance is mine…'

'I will repay, says the *Lord*.' Mark finished the biblical quotation for him.

Podevin paused. 'All right! But if he comes after me…'

'But we think we can you get into Tugumir's castle, find out what we need to know and get out again without killing him.'

'Yes. If that's what I have to do. But you haven't said exactly what you want me to find out. Or why it has to be me.'

'It's you because Emma trusts you—this information is for her, not Boleslav. Or Mladenic for that matter.'

'He'd only blab it to his father anyway.'

'He's simply concerned for his own safety,' said Mark.

'Why so concerned with everyone else, all of a sudden? You haven't forgotten they killed Wenceslas?'

'No, I've not forgotten, but I have to try to understand. Frankly, the young Boleslav would have made a better priest than prince. And Emma isn't the best wife for him.'

'So, it's Emma's fault, is it?'

'I did not say that. Emma is who she is. And Mladenic is who he is. They just need to learn how to get along together. And they will,' Mark said, but the sadness in his voice made Podevin wonder if Mark expected them to get along or just hoped for it. Either way, he had more to say. 'But all this is beside the point. You need to be sure you can complete the task.'

'You still haven't told me what it is. Get into the castle, not kill Tugumir, and get out of the castle—there, done it in an instant.'

'Then give me the documents proving Tugumir's plotting with Drahomira. Tell me who he's going to marry. And tell me if there's anything else I need to know so we can convince Boleslav.'

'Ah.'

'It has to be you. Like Wenceslas, you speak and read German. We think the document might be written in German, as it comes from Saxony. If he's been in communication with England, we might even need your Anglo-Saxon to check how far Emma's life is in danger. Apart from that, you can fight like a warrior. And, I hope, move across the ground like a scout. And you're loyal to Emma.'

'My Anglo-Saxon is rather rusty.' So was his German, if he was honest, but he had more practice in that language.

Mark continued as if Podevin had not spoken. 'If she can show a conspiracy, then Boleslav can deal with it. If it's just talk, then she will at least know it's just talk.'

'So, it's all right for Boleslav to kill Tugumir, but not me?'

'You kill Tugumir, and you'll have everyone after you. If Boleslav does it…'

'He'll just have another death on his conscience.' Podevin finished the thought. 'When do I start?'

'Tomorrow.'

'So, why didn't she mention any of this when she saw me?'

'I understood you were concentrating on other things! Besides, she didn't know,' Mark said. 'Come on, we'd better get back to the others and explain something of why we want you to go.'

'We could just say I've outstayed my welcome.'

'No, we can't. You'll have to come back here afterwards. Just because you weren't recognised in Prague the other day doesn't mean there is no-one around who can tell who you are—or were. No, you'll have to return here. At least until you can give your report. I'll be going back and forth when I can until Priby's better. I don't suppose it'll take that long.'

'What will? Priby's return to health. Or my trip to—where? You haven't said where I'm going? Tetin? Budec?'

'You haven't asked.'

There was a pause.

'I'm asking now,' said Podevin.

Mark looked off into the middle distance. 'Budec.'

'I see.'

'So do I. But I think I see differently.'

'You think someone will recognise me.'

'Oh, I think the chances of that are very slight. You've not lived there since you were seven. But I just wonder whether you will be able to cope with seeing your father's castle.'

Podevin looked at the monk. Mark had spoken quietly, as he often did, but something in the words troubled Podevin. He could think of no words to comfort the older man, as he had no idea how he would feel. At that moment, all he felt was excitement that Emma wanted him, Podevin, to go there and find a conspiracy. He'd do it.

They returned to the girls' chatter, to the crackle of the fire. To Lyudmila tending it, while issuing her orders so that everyone would sit at table and eat at the same time—except for Priby, who would, for a few days yet, be lying on her front. To Krok quietly sitting, checking his snares, sharpening his knife, or just trying to ease his aches and pains. The hut was no longer a leaky old hovel, but a watertight home and, for the past months, his home too. Funny, he had not realised how comfortable he found living here until he was about to leave—until the realisation that he might not come back from his trip.

There was no question in Podevin's mind about not going. Even if he had not been in love with Emma, in his mind she was still the person to whom he owed his loyalty. Despite Krok's questioning words down by the river. Oh, he had waited for Podevin and had been very sharp with him. Mark was just round two of the questioning! Whatever his feelings, Podevin had to accept he owed Emma his life, which put him in her debt. He could not refuse the task. He would not refuse.

They ate. Mark, without irony, appreciated the fish. Afterwards, the four adults talked. Podevin's disappearance just as he was getting useful was going to have to be explained, and Mark was against lying for the sake of it. So, Lyudmila and Krok were told the truth. Lyudmila wanted safety; Krok wished that great events would not keep troubling his world. They both seemed more loyal to Mark, who was only a monk, than to Princess Emma. However, when Podevin thought about it, even that made sense, as it had been Mark who had provided the practical help ever since Wenceslas and Podevin had made that first, fateful, visit.

'Couldn't Boleslav just call Tugumir back to Prague?' asked Krok.

'Yes,' replied Mark, 'he could. But someone as canny as Tugumir knows how to guard his tongue. Even when plied with drink. And he's not likely to bring anything with him, showing that he's involved with a plot to kill the person he's visiting. He'd leave all that at home.'

'Home?' said Podevin.

'It's been his home—or one of them—for a long time now,' said Mark. 'And for all Wenceslas did for you, he didn't give you Budec.'

Podevin opened his mouth to defend the implied criticism of Wenceslas, but could think of nothing to say. He realised, too late, he had just shown Mark a reason to be worried about this journey. Budec was his childhood home. The memories might be blurred with the later ones of learning with Blanik and Wenceslas, and there were some he knew had to be dreams because he saw his mother in them, but others… He shook himself. He must concentrate on the present. They were talking about when and how he should go. On foot? Should he hire a horse? Should he be a peasant until he arrived in Budec—which meant no horse, of course—or could he dress as a knight, or squire, or merchant?

All the options from higher up the social scale were rejected. Podevin would have to go on foot, as best he could. It would only take a couple of days if he moved fast. A horse, galloping up to the gates would only raise suspicion. Another option of there being two of them was addressed; there had been two of them when they went to Prague. But then, they had not known whether Podevin would be recognised. It was always easier for one person to creep into, and out of, a place than two. Talk also covered practical matters, food and drink. He could carry enough to get him there, but four days' worth of dried meat and bread? That was possible, but not four days of drink. And four days' worth assumed Podevin would find everything out instantly. Then Podevin noticed Mark had not said anything for some time.

'There's something you're not telling us.'

'Remember Mabel?'

Podevin cast his mind back to when they had first brought Emma to Prague. 'Yes. Yes, I do.'

'She's at Budec with her Stanislav. He's Blanik's cousin, remember? They'll help you.'

'We have a spy in the enemy camp already?'

'So why doesn't she sort this out?' asked Krok.

'She can't read Czech or German. Her husband can't read at all. She has no reason to be inside the castle. Unfortunately, we do need someone like this young man here.'

This young man was finding it difficult not to feel like hiding away. It was nice to be needed, but the memory of the last time he saw Budec kept flooding in. Before he could dwell on those times, the conversation turned back to practicalities.

'Live on your wits. Go hunting!' said Krok.

'I can't hunt and find out what Tugumir's up to!'

'No,' Mark sobered, 'but more missions have failed because people get hungry and thirsty than for any other reason. Set up camp outside Budec and leave a cache of food and drink behind, so you can come back to it afterwards. And, one last thing, Podevin—and this is why there's the hurry—we think Tugumir's in Tetin just now. We're as sure as we can be he's left the documents in Budec, but we might be wrong. Either way, we've got to try.'

'I could always go with him—stay in his camp,' said Lyudmila.

Podevin noticed Krok look at her sharply when she said this, and look away again. He shrugged, assuming Krok just didn't want his wife wandering off. Mark did not like the idea either.

'You're needed here. You need to look after Priby—and the rest of them. Krok as well, who, if I'm not mistaken, will be tempted to do too much while Podevin's away.'

'So, he's coming back, is he?' said Krok.

'If you'll have me.' Podevin grinned.

Krok smiled and the moment passed. Besides, Mark was talking about getting back to Prague. It was a busy evening, sorting everything for Podevin's trip but, by sundown, all were ready for bed. However, as he lay awake, Podevin could no longer dismiss the memories…

Chapter 36
Trouble with the Saxons

A.D. 921

He was seven years old again. His father had explained it all—apart from having to promise to keep out of the way 'whatever happens', Podevin felt very grown up and proud. His father was one of King Wenceslas's bodyguards. Wherever the king went, Daddy would go too. Of course, Podevin would have to stay behind with the women and all the baggage, once the fighting started, but, for now, he could stay with Daddy and listen to the grown-ups talking. Not that many of them talked. Mostly, they just followed the king and Blanik. Daddy said Blanik was a very important man. Not as important as the king, but Blanik was in charge of Prague Castle when the king wasn't there.

'So why isn't he there now?' Podevin asked.

'Because the king wants him here. We have to tell the Saxons they can't just keep taking our money.'

'And then we can go home?'

'Back to Budec? Yes, we'll go home soon.'

That was the end of that talk. The king had stood up and wanted to see how the soldiers were disposed—that meant where they were standing to fight. Podevin looked around the field; it was covered in soldiers. Daddy pointed at Duke Radslav on the right wing. Duke Radslav had lots of soldiers too. He was doing a lot of shouting. The king turned to Blanik and Daddy and raised his eyebrows.

'That's one way to exhort, I suppose.'

'He is an old-fashioned warrior, sire,' said Daddy.

The king turned back to look at his troops. He was fourteen, so was old enough to fight. Podevin could not wait to be fourteen and grown up. Wenceslas shielded his eyes with his right hand, and looked towards the trees up the hill. Podevin's father had already said that was where there would be a nasty surprise for the Saxons.

Once Podevin was removed, away from the battlefield, what he imagined, what he knew, what he had been told and what he had overheard, all came together as if he was there. He was the eagle, seeing how the armies were arranged. The Bohemians having the first advantage as they held the higher ground. How men's shouts and then screams drowned out all other sound. How the experience of the Saxon generals showed in bringing up the second line in a narrowed focus, so that they came up against the weakest part of the Bohemian army—where Radslav's and Wenceslas's forces met in the middle on the Bohemian line. How that join gave.

He could not have seen Saxon reserve forces then press on Wenceslas's side, forcing his own bodyguards to fight for their lives. How Blanik had to commandeer a horse to dash to Radslav, who was fighting in his own front line, and command him to withdraw his troops before withdrawal stopped being an option, and rout happened on the left flank. How Blanik dashed back across the line to see a troop of Saxons break through the Bohemian line, targeting Wenceslas. And how Podevin's father, in defending his king, took a wound in his side from a mace that meant he fell and had to be left as the Bohemians withdrew up the slope.

The rest of the battle went to plan. The Saxons charged up the slope and were met by the arrows of the concealed archers. The furious volleys, and the renewed strength of the Bohemians meant the Saxons, for all their discipline, had left the field by mid-afternoon. They retreated to their camp on the far side of the river. What happened there would not concern Podevin.

Nothing concerned Podevin. His rising panic as he scoured the faces of the exhausted bodyguard for his father. His breaking from Blanik's grip as the castle constable tried to explain. His run down the hill, through the trees, stumbling over stones, tripping over roots, grazes from brambles, scratches from twigs. All ignored in his desperate pleas; if only he could get to his father again. He'd be good. He'd always do as he was told. Only, please, please, please make it all right. Podevin ran past the others; those trying to find their loved ones; those looking for what booty they might steal before order was restored. The ravens, already gorged, barely bothering to hop out of the way as he ran past. And all the time screaming: 'Daddy! Daddy!'

Then a bloody arm raised. Even as he scrambled over the other maimed bodies, the arm dropped again. He saw the gaping dent in the armour. The blood-soaked ground. Even blood in Daddy's mouth. Daddy not able to speak, not able to get up. Daddy just able to move his arm to tell Podevin to cuddle him. But Daddy's face was cold, his armour was cold. The hand on the back of his head was cold and it didn't move like it used to. Daddy always used to stroke his hair. Daddy was able just to put his arm around him and not even tell him off for crying his hot tears because Daddy was hurt.

Daddy had turned his head. He wasn't looking at Podevin anymore.

'All right, Rostislav, it's all right. Don't speak. We'll get help.' Podevin heard the king's gentle tone.

His father shook his head. He managed to get his shoulder off the ground. 'Look…after…him.'

And, suddenly, the arm round Podevin felt heavy and didn't move anymore. Podevin lifted his head. He looked at his father—the soft grey eyes were open, but they stared into the sky. And other hands were touching him. They were trying to take him away from Daddy!

'No! I want to stay here. Leave me alone.'

'Come on, Podevin. You can't stay here.'

Daddy had always said that Podevin should obey his king, but he hung onto Daddy as hard as he could. Wenceslas unpeeled his hands from Daddy's chest and picked him up. Podevin buried his head in Wenceslas's cloak and howled again.

'He died so I could live, Blanik.'

'Yes, sire. But what the hell was the boy doing here in the first place?'

'He's not the only one.' Wenceslas looked about the bloody field.

Other children were being comforted while wives screamed their anguish. A few had the energy to shake their fists at Wenceslas or shout obscenities. Those corpses still unclaimed were considered fair game for scavengers, whether human or feathered. The wolves and others would wait until after sundown.

'But he was the only one without a mother.' Blanik paused. 'So, what are we going to do with him?'

Sheer exhaustion had stopped Podevin's howls. He stiffened.

'We fulfil his father's dying wish—we look after him, don't we?' These last words were addressed to Podevin, who looked into the king's dark blue eyes, and tried to blink away his tears.

❧

The walk back to the king's camp took a lot longer than the run to the battlefield, and not just because Podevin was too tired to think of running. The king had set him on his feet, so he had to walk, but he could walk clinging onto the king's hand. They stepped over bodies, avoided pools of blood—fewer now the ground had had time to soak the spillage away. Those who would live had mostly gone. It was, it seemed, Blanik's job to organise parties of people to carry their comrades back to the camp. You did not argue with Blanik, but he couldn't be everywhere. Some wounded, who might have lived, mysteriously died where they had fallen. Nobody said anything to Podevin back then but, as he got older, he understood there were people who valued a ring, a jewelled chain, or even a fine sword, more than helping someone who was injured. That night, others who could not be moved were luckier, as they had someone to sit with them. A few were starting fires, preparing to sit out a long night; either the wounded man would die that night, or he would live. Wounds were patched up as best they could be. As the king made his way back to the camp, he would stop to offer a word here, squeeze a shoulder there.

So many people wanted to talk to the king; who would have castles and lands, or huts and farms, now my husband, now my father, has died serving you? Would the king ensure this person did, or that person did not, get his land, his animals, his home? How did the king think she would survive now her husband, her son, her father, had died? All the time, the sinking sun cast cheerful orange rays over the dead and the dying. The evening dampness, as gentle as a sigh, insidious as a rumour, crept through shoes and into feet and ankles. Podevin sneezed.

'Come on. We need to get you to a nice, warm fire.' The king grasped his hand more firmly, and they set out through the woods.

There were fewer bodies here; the Saxons hadn't charged that far, but one or two Saxon spears had found a mark. Podevin shivered as the temperature dropped in the dappled sunlight. They came out the other side and saw the camp. The flags fluttering and the crowd by the king's tent.

'It seems we have visitors,' said Wenceslas, checking his stride.

He looked at Podevin, half asleep but still clinging to the exhausted monarch. An older woman approached.

'Sire,' she said, holding out her arms.

This time, Wenceslas allowed himself to be relieved of his burden, and Podevin was lifted up and found himself in a softer berth.

'Shall we see if we can find you some food, little one?' the matron murmured into his ear.

Too exhausted to object that Daddy always called him his 'big boy', Podevin allowed himself to be carried round the back of the king's tent, where another fire blazed and there was food and drink. And, unlike the scene on the other side of the wood, here was where the heroes had come back from the fight, where they were reunited with lovers, or arms were flung round maternal necks and holding tight. Fathers slapped sons' backs or arms. Minor wounds to arm, leg or torso were tended.

'You can tell everyone you got those scars in your first battle!'

The wounded warrior, just out of boyhood, grinned back, slipped away from his mother's ministrations and wandered, over-casually, towards another group, another fire, where a comely girl was paying, at best, semi-attentive service to her father's account of the battle. Podevin yawned, then returned his attention to the food in front of him.

Tents might provide shelter, but they are not soundproof. Just as he had not understood the need for the young soldier to leave his mother and go to his girl, Podevin certainly did not understand the import of what he heard through the canvas of the king's tent. Later, he would have cause to know and recognise Prince Otto but, for now, he was just another voice, out of sight, in the king's tent, talking to Wenceslas, and saying things Podevin did not understand at all. He heard the king's voice too.

'That's shut them up. They should have known Wenceslas speaks German!'

It was one of the men round the fire with Podevin who spoke, but then they all quieted as the king's voice was raised. The man started translating for the benefit of the others.

'So, you decided—you decided—that I needed to be taught a lesson. That I needed to lose some land. Have I not paid my tribute? Was there any excuse? I assure you, my prince, my emissaries will already be at your father's court, seeking an explanation. Will they get one?' Wenceslas didn't wait for a reply. 'Will Podevin get one? Will he get an explanation as to why he is now fatherless?'

There was a mutter, but Wenceslas hadn't finished. 'I think you should explain. Blanik?'

The matron who had taken Podevin under her wing did not wait for the constable to appear but gathered Podevin up, roughly wiped his mouth with a cloth, and took him round the side of the tent. The matron put Podevin on the ground but held onto his hand, staring Blanik in the eye. He shrugged and allowed them to precede him into the tent.

It was silent. Podevin recognised many of the bodyguards. He drew in his breath—when he had last seen these men, his father had been with them—felt his hand squeezed, a gentle reassurance that someone here was on his side. But the king, sitting behind a table, was smiling at him too. He spoke to the man standing in front of him.

'There you are, Otto. A child—one of many—who has no father tonight because of your recklessness. Do you wish to explain why? Because I'm sure I haven't understood your reasoning thus far.' Wenceslas still spoke German, but Blanik bent down and told Podevin that the king was cross with the other man, not him.

The man, who also looked cross, stared at Podevin. Podevin stared back. The man took one step towards him, and Wenceslas's entire bodyguard stiffened; hands went to hilts. Even Wenceslas went very still. But the man said nothing.

'We're waiting, Otto. All of us are waiting,' Wenceslas said.

But the man still said nothing; he just spat on the ground and left the tent. His gang went with him. Podevin heard them talking in their language. They did not sound happy.

'You've made an enemy, sire,' said Blanik.

'Saxony is always an enemy, except when they need us as a buffer against the Magyars or as allies against the northern rabbles.'

No-one had a reply to this. Podevin looked up at the matron, who smiled down at him. But, as she started to curtsey, ready to take the boy away, Blanik spoke again.

'So, what are we going to do with him?'

'As I said, we're going to look after him, Blanik. As his father requested.'

'But, sire, it's not as if his place is in the kitchens. And he's too small to train as a warrior with the other apprentices.'

'But he could be a page at my table—at least until he grows up enough to be a bodyguard. And you could train him, and tutor him.'

Podevin looked up. The king was looking at the constable. Blanik turned his head slightly so he was looking straight at Podevin.

'Can you hold a cup?' Podevin nodded. 'How about a jug?' Blanik pointed at the pitcher of wine that stood on the trestle table in between him and the king.

The other bodyguards stopped talking. They were looking at him as well. Podevin let go of the hand that was holding him. He reached for the pitcher. He touched it with the tip of his fingers.

'Unfair, Blanik.'

The king leaned forwards, grabbed the top of the pitcher with one hand and twisted it so the handle was in Podevin's reach. Podevin grasped the handle, pulled the pitcher gently towards him. And lifted it. It was heavy, and full of wine. The king held out his goblet. Biting his lip with the effort, Podevin poured.

'Whoa, stop!'

The wine slopped down the side of the goblet as Podevin straightened the jug. He looked up at Blanik, who shrugged slightly, but said nothing. One of the other knights came to Podevin with a goblet. This time, Podevin was more careful and only a couple of drops were spilt. Two more goblets then appeared. He filled them. Then he set the empty pitcher down.

He looked from the king to Blanik. The king was looking at Blanik as well. Blanik had his hand over his mouth. Then he put his hands on his hips as he looked around the tent at all the men. The bodyguards were smiling. Eventually, Wenceslas spoke.

'Well, Blanik?'

Blanik said nothing for a moment. Then: 'You have a page, sire. One who can wait upon you at table, at any rate. And I, it seems, have a new tutee.'

Wenceslas turned and looked at Podevin. 'Well, page, you'd better come with me to see the troops.'

'Not so fast!' A new voice spoke, and a new person stood in the doorway of the tent.

'Queen Drahomira expects an audience. Now!'

A youth Podevin would come to know as Duke Boleslav, the king's brother, swaggered into the tent.

'Well, well, my noble brother, swigging wine, carousing with his mates, while those who did the hard work have to make do with what they can find outside.'

Boleslav hitched his fur cloak, trimmed with ermine, so it sat more comfortably on his shoulders, his hard brown eyes darting from one knight to another. Podevin shrank back. The tent was silent. Boleslav grabbed a goblet, drained it. Put it back down, none too carefully.

'What? Has nobody anything to say? Our mother is waiting, Wenny.'

Wenceslas didn't move. 'We have nothing to say to mere messengers…Bolly.'

'Mother told you not to call me that.'

'And I'm telling you to address me properly.'

The brothers glared at each other. Boleslav's gaze dropped first. He turned.

'I'll tell Mother that you refuse to come, then.'

'Tell Mother what you like—you usually do—but I will attend her once I've seen to my duties here. As I said I would this morning. Also, you two might be members of my council, but it's *my* council; you sit there at my pleasure.'

Boleslav reached the tent flap. Lifted it. Paused.

'You can't sack us, Wenny. Not unless you want a civil war. By the way,' he said, turning his head, 'I don't see Rostislav here.' Podevin started as he heard his father's name, but Boleslav carried on, 'The queen, your mother and I, have acceded to Duke Radslav's request; Tugumir is pardoned and restored to his stepfather's lands and titles. You weren't there, so we went ahead without you. Oh! Before I go, Radslav's decided he owes you nothing. It seems you're a lily-livered milksop who couldn't fight a battle against a bunch of petal-flinging maidens. I think that's quite an apt description, don't you?'

And with that, he was gone.

'By God, sire, it was Radslav's fault the Saxons came so close to you!'

'How dare he!'

'Sire, you'll need to get rid of him before he does real mischief!'

Wenceslas looked round at his indignant bodyguards. Alone amongst them, he appeared relaxed. He was still sitting at the trestle table.

'Gentlemen, much as I thank you for your support, Boleslav is still my brother. And, for the moment, he is right. But you know our plans. Once I reach my sixteenth birthday, my father's will states I can rule and not just reign. Until then, my brother can be contained. Besides, he would do no mischief without our mother's express consent. And, it seems, we are required to attend to our mother the queen. But first,' Wenceslas drained his cup, 'let us thank our troops.'

Finally, Wenceslas rose to his feet. 'Come on, page, you'd better walk with me.'

Chapter 37
Journeying Out
A.D. 936

The morning after the discussion about him going to Budec, full of memories and breakfast, Podevin pulled on his no-longer-new, but still serviceable, leather boots. If he was going to be traipsing through forest and swamp, he needed something on his feet that could cope with the wet. He wondered what Duke Radslav now made of his protégée Tugumir, but shook himself.

It might still be dark, but everyone was up. Even Priby, lying on her pallet of straw and bracken, was awake and watching him. He went over to her.

'Let's see if Mark can't have you up and about before I get back, hey?'

She grinned up at him. 'Mark says I'm getting stronger every day.'

'It must be all the food your new sister gives you!'

Maria was standing by with a bowl of broth, ready to help. Priby was a cute child, thought Podevin. She deserved better than growing up in a world where wars could be started at the whim of an idiot like Boleslav, or a turncoat like Tugumir, ready to overthrow any peace and order just to advance their own selfish agendas. Well, this time, Podevin would be ready for him. This time, the Pribys and Marias of the world would get to grow up without war being a constant companion. But he was delaying their breakfast. He stood. Time to say goodbye to the grown-ups. They stood awkwardly together.

He walked across the hard earthen floor, skirting the fire. Lyudmila held his cloak, while Krok was standing, not leaning on his staff.

'Here you are.' Lyudmila spoke first. 'You'll need this. It's chilly at night, even if the days are warm.'

'You're babbling,' said Krok, but without anger.

Lyudmila hugged Podevin. Podevin glanced at Krok before wrapping his arms around the normally sensible woman. She leaned back, her eyes moist. 'You come back to us, you hear?'

Podevin nodded and let her go. Embarrassed, he turned to Krok, who held out his staff. 'You'll need this to fight your way through the paths. And for when you're tired.'

'But it's your staff!'

'Today's job is to make another.' The other man grinned. 'Now, off you go. Give my wife a chance to blink back her tears.'

Podevin nodded and picked up his pack. He was travelling as light as he could with Lyudmila's provisions, Mark's purse—the money came from Emma, enough to keep him going for weeks—and Krok's staff. But he had a long walk today if he was to get anywhere close to Budec by nightfall tomorrow.

He decided to avoid the mountains and follow the Vltava on its way north, then skirt, if he could, the town of Levy Hradec. Quite apart from the obvious implication that the place was where Wenceslas (and now Boleslav's) chief clerk came from, Podevin had no idea how sympathetic its people might be to Boleslav or Tugumir. If he was recognised there, it could be fatal—if not to Podevin himself, then certainly to his attempts to find out what Tugumir's plans were. However, he was not averse to hitching a ride on the back of a cart. A load of hay and other foodstuff going from one farm to another. It was going the right way, and a couple of coins bought the driver's complete silence in the conspiracy.

'Running from a woman, eh? Or to one?'

'Something like that.' Podevin grinned.

'Yeah. Thought so. I can always tell. You ain't shabby enough to be a peasant.'

Podevin merely raised an eyebrow.

The driver spread his arm wide to the fields. 'Always stuff to do for the lord of the manor—if there ain't any wars, that is.'

'I could be a forester?' said Podevin, more to get a reaction than in any serious attempt to claim Krok's role.

'If you lived in the forest, you'd soon look greener than you do. Unhealthy places. Give me the wide-open spaces any day.'

'Spoken like a true farmer!'

'Me? Just a wagoner. Plodding from Prague to Levy Hradec, from Levy to Prague. If they make it worth my while, I'll even follow the Berounka river to Tetin, but that's a three-day journey and with no guarantee of a return load.' The man shrugged.

For all his talk of the wide-open spaces, he seemed content with just plodding back and forth every week between the two towns. Further questioning from Podevin discovered that he had never even thought of going into business for himself; he was content to do the bidding of others. Not that he put it that way. He could never get the money together to buy a full load; he did not have the contacts to make the sale at the other end; and besides, if he went into business for himself, he would lose the work he did for the merchants in Prague, wouldn't he? Podevin wondered whether it was so clear cut but held his peace. If the driver had been more business-minded, he might also have been more curious about Podevin's mission.

The wagoner did have one useful contact; for a night's stay when it looked like rain, just south of Levy Hradec, there was a mill run by a widow.

'Called Libuse, like everyone these days. Just say Jan the wagoner sent you.' He flicked the reins, and he and his cart ambled off towards the local farms.

Of course, Queen Libuse was the founder of the Bohemian state, so, yes, there were lots of Libuses, but this old woman, with several teeth missing, looked nothing like a beautiful, elegant queen.

'Jan sent you, did 'e? No better than the rest of 'em. Let's see yer money. I suppose yer want supper? No reduction if yer don't.'

Podevin handed over the rather steep price for a night's rest and, thinking his food would last better if he did not tuck into it today, said he would indeed like supper.

ৎৎ

The sun was up. Podevin rubbed his eyes. Then the back of his neck. Then he eased himself upright.

'Now I know what it feels like to be Krok,' he said to himself.

He'd been kept dry by the old woman's hospitality, but hardly comfortable. Breakfast was no more than hard bread with some honey and small beer. Better than nothing, he thought, as he thanked the old woman. She'd had a thought. It seemed 'loads of folks' were tired of walking everywhere and usually hired one of her 'fine beasts'. Given her definition of a 'fine, comfortable bed', and her prices, Podevin declined the offer. Then, trudging towards the forest, he headed to Budec.

The main road would go east first, following the river, and then skirt the hills and forests, but Podevin reckoned the short route through the woods would be quicker and easier for a man on foot—and for one who now wished to avoid company. A man, coming out of the forest, with a load of firewood, eyed him suspiciously but answered him readily enough when Podevin hailed him to check his route. Avoiding company was one thing; trying to duck out of sight would only make people even more suspicious.

Podevin stopped at a stream. He drank deeply, getting the taste of the stale small beer out of his mouth. He pressed on. Walked an hour, stopped for ten minutes or so. The woodland tracks were kind and led him to Budec by mid-afternoon. Early falling leaves brushed his face and softly scrunched under his feet. Blinded by childhood memories of kicking his way through leaves—possibly in these very woods, as his father somehow seemed to be with him in his mind—he checked his initial temptation to walk right up to the castle. A bit of scouting was called for, or, at least, some sitting and observing. And he had an excuse; he had not eaten all day and, now he had reached his destination, he was hungry.

Part of his mind worried that he ought to feel nervous, but his body decided that food came first. He unpacked his bags and tucked into the provisions from home. From his vantage point, he could see the road from Levy Hradec as it came round the hills into the town.

He could see the wooden castle and palisade wall. He could see dots moving around—presumably guards—on that wall. As he sat there, beginning to squint into the setting sun, he saw people on their way out of the town. It was, presumably, still considered safe enough to spend your nights outside the walls. At least they were not expecting marauding bands of Saxons. Podevin realised he had made his choice; tonight, he would bed down in the forest. He retreated from the pathway and looked for a likely spot.

A dry patch of ground, a little raised from its surroundings, suggested itself. There was a convenient tree with a forked branch so he could lean a long length of wood into it and start on his shelter. The wind appeared to come from the town—a pity, but he would not see much while he was asleep anyway—so he put the back of the shelter facing west, with a solid base of mud from a nearby stream, and covered it with the available bracken and dry reeds. Then a few heavier branches, in case the wind increased in the night, and he was secure.

He lit a fire on the other side of the tree; not too far from the shelter, but not so near he'd burn his toes overnight, and settled down. For a few minutes, he watched the fire-smoke meander its way up into the woodland canopy and let his thoughts drift back towards home. For the first time since Wenceslas's death, he found he was praying. He prayed for Lyudmila and Krok, for Maria and Priby. It was important to him they should be safe. He prayed that Krok would soon be pain-free. He prayed for Brother Mark—that he would keep faith with his role of protecting Emma. He prayed for Emma; of course he prayed for Emma, but his thoughts were conflicted. Was he praying that she would be free of Mladenic, or that she would be queen someday? He could not resolve the conundrum.

The fire snapped. A branch must have been damper than he had realised. He got up to check in the fading light, but the fire quietened down and no sparks lit up any brushwood. It was time to add the bigger logs, the ones that would burn well into the night, keeping anything away that might like to snack on him or his provisions. Podevin sighed, settled back down and refocused his thoughts. He had arrived in two days, as planned. Mabel would be looking out for him. All he knew was that Mabel would be shopping near the gate one hour after it opened in the morning, as she did every morning. But, ever since Beatrice had sent her a message, she would also be looking out for him. Podevin yawned. By sunrise, he'd better be up and ready. He could smell the sweet pine as it glowed in the fire. He settled down. He slept.

One advantage of building your shelter with its back to the setting sun, is that the rising sun will wake you as soon as it pokes itself over the hills. He washed himself in the stream as best he could and ate his breakfast. Now he was nervous—as on the days when he knew Wenceslas was going to come to watch him practise his warrior skills. Only today, the test would be stiffer.

The staff would be part of the disguise. Once again, he was to be Krok. If he could not fake a limp, he could stoop. He could ask for bread. He could be recognised as a long-lost friend from Prague—the secret of good duplicity was to stick as close to the truth as you could—and Mabel would lead him home to meet her husband. Podevin chafed his hands together. Plans always sounded great, especially when you had someone like Brother Mark doing the expounding, but, when it came time to enact those plans, doubts ensued. What if Mabel, or more likely, her husband, had joined Tugumir? What if, for whatever reason, she failed to go to the market today? What if, by some fluke, he was recognised?

A deep breath. This was getting him nowhere. There were people on the road to Budec. He had better get going, or the plan would fail simply because of his tardiness. He left the camp—he might need it—picked up the staff and his bag, left all the provisions he would not need tied in a bundle on one of the higher, flimsier branches, said a quick prayer, and made his way out into the open.

Chapter 38
A Budec Welcome

'Krok! How wonderful to see you! How's Lyudmila getting on? And little Maria? Only she won't be so little now, will she? You must bring them with you next time! I'm sure Maria would get along with my three—and another one on the way.' Mabel patted her bulging midriff and leaned towards Podevin.

At least she'd lowered her voice, marginally, for the last statement. Podevin vaguely supposed that married men were less embarrassed about such conversation, but he wasn't so sure he could cope. The Anglo-Saxon former lady-in-waiting prattled on in almost flawless Czech, inviting him to her home, where Stanislav would be soon, as he was due to be off duty.

Their married quarters were comfortable and came with servants, who brought beer and meat almost before Podevin had a chance to sit down.

'Inform my husband as soon as he arrives that we have a visitor. Oh, and you'll need to get more bread in.'

The servant was dismissed.

'Phew! I'm new to all this,' said Mabel once they were alone. 'How'd I do?'

'A bit chatty, but you're all right,' Podevin said.

'But I was so nervous! I was afraid I'd never recognise you, but I needn't have worried. You haven't changed a bit. Well, older of course, but no grey hairs, not even in your beard—not yet anyway. Life in the forest agreeing with you? Has Emma, I mean, Princess Emma, sought you out yet? As soon as she gets rid of that milksop of a husband, she'll be after you. Then you'll have to look out.'

'Madam.'

'I mean, it was so obvious to all of us, back when you first met in Augsburg. I couldn't believe it when Wenceslas insisted Emma was to marry that child. I mean, what was he thinking?'

'*Madam.*'

'I don't know. Maybe he's grown up into a fine figure of a man, but I doubt it.'

'MADAM.'

'Sorry.' Mabel opened guileless blue eyes wide—presumably it was the expression that had ensnared Stanislav, but Podevin was terrified. He had to find out who else knew of his visit.

'Hello, my lovely, has our guest arrived?' The new voice spoke with a mature authority.

'Oh, yes, but he hasn't said much.' Mabel jumped up and embraced her husband.

'I doubt he's had the chance.' The still-besotted husband emerged from the welcome and poured himself a drink. 'Why don't you go and check lunch is on its way?'

Mabel opened her mouth, but her husband raised an eyebrow, and she closed it, glanced at Podevin, and left the room.

'Her heart's in the right place or she wouldn't have brought you here. And if she didn't stop talking all the way, then it doesn't matter, it's her way. Everyone round here knows it's only Mabel and her chatter.' Stanislav sat down opposite Podevin.

'I was a bit worried. I didn't expect to be told your good news within a minute of meeting her. Congratulations, by the way.'

'Thank you.' Stanislav drank.

'Where are they?'

'Hmm?'

'The children.'

'Oh, up at the castle, I expect. Mabel's in charge of that. They run a sort of group thing with a few other mothers. We aren't quite in the "send them away to be educated elsewhere" class—not that Mabel would ever countenance that—but she doesn't say no to a couple of mornings a week without them and enjoys the days when she has a dozen to cater for. Works for us. Another sip of beer?'

The change of subject was abrupt, but Podevin accepted it, even as he refused the drink. Perhaps it was the memory of what he'd been through over the previous days, but he was not completely sure of Stanislav. Why should he be? He had not seen him since the journey from Augsburg and, while Mabel might be loyal to Emma, Stanislav could easily be loyal to Boleslav, to Tugumir, to…whomever.

'You look worried.' Stanislav poured himself the second drink Podevin had refused. 'You shouldn't be. If I'd wanted you arrested, I'd have had you picked up last night. Mabel wouldn't have known a thing about it. Believe me.'

'Oh, yes, I would, Stanislav Blanik! You could never do a thing like that without me getting it out of you!' Mabel, making no effort to disguise the fact she had been listening at the doorway, sauntered back into the room.

Stanislav grinned into his beer as Podevin's eyes darted from him to her and back again.

'How did you know where I was?'

'I didn't—wasn't even looking for you—but to be here so early, you must have camped out in the forest overnight. Comfortable?'

'Yes. I've slept under the stars before.' Podevin paused. 'Blanik? I knew a man by that name.'

'Cousins. Sort of. Part of the reason why I was allowed to marry this girl.' This girl feinted a clip round his head, which was easily fended off. 'Got me out of the family's clutches—a cousin on the other side who had twice her girth ten years ago.' A quick nod to Mabel, who was aiming more blows at his head, not that any landed. 'Hey! I preferred you! Always have and always will!' Then, in a change of tone, 'Hope her husband's happy.'

'He was poor; he wanted the farm.' Mabel shrugged.

She was standing by her husband, his arm round her waist. She had made her choice and was happy with it. Podevin finally relaxed. It was all right; he was among friends. Not that it made his job any easier, but he did not have to worry about Stanislav's or Tugumir's cronies coming to get him in the night. Of course, this meant Stanislav was playing a dangerous game too; he had a wife and—how many was it?—children to worry about.

'Why are you risking everything for me?' Podevin asked.

'We're not risking anything. We're just taking in a friend of a friend. What he's up to in Budec is none of our business,' said Mabel.

'I need your help, or Stanislav's, to complete that business.'

'But if I talked about my job, how was I to know what use was to be made of it?' Stanislav's innocence was so palpable, that Podevin had to laugh.

'All right! But I hope you are never called upon to tell the tale!'

'Dear, shouldn't you be off to get the kids?' Stanislav gave his wife another squeeze.

She gave him a kiss.

'In other words, "man-talk". Don't worry, you'll only bore me! Lunch in half an hour.'

He watched her leave, then turned to Podevin.

'Well?'

'Well, what?'

'You have questions.' Stanislav leaned back and took a long pull at his beer, never taking his eyes of Podevin.

Podevin shifted, now wishing he'd accepted the offer of a second drink.

'I suppose there are a couple,' he said. Stanislav raised an eyebrow, inviting him to continue. 'Blanik. Any idea about him?'

If Stanislav was surprised by the question, he only gave it away by his pause before answering.

'As soon as he knew it was a lost cause, he got as many men out of Prague as he could. Boleslav's supporters were already shouting that Wenceslas was dead. As far as I know, they're all in Saxony, so what they think about this war kicking off, I don't know. And, to answer the next question, what about me? I was there, but quartered in the town, thank God! Definitely not close enough, or senior enough, to be told any plans beforehand. Loyal enough to guard his castle, but not close enough to travel with Tugumir when he goes off to Tetin.'

'But why here in town? Surely you do guard duty?' A nod, so Podevin pressed the point. 'Guards live at the castle—you do guard duty, but you're here.'

'In a place where we can plot rebellion.' The nonchalant smile still in place, Stanislav put the empty tankard on the table and leaned forwards. 'Family life, if no longer family connections, means I'd rather earn less by paying for this place than take free board and lodging at the castle. Besides, wonderful as some of my colleagues are, there are others I would not share a spoon with, much less my living quarters. You'll find there's quite a few of us down here. And Tugumir doesn't mind. A vanguard in town in a surprise attack is no bad thing.'

'Vanguards have high casualties.'

'So? We'd better make sure there are no surprise attacks, hadn't we?' Stanislav paused. 'What's the plan?'

The plan, as concocted in a forest hut, could not stand in its entirety when faced with an intimate of the castle, but the broad outlines remained the same. Podevin needed to be the man inside; he needed to be the one lifting the plans.

'There are plans, then?' Podevin asked.

'Oh, yes, we all know there are plans, but what they are, no idea. I'm not, as I said, part of his inner circle.'

The tricky part, always the tricky part, was going to be getting Podevin out again without being discovered, and with Stanislav doing no more than looking the other way for as brief a moment as possible. Stanislav's solution was simple; Podevin was to become a clerk. Clerks wandered about at will (not quite, but it seemed like it to the knights), and often had parchment in their hands. Podevin could read, so he could be a clerk. He just needed to look like one.

'And not too much ink on my fingers!' Podevin remembered Prague Castle's chief clerk being very fussy about ink splodges on vellum. 'I'll need to be reminded where the scriptorium is. It's a long time since I lived here.'

'You'll need that anyway, as all the copying is done there. Why the frown?'

'I could fool a knight that I was a clerk, but fooling a roomful of clerks that I'm one of them, is another.'

'They won't be there. That's the beauty of the scheme! They're all off on a tax-collecting exercise.'

'But surely there's at least one left behind?'

'Ill. Tummy trouble.' Podevin thought that was a little convenient, but Stanislav just tapped the side of his nose. 'What you don't know, won't kill you. We just need to work on your story and it's all sorted.'

But the work would have to wait as, with squeals of 'Papa! Papa!', Stanislav was inundated with small bodies. He did not appear to mind the interruption.

∾

The next day, with Stanislav on early duty, Podevin made his way to the castle. His boots had been cleaned for him; no clerk would have the sort of muddy boots that had travelled all the way from the forests of Prague. He tucked his dagger into the right one. Clerks only carried knives for sharpening their quills—and to help with food—so his was too long and had better not be visible. His dusty brown cloak was typical of all clerks; hooded like a monk's. In so many places, clerks were monks. They had access to enough learning to read, write and do their sums. In other places, they just looked like monks, or what everyone thought monks should look like: pale, inoffensive, heads bowed, keeping out of the way, spending their lives inside and scribbling constantly. Podevin reflected he was lucky to have the learning and the skills of a knight, and a forester, and… He shook himself. His skills were no good if he failed.

Clerks were not knights, but they were important enough not to travel on foot. Before anyone could become suspicious, Podevin made his way through the gates, his face buried in the parchment Stanislav had procured for this purpose. He nodded at the guard and kept walking. Then to the left, through the doorway—only the briefest of hiccoughs as the iron latch resisted his twisting at the handle—and he was in. He pulled the hood from his head and puffed his cheeks out as he sighed in relief. He also needed to allow his eyes time to adapt to the dingy light.

He shrugged away the odd feeling that this was home. Yes, he had been born here. Yes, his father had owned this place. But no, without Stanislav's directions, he would have no chance. Left and down the steps to the scriptorium. As predicted, the place was deserted. Podevin shut the door behind him and prowled around the desks, checking each clerk's work. Nothing. By which he meant nothing like what he was looking for. Just tax receipts and loyal letters to Prague. Almost as if it was ready for a visit from the new king himself. Podevin paused. He checked the shelves and cupboards behind what must be the chief clerk's desk—it was on a small podium, high enough to enable the chief clerk to check everyone was doing their work. Vague sounds emerged from outside, typical of a busy castle, with important people coming and going. One last look round, and Podevin headed out. No-one expected incriminating documents to be left around for anyone to pick up, but it had been worth a try. Now for the more difficult part: Tugumir's rooms.

Did clerks go the main way or by the back stairs? Podevin reflected, then headed left again out of the door. He had never bumped into a clerk when he was Wenceslas's page, so they must, on the rare occasions when they moved out of their hidey-hole, have gone the back way. A kitchen wench, carrying a pitcher of water, scuttled by. Podevin shrunk against the wall, but she barely gave him a glance. Another one scampered past him, warm water splashing from her jug. He found himself following them, intent on his mission and keeping out of the way. Stanislav's directions were great, but being able to follow someone on silent feet was better; tracking skills could be useful inside as well as out. He did not need the bed chamber but the outer rooms. So he ducked aside and entered.

Whatever the man's ambitions, Tugumir had done well for himself. Tapestries hung on the walls showing hunting themes; that must be silver plate in the cupboard. Loads of it. Podevin felt his anger rise. This was the man who had killed his master and was still plotting. Every cupboard door he could see, Podevin opened. He lifted every tapestry and checked to see if it was covering any holes in the wall. And he opened every door to see where they led. Every door bar one. There was noise through there. A lot of moving around. A squeal? A protest swiftly quenched? A splash? What was going on in there?

Chapter 39
Plans Made, Plans Changed

Podevin waited, the fear of discovery fighting his curiosity. He had found nothing. If those wenches were having a party, they were taking a big chance—more likely, one of the knights left in charge was making free with Tugumir's private quarters. Podevin took yet another turn around the sumptuous rooms. But there was nothing to link Tugumir with the latest plot; he might as well admit it.

Then it all went quiet in the room next door. Giggling footsteps passed by. Podevin froze, ears straining. He had to check the bed chamber. If there was nothing there, what was he to do? He could not, absolutely not, go back to Emma having failed. He tried the last door. It opened, and he stepped through. He pushed the door closed. There was a slight clang as the latch dropped into place. He froze again. More silence. He turned.

Tugumir! He was in the bath, but with his eyes closed and a half smile of contentment on his face. The bed covers were rumpled and his clothes were on the floor, presumably waiting to be picked up— not a knight's job. Tugumir was not supposed to be here, but there was also a parchment left on the dressing table. Podevin would have to go farther into the room. Step by careful step, while his half-brother dozing in his bath, he managed to take the parchment. A swift glance.

Your Majesty is most generous to her humble servant. As I find myself in the position of widower, you are most kind…

He did not need to read any more. This was it. Now, all he had to do was get it to Prague.

'Ah! Greetings, my friend. I want that sent off as soon as possible.'

'Of course, sire!' Podevin bowed, secreting the parchment within the folds of his cloak.

'Sire! It'll be your majesty, soon enough.'

'Of course, your majesty.' It stuck in his throat.

'Just a minute. Who are you? Where's Bron?'

Podevin thought quickly: 'He's ill, sire. He sent me.'

'Don't be ridiculous! He rode in with me not half an hour ago… Wait. I know that voice. Podevin? My little rat of a half-brother has been hiding here all the time?'

As he was saying this, Tugumir clambered out of the bath. Podevin froze. He looked at the door. Too far away. Even naked, his brother was all muscle, height and breadth. What could he do? Tugumir was not going to let him walk out with evidence of his disloyalty, was he? A weapon, anything! Tugumir bent and straightened up, swinging his battle-axe. Podevin moved, put the rumpled bed between them, and almost tripped over Tugumir's abandoned sword belt.

'You're going to die, little brother. And how appropriate—here at my home.'

The damned cloak was in the way. In two seconds, Podevin had untied it and dropped it to the floor, along with the now crumpled parchment. Tugumir was advancing slowly, mouthing curses. Podevin bent, the belt had a sword attached. A sword was a poor second best against an axe, but Tugumir was not worried about a fair fight. He had not been concerned when they were children together, so why should he be now?

Tugumir advanced. Podevin scrambled over the bed, so busy keeping his eye on his adversary, he all but stepped into the bath. Tugumir retraced his steps.

'You're doomed, Podevin. The king wants you dead. And you'll be the one discovered with a parchment detailing your treachery.'

'Queen Drahomira knows she was dealing with you!'

'We've never met. Not in person. And we all know you'd do anything to get your castle back. It's you the king wants dead, not me.'

While they'd been talking, Tugumir had kept stalking him. He was too close! A wild swing with the axe, and Podevin ducked away, flailing his weapon at his foe. It missed, but so did the axe.

'Stand still, you brat!'

Another swing, another dodge, but, this time, he had to use the sword to block the axe. A mistake. The sword jarred his arm as it flew off to the other side of the room. Podevin backed away from the bath; the table jutted into his back. The sleeve of his jerkin was turning red—it didn't hurt, yet.

Come on, lad! Think! If you give the other man the advantage, he'll take it! If you've got nothing else—pretend! Blanik's voice sounded in his head as if his tutor was in the room.

The table; there was a goblet. Podevin snatched it up and threw it. Tugumir was distracted for less than a second but it was enough. Podevin ducked down to his boot. No time for refinement. The dagger flew through the air and hit his brother's chest, stuck there. He had to retreat as the axe swung. Tugumir was still alive! The dagger still in his chest, he took two steps forwards. Only the bath was between them. Tugumir took another step, his face twisted in a grin. Podevin heaved the bath sideways, a desperate attempt to stop his brother's approach. The axe swung again as the water sloshed at Podevin's feet, but something went wrong. The axe clattered to the ground, missing Podevin as its owner toppled forwards.

A splash. A gurgle. And a new silence. Tugumir was face down in the water. Podevin stood over his brother, pushing him down, keeping him under the water as his struggles grew weaker. Even when Tugumir was still, he held him there, making sure. His chest heaving, his arm hurting, the water still accepting drops of red blood. He stood and looked at the naked body in the water. The half-brother who had taken everything that was his, including his king, was dead. He felt no better. He felt no worse. He leaned on the table. A second, unnoticed goblet. He gulped the wine. Wiped his mouth with the back of his bloody hand.

He ripped at his sleeve. He would now have scars on both arms! This was a deep cut, and needed binding. With his left hand, he pulled at the rumpled sheets. He went for the sword belt and found a dagger. He was not ready to remove his own from his brother's body. Using the new dagger, he ripped the sheet to strips and, using his mouth and his left hand, he managed to bind his wound so the blood stopped dripping out. Then, gasping for breath, he sat on the edge of the bed.

'Vengeance is mine, says the Lord, I will repay.'

As far as Podevin could see, the only repayment Tugumir had been looking for was the kingdom itself. He stood, looking down at the man who had haunted him and hated him. It took noise outside the door to rouse him. His cloak! The parchment! He dived over the bed, wasted precious seconds tying the cloak round him and stuffing the parchment into his jerkin. His dagger. What could he do about his dagger? Nothing. He couldn't face retrieving it. He would just borrow his half-brother's. Podevin dashed back through the outer room. The noise was repeated—just a tap, someone checking to see if their lord and master was all right. Podevin went back into the corridor, after one last check of the outer room; yes, he had left the tapestries just as he found them.

'Hey! You! What's going on?'

The guard; goodness knows where he had been on Podevin's way into the bedroom. Not at his post, that was for sure, but now he stood at the door to the bedroom. The girl by his side. She was holding yet another jar of hot water.

'Oh! Um. I'm just going to make some corrections. He's not to be disturbed.'

'But he asked me for more water,' the girl said.

'That was then. I only know what he told me.' Podevin shrugged and turned away.

Whether they opened the door now or later, he wanted to put as much distance between himself and any questions they might want to ask him. He strode as fast as he could, without running. He made his way round the corner and almost bumped into the second serving girl.

'In a hurry?'

Podevin showed her the parchment. 'Corrections,' he muttered.

'Oh, he won't be in a hurry for those—he has other things on his mind. Like her.' She nodded down the corridor in the direction Podevin had just come from.

Podevin opened his mouth to reply, but a scream cut him short. The girl took one scared look at him and ran towards the noise.

Podevin fled in the opposite direction. Ducking in and out of corridors. Turning left and right. Avoiding people—too late, he remembered his cloak had a hood, tried to pull it over his head one-handed while he ran, but it fell off again. He concentrated on running.

Somehow, he was back outside.

'Podevin! What the hell happened?' It was Stanislav, rushing in from the gate.

'Tugumir's dead. He recognised me.'

'What? You killed him?'

'You said he wouldn't be there! So did Mark!'

'I can't know every change of plan. He made enough noise coming in the gate. How come you didn't hear him?'

'I didn't know it was him! He was in his bath.'

'And you were seen?' The shouts from inside were getting louder. 'Knock me out!'

'What!'

'Knock me out, or I'll have to kill you!' Stanislav was frantic.

'And then just walk through the gate?'

'No, the postern gate I told you about. Back that way. And don't stop until you're well clear of Budec.'

Podevin took a deep breath. 'All right,' he said. 'You're sure?'

Stanislav nodded.

Podevin picked up a large stone. 'For God's sake, look away,' he said.

He swung the stone. Stanislav dropped, and Podevin ran.

Clear of the castle, he shed his cloak. He ducked round the dry moat and made his way back towards Mabel's house. It was dangerous, but he needed only a minute.

'Where's my bag?' he said as he went through the door.

He'd run the whole way and was panting hard.

'Where's Stanislav?'

'Knocked out. I'm sorry. It all went wrong. Tugumir was there.' Podevin paused. 'He's dead. I killed him.'

'Oh, God!' Mabel's mouth opened in a wail.

'No! Tugumir's dead—not Stanislav. But he made me knock him out, or he'd have to kill me. I'm sorry. Just give me my stuff and I'll go.'

'Not Stanislav? Sure?'

Podevin, frantic now, repeated that Tugumir was the one who was dead. To her credit, Mabel recovered fast.

'They'll shut the place down. You can't outrun them.' She peered out at the street for a second before coming back inside, then stared at his arm. The makeshift bandage was red. 'You're not going anywhere until we sort that arm. You're just as safe here as anywhere else. You go at nightfall. Take the direct route back to Prague.' A sudden thought. 'You've got it?'

Podevin drew the parchment from within his tunic. It was a little stained from his sweat, but blood-free and legible. Mabel waved it away.

Podevin mused. 'You're right. What you don't know, won't kill you.' A second thought. 'Mabel, if it helps Stanislav, tell him to give my name. Once he comes round. I'm already wanted—another crime won't matter.'

'What were your other crimes?' She was bustling about, gathering stuff.

'Mainly being Wenceslas's page.' Podevin shrugged. 'Where do I hide for the rest of the day?'

He realised he was putting himself into the hands of someone who, until recently, he had only thought of as a silly girl who had slept with the first boy she came across in Bohemia. Mabel was a competent nurse, but one who ignored his wincing as she pulled his makeshift bandage from his arm, making the wound seep again. She cleaned it up, tied the new bandage competently, and tighter than he had managed himself.

'Keep that on until you get back and someone better qualified than me can tend it.'

He nodded, obedient, and yawned. Probably a reaction to his recent experiences, and he did not object to being led to a hay rick out behind Mabel's house.

⁓

'You're lucky he has a hard head.' Mabel laid his supper down with less gentleness than she'd provided his lunch.

'I'm sorry. I've never had to knock someone out before.'

'Oh, he'll be fine. He just has a headache. They brought him back an hour ago.' She paused. 'He's saying he can't remember.' She let the words hang.

Podevin had spent the afternoon asleep. Using his left hand, he was tucking into the food with gusto, but he heard the hesitation. 'If he can forget until tomorrow, that's all I need.'

Mabel nodded. 'Finish up. I won't be out again—they're a suspicious lot out here.'

'I'll give you time to get home. And wait for full dark. Then I'll be off.'

'May God go with you.'

'And may He protect you.'

It was only after she had gone that Podevin realised he had meant the pious, formulaic words.

હ

If the Great Bear moves about the sky, at least it always points north. Once he'd visited his camp and collected his provisions, Podevin moved eastwards, following the route he had taken to get to Budec, but in reverse. Mabel had said to take the direct route. This was as direct as he could cope with. Besides, he had a plan. He stumbled no more than occasionally but stopped several times to check that there were no sounds of pursuit. As the sky moved from inky dark blue towards the grey of a damp autumnal dawn, it was time for him to think about finding a hidey-hole for the day. Or keep moving and get home faster?

He checked his bags for food and made a frugal breakfast. He compromised and lay down, well out of sight of the road. It was a disturbed snooze, as he kept hearing horses snorting in the distance. He started awake. Wide awake. He might as well move, as he was not going to get any more sleep. He was a scout, a tracker, wasn't he? He could move without being seen.

However, this time, he was the hunted, not the hunter. Now he had to assume everyone was against him. Snapping a twig could be fatal. The lack of night-time pursuit meant nothing. How much could they, would they, get out of Stanislav and Mabel? What a fool he had been! How could he have not foreseen that Tugumir might have changed his plans? He ducked behind a tree, hiding from…a deer. He was getting jittery on top of everything else. Thinking about it, he had not gone there to kill Tugumir ('Is that true?' He could hear Brother Mark's admonition as soon as he had the original thought). Either way, he hadn't planned the killing, and he had allowed, even told, Mabel and Stanislav to give him away. Fine words when he was on the cusp of leaving town and not thinking beyond getting away, but now there was going to be a real hue and cry after him. Not just a page, an inconvenient servant who had been missed in the initial purge—a footnote on a *coup d'état* whom it would be nice to have out of the way—but one who had made trouble. He had killed someone who, for all Boleslav knew, was a loyal supporter of his regime. All he could do was press on, go back to people who had no expectation of being part of Bohemia's troubles, and hope he could get the parchment to Emma before he was caught.

Perhaps it was the logical conclusion of his meandering thoughts that made him relax. He was a dead man. He had tried to do his best, but, call it his lower nature, call it an accident, he had failed. He had been specifically told not to kill Tugumir, who would not be there to be killed in the first place. Just get the evidence. It would be easier if he could be killed in combat but, he shrugged, he could not hope for that; he could only hope Emma's position could be secured by the parchment he carried.

His decision to return to the mill had no logic, other than it was nearby and there was the possibility of stealing a horse. Even if the animal could not be persuaded to go faster than a trot, he would still get home quicker. There was an animal tied to a post outside the mill, the barn close by. Podevin wasted half-an-hour in hiding, waiting for movement, but there was none. The mill wasn't being worked. Maybe the old woman was out? Given what else he had done, taking a horse was nothing. He didn't want to see anyone. He scouted the barn and found a bridle he could use—was he going to have to ride bare-back? A saddle—he needed a saddle. In the far corner, its leather uncared for, cracked and peeling, but better than nothing. However, with only one arm, he could not carry both it and the bridle. Why not just bring the horse to the equipment?

He expected to hear the old woman's screech every second, but nothing, not even when the horse whinnied as he took three goes to get the saddle on its back. Not even when he had to let it feast on the hay and oats scattered in the barn. Once he was able to mount up and leave, they made progress. The animal even consented to canter for a while. When they came near any villages, he left the road and skirted round, keeping to woodland when he could. It was late afternoon when he finally reached his forest home.

Chapter 40
Back to the Forest
A.D. 936

Podevin had been away five days and not slept since the previous afternoon. He was painfully aware of his arm. The two girls running around, squealing. There was a mother, and, somewhere, there would be a father. Podevin watched, out of sight and behind bushes, unable to take those final few steps.

'So, it went wrong then?' Krok was standing beside the bushes, a string of rabbits hanging from a pole.

Podevin sighed. 'What gave me away?'

'The wind.'

'There isn't any.'

'True. So why did that branch move? And,' Krok had a smile in his voice, even if Podevin couldn't see his face, 'there's several great big hoofprints in the mud pointing this way. Which I've covered. You're getting tired and that's when you get careless.' Another pause. 'You're injured! You'd better come in.'

'But I killed him!'

'Yes, and the whole world is after you. And you killed the local miller, and her friend. And they think you're headed for Prague.'

'How do you know?'

'Remember the license you and Lyudmila bought? We used it. Mark stopped to have a word with her.' Krok nodded towards their home.

'So Mark knows.' A statement. Then: 'Hang on. The miller's dead too?'

'She sheltered you. She didn't report you. They hanged her.'

Krok's brief sentences made the mill's silence easier to understand, but why would anyone leave a horse behind? They must have noticed it, or maybe it just wasn't a war horse, so they left it to starve? Or was the mill being watched and he had walked into a trap? But Podevin was sure he hadn't been followed. Positive, in fact. He had to shake himself to stop falling off the horse, which, now it had stopped, was disinclined to go any farther.

'Sorry, Podevin.' Krok interrupted his thoughts. 'Come on, let's get you inside. There's a whole load of troops in Prague from Tugumir's place—all after vengeance.'

'But if you allow me in, then you're a part of it.'

'And where else are you going to go? Prague Castle?'

Krok's logic did what his own thoughts could not. Slipping off the animal's back, and abandoning it into Krok's care, Podevin walked back home to a rapturous welcome. Priby was ecstatic at being able to show him she could now walk around—her back was healing and all the maggots had been removed. Maria wanted to show him how well she was looking after the ducks. Lyudmila was just happy to see him home safe and was absolutely not going to hear tales of his adventures until she had seen to his wounded arm and he had some decent food inside him.

The tale was simply told, once the two girls were in bed.

'You idiot,' Krok said, but there was no venom in his voice. Then: 'You had no choice.'

'It'll be all right. You're safe here,' Lyudmila noted.

'Neither of you seem bothered.' Podevin felt he was stating the obvious.

'You mean, as our former lord, we should seek vengeance for his death? Hardly,' said Krok. 'But we'll have to keep you out of sight for a while.'

'Why?' said Lyudmila.

'Because where are they going to look, once they don't find him in the city? And, as Mark told us,' Krok looked at his wife, 'they're already turning the castle upside down. They know you've stolen a horse. So, they're looking for that as well. Then they'll start on the town, and then...' He let his voice peter out as the implications became obvious, and Lyudmila's face whitened with horror.

'Don't worry, I'll go.' Podevin made to stand.

'Not now! Tell him, Krok!'

'You're safe for tonight. How many of them would want to come out here when they can't see their hands in front of their faces?'

It was not quite true, of course. There was moonlight and, even if it was cloudy, it would never get pitch black. If it was light enough for the owls to hunt, it was light enough to allow a skilled scout to move through a wood, but it was that word 'skilled'. It took training to know what movement was a mouse, or a deer, or a man, armed and out to kill you. But Podevin said none of it. Whatever Boleslav was, he was not stupid. Boleslav could easily keep enough guards on the palisade wall, in case Podevin was thoughtless enough to try a solitary night assault on Prague Castle.

'But I will go tomorrow. No, Lyudmila,' Podevin said, as she started to object. 'You have to think of Maria and Priby. I have to think of the parchment and getting it to Emma.'

'You'll never do it.' There was a sort of calmness about Krok that Podevin could not place, even though, in the back of his mind, he knew he had heard the tone before. 'Give me the parchment.' He held out his hand. Podevin reached inside his tunic and half drew the letter out from its hiding place before he stopped.

'What are you going to do with it?'

'Safe keeping.' Still the same calm authority. Podevin handed over the parchment. Krok put it down. Podevin looked at him. 'I'm not going to hide it while you're watching, am I?'

It made sense. Podevin nodded and yawned.

'Bed,' said Lyudmila as if she was his mother.

Podevin was too tired to object. He could have one good night's sleep before hiding out in the forest. He was sure he would have to have another conversation with Krok. There were some details that had not been sorted. But that would have to wait until tomorrow.

❧

As soon as he woke, he realised that he had not thought about where he was going to hide, nor how he was going to communicate with Emma. Was he supposed to draw the hunters off while Krok took the letter to Emma? Or was he just to disappear without seeing Emma again? And what about the horse? He couldn't leave it to be found, not anywhere near here, anyway. He groaned. The failure of his mission haunted him. All he had managed to do was endanger everyone who had helped him, and get the whole of Boleslav's army after him.

Lyudmila rushed into the hut. 'Get up! They're combing the forest!'

'What? Who?' Podevin was out of bed in answer to Lyudmila's order, but jerking out his words in his confusion.

'Soldiers from Prague and Tugumir's lot from Budec. They must have camped out last night and started before dawn.'

'Hell!'

'Hell won't help you—and we'll save the praying for now.' Krok looked drawn and tired. 'We need to keep them away from here. They'll torch the place as soon as look at it.' He turned to his wife. 'If nothing else, you have meat for weeks, just salt it well.'

'The horse?' Podevin asked.

Krok nodded. 'What else could I do? We can't feed it, and letting it go to be found—given they're assuming you're the one who took it... Was anyone watching the mill when you went back?'

'Someone must have been.' No good thinking now what he ought to have done or saying it was his first mission.

'What's past is past. We have to deal with today.' Lyudmila thrust a package into Krok's hands. 'Even if you don't eat here, you need to keep up your strength.'

He smiled in thanks. She had another package for Podevin. She also checked last night's bandage; at least no blood had seeped through the cloth.

'The girls want to say goodbye.' She motioned towards the fire, where both girls stood in silence.

Podevin went over to them.

He squatted down, allowed Maria to fling herself at him. He opened his arm for Priby to approach as well.

'You're always going away!' sobbed Maria.

'But I've always come back before.'

'Are we going to see you again?'

Podevin's 'of course' caught in his throat. 'Sorry, sweethearts. I don't know. You just be good for Mummy. All right?'

He gave the girls an extra squeeze and released them to hug Krok. If they were a bit more casual with their goodbyes to him, it was because they knew Krok would come back; but he was fierce with his hugs, and also told them to be good for Lyudmila. Then: 'Let's go!'

'Hey! What about me?'

The intensity with which Krok embraced his wife was almost embarrassing. Podevin turned away, but, for all its fierceness, it was over quickly. Podevin was given a fleeting hug too.

'Look after yourself,' Lyudmila whispered in his ear, and then she was releasing him and propelling him to the door.

Within a couple of steps, Krok reached to the side of the path and cut off a branch. He was careful to cut it deep in the bush, so the wound was hard to see and invisible to the casual observer. He handed it to Podevin. Brushing over their tracks, they retraced their steps to where Krok had found Podevin the previous night. Krok then cast around. Podevin watched.

'Not bad. Unless they're experts, they won't discover you were here. But we'll make sure.'

They retraced Podevin's steps some way farther, brushing their tracks into oblivion, until they came to a big fork in the track and took the other one, leading away from their forest home. It also led away from Prague.

'I thought I was supposed to be trying to get to Prague.'

'But they also think you're not much good and make mistakes.'

'That's true enough.'

'Hey! Not so down—I said they'd need experts, didn't I?'

'But if I hadn't—'

'There would have been something else. They've wanted you since before you came to live with us. Sooner or later, this would have happened and you know it.' Krok paused. 'We know what it's like, being an inconvenience to a lord and master.'

They abandoned the branch and, despite Krok's reliance on his staff, picked up speed and went round the forest so they would soon be heading towards Prague.

'But if I know it, what about you?' Podevin asked.

'I am to abandon someone in need?'

'You didn't do it just because Mark—or Emma—asked you. Why?'

'Maybe because I knew I could take a knight down a peg or two? Maybe I liked the idea of having someone to help me? Or maybe—' Krok stopped. Straightened as best he could. 'I'm dying, Podevin. Brother Mark can dull the pain, but now I need so many herbs that I'm useless for anything else. You know,' he still wasn't looking at Podevin, 'I don't really care about your foreign princess. I don't care about your parchment. I don't even care about your feud with Wenceslas's killers. But I do care about Lyudmila and Maria, and Pribyslava. So, wherever you end up, whatever station in life, you're to look after them. See they're all right. Or I will haunt every dream, every thought, and every step. Understood?'

At that, Krok did turn. His eyes bored into Podevin, who tried to make light of the situation. 'We'll get out of this. You'll live for years yet.'

'Promise me!'

There was no way out. 'I promise. I'll look after them when you're not here.' Even as he said it, his memory of the last promise—one that his failure to keep had landed them in this mess—surfaced. This one he'd keep, or die trying.

Krok nodded once and turned back to the path to lead the way. Podevin only then thought it was odd. Krok leading the way without getting him, Podevin, to do the work.

❧

They travelled in silence for another half hour.

'We'll stop and eat here.'

It was the base of an oak. A stream gurgled nearby. The birds chirruped; the breeze rustled the leaves. The oak was already starting to turn, its leaves fading to yellow or brown. Podevin eased his jerkin off his shoulders—travel, especially at the speed they'd been doing it, was hot work. A sparrow landed nearby; Podevin gathered up a few crumbs.

'And how easy do you want to make it for them?' Krok spoke quietly.

At least one of them had not forgotten why they were out in the forest.

'Ah! Perhaps not that easy. Sorry, birdy.'

The crumbs went into a bush instead. No doubt the bird could find them if it was that hungry.

'But at least it's told us they're not too near.' They both smiled. Krok reached inside his top. He drew out the parchment. Looked at it. 'I've already said I don't care about this. So you'd better have it back. We'll get you to Emma or Mark. He's probably the only one with access to her now.'

'Why?'

Krok looked at him with a pained expression. 'Emma is in confinement. Mladenic has already announced that "the kingdom waits in eager anticipation." It seems her husband has decided the princess will await the birth indoors.' Krok's tone was ironic.

'But how can they know so soon?'

'Don't ask me! I'm just a peasant, remember? I have no idea about how these things work.'

Podevin understood—anything to keep Emma out of the way. And heaven help her if she did not turn out to be pregnant! Whatever he felt for Emma, most people would be getting on with their lives and not bothering about what was or was not happening in Prague Castle. After all, here it was calm and quiet. Then, with a sharp cry, the bird flew away. They both froze.

Silence again. The breeze in the trees. Far away, a squawk. A pigeon lumbered its way across the forest. Then another squawk.

'Go on. Up you go. You can climb?' Krok pointed at Podevin's arm.

The tree would be an easy climb, its lower branches just in reach.

'What do you mean?' But Podevin was reaching up with his right arm, checking he could reach without straining.

'Spy out the land. See how close they are. Which direction. And, whatever happens, look after yourself—and them.' Krok had a lopsided, half-smile, but what shone in his eyes was an unfathomable sadness. 'Go on,' he repeated. 'Quick and quiet.'

Podevin nodded, stuffed the parchment back into his jerkin, and heaved himself up into the branches, favouring his left hand and trying to fathom Krok's idea. If height gave him vision farther afield, it would only be to look down on the forest canopy—unless there was a whole army about in the woods, it would be difficult to see evidence through the branches. The leaves were changing colour, but not dropping in vast numbers quite yet. Later in autumn or winter, he would be seen clambering up the oak. It might be a suitable hiding place, if he could not be traced to its base, but for how long? However, they had come to the edge of a more open part of the forest. He could see gaps in the trees, even some tracks, and, in all directions, or so it seemed, spears—more like pikes with their points and hooks and blades—men on horseback directing the prodding and poking in the undergrowth. They had worked their way into the forest from Prague, but the line must end somewhere. If he climbed a bit farther, perhaps he could work out where? A few branches higher would mean he needed to worry about the thinner branches breaking under his weight. He could get round this cordon and get the parchment to Mark—that was it! Podevin began to scramble down, no longer caring if a branch tore at his clothing or scratched his hands or face.

Krok had gone, and left his staff behind. Podevin picked it up and lurched down the path after him. He had gone fifty yards before caution and sensibility awoke—how could he know which way Krok had gone? He retraced his steps. In his unthinking mode, Podevin had assumed Krok would have known which way was away from their pursuers but, when he examined Krok's tracks, Podevin could see the man had headed straight for the nearest party of hunters. The fool! Surely he knew better than that? And how come he, Podevin, had not seen Krok move from the tree? But none of that mattered now. What he had to do was get to Krok before it was too late, and then guide them both round the hunting pack and…

The horn. It was sounded at the end of a successful hunt. People crashed through the forest, calling to each other, not caring about noise. They found a clearing; they moved out of the forest. Torn between wanting to find Krok, and fast, and wanting to know what was going on, Podevin wasted precious minutes crouching in the undergrowth, waiting for the sounds of movement to end. Only when he was sure the search party had gathered did he push his way out, catching his hand on some nettles. Grabbing a dock leaf, he rubbed it on his hand as he moved forwards, trying to trace Krok's movements in amongst all the other muddy footprints. It was easier to keep checking right and left, to see if Krok had moved off the path, but, as far as Podevin could see, he had not deviated. He could hear the unmistakable bark of orders.

'Captain, you may take your troops back to the castle. I'm sure the kitchens will have plenty of meat for you and your men.'

Podevin did not catch the rumble of the reply but, when he crept to the treeline, he saw the troops were already marching away down the dip in the direction of Prague Castle. There was just a gang of about ten left. Podevin recognised them. Knights, four of them, from that day when Wenceslas's reign came to an abrupt end. It was just them and a few guards holding a peasant—or somebody—roughly. The captive was on his knees, making no attempt at escape. Podevin tried to see who it was—dreading, refusing the thought that would not go away—but either guards, knights or horses kept blocking his view. Podevin searched for a name; Cesta? Either way, he seemed to be the leader of this pack. He faced his prisoner. Podevin had a clear view of the man trying to look impressive on his horse; the sardonic smile, the black brow, there being no gap between his eyebrows above his flattened nose, the scarred cheek—the man who had stood next to Tugumir at the scene of Wenceslas's assassination.

Chapter 41
To the Death!

Emma took a deep breath. She had not known whether she would be admitted, despite having Brother Mark's comforting presence with her. After all, as a supposedly pregnant woman in Boleslav's family, never mind his court, she was supposed to be resting. Ever since one of her Bohemian ladies had reported to Mladenic that Emma had been 'violating her confinement', the reprisal had been immediate, vindictive, and complete. After her husband's single, solitary visit, Emma ought to be with child. If she was not with child, it must be down to her not following her husband's orders, mustn't it? There had not even been a chance to see Mark until today. However, Mark's news and his update on the hunt for Podevin, which her husband had sanctioned while she had been out of sight, meant, parchment or no parchment, they had to take the risk.

With the two of them asking, even daring to insist, on admittance, Mladenic, in his father's and Radslav's absence, and glorying in his role as acting constable, decided to be gracious. It had been a shock for Emma, arriving back from following the hunt—was it a week ago?—to find Radslav gone, Mladenic in residence and in charge. In her quarters, she had plenty of time to think. She realised the young Boleslav's promotion out of harm's way had not been unexpected. The heir was no fighter and would have seized any excuse to stay safe in Prague. In fact, given his father needed Radslav's expertise on the field of battle, it had been inevitable that the swap would be made.

The only surprise, on reflection, was that it had taken so long. There had been brief, but frantic, provisioning, and setting out to deal with the latest Magyar raid. Emma had been told by Mladenic to go to her quarters while he awaited the result of the latest 'disruption to the Kingdom's peace and security'. Not one scrap of information had come to her rooms, but the arrival, and setting out, of so many troops over the previous hours and days could not be done in secret; and Mark had come to her as soon as he knew all about what was going on.

'Ah! My dearly beloved wife! How good of you to grace us with your presence—given your condition—despite my orders for you to keep to your rooms.' The heir waved them towards the throne.

The young gentlemen with him tittered, as was expected of them.

'Husband,' Emma began, 'if I could have a word in private?'

'In private? What could you possibly want to say to me that could not be said here?' The hand came up to cover, but not touch, his mouth and nose. The face then turned aside so eye contact could be avoided with her, but not with his companions. 'No, don't speak! Let me guess! You're going to tell me the child you're carrying isn't mine.' Mladenic pretended to sob. Two of his fops went so far as to applaud his acting.

Emma gasped. It took all her willpower not a send a pleading glance in Mark's direction. The applause died and she became aware of the stillness in the hall.

She licked her dry lips. 'Sire, how can that possibly be? Any child of mine is yours.'

'Very pretty. However, we have heard…rumours. All this hunting in the forest. Hunting what may we ask? There is hardly an overflow of meat in our kitchens.'

'Given I spend most of my time in my rooms with my ladies, sire,' Emma ground out, though she was aware of the sweat under her armpits and running down her sides. 'It would be difficult for me to meet anyone without your highness's knowledge. However, we have other information we seek to bring you.'

'No, you don't. You just want to pretend to be a man and deal with manly things. All I am saying is, if you go off into the forest alone, where no-one knows who you meet, or what you do, how can I be sure that child in your belly is mine?'

'Sire,' Mark interrupted, 'these are dangerous words. If you have proof against my lady, and her fidelity to you, then you must bring it before the court and let her be tried.'

Thanks! Emma thought. *As if I didn't already feel guilty enough.* She tried to keep her face blank, looking at Mladenic, waiting for his reaction. In the silence, they heard distant sounds of another arrival, or departure. People were going backwards and forwards all the time now the country was gearing up for war. If the castle constable needed to be told, someone would no doubt whisper in his ear. However, Emma had other concerns just now. She risked a glance at Mark. He looked relaxed, which infuriated her. It was Mark who'd told her rumours like this were deadly, never mind truth. It was no time for games—they had to turn the conversation to the plot!

'Sire?' said Mark again, ignoring Emma's gesture to shush him.

'If I say a thing, that should be proof enough. I could have her arrested now. I'm in charge. I can do what I like. And I never wanted her in the first place!' Mladenic paused, as if a thought had flitted across his mind. 'Anyway, we can have a trial. Trial by combat. She wants to be a man, so doesn't need a champion—and I choose Tomas as mine.'

'Sire!'

'You can't!'

Emma was surprised that one of the fops echoed Mark's objections. But he was quickly shushed as one of his companions stood, taking his sword from its scabbard. A thin smile on his lips, he advanced towards Emma.

'Husband! I am unarmed.' Emma kept the closest of eyes on Tomas's sword, now swishing left, now right. She backed away, one careful step at a time.

'Should have thought of that when you came here, shouldn't you?' Mladenic said, looking at his fingernails. 'Get on with it, Tomas.'

'My lord. I was not aware it was considered honourable for us to kill unarmed ladies?'

Even as Mark spoke, a second young man leapt to his feet, drew his sword and held the blade to Mark's throat. 'You were saying, monk? They say this dragon bitch killed her first suitor with her bare hands. Now's her chance to prove them right.'

Emma looked round; the guards were not about to protect her. And Tomas was not going to let her get anywhere near a weapon.

It was Mladenic's turn to give a little titter. 'This is going to be such fun.'

Then one of the remaining fops moved. 'Let's make it a little fairer, shall we, cousin? Unless you really want to be known at home for killing unarmed women.' Avoiding both Mark's antagonist and Tomas's eternally moving weapon, a third young man, this one barely more than a boy, approached Emma. Holding his sword by its blade just below the cross-guard, he gave it to her, grip first.

'Oh, all right, Mikael. But don't look for any help from me in the future.'

Tomas kept his sword moving but allowed Emma to take the prof-fered weapon.

'Beware his dagger,' Mikael hissed as he carried on walking towards the back of the hall, away from his former friends.

Until the young man's warning, she had not noticed Tomas's left hand was hidden behind his back.

The distraction of smiling a thanks at the young man was enough for Tomas to close the gap. Emma barely had time to get her new sword up to parry the first blow. She danced away, giving herself time to look at her opponent. Mark, with a sword still at his throat, had also retreated. Blades clashed. Tomas was good, but she'd met his sort before. Their blades clashed again, but she wasn't letting him turn it into a trial of strength. She kept moving. Her brain registered a draught as the door to the hall opened, but she could not afford to be distracted. Her headdress had slipped. Furious, she tugged it from her hair, wrapping it round her left hand, simply to keep it out of the way.

'To the death!' Mladenic yelled as the combatants paused.

Tomas smiled. He was stepping closer. Emma realised why she'd received the warning. Tomas's sword was still dancing in the air, no doubt as a distraction. His killing weapon of choice must be the dagger he kept hidden behind his back.

'Get on with it.' Mladenic again, eyes bright, breath panting, excitement glistening across his face as he leaned forwards. 'I've not seen any blood yet.'

Sword dancing, dagger still hidden, Tomas moved forwards. Emma stepped back onto the hem of her dress. She stumbled, but managed to hold her sword in front of her as Tomas seized his chance and leapt at her falling body, whipping out his long dagger, ready to kill. Her useless headdress was the puniest of shields, but it was all she had, as she used her left hand to block the flailing sword. She used her own sword against the dagger, turning it aside as Tomas landed on her, forcing her to fall back to the floor. She landed so hard, the breath left her body.

A moment of stillness. She dragged air into her lungs. There was pain beginning in her left hand and a weight on top of her. A weight that was not shifting. She grunted as she forced it to slide off her. The weight took her sword with it. Tomas's forward momentum meant he had been unable to stop himself when Emma's desperate defence blocked his attack. Her sword had pierced his ribcage, traversed his heart and emerged through his back.

Emma stood. There was a red stain on her bodice. There would be a bruise on her chest where the sword's handle had jarred her ribs. She moved to the body and tugged her borrowed sword from it. She was still facing the throne and its shocked but speechless occupant.

'Trial by combat. To the death, my lord, as you ordered. I think I am vindicated,' she said, but there came no reply.

Mladenic barely gave her a hate-filled glance before looking over her shoulder at the back of the hall. Mikael was still there, wasn't he? But that draught she had felt while fighting for her life? Who had entered the hall?

'I wonder what she would do in a fair fight?' a new voice said.

Emma turned and dropped into her deepest curtsey. How long had the king been there, talking with Mikael? With his bare hand, Mark guided the now unresisting sword away from his neck and bowed. The fops turned and gaped. Mladenic gulped, forgetting even to stand.

King Boleslav advanced into the hall, his pace measured, his left hand on his sword hilt. As he passed Emma and Mark, he used his right hand in an upwards movement—they both stood. Boleslav walked round the table, towards his son. Mladenic remembered his etiquette and retreated, vacating the throne, his face as white as the ermine trim on his fancy cloak.

Boleslav sat. 'You will be pleased to know we have returned, having dealt with the latest raid.' He glanced at the fops as if they were unruly children, caught engaging in an infantile tantrum. 'I don't need jesters in my court. Depart. And take your friend with you.'

They looked at the heir, but he refused to look them in the eye. Their usual flamboyance forgotten, they gathered round Tomas and lifted his lifeless form.

Boleslav glanced at the remaining young man. 'Mikael? You had better claim your sword.'

The young man approached from the back of the hall. Emma looked round for some way of cleaning the weapon, but Mikael held some cloth in his hand.

'You're injured, my lady,' he said on coming up to her.

'It's nothing,' she replied. 'Thank you for the warning.'

'I knew him all my life. But I can't say I was ever fond of my cousin, even when he got me my place in court.' Mikael paused.

It was his smile that did it. She remembered; he was one of the squires Emma and Podevin had trained. One of those initially unhappy about being taught by a woman…

'You've grown,' she said, but grew aware of Boleslav's glowering look. She handed over her sword. Mikael bowed to her, and to the king, before stepping back.

Silence. Emma risked a look at her hand. Mark came up. Her head-dress was useless cloth. Mark tore it into several pieces and used what he could to bind the wound. The king waited until they had finished. His son, having not been addressed, had to wait as well.

'So,' the king's voice was mild, putting Emma on instant alert, but he was addressing Mladenic. 'You can do what you like, can you? I was not aware I had given permission for you to put your wife on trial—or were you looking to be a young widower? Speak up! Or do I get your wife to tell me?'

'It was a joke! Just a joke! Of course she's carrying my child!'

Boleslav pretended to think. 'And this was such a funny joke, you forced your wife to fight for her life against one of your swordsmen?'

'Tomas hated women. He should have—' Mladenic stopped, and reconsidered his words, 'known it was a joke! Of course, he wouldn't have actually killed her! She's the one who killed someone! Not me!' He was now pointing at his wife, but his hand was unsteady.

'And you are minded to seek vengeance? Should I hand you *my* sword?' His father's voice was contained, but the son gave no reply. King Boleslav looked up at Mikael. 'And you? Do you wish retribution? It is, after all, your cousin whom the Princess Emma killed.'

Mikael stepped forwards. Emma could see he licked his lips and paused before speaking, but his voice was clear. 'With respect, sire, my cousin was killed in a fair fight and—if I may—by unfairly and wrongly supporting a vile accusation against the lady. He deserved his death. My lady is innocent.' Mikael bowed and waited.

After that, Mladenic would never have him back, but what could Emma say now?

'Very pretty!' said the king. 'You may go. Perhaps you'd better join the princess's bodyguard.'

'Sire?' Emma was puzzled. Why, after all this time, did she need extra bodyguards? Not that she was about to refuse Mikael's support, but the king spoke again.

'The castle constable needs her own troops. You have inspired loyalty. I like that. Provided I see or hear nothing that is disloyal to me, I think you can take charge here!'

'But—but she's a woman,' Mladenic screeched in shock.

'I had noticed, my son,' came the dry response, 'but she can fight like a man. And young Mikael here tells me there are others he can find who would fight for her.'

Mikael leaned towards Emma. 'I had to tell him why you and Tomas were fighting. And why you had my sword!'

Emma nodded, not daring to speak, just very grateful for her life—Boleslav could just as easily have decided to have her killed. However, Mladenic had not finished; he was now crying that she should not have even left her rooms, but she and her monk had forced their way into the hall. Mikael opened his mouth to speak, but Emma shook her head; let the king make up his own mind.

'With child? Yes, that could be a problem. Shall we allow you to call on Duke Radslav if and when needed, or when we are not available?' Mladenic's shoulders slumped. Perhaps he realised this was not going to be his day. His father then decided to address Emma directly. 'So, why did you enter the hall?'

'Sire,' Emma bobbed a brief curtsey to show appropriate subservience, 'we've been trying to get information for a while, but now you are here...' She gestured to Mark, who was able to give a succinct summary of what was known about Tugumir's plot. Boleslav listened in silence.

A silence filled by Mladenic mouthing, 'Why didn't you tell me?' at Emma, who could only reply with a shrug. What had she and Mark been trying to do?

'So why have *you* got this information, monk?'

Mark took a breath. 'We, that is myself and my lady, and some others, have, as you know, maintained contact with Queen Matilda, with, if you recall, your approval. There are other people in Saxony who have contacts at court here, who seem to think King Otto would prefer a different ruler in Bohemia. We heard about it, but needed proof, before telling, or trying to tell, your son, in his role as constable, about what we knew.'

A pause. A horrible pause before the king spoke.

'Right! You, my son, will come with me, and you'd better bring your friends. They can fight in the front line, or face my further wrath about your joke! We're going west—to fight. Radslav's in charge of mobilising our resources around Prague. You, Emma, as of now, are castle constable. You two,' another change in focus as his gaze encompassed Mark, as well as Emma, 'will tell Radslav what you've told me. As for your plot, I need proof! Get it!'

The king swept out of the hall with his son bleating beside him—or, rather, bleating until he was told to 'shut up!'

Radslav appeared from the back of the hall. 'I don't know about you two, but I need to sit—and I need some food. Before we do anything else.'

'Anything else?'

'Like try to stop that man-hunt in the forest. I need those troops to fight the Saxons! Not trying to chase down one, solitary outlaw! And, don't worry,' he continued as the hall doors opened for the food Radslav must have already ordered, 'not everyone will be happy with you being constable, but you'll cope.'

Yes, Emma thought, they had to get that parchment; only after that could she afford to worry about if she was pregnant and who the father was.

Mark leaned towards her. 'You might have won that trial by combat, and your husband may say nothing ever again—the king neither—but your penance is to pray every day that your child looks like you!'

Emma nodded. Given the way things had turned out, a cut hand was a small price to pay.

Chapter 42
Triumph and Disaster

'Well, pageboy. Thought you'd get even, did you? Well,' the last word was long, drawn-out, 'you're going to find out what we do to little murderers, aren't you?'

'Little?' thought Podevin. That was rich. He had always thought of himself as reasonably tall.

'Well? Answer me!' Cesta's shout was accompanied by a blow from one of the guards. The prisoner fell forwards, or would have done if he hadn't been held so roughly and so firmly.

'No, sir. I mean, yes, sir,' he said.

'Well. Which is it?'

'Yes, sir.'

Podevin's dreaded thought had turned into fact. Krok had somehow wandered into the hunting party and... Podevin squared his shoulders. Now there was no choice. He made to step into the field.

'You killed Tugumir.'

Podevin halted at the words.

'Yes, sir. It was my duty as Wenceslas's page,' Krok said, clear and defiant.

Podevin never wanted to remember the next ten minutes, but never forgot them. He worked out afterwards that it must have been only that long. In a blinding flash, he realised what Krok was doing—and he, stupid as ever, would only be killed too if he broke cover. He was rooted to the spot. He watched as they dragged Krok no more than a dozen yards, before deciding that an old beech tree would do. A hanging. Oh, it was competent. These people had done it before. The rope thrown over a convenient branch and tested that it would hold. The noose, expertly tied, placed over Krok's neck and tightened, but not too much. He was not even going to be blindfolded, just hauled up so he started to dance in the air as his windpipe was constricted. Then a shout from one of the guards who was facing Prague.

'She's coming!'

A frantic look. 'But the king's son said—No! Get on with it! She can't argue with a dead body!'

The guards grabbed a leg apiece and pushed Krok upwards so he could gasp a lungful of air, but this was no reprieve. Almost before he'd opened his mouth, the guards jerked his body down again. Snap. Almost like a dry twig breaking underfoot, Krok's neck broke. His body still jerked, but the life had left it.

The party turned to leave, but they had left it a fraction too late. There were new arrivals. Cesta tried to prevent them seeing what was behind him but, when it became clear he would either have to draw his sword or knock Emma off her horse, he desisted. Ashen-faced, she rode forwards with her two companions. The hanging party drew back. She looked at the now still body.

'Cut him down,' she said. 'Now.'

Radslav snapped his fingers at the guards. 'You heard! Do as you're told!'

The knights looked at Cesta. A mistake.

A full-bodied roar: 'Whose orders do you obey here?' The guards jumped, glanced from one horse-backed authority to another.

'The princess, my lord.'

'Then get on with it,' Radslav hissed.

Emma rode back towards Cesta and his gang.

'And whose orders do you obey, Cesta?' Her words were silky smooth.

'King Boleslav's, my lady.' Cesta smirked.

'And in his absence?'

'His representative.' This time, a shrug.

'And who is that here in Prague and its surrounding countryside?'

'His son.' Cesta licked his lips as if he needed a drink. He was looking puzzled, as well he might be, not having been in Prague when the king issued his latest orders.

'No. His son is with his father. Try again.'

Cesta was trapped. He looked away, stunned at the change in his fortunes.

'I said, try again.' Emma's voice was still low, but her eyes had narrowed.

'You, my lady?'

'Yes. Me. The castle constable.' Cesta gaped at Emma's words. Involuntarily, he looked towards Duke Radslav, but there was no comfort there. Emma decided to temper his shock. 'Yes, when I am absent, or indisposed, Duke Radslav will act for me.'

A pause. Cesta licked his lips again. The guards had finished their grisly task and stood over the body, awaiting further orders. Emma broke the silence.

'And why was I not informed of the nature of this hunt?'

'Well, my lady, it's like this,' one of Cesta's companions stuttered into speech, 'we did not see that, with you being a lady, and in your, er, delicate condition, that you should be troubled with our little problems. After all, we had traced him here, and we knew his life was forfeit, and we thought all we needed to do was just—'

'Get it over without a trial, without telling anyone who could act as judge, without going through the proper procedures?' Emma faced the knight, who decided he had nothing more to say. 'Hmm? And I suppose you know the penalty for taking a life without the proper legal sanction?'

The man looked away, avoiding Cesta's glare, as well as Emma's. Emma kicked her horse's flanks and it trotted forwards obediently. The men barring her way wisely stepped aside and allowed her to approach the body. She stared down at him. Krok lay there, in peace and in no pain. At least the quick death had spared him the protruding tongue and the red face of strangulation.

Silence. Her horse pawed the ground, impatient to be moving. Emma glanced to her right, where Radslav and Mark waited.

'We'll bury him here. And raise a chapel over him, dedicated to him, to Podevin. Where his soul can be prayed for. This lot will pay for it.'

'This lot' did not like the idea. 'This lot' started to object. But 'this lot' did not get much choice. They all knew they could have waited for the full court to convene and tried to overrule Emma's judgment. They could try to explain to King Boleslav why they had not followed the correct procedure. They might have been excused; they might have been able to argue their way out of a tricky situation. On the other hand, if the king was not in a good mood, if the king felt he was short of funds—and when was he in a good mood, and when had he ever not felt short of funds?—then they would be fined, or have their lands confiscated, or even be imprisoned. On balance, raising the money to bury him and build a chapel over him was the cheaper option.

Mark collected their purses.

'I know a family who'd be able to help provide the wood for the chapel, and the coffin,' he said to her.

Emma nodded. 'I'll leave it to you.' She turned her horse, ready to depart.

'Madam,' Mark's voice was respectful, but firm. She halted. Turned back to him. 'We need a guard to stand vigil until the burial can take place. I know he was a wanted man, but people may wish to pay their respects, with your permission, of course. They may wish to view a body unmarked by beast or bird.'

In his hiding place just inside the forest, Podevin gasped. How could he have not realised? He would have to tell Lyudmila and the girls. They would need to come here—but how to do it without getting them arrested? His thoughts tumbled over each other in a mixture of guilt and anger, and shame that Emma still did not have the parchment.

But it was too late. She was on her way. Her head still held high. With Radslav at her side, the knights and some of their guards followed in sullen silence. There were just two guards left—and Mark.

'You stay here. I'm going to find some herbs to keep him sweet. Then you can find firewood.'

Mark moved into the forest. Podevin waited.

'Well?' Mark spoke softly.

'I've still got to tell them.'

'Tell them what?'

'That they caught and hung him as me.'

'He was a dying man, Podevin.' Mark paused. 'And be grateful. He knew what he was doing, and remember, always remember, he did this so you could live—so live!'

Mark turned away and began searching the ground.

'What are you looking for?'

'Anything—just so those fools don't suspect I needed to go to the forest to see you.'

'Oh.'

'Off you go.'

'Wait. You'll need this. At least, I hope you do.'

Podevin reached inside his jerkin and pulled out the parchment. Proof that there had, indeed, been a conspiracy. In silence, he handed it over. Now, of course, with Tugumir dead, it might well be a waste of time, effort and lives, but, somehow, it was important to him that Emma knew he had succeeded in his mission, if only in part.

With no further words between them, Podevin went. His feet found the path back towards Krok's family in the gathering gloom. Back in the days when he had first come to the forest, he had fancied all sorts of witches and goblins in the shadows, but now they were just tree roots and bushes, and puddles and trackways and branches broken off in old storms. Krok was dead. Not even a boar, of all things, snuffling its way through the leaf litter, could worry him now. He sighed. He had a tale to tell, and he did not know how to soften the blow it would bring.

Chapter 43
Penance

His arrival back was enough. That he was alone was enough. That he stumbled in through the gateway, paused and looked at the family in the doorway as they sat around the fire eating supper: it was enough.

Lyudmila looked up and read the news in Podevin's face. The girls were told to go on eating—so, of course, not another mouthful reached their lips. Lyudmila stood up. Her 'no' was more a moan than a statement. She crossed the rush-covered floor. Podevin, in one of those odd, inappropriate moments, noticed the rushes were new. They, or Lyudmila at least, must have spent the day gathering and spreading a new floor covering. As she came to him, she was still saying no, increasing in volume with each repetition. By the time she reached and clung to him, it was a full-throated wail. He stood. If she wanted to beat him, to kill him, it was fine. But she just clung and howled.

'I've made your clothes all wet,' she said, gulping back her tears at last.

It was true; there was a patch of salty dampness on his shoulder.

'It doesn't matter.' He paused and slipped into fatherhood. 'But the girls do.'

And, sitting on a bench, with Priby on his left, and Maria on his right, he told Krok's story. He told them how he had first met Krok, years ago when Maria was just born, but he also told them about the later Krok, the man who knew he was dying. Podevin spelled it out for himself as much as his listeners. The painkilling herbs were not working any more. The injuries were more troublesome with each passing year. He also told them how Krok had taught him all he knew. He told them how Krok loved them all and wanted to look after them but knew he could not.

'So, now it's your job?' Priby had leaned on his shoulder and looked up at him with her big, dark eyes.

Podevin smiled but, without hesitation, said, 'Yes, now it's my job.' He glanced up at Lyudmila, who was pretending to be busy with clearing away and tidying up. 'Yes, my job now. And it's time you young ladies were in bed.'

He let Lyudmila sort the bedtime routine while he mended the fire. The flames crackled and danced, in defiance of his mood. He heard the muttered conversations, relieved to recognise Maria's voice. She had been very quiet, silent even, during his talk about Krok. Podevin sighed and put his empty bowl aside. He supposed he must have been hungry; it had been full a few short minutes ago.

Lyudmila came across to him.

'Will they sleep?'

She shrugged. 'They're tired enough. There will be more tears in the morning.'

'From you, too.'

'Maybe.'

Podevin looked at her in surprise that she might shed no more tears for her kind, competent husband.

'Life goes on. Look,' she turned to him, 'you don't have to take us on, just because Krok's dead. I don't want you to hang around here— staying on—all the time wanting to be elsewhere in that fancy castle of yours. What's there to smile about?'

'That's just what my castle is—a fancy!' Podevin patted the bench beside him. 'Emma's gorgeous. No, let me finish,' he said as he felt Lyudmila stiffen, 'and, in another life, I'd be married to her, and we'd be raising little dukes to inherit our lands. But she is a princess, and married. So, the only realistic alternatives for her would have been her current husband's father or Wenceslas. If he hadn't been so stupid about going to Rome, all of this might not have happened. Now what?' For Lyudmila was staring at him.

'You know, Podevin, that's the first time I've heard you criticise Wenceslas.'

'Is it?' He shrugged and, uncomfortable with Lyudmila's direct look, looked into the fire. 'Besides, Maria may not be my daughter, but she is my flesh and blood. It's time I began to know her better—and her adopted sister.'

'You've changed, Podevin.'

'Hmm? Maybe. But I've killed my own brother, and watched another man hang so I could live. If that doesn't change me...' He picked up a stick and poked the fire.

Lyudmila took the stick from him.

'Let it die down. Or we'll have to spend tomorrow gathering more wood.'

'You haven't asked to see the body. Mark thought you might.'

'Yes. I want to see him. To say goodbye.' Now it was Lyudmila's turn to stare into the fire. 'And to say sorry. If I'd just gone with Tugumir willingly—been content to be another one of his women—Krok wouldn't have been beaten in the first place, and we wouldn't have had to run away.'

'And you wouldn't be living here, and you wouldn't have met me.'

'Now there's a mixed blessing!'

'But Maria and Priby aren't.'

Lyudmila glanced towards the quiet, whether sleeping or not, girls. 'No, they aren't. And maybe Mark can give you better answers than me, but what's done is done.'

They left the conversation there. It was dark. There was nothing to do but go to bed. If Podevin heard tears from Lyudmila's bed in the night, he knew better than to interfere. There would be enough to do at first light. He hoped everyone would be able to eat breakfast. He hoped he could be a better father than guest.

❧

He woke at dawn to realise Lyudmila was already up. She was tending the fire and had brought water in.

'I want everything ready for Krok,' she said when she saw he was awake. 'He's coming back here.'

'Lyudmila.' Podevin clambered out of bed.

'We'll lay him out. And we'll find a proper place to put him.'

'Lyudmila.'

'And we can visit when we like.'

'Yes, but not here.'

'He's not coming back here? But this is his home!'

'The whole forest was his home.' Podevin was now close enough to put his hands on her shoulders. 'We can go to see him. Mark has it sorted.' Podevin fervently hoped that was true. 'He will be buried at the edge of the forest, and a chapel built over him.' He did not say, did not know how to say, that the chapel would be dedicated to someone called Podevin, but some things, he told himself, had to be left to Brother Mark.

'Come on,' he said. 'It's time we got those girls up.'

❧

A bright early autumn morning, the sun creating dappled patterns on the forest floor through the branches. Leaves mainly still hanging on, but not for much longer. If you were quiet enough, you could catch the birds and mice gorging themselves on the berries and nuts, hinting at the harvest to come. But the pathways only echoed the sound of four sets of feet dragging their way to a final meeting. Lyudmila carried a basket of herbs. She had ignored Podevin telling her Mark had gathered herbs the night before. It was her job, and she was going to do it.

It was still quiet and bright when they arrived. Mark stood to welcome them, motioning to the guards to stand back. These were different guards. The body had been laid out on the ground with a cloth under him. Lyudmila approached, the girls just behind her. Mark stepped aside. She knelt. Mark motioned to one of the guards. The guard brought up a pail of water and placed it where Lyudmila could reach it. There were no tears. Mark knelt between the girls, one arm around each. Podevin could not hear what was being said, but Priby and Maria were nodding as the three of them watched Lyudmila clean Krok's already cleaned face with the herb-infused water. Mark looked round and saw Podevin standing apart. For a few seconds, he released his hold around Priby's shoulders and beckoned Podevin closer.

Podevin approached, each step more leaden than the last. By going to the other side of the body, he could still keep some distance. He looked down at where he should be lying. Looked up at those who should not be bereft.

'We will have a burial service here later today. But, for now, we will kneel and say some prayers.'

Another glance in Podevin's direction from Mark and Podevin dropped to his knees. The grass was still damp from the morning's dew. The creeping cold and wet gave him something to think about as Mark led the prayers. Not a sound from Lyudmila, but Podevin could see the tears falling down her face as she gazed at her husband. Maria's slight form was shaking as she, too, wept for the only father she had known. And Priby—only just getting over, or getting used to, the idea her own father was dead, and her mother and brother had left her—now had to come to terms with the fact that her substitute father was also dead.

'And as we commit this man's soul to your care, we also pray your blessing on Lyudmila, Maria and Pribyslava, as they continue on this earth under the care and protection of Krok.'

Podevin smiled grimly to himself. Even in his prayers, Mark was aware of the guards. Perhaps he really was to become Krok? No castle, no lands, just a forest and a family. Life, he realised, moved on. Mark was now talking with Lyudmila, and Podevin was the only one on his knees. He stood. Waited. He had to have a word with Mark, even if Mark was not desperate to have a word with him. Eventually, Mark sent the others off. Podevin walked away from the guards; what he had to say they did not need to hear. He joined Mark.

'You're a free man.'

'Pardon?' As ever, Mark had surprised him.

'You are no longer being looked for. They think you're dead.'

'But Emma?' Podevin said.

'As you saw yesterday, knows better, and knows not to enlighten them. There might be good brought out of this.'

'But Krok's dead!'

'Not so loud!' Mark hissed. 'Yes, Krok is dead, but how many times do I need to say this? He was dying anyway. He'd made it through last winter but, without a miracle, he wouldn't have made the next.' Mark paused. 'What happened?'

As they wandered towards the trees where the family waited for him, Podevin told Mark how they had both gone on the run in the forest, how Krok had led them away from home, sent Podevin up that oak tree and gone straight into their trap, pretending to be Podevin. If only Podevin had not pretended to be Krok on that visit to Prague!

'You couldn't have done much else,' Mark reminded him. 'And now, you will have to pretend to be Krok again.'

Podevin nodded.

'And, once this chapel is built, I'll marry you to Lyudmila.'

Podevin did not even flinch. Emma was, as he had told Lyudmila last night, a fairy tale. He had loved her, he loved her still. At one time, he'd had far-flung plans to marry her, but she was married to the Bohemian heir. Podevin was not yet prepared to hope that Mladenic would enable her to forget him, but he could hope that Emma's husband would, one day, make a good king.

Mark interrupted his thoughts: 'Time you went. The burial is this afternoon. You can watch from the forest but not attend. No! I said not attend. If Lyudmila can accept it, so can you. Off you go. Once all this has calmed down, I will visit. Until then, you make no attempt to get in touch.'

Podevin nodded, and walked back to the forest with his family.

⁊

It was easier, at least in some respects, to live in the forest without Krok being there. For a start, there was so much that had to be done. The routine chores: the collection of food, whether it was nuts and berries or the crops they had grown, or checking the traps, or collecting the fish. A hard day's hunting or fishing kept Podevin away from home for the day, and a hard day's work at home meant both adults were too tired to lament, or blame, each other. Also, the girls needed looking after; there was the shock of realising Priby must be the older one by a couple of years—she was merely undernourished but was now growing fast. At least the two girls got on well together and they were both old enough, and fit enough, to contribute to the daily work of making sure they had enough to last through the winter and the coming spring. There was other work as well, like providing wood for a chapel. They had plenty of supplies, not just because it was a forest, but because Krok—though Podevin had no idea how the man had done it without the regular use of a packhorse—had made sure there was plenty of seasoned wood stockpiled. Of course, Podevin, with Lyudmila's help, had to cut down trees to replace what was taken away, but even that was welcome, if backbreaking, work.

However, tramping the forest paths and byways alone through the fruitful autumn, frosty winter, and the following spring, gave Podevin time to think. He could be thankful he had been well taught; the signs and spoor he noticed subconsciously, his hearing attuned to the forest noises, or its unnatural silences. He could think about Emma; Princess Emma, one-day-Queen Emma, Prague Castle Constable Emma. It had been fun, mostly. Apart from when they were attacked by those bandits, and there was also the escape from Stara Boleslav. Those bits had not been such fun, but sharing the litter had had its moments!

Shaking his head to clear it of memories, Podevin retrieved a rabbit from a snare—a nice clean kill—and reset it. He looked up. He was by the edge of the forest, and why not? Rabbits needed open grassland for their grazing. The sunlight filtered through and, at this time of year, newly grown grasses, light and vivid against the darkened, over-wintered stalks of last summer's crop, reminded him of life's endless coming and going. He could see some people making their way from the castle. No doubt Mark and Emma were off to inspect progress on the new chapel. Emma was a mother again now; a daughter, but no signs yet of child number three. She was, however, still in charge of Prague and its castle. Mark had kept him and Lyudmila up to date; Emma wasn't happy exactly—having a husband who wanted to kill you precluded that—but she was, in her husband's absence, 'more contented with her lot'. She had her bodyguard. Mikael had been true to his word so now, for every Anglo-Saxon, there were two Bohemians, but they all owed their loyalty to Emma.

Podevin ducked back into cover. He could get to the half-built chapel before them and find out something of what was going on. Emma's bodyguard would not be looking for a forester, and they were making too much noise to notice him anyway.

☙

'So, you see, my lady, we are making good progress.' Mark and Emma had dismounted and were walking to the chapel by themselves.

'Yes, but I had hoped for better,' Emma said.

'We are waiting for more workmen.'

'And more funds?'

'No, the funds have been provided.'

Podevin listened, growing puzzled. Had they fallen out? It did not look like it, but the conversation was formal, as between consort and courtier, not two friends.

'They're already calling him a saint, you know—like Wenceslas.' Now Podevin could see Emma's smile.

'The dead can sin no more.'

'It's the idea of a living saint that worries me!' Emma raised her voice. 'We know you're there—watching us!'

Taking his cue, Podevin stepped out into the light.

Acknowledgements

Firstly, thanks must go to my sons, Alastair and Jonny for giving me the idea and impetus for this novel in the first place. It was they who wanted to know 'who was the page' in the Christmas carol 'Good King Wenceslas.' Who was it who had to carry the provisions out to the peasant in the cold winter snow? Of course, so much of tenth century Bohemia is lost in myth and legend—I've made up a lot of the tale. But there was a Wenceslas, who was killed by his brother. There was a page, who was called Podevin, and he did have to go on the run. Emma is also based on a real Anglo-Saxon princess, but her friendship with Podevin? Well, it makes for a good story!

I must also thank Alastair for producing such a wonderful illustrative map of Podevin's Bohemia.

Thank you also to all those who read and commented on earlier versions of the story as it developed over the years. The Lakes Writers Group, convened by Andy Chamberlain and Mark Finnie, and the Durham Christian Writers, convened by Ross and Dorothy Hamilton, were both very helpful and encouraging as I learned my craft. In later years, members of the Lichfield u3a writers, led by Veronica Birkett and latterly by Marilyn Sands, have read and commented on whole drafts—way beyond the call of duty, so my heartfelt thanks to you all.

My editors Amie McCracken, and Annie Percik have been extremely helpful and professional. As have my peer reviewers at Resolute Books: John Stevens, Sue Russell and Sarah Nicholson. Thanks also to Liz Carter whose cover design is wonderful. Last but not least, heartfelt thanks to Sian and Jonathan who not only provided support when I needed it most, but also have been an unfailing source of encouragement. All of you have been gracious and supportive as you did your best to get this novice novel writer over the line—I had no idea what I did not know!

To you all, named and unnamed, who helped get *Warrior Princess, Errant Page* to the starting line of being an actual published book, thank you—and here's to the next one!

About the Author

Originally a 'Shropshire Lad,' Nigel has long harboured ambitions to be a writer. However, life intervened, and the later 1980s saw him teaching Maths in Botswana. On returning to the UK, he continued teaching for a while before going to Durham to get a PhD in Theology and working for Durham Diocese as their World Development Officer.

Now living in Lichfield, Nigel writes a short story each month, some of which end up on his website www.nigeloakleywrites.com and is scribbling away at the second story about Podevin and Emma.

About Resolute Books

We are an independent press representing a consortium of experienced authors, professional editors and talented designers producing engaging and inspiring books of the highest quality for readers everywhere. We produce books in a number of genres including historical fiction, crime suspense, young adult dystopia, memoir, Cold War thrillers, poetry, and even Jane Austen fan fiction!

Find out more at resolutebooks.co.uk

for the joy of reading

Printed in Dunstable, United Kingdom